TOME OF LORE
SACRIFICE

DANIEL M MELCHIOR

First Paperback Edition

ISBN 978-0-9919343-0-0

Cover Art
The Triumph of Death
Pieter Bruegel the Elder - 1562

Driftwood Publishing
Sooke, BC
Canada

To Bryan,

Thanks for all
of your support.

Your Friend,

Dan Mehrtu

Table of Contents

Preface

I began writing this book back in 1996 after waking from a lucid dream. I sat on the edge of a riverbank and witnessed men diving into the cold water looking for the representation of their soul on earth in the form of a glowing stone. For anyone who has experienced lucid dreaming, it can be quite exhilarating, and at my wife's urging, I decided to write down the dream which became the seed of inspiration for my novel.

Due to the nature of my day job, I have spent many days on the road travelling across this great country and have found myself buried in my notebook flushing out the characters and ideas that inhabit the world I've created. And with that, I owe my love and thanks to my wife and children for putting up with my absences, but in return I give you this novel which has manifested my thoughts for the past seventeen years.

Dan Melchior

Map

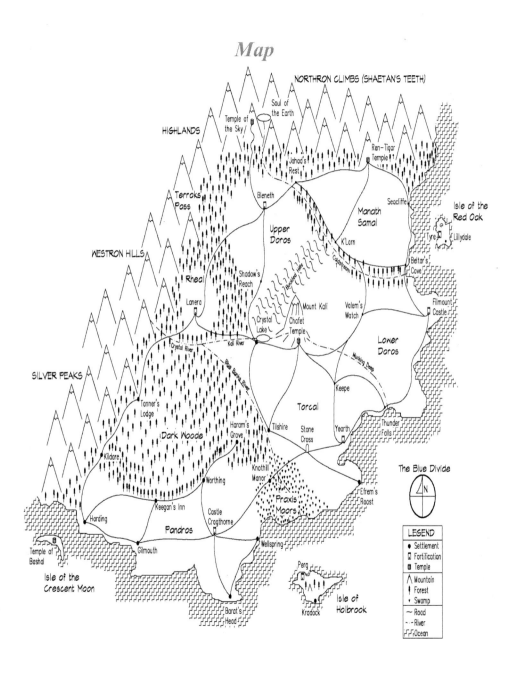

Prologue

Because I consider myself a fool, my advice can be freely given; how you take it is up to you. Here it is: I would not recommend enlisting into service for any King, Queen, Liege-Lord, High Priest, Lore Master or whoever demands obeisance upon a bended knee or by a reverential kiss upon a pig-fingered, gem-encrusted hand that has more than likely never wielded the very weapon you are pledging in their service. No matter how great the prospect conjures the illusion of glory and honour, nothing is worth losing the women you love, or the children you will never know, for the reward of scars that will etch every inch of your prematurely-aged body or the distant memory of a peaceful night's sleep. I am more than willing to discard my well-used armour along with those childish dreams of glory and honour and replace them with the vows I swore thirteen years ago (not on bended knee) here in the Temple of Bashal on the Isle of the Crescent Moon, the furthest place from where my life began, to bask in the sunshine and enjoy the privilege of being the only man in history to be given those Rites.

The name given to me by my mother and father, the same as my wonderful old grandfather, and the name I expected to pass onto my firstborn son, was Thomas Cartwright. Now, I will be simply known and buried along with my holy sisters as Brother Equinos, and the only weapon I will ever hold again in my non-maimed right hand is the newly written and finally completed, *Tome of Lore*. It is the single greatest collection of knowledge, morals and spirituality harvested by the wisest minds over the past millennia, condensed, revised and edited by a living God, whom I called friend; however, it also contains the most contentious sources of war during the same span of time. The copy I now hold in my ink-stained hands is precious to me as I have personally aided in the writing of this particular edition, and in fact, the events that shaped and changed my life forever have now become a part of it, even as I write down these words that now form the prologue to these same events.

I will begin the faithful narrative of my life (as it stands to date) with those specific contentious sources of war that predate mankind, and begin this uncompromising book, but it first must be understood that as a former soldier, I can make no claims to be either a tutored writer or non-biased historian. I will leave those excellent professions to the remaining Lore Masters and their Acolytes residing in the Temple of the Sky in the Northron Climbs, who continue to dedicate their cloistered lives to the precepts dictated by the God, Thayer. Their Library, which I had the privilege of glimpsing briefly in my youth, was reported to fill the entire mountain under which they command an unobstructed view of the pristine Lake named, *The Soul of the Earth.* Hopefully, they are nearing the end of the Temple's refurbishments after it suffered dearly at the hands of my unexpected and short visit.

Two sources of contention I have already named, Bashal the Goddess, and Thayer the God. The last source has been the catalyst for every armed conflict that has torn this beautiful land into the many smaller provinces that exist today, each being ruled by its King or Prince. Or High Priest as in the case of Mount Kali, hub of all the Provinces, and supposed ancient birthplace of the God-Creature Eth. There are no coincidences in the naming of that foul beast which came from the ancient language of the desert tribes, lost in the dry sands beyond the Westron Mountains, the word 'Death', or more specifically 'D'Eth', which translated as 'Of Eth'. For those of you reading this narrative without access to a complete copy of the *Tome of Lore*, I will retell the ancient saga of the three Gods that once roamed this land, before man emerged from the cold cistern lapping the black rocks which surround Mount Kali. The shores of that lake are now dead – salted and choked, but once, lifetimes stretching back beyond imagination, the shores were bountiful and rimmed by a lush garden where mankind first learned how to love, how to grow, and of course, how to die.

Excerpt from the Tome (Book of Creation):
Thayer waded slowly into the cold lake water nestled serenely in a hidden valley high up in the Northron Climbs. Cradling His creation in anticipatory and well-scarred hands, He whispered the words of Lore into the dull stone surface in His latest attempt to bring life to the lifeless. The green-coloured stone glittered fitfully in the pre-dawn hour,

3

reflecting His half-smile on the dark, still surface of the water. As the stone's spark extinguished, He let it slip back underwater, drowning His frustration alongside the myriad other failed attempts littering the lake bed.

The Stone of Knowledge briefly flared to life around His neck as it registered this latest failure, and into the following darkness, Thayer studied the millions of stars overhead that mocked His inability to solve that which His Mother did effortlessly; creating life from nothingness. Raging at the stars in futile defiance of this one problem that continued to elude His God-given ability, His tantrum quelled when He spotted the small fiery object, reflecting its silent arc on the rippling waters around Him. Thayer thanked His Mother for granting Him this most precious gift, and strode south to claim the long sought-after solution to His only unsolvable puzzle.

Bashal stirred from mournful reverie, hearing a pitiful cry of sorrow, wailing softly in the silent spaces held between each of the crashing waves that thundered along the battered shoreline of Her island. She discreetly observed the source of the sorrow who was a mother that paced fretfully among some slippery rocks, and tried without success to retrieve the small, lifeless body that floated face-down in a tidal pool. Moved by compassion for the distraught mother, the Goddess scooped the newly born body from its watery grave, called its confused soul back from its first flight, and placed the tiny reawakening body back into the soggy nest, now moved up out of harm's way. The mother preened and squawked its delight, unafraid of the benefactor that moved swiftly away.

Bashal dared not revel at the familial reunion as the pangs of yearning overtook any feelings of joy, and sent Her stumbling blindly into the surf, ranting madness at Her Mother who dared to continue to mock Her barrenness by showing the ability in the smallest of fragile creatures. She wanted to know why Her Mother continued to deny the child that was rightfully Hers. Frustrated and furious, She plucked the final red-fletched arrow from Her quiver, whispered powerful words into the gilt runes that decorated the arms of Her bow She had named *Silya*, Seeker, and let it fly in search, once more, for the answer She knew did not exist. Shock stifled Her choking despair as the last arrow, Her last hope, curved back upon itself, away from the open ocean, and angled upwards behind Her, streaking towards a bright object that was falling from the Heavens. Shaking with hysteria, Bashal ran north to claim her long sought-after child, discarding Her now-useless bow in the surging tide.

Beady crimson eyes peered heatedly from within thick foliage that hid the bright golden scales decorating Eth's long, sinewy body; heavy claws clenching the moist loam in hungry anticipation. A musky stag, nostrils flaring, eyes black with anger, approached the barely-hidden God-Creature slowly, displaying its majestic crown of antlers in warning to this would-be interloper. The God-Creature bridled at the stag's display of hubris and unleashed Its Will upon the woodland guardian. Falling under Eth's heady

5

spell, the stag lifted its antlered crown in supplication and exposed its throat as commanded. The God-Creature pounced furiously and lifted the kicking sire above the treed canopy on well-muscled wings, crunching on neck bones and drinking the hot blood down its parched throat.

Its joy fell along with the still-kicking corpse as It sensed wrongness from above. The God-Creature panicked upon seeing the fiery object falling in a destructive path towards Its home and towards all of the precious articles It had taken a lifetime to procure and hide within the warren of tunnels snaking into and under the mountain. And then Eth sensed movement north and south, and realized that It was too late, that It was being ambushed on all sides for Its precious objects, and from those that It had suspected least of all; family, the other God-Creatures that inhabited this land. Alighting on the mountain's lip, a last thought penetrated Eth's hate-filled mind before consuming them all in a furious conflagration; *I will never release you from this betrayal.*

That fateful day three Gods clashed at Mount Kali in search of, and in defence of their Creator's Gift; instead finding immolation and destruction. Knowledge, Yearning and Fury combined to give birth to mortal creatures from the pure, baptismal waters that lapped the God's final resting place, known then as Immortals Tarn.

A man and a woman, each carrying the desire to procreate, the thirst for knowledge and the need for self-preservation crawled naked and helpless into this world and found paradise. A paradise that now included greed, deceit, magic and murder.

***

As in the Tome's Excerpt of man's first appearance, my story begins with naïveté bred from ignorance, but all that was about to change.

ONE

Heeding the Call

The serpent uncoils.
Master of discord, It sows,
Bleeding a trail of chaos.
~Book of Eth

"Higher you idiot!" I'd soon learn that they were words to live by in the years to come.

Idiot, now I feel the fool, but then, seventeen and full of myself, the only idiot I knew was the one ordering new wheels on his cart in the middle of winter without steel trims. My father's business seemed to be doing fairly well, mostly due in part to the spindly fool who yelled down at us, who undoubtedly would be back again for new wheels before the season ended.

We should finally have enough money this year to send my younger brother to a Temple of his choosing and still have enough to build the extension on our house in the spring for me and my future Mrs. Cartwright. My father and mother, bless their eternal souls, had their combined eyes settled on Maura, our local Innkeeper Mr. Salt's daughter, and by the Gods so did I. Her eyes were molten laughter and her smile killed me at ten paces. I couldn't keep her out of my mind as I worked and thus the present, "Higher you idiot!"

"Aye, Sir." My usual reply. I looked across at my dad struggling on the other side, and I noticed he looked unusually tired as we took the curses doled out from our idiotic patron, Mr. Scat. I remember my father's eyes looking down-trodden and his complexion sallow, and curse my memory but I'm sure that was the precise moment when I decided that my present circumstances required vast improvement.

He winked at me, and I at him as we settled that old and rotting cart onto the new set of unshod wheels. My father implored him to at least replace the axle supports and the rusted springs, but Mr. Scat just swore at my dad and accused him of trying to rob him of every last coin. The minimal costs were always too unseemly, even though Mr. Scat's mill had produced more flour that year than any other due to our bountiful harvest (his new inlaid, brown velvet coat notwithstanding). Besides his mill, he had been raised to Lordship status only yesterday, despite the controversy surrounding his brother's death.

The cart settled noisily on the creaky springs as my father and I just stood aside and watched, fingers crossed and hidden wards etched into the air behind our backs. Mr. Scat sniffed the air and examined the mended upholstery studiously while shifting his weight back and forth to test the seat as my younger brothers hammered the axle pins into place. He ordered my dad to throw the old wheels in the back as he wasn't giving them away, unless of course my father wanted to pay him for them, then he could settle his accounts as fair trade for servicing a *Lord*. I threw the wheels in the back as Mr. Scat sniffed, obviously displeased, and threw the owed coins into the mud at my father's feet. As he drove off, scaring away the few birds, he promised to return and force us all into the militia.

That was the moment I turned and said, "I'm leaving dad. I can't stay and bow my head to the likes of Scat, besides, the King needs me." There are certain moments in life that are etched into your mind for eternity, filling your soul with joy or regrets, and that day, that very second, I saw whatever life that still existed in my father, drain from his face as he stood still for a moment, nod his head in acknowledgment, and then walk stoop-shouldered back into our house. I didn't know then the regrets that would comprise my life, but I also knew that I couldn't stay and be faced with a life full of "Higher you idiot!"

The night before I had been at the Inn's tavern, The Salt Cellar, enjoying a pint and the sight of my Maura as she served them, when a strange man entered and sat by himself, ordering a flagon of wine from out-country, which he knew the Inn apparently stored in their famous cellar. Not a strange sight in and of itself, but this man wore the King's Colours, which hadn't been seen in our village for quite some time, not including the Excise Man, who everyone knew and was seen regularly each quarter.

Just then Mr. Scat preened his way into the tavern, sporting a bright red sash declaring his new appointment as

Lord Scat. So it was true. It had been widely discussed among the women that his brother's recent death had in fact been murder, and more than one had looked to the younger Scat as the obvious perpetrator of the crime. However, since the body had been discovered floating in the river, no proof of murder could be found and the official cause was put down as drowning.

His *Lordship* called Maura over and as he ordered a drink, he placed a coin as close to the wall as possible so that she had to lean in to pick it up, and as she did, his hands caressed her buttocks. She stood quickly and grabbed his hand, slamming it back onto the table hard. He triumphed a greasy grin around the room, while slicking his black hair back over his balding pate. As our eyes met, his grin faded. He shook his head and mouthed the word 'Bitch'. Before I realized I was standing, a strong arm pulled me back to the table and to our conversation. My cousin Kay whispered into my ear that he wasn't worth it and I nodded in agreement.

I turned back to my friends and continued our heated discussion about the 'new' Lords who seemed to enjoy their newfound status at our expense. They prodded me insinuating that I should be raised too as the King seemed to be favouring the wealthiest merchants. I told them that he favoured only those that traded on the mainland, off of 'Red Rock'. The name suited as it was steeped in our blood, but was actually named after a giant oak tree in Tyre that supposedly grew only red leaves. Our bitter derision turned to surprise as the stranger spoke up.

"It is red. I've seen it for myself, and indeed it looks as if it's been fed on nothing but human blood." He turned back into the booth, drained his drink and refilled it from the glass bottle occupying the role of guest at his table. We didn't know what to make of him, so on an under table bet, I approached the man hesitantly and was ushered onto the bench opposite just as his plate of food arrived. He dug into the juicy roasted mutton, draining rivulets of grease over his grey-streaked beard and onto the red and blue sash hanging loosely across his chest.

"I want you to tell your friends that the King has issued forth a proclamation for enlistment. I've posted it on the Inn, but if any man of reasonable age doesn't voluntarily enlist, their family's taxes will rise tenfold in the coming year, and likewise if they do join, they will be spared next year's taxes in gratitude." With that bold statement he smirked and polished off his drink in four easy gulps. He offered me the remainders of food off his plate which I gladly accepted and made the remaining roasted potatoes disappear down my throat faster than his drink.

"Sir, might I ask why he is enlisting more men? Surely Tyre is already full." I ordered another drink and waited for his answer.

"Young man, have you ever been off this island?" He asked, but I heard no humour in the question.

"No sir, there's never been any need to leave." I looked over at my friends who had engaged back into derisive laughter, darting smarmy looks over at Lord Scat.

"Son, there is a lot to see out there, more I suspect than you have ever imagined. I've seen endless mountain ranges capped in never-melting snow. Torrential rivers, blue as topaz, grey as stone and some as colourless as your face. I've encountered creatures in inhabitable areas that were as cold and inhospitable as their environment and could eat a man whole. And women." He piqued his eyebrows as Maura served my drink and flashed a toothy smile, obviously impressed that I was conversing with the strange Lord.

"Thank you, but I don't need other women. One will do nicely." I responded too quickly. He merely grinned and resumed drinking his wine. "But my friends might want to know more." I sheepishly added, hiding my smirk behind the mug of beer.

"Ah well then, there are women whose skin is as dark as earth, olive skinned beauties and some as white as fine porcelain. I've seen eyes of every colour to match a merchant's gem collection. But all of these aren't the answer to your first question." He sat back on the bench and let out a slow belch. "Where there are people there are conflicts, and where there are Kings there are wars. Wars to defend borders and wars to defend those who can't defend themselves. Such is a war brewing now, off island, and at stake are not only the King's lands, but His subject's lives as well. Some have already been stolen by a cruel and barbarous Queen, whom it is rumoured," he leaned in closer, "feeds on her victims flesh." The room seemed to grow colder suddenly.

"Their flesh?" My voice failed to emit much more than a squeak.

"Aye lad, I've heard whispered tales of the devastation she's left behind and it's enough to chill my soul." He inscribed the God's protective symbol in the air above the table. "Thayer save my eternal soul, but yes, she is said to command an unholy army." He looked down at his dinner, and slowly pushed the plate away. "Your King needs help to stop this abomination. You wouldn't want to see your family eaten alive, would you?" The question hung between us.

It was at that point I realized the room had grown quiet and a rapt audience hung on the stranger's every word. He stood and surveyed the people staring at him, incredulity plain on more than one face.

"Queen Mordeth is an abominable creature." He held the room with each word. "She wields an unholy power over her followers, and they eat the innocent in her name. I am not the only man that wishes to see the colour of her blood." He walked to the bar that centered the room. "Your King needs every fit man at his side to see this murderess thrown down. Innocent people need protecting and in answer, King Arian rides to their salvation." Mr. Salt, Maura's father, handed the man another drink, spilling beer from the lip as his hand shook.

"I can see by your faces that you don't believe me because you don't know me. I am *Lord* Trevor," he eyed my friends at the adjacent table, "and King Arian is my brother." He pulled forth a signet ring attached to a golden chain buried beneath his clothes and held it out for all to see. The symbol of a giant oak tree was all that I caught as he swept it by slowly.

"Your King needs you. I need you. Your people need you. You all know Lord Fiongall, and he would have been here in my stead, but he has already gone ahead of the main army in search of Queen Mordeth. Lord Scat has been ordered to remain here and raise the militia, just in case things go badly." He drained his beer. "I leave at first light to join the King's army. We'll arrive at Ambrose Harbour on the coast two days after that where we've arranged transport to the mainland. You'll not be alone lads, the King is determined to engage the Ren-Tigarians."

Mouths gaped at this unexpected revelation. Everyone had heard tales about the Ren-Tigarians, a sect of mysterious priest-warriors who lived in the Northron Climbs claiming to be disciples of the true teachings of Thayer. After their failed 'Great War' a hundred years ago, they withdrew behind the walls of their Temple and decreed not to interfere in the affairs of man again.

"My Grandmother, Queen Isobel, used to quote Lore to us as children, 'When darkness falls upon the innocent, the

Creator's light shall set them free.' Alas, she is no longer
here, but her wisdom fills my thoughts of late." He walked
slowly back to the booth. "You have until tomorrow at dusk
to make your decision."

I noticed the empty table where Lord Scat had been
sitting. It didn't dawn on me then that he had left during
Lord Trevor's announcement, but it bothered me that he
wasn't there to see our excitement at this new prospect. My
friends and I stayed until closing asking Lord Trevor as
much information as we could about Queen Mordeth and the
famed Ren-Tigarians. We left quietly, trying not to disturb
old Mr. Partridge who had passed out at his table again,
spectacles lying gently next to his grey-haired head. After
planting a kiss on Maura and having the door slammed in
my face by her father, I said goodnight to my friends and
made my way back home in the crisp winter air, crunching
frozen snow under my boots. I turned a couple of times,
convinced that someone was following and quickened my
steps home to imagined ghoulish shapes of flesh-hungry
hordes hunting me.

I awoke the next morning, heart racing and sheets soaked
with sweat as images of babies being eaten slowly faded in
the growing daylight. I knew I had to do something, but
then again, I was an impressionable young man with the
world, and a future bride to impress. I began packing my
few meagre belongings and was stowing them away when
my father called me to help as Lord Scat had arrived for his

new wheels. After I told him I was leaving, my father fell into a foul drinking mood that only fed my own anger. I know now that his depression was based on his fear of losing the only thing he cared for, his family, and his connection to the future, and I suppose me as well.

It turned out that our family name didn't end with me as my parents had been smart enough to brood a large family, and eventually my brother-in-law took over the family trade along with my older sister. My younger brother eventually decided not to join a temple, and instead was smart enough to join the kitchen scullery in Tyre.

My shattered beliefs have slowly been restored over the past thirteen years, but back then, I heard the call to glory and answered it whole-heartedly.

TWO

Off Island

Yearning burns,
And withers the heart.
A wasteland of cold despair,
That hope can never repair.
~Book of Bashal

I'm not one to preach advice, but never let anyone convince you that leaving home and going abroad is easy, especially at seventeen and completely naïve of how the world works. I was well muscled due to the heavy labour of my father's trade, but I was nowhere near ready for battle, let alone ready to leave my family or face my betrothed. My youngest sister was not quite three years old and wailed at me not to leave. Obviously she was wiser than my seventeen years.

Nevertheless, I managed to pack everything I believed I would need into a small cloth bindle that I carried on the end of my new weapon. My father, knowing my mind to leave, had retrieved from the wall of our workshop a long ash spear with a steel head, wrapped in an old rotting cloth. The shaft was the colour of dried blood and from the look of the rusted steel head I had presumed the shaft would snap in the first melee. I took it to my friend Jared's father, who was our local smithy, and asked him to hammer out and hone the edge. Thus I left home and the only life I had known with an old spear, a change of clothes, a small carved Thayer amulet my mother hung on a leather cord around my neck, and a handful of coins my father pushed into my hand. My mother cried, my siblings cried, my father drank.

Maura on the other hand, looked like a badger flushed from its den. "You miserable sack of goat shite!" Maura, arms buried beneath her breasts, shot me a look that would have frozen my blood if the very sight of her hadn't started it to boil. My mind reeled with the implications of leaving and I hoped that when I returned Maura would still be unmarried (the Gods forbid she entertained any of Lord Scat's attentions). I mouthed an oath touching my amulet and stopped in my tracks.

"Maura, you know I'll never make anything of my life here, trapped between changing wheels and bowing to *Scat*." I dropped my bundle and heard the heavy spear head clunk on an exposed rock. A quick look confirmed the edge not to be damaged and still sharp.

"Thomas, you should be my husband and raise a family. That's not something to run away from." Her dark eyes chastised me. "Sooner or later you'll realize that the world doesn't revolve around Thomas pig-shite Cartwright." She stormed back into the Inn.

"Maura!" I retrieved my bundle and followed her into the dark tavern, placing it in a chair by the door. I saw old Mr. Partridge perk up from his table and raise a drink in greeting. He laughed through over-sized spectacles while eating his eggs and toast. I chased her into the kitchen and grabbed her by the arm, "Maura, please."

I turned her around to face me and saw the tears ruining her beautiful face. I held her close and rocked her back and forth as she sobbed into my chest. Her warm body awakened hidden desires in me and she recoiled violently.

"How am I supposed to continue on here when everyday I'll be imagining you lying in a ditch somewhere bleeding to death?" She was genuinely mad at me, and being the young oaf that I was, just shrugged my shoulders and stared into her big brown eyes, not saying a thing. I tried my best smile. "Follow me." She graced me with an answering smile.

As she dragged me up the stairs and down the hallway to a small room that she locked behind us, she calmed my fears of her father by explaining that he had travelled to Tyre with Lord Trevor at daybreak, carting barrels of his best wine purchased with rare gold coins, and wouldn't be back until tomorrow. Her mother was in the next village visiting a sister who had just given birth.

We didn't speak again as we undressed slowly to enjoy our last afternoon together, naked and sweaty beneath some old scratchy woollen blankets. I would remember that afternoon fondly during my following years of self-torment, and use its pure indulgence as a balm against my many dark regrets. I could recall every curve of her young, shapely body, the smell of her hair, the feel of her hands pressing against my lower back and the warm sensations of her womanhood. The sun was setting as I left the tavern, smiling among the last cartful of hopefuls leaving our village to the wagon driver's warning bell. I waved at Maura and kissed the air until losing sight around the first of many bends in the road. Sitting back against the rocking wood railing, I felt under my shirt for the leather thong around my neck which now contained a lock of her hair wrapped lovingly in silk beside my Thayer amulet; two wards against evil.

I sit here at my desk, more than a decade later, and the smell of her hair still floods back the soft memories of that magical afternoon. It is painful to place it back within the golden locket it now resides in, but my fresh tears keep it company as the amulet is long gone.

That trip to the coast would remain in my mind as one of the longest journeys I would ever take. I was constantly at war with myself to leap off the back of that rickety cart and run back into Maura's soft embrace, but my youthful cowardice rooted me against the hard wood railing. The other boys, for I could not call that rabble men, filled the remainder of our trip with boasts of bravado that heartened everyone and filled our minds with dreams of glory and riches that would see us each become a king.

It took two days to reach the coast, and by then I had eaten all of the food Maura had given to me as well as the loaf of bread I stole from our pantry, although circumspectly, I realised my mother had baked it specifically for me, as it had been filled with crumbled goat cheese which she knew had been my favourite since childhood.

Ambrose Harbour teemed with activity. Men, women, children, prostitutes, hawkers, sailors, merchants and thieves stalked the causeway. My natural size cleared a path in front of us, that and the way I turned in slow circles taking in the sights, bringing my shiny spear head swinging over people who ducked and swore while trying to avoid it. Ships crowded the harbour, some just docking, but most were rowing out past the harbour inlet to pick up the winter winds that would fill their multi-coloured sails and drive them away, toward the mainland which wasn't visible through the fog today.

Kay grabbed my arm and pointed to a ship tied up at the end of the docks that was being loaded with supplies. Lord Trevor stood at the end of the gangplank leading onto the ship conversing with a gnarled and twisted older man with grey greasy hair that he kept patting back over his tanned eggshell. Lord Trevor caught my eye and waved me over, the other boys from my village following in my wake.

"Very impressive Mr. Cartwright, you're lucky one of these sailors didn't knife you before you cut their halyards." The hearty laugh escaping his barrel-chest lightened my mood and I couldn't help myself but embrace him in a cordial hug that he returned solidly. "Well met Mr. Cartwright! Well met!" He patted me on my back as I introduced the sorry lot that had escaped from my village.

He shook each person's hand, repeating their name and then showed us onboard the *Merry Widow*. "Mr. Mange here was just telling me that we should reach the mainland within three days, good weather permitting of course, this being so close to the end of winter."

What I mistook as a misshapen hump on Mr. Mange's shoulder turned and looked at me with baleful, rheumy eyes. "Well my day's young sir, looks like Beatrice has taken a fancy to you." Mr. Mange cackled as the old cat meowed into his ear and settled back into his neck. I swear that cat had less hair than Mr. Mange which wasn't saying much for the cat. I followed them onboard and was introduced to my berth for the next three days, which was to say a swale of hay next to a pile of tarred rope that would become a depository for the entire contents of my stomach.

I don't know which I blamed more, the roiling winter seas or the pathetic excuse for liquor that was passed among the men on board that tasted vile and smelled of goat urine. Those three days on board definitely lasted longer than the cart ride to the coast, but without the constant urge to flee as there was nowhere to run. I didn't know my stomach could hold that much fluid, but after awhile I stifled my gags by sucking on a rag soaked in seawater.

A man has never been happier than I was that day when we spotted land and hours later, wobbled onto shore and kissed the ground holding my amulet in my shaking fist. I spat out bits of sand over the next couple of hours that had found its way into my teeth as I profusely thanked Thayer for allowing me back onto solid ground. My friends and I celebrated the crossing that night in one of Seacliffe's local taverns called *The Seawitch*, which reeked of old fish, and later offered back to the ground everything in our still-swooning stomachs. My teeth were beginning to protest the constant regurgitations through a series of shooting pains that tore at my jaw.

Only five of us from our village remained true friends during the coming months and years. Graham's dad was a carpenter, but he didn't retain any of what his father had tried to teach him. Kay was my first cousin, and his face or his brother's had forever been intruding into our workshop, so much so that my father considered them long-lost sons, despite their reluctance to actually work. Kay split his time between our workshop and the smithy with Jared where both grew shoulders and arms seemingly overnight. Geoffrey's father was a baker, and his love for Lord Scat was worse than mine as his father was indebted up to his eyes for the milling.

For some unfathomable reason Graham and Geoffrey had not been affected by the sea travel, but Jared, Kay and I had headaches for several days, the liquor notwithstanding. I had started a debate that lasted most of the first day, convinced that we had been poisoned by the ship's crew. Lord Trevor swiftly got wind of this and drew me aside.

"Son, I've heard rumours that you're spreading dissention among my men." Lord Trevor whispered into my ear as we stood freezing on the deck by the railing.

"I'm sorry Milord, but Kay and I have been miserably sick, more so than any onboard." I paused catching his eye.

"Careful lad, those words are mutinous and could see you swimming home." He swung my head back to show me we were approaching two days away by ship.

I gulped and forced my gaze back to him, quickly thinking. "I apologize, the food has been excellent and the lodgings beyond compare." I managed a weak smile.

"Good to hear it Mr. Cartwright. Now make sure your friends think the same." He pushed me forward where I made my way below decks to relay my new sentiments. I glanced back as I descended the stairs and saw him relaying my feelings to Mr. Mange. Beatrice saw me and hissed. Mange only nodded and limped his way back to the wheel deck.

Early the next morning, our troop marched into the outskirts of town to an abandoned farm, sea at our backs, and spent the next several hours complaining about footwear, hunger, and the unknown enemy. We were completely innocent of the way the world turned, the way it bled, the way it was unravelling at its very seam. Our immediate concerns were for a hot bowl of food, a flagon of *decent* ale, and a wench we might spot falling out of her blouse.

Lord Trevor delivered our reality upon a tray that had us hip deep in horse manure before noon in the hastily erected way-station for the assembling army. Seacliffe was a bustling harbour town whose claim to fame was a clear view of the very island we had just left, and a pasty white meal-fish. That's what we called the crap we were made to eat for the next two weeks made from a batter of some kind of bottom fish they pulled from the sea every morning and by noon had created a texture-less mound fried in a pan with a pinch of salt.

As we choked back another lunch, Lord Trevor approached our group to give us the very good news that we were departing from the town tomorrow and making our way inland for the next couple of weeks. "Pack lightly." He snarled, riding past us on his way to the Mayor's house that dominated the town's skyline with its blue tiled roof and golden mermaid mounted on its peak pointing to the ocean. The whole afternoon was spent packing crates onto the carts that would be following behind us.

He appeared again later in the evening as we sprawled exhausted in the barn we had converted into our barracks with an armload of weapons wrapped in a sack that he dropped into the center of the room.

"I bought these from the Mayor in gratitude for the use of this farm. Grab what you can." He boomed as we ripped open the cloth and swarmed the pile, snapping up anything that our dirty hands could clamp down on. "Most of it is probably shite, and will more than likely snap at your first parry, but better one of these breaking than one of your thick skulls."

I tested my grip on the sword I had grabbed, unsure of the feel of the sheath as it looked like it was made from the skin of some strange fish, but it stuck to my sweaty palms like honey. I gave a surprised look around and noticed everyone studying their own new weapon, and unsheathed it slowly. The blade was dull, having no sheen at all and I despaired at having to spend more of my own money to have it sharpened. Disappointed, I looked to the pile, but all the weapons had been claimed. My sword was completely unimpressive and the hilt appeared to be wrapped in the same fish skin as the sheath. I touched the blade edge to test its sharpness and as I did, my vision swirled slightly and I thought I heard soft, distant humming. I was surprised to see a line of blood marring my thumb.

"Beautiful." Lord Trevor whispered into my left ear as he appeared out of the ether behind me. I jumped and eyed him curiously as the humming suddenly stopped. "May I?" He questioned, grabbing it from me. He palmed the hilt and turned it over several times, eyeing the blade closely, and the hilt particularly. "In my lifetime I would never have believed it." He hefted it with one hand and then with both as he moved into a corner beside a table that held both water and bread.

"Sir, I don't understand. Yours is much nicer than this shoddy one." I shrugged noncommittally and crossed my arms over my chest.

"You obviously have a great history with swords Mr. Cartwright, yes? Then please indulge me with your expertise." A cunning smile played across his face as he briefly met my eyes, then returned them to the blade. "No? If I'm not mistaken, this blade was crafted by a master swordsmith. I've seen many similar inferior copies." His last words hung in the air as he spun around blurring the blade in an arc to completely sever the leg of the table. Our water and bread crashed to the floor. The leg had been cleanly cleaved in two. "Yes I knew it...the blade you see is unbelievably strong, and yet incredibly light."

I took the blade back and was amazed to see no visible damage on the surface. A group of admirers had grown around us and more than one offered a trade plus whatever valuables they had brought with them. A couple of boys even tried to cut the other legs off with their swords before Lord Trevor yelled at them to stop. He chastised them about destroying the furniture and not being able to replace any weapons that they decided to break. Lord Trevor grasped me by the elbow and led me toward the door leaning close to my ear.

"Mr. Cartwright, guard this unexpected treasure closely. Trust me when I say that you will never see its equal in your lifetime." He busied me out into the cold night air. "Do *not* let this fall out of your possession, especially to the likes of one of these untutored louts. I will have to explain this in more detail to you at a later date." And with that he mounted his horse and disappeared back into town.

After he left one of the younger men snapped his sword in two trying to hack at the table legs again. He disappeared outside and buried the pieces deep in a manure pile we had worked on the other day. Looking rather shaken and upset he disappeared later that night into Seacliffe and wasn't seen again.

THREE

Inland

All-seeing.
All-knowing.
All-empty.
~Book of Thayer

W e marched slowly for the next two weeks into the
middle of Manath Samal and into training
grounds that appeared old and well used. Men
from all over the province swarmed to the King's summons
and at the end of our first day I heard one of the cooks
complaining that all of us ranged just over two thousand
souls, including ground soldiers, cavalry, archers, recruits,
cooks, armourers, blacksmiths, laundresses and a few crazy
zealots who claimed no allegiance but were drawn by the
crowds and the prospect of free food.

We were immediately set to work, not that the previous
weeks had been remiss from constant cleaning, horse duty,
food gathering, and general labouring which included setting
up our camp every night, and then clearing away all
remnants before we were on the road the next day. It was
now nearing the end of winter and we could see the land
slowly coming back alive around us. We had started a basic
fighting and training regime during our inland march that
began every evening just before dinner and comprised of

exhaustive defensive drills which ended in a random sparring match using heavy wooden staves.

Lord Trevor usually resided as judge at these matches, but on the night of our arrival at the training grounds a group of seasoned soldiers joined him to witness the event. They stood together and eventually hand-picked two of us and that was how I found myself squaring off against my cousin Kay. We had been pretty much even-matched since we started the sparring event and had fought each other occasionally, but tonight's fight was different as we found ourselves facing off wearing borrowed armour.

I was half a head taller than Kay, but he was wider in the shoulders, and consequently hit a little harder than I did. But he couldn't match my reach. As we circled and flourished our staves, the soldiers spat bits of advice, commenting about our mother's teats and our lack of courage. Kay came at me first with a quick underhanded slash that I countered easily, returning it with a forward stroke that would have knocked him unconscious if he hadn't countered with an equally fast block. Their comments ceased and we knew we had everyone's attention. Kay attacked again and reversed a swing that would have taken out my legs if I hadn't anticipated the attack and jumped clear. It was my turn to put him on the defensive with a series of well-timed hits and thrusts that ended with him on his knees, panting heavily through the slits in his helmet.

"So that's the way it's to be then?" Kay asked pushing himself into a standing position. "So be it."

31

He unleashed a fury of whorls and thrusts that had me stumbling back, barely deflecting each blow that would have given me bruises if I wasn't wearing the armour. He ended with an over-handed blow that forced me to my knees, holding the stave doubled-handed over my head in a protective stance.

"Enough!" Lord Trevor was standing close to us. "I don't need you two killing each other tonight. Go back to your camp but leave the armour here." With that he strode back to the hard-faced soldiers who began discussing our match with him.

Kay offered his hand and pulled me to my feet.

"I wonder what that was all about?" Kay asked as we removed our stifling helmets.

"I don't know, but you had me worried, cousin." I studied his grinning face. "I thought you were trying to kill me."

"I was." He said wolfishly. "I imagined you to be one of the Queen's soldiers."

"By the Gods, that was an impressive show you gave us!" Graham strode up holding two cups of something. "I hope it wasn't all for my benefit!" He laughed as we downed the cool beer. "I think you may have attracted the attention of your betters." He thumbed over his left shoulder where Lord Trevor was shepherding out the soldiers. I swore I saw a coin flip in the air and land in his hand.

"I don't know about you, but I could do with another beer, but back at our camp." Kay suggested as we removed the armour and placed it back onto the armour trees flanking the gate into the arena.

As we approached our camp, our friends spilled out from every sluice valve and clapped us on the backs for our demonstration. My mind kept racing back to my mysterious sword and the affect it would have made on Kay's armour, but that image was interrupted when I smelled the roasted mutton and potato stew. Saliva raced down my chin.

"Lads, let's raise a cheer to our two knuckleheads that put on a show worthy of Lord Trevor's training." Graham smiled, encompassing our entire party with a raised mug. "Cheers!" He drained it in one smooth motion, which was mirrored by everyone sitting around the fire.

"Easy now, not too much boys." Lord Trevor said entering the glow of fire. "You've a long day again tomorrow and the Gods know that it'll start early enough." As he said that, he scooped a cup from of one of the youngest men and drained it in one smooth motion. "Thomas and Kay, after you've eaten meet me in my tent." He turned and melted back into the night.

"Shall we stay up for you Sirs, or will you be indisposed for the night?" Graham mimicked a kiss to the buttocks.

"Stay up if you like, I still need to clean my weapon and your guts will do nicely." Kay stretched his shoulders, grinned and filled his bowl with the steaming contents from the pot hanging over the fire. "Envy suits you Graham, the colour matches your hose." He began laughing as he dipped some bread into the stew and gobbled it up.

"Why do you think those soldiers were so interested in you two?" Geoffrey, who was the youngest, had a hint of a moustache growing on his upper lip which looked more like dirt than hair.

"They probably just needed a good laugh." Jared's mane of blonde hair resembled an unwashed dog. His grim face belied his age, appearing ten years older than the rest of us. Perhaps it was his full beard.

"Why don't we ask Lord Trevor himself? Kay, are you ready?" I wiped my mouth on the sleeve of my tunic eager to go and find out why we were being summoned, and avoid cleaning up after eating.

As instructed since leaving Seacliffe, we both strapped on our new swords and walked from the light of the fire to the middle of the camp where Lord Trevor's large blue and white striped tent stood. The flaps were closed, but the torchlight within shadowed his movements. I coughed as we approached and Lord Trevor invited us in. A guard materialized at the entrance, pushing his way outside and into the night.

We had to cover our eyes as we entered the tent so the light didn't temporarily blind. Something triggered a defensive reaction in me, but before I could draw my sword, Kay's firm grip held me fast.

"Is that anyway to meet your King?" An unfamiliar voice questioned with a hint of steel in it.

"You'll have to forgive them Sire, but I didn't tell them you'd be here." Lord Trevor sat down in a high backed chair beside the man he addressed. My first impression was of great strength, and a casual confidence that filled the large tent. "Thomas, Kay, this is my brother and your liege-lord, King Arian."

Simultaneously, I was compelled to my knees and filled with terror, so much so that my mouth went dry and my palms began to sweat. My mind swirled with the implications as I had never imagined seeing our King, let alone meeting him in such a private setting.

"Stand gentlemen and gather a seat." Arian said calmly as we stood and I got a clear look at this man. He was garbed in brown riding leathers that were indistinguishable from any other soldier and looked travel-worn. The only mark of office he wore was a large signet ring hanging around his neck on a heavy looking chain, and a single golden ring in his left ear. His eyes sparkled keenly in a face that sported a brown beard. He looked younger than Lord Trevor, but that could have been because of the grey that streaked the other's hair. Kay handed me a folding chair that we drew close to an urn burning wood in the middle of the tent.

"That was an impressive demonstration we witnessed," Arian smiled with a full mouth of unstained teeth, "for two untrained young men." He tucked the signet ring back into his tunic and picked up a goblet from a table beside him. "Welcome to our army." He glanced over as his younger brother rolled up a parchment, sprinkling sand on the drying red seal. "May I?" The King outstretched his hand to me.

Confused, I blinked, and then fell to my knee ready to kiss his ringed finger.

"Your sword Thomas, not your lips." I stood up, feeling embarrassed. "I was just telling Arian about it." Lord Trevor poked his head outside of the tent flap and relayed quiet instructions to the guard, handing him the sealed document.

I unbuckled the sword and handed it to him with both hands.

"Incredible. Trevor, where did you say you found this?" The King unsheathed the sword and studied the blade.

"Seacliffe, if you can believe it." Lord Trevor sat down beside his brother and bent his head in to examine the blade once more. "I didn't recognize it at first because of the strange hilt and scabbard." The King fingered the strange fish-skin hilt and scabbard and made a surprised look with his eyes.

"Amazing material. I wonder if he became a fisherman?" The King smelled the hilt, which raised my eyebrows. "I suppose you couldn't throw some light on this Fen?" The King asked as he continued to examine the hilt, holding the blade upright at arm's length.

"It will need proper identification, but the blade does look old." A disembodied voice came from behind us, causing us to turn quickly and knock the folding chairs over. A man dressed all in black stood at his ease against a tent pole by the opening. Only his eyes were visible as he wore black folded material to cover the remainder of his face. An open, lidless eye was woven in gold thread into the black cloth above his dark eyes. "Please gentlemen sit down." The man picked up and opened our overturned chairs.

"You boys are feeling a bit jumpy tonight aren't you?" Arian laughed quietly. "This is Fen Gisar and yes, he's a Ren-Tigarian." The black-clad man bowed at the introduction, then sat cross-legged on the ground beside the King. Arian handed the sword carefully to the Ren-Tigarian. He turned it over and over in his hands and eyed the blade closely. He reached under his face-covering, licked one finger, and wiped it along the blade near the cross-brace.

"You can barely make out the character." He pointed to an insignificant mark that I had assumed was a flaw in the blade. "It is the mark of Al-Shidath." Fen's eyes studied me. "We know he was killed during The Great War, but neither his body nor his sword were ever returned to the God." He returned the blade to King Arian, hilt first. "It appears you've finally found The Sword of Prophecy."

"Perhaps he didn't die and decided to live in Seacliffe?" I suggested into the sombre atmosphere just as a piece of wood snapped loudly in the fire pit, startling me and throwing up sudden sparks.

Fen Gisar gestured with a warding sign at the pit. "Boy, you shouldn't speak ill of the dead." His stern eyes chilled me despite the fire.

"Come Fen, the boy isn't aware of your bloody customs, are you Thomas?" Trevor asked. After a quick refute,

Trevor turned to Fen. "He wouldn't know anything about your warped system of rules." The two men stared at each other in gathering silence.

"Enough." Arian broke the tension and handed the blade back to me. "Regardless, it has come into Mr. Cartwright's possession and there it will remain until we can study this further and verify it properly." He settled back into his high-backed chair. "We have other needs that take precedence over an old sword."

Understanding the waved dismissal, Kay and I bowed to the King and made our way out of the tent and back to our camp. All around us men were settling in for the night. When we returned, only Graham was still awake, poking a stick into the dying embers of our fire.

"Well, you've returned sooner than I would have thought, and your knees look rather unscathed." His smile dropped as he registered the grim looks on our faces. "What happened?"

Kay and I exchanged looks, and then shrugged our shoulders.

"We've just met the King." I said evenly, not revealing the unsettled feeling I had in my stomach. "And a Ren-Tigarian priest named Fen Gisar."

Graham didn't know how to respond, he just kept switching his gaze from one to the other looking for the telltale smile that would reveal our joke. "Bullshit." Again he waited for confirmation. "Why would the *King* want to see you miserable turd sacks?" He sneered a little too quickly, revealing jealously at missing out.

"I don't know," I admitted, "but I think it had to do with my sword."

Kay shrugged. "I'm going to bed, after I clean my *insignificant* sword." He turned to his bedroll, pulling out the oil cloth he kept tucked in his belt, a trick he learned from his days working with Jared's dad.

"Your *sword*? You've got to be kidding." Graham's face was filled with doubt. "I don't believe you and I don't really care and I'm going to bed too." He threw his stick into the fire and turned over in his bedroll, showing me his back. I sat for awhile on a log and stared into the dying embers before climbing into my bedroll. As I lay there restless, I watched a shooting star blaze across the night sky and made a wish to Thayer to help me learn the true meaning of my sword. I finally fell asleep to dreams about black ghosts sneaking around in the dark, always slightly out of focus, trying to steal the sword that hummed strangely in my hands.

FOUR

The Temple of Ren-Tigar

What are we?
The Gods remained silent.
We shall make some noise!
~Book of Man, 1st Century

O ur army spread out in formation along the base of a mountain and stared awkwardly up at the steep rocky path leading to massive walls encircling the legendary Temple of Ren-Tigar as King Arian, Lord Trevor, Fen Gisar and three other Ren-Tigarians (we had just learned they were traveling secretly with us), approached the Temple and bowed before large wooden doors studded with black iron spikes as a warning to any who approached that they were not welcome. Splashed across both doors in blood-red paint was the large symbol of Thayer, matching my own amulet, and it reminded me of a giant angry eye staring down in judgement.

Mounted on a pole high above a curved red roof structure that was barely visible above the grey walls, a flag with a sinewy black dragon outlined in gold on a red field seemed to come alive as it snapped in the cold mountain air. A column of grey smoke belched above the Temple and was lifted on the same wind currents, blowing west to mix with the fog shrouding the thickly treed mountainside.

The Ren-Tigarians accompanying King Arian removed objects from within their clothing, raised them above their heads, and began swinging them in slow circles to produce a high-pitched wailing that reverberated down the slope. As suddenly as they started, they stopped, and replaced the objects within their clothing.

A loud click could be heard as the locking mechanism was released within the wooden doors and a smaller man-door swung open, revealing a small man dressed in matching grey to the other Ren-Tigarian's black. He stepped over the sill and approached the lead Ren-Tigarian, who I assumed was Fen Gisar. After exchanging bows and informal greetings, Fen indicated the other Ren-Tigarians behind him, who bowed in turn.

Fen introduced King Arian. The King approached slowly and bowed a similar greeting to the small grey man. The man approached the King, getting quite close, and appeared to smell him. The King was turned slowly by the small man, examining him carefully, and once satisfied, bowed a formal greeting. The small man then turned to Lord Trevor, produced a fan which he unfolded slowly, and used it to block his view of Lord Trevor's face, shunning him publicly.

The grey man walked back inside the small man-door, still holding the fan, and was followed by Arian and the four Ren-Tigarians. As the last man stepped through the door, it slammed shut and the locking mechanism could be heard reengaging. The noise echoed in the stillness.

Lord Trevor stood alone, staring back up at the red accusatory eye. He turned on his heel and made his way back down the mountain path. Even from my distance at the front right flank I could see Lord Trevor's face growing red with anger as he approached.

"What in the name of Petra's arse are you doing? Set up camp!" His barked order was heard throughout the army as the lesser Lords instantly perked up and dismissed their rank and file to follow his command. Lord Trevor jumped onto the back of his big black warhorse and raced away. He didn't look back, disappearing into the thick forest.

We spent the next several hours erecting shelters, staking picket lines for the horses, setting up the canteen as ordered by the head cook and his staff, and finally digging the dreaded latrines. Darkness was draping the mountainside as we put the final touches to the camp. Graham bumped my elbow and we watched as Lord Trevor returned, handed his horse off to a groom and disappeared into his tent. Our interest was piqued at his earlier outburst, but our conversation was of a more immediate interest - food. It amazed us how much our army consumed and we had started to bet on the type and amount of game the archers would catch each day. Jared seemed to be on the current winning streak with today's four doe and three pheasant.

Kay appeared out of the growing darkness. "Thom, Lord Trevor wants to see you." I put my empty bowl down and followed him, shrugging my shoulders to my friends in confusion. After our sparring match, Lord Trevor had taken Kay on as his new squire-in-training.

"Did he say why?" I asked, but he just shook his head as we approached the tent. Kay pushed open the flap and showed me in.

"Good you're here. Kay, can you please see to this?" Kay grabbed the offered breastplate and left, fingering a dent that looked new. "Thomas, there are certain things I need to tell you about the Ren-Tigarians, as it may concern you in the days to come. Please pull up a seat." He indicated the folding chairs, so I grabbed one and set it up next to his table. "Have you had a chance to eat?" He asked digging into a bowl of the same stew which I noticed had more meat than ours.

"Yes Milord, I had just finished when Kay found me." I noticed the tension on his face. "Can I get you something to drink?" Since that first night in the tavern when I had befriended him, and subsequently after when I had claimed my strange sword, Lord Trevor had treated me like a long lost nephew to the consternation and derision of my friends.

"Thank you," he motioned to a table where a pitcher glistened next to the tent opening, "and please, help yourself." I filled two mugs and returned to the table where rolled up parchments littered the surface. Lord Trevor stopped eating and sat back in his chair. He eyed me sideways, leaned forward and downed the offered beer. He held the empty mug out to me, so I refilled it and sat down again. "You must have noticed the way I was treated by the

43

Temple Master today." His eyebrows lifted high onto his forehead as the question hung between us.

"I was pretty far away." I trailed off, trying to hide my lie.

"Surely you saw that little rat mock me?" The pain was evident on his face as he mimicked the fan-in-the-face gesture. "I was around your age when I first entered the Temple, as an initiate, but that was a long time ago." He pulled out and filled his pipe, then lit it with a switch from a glowing brazier. "A lifetime ago." He puffed out some smoke and then drank again from his refilled mug. "As second son, I had to prove myself to the world. I wanted to be trained in Ren-Tigar and become a warrior-knight," he blew a smoke ring up into the tent, "but I never completed the training." He smiled. "A messenger arrived from Tyre with the news that my father was dying. I had been away for over four years, shut-in behind those impregnable walls and I hadn't had any news from home since leaving, and had no visitors, so this was a bit of a shock.

"My father, *their King*, lie dying and they had the gall to forbid me from leaving." He tried another smoke ring, but it dissipated with his angry breath. "So I decided then and there that nothing on this earth would stop me from seeing him before he died. I managed to escape, but was pursued by Fen and his Hand of three." He let out a laugh and slapped his thigh. "Can you imagine being chased over hill and dale by men who had been trained to kill with a finger?" His laughter died down. "You see Thomas, it is against their most sacred teachings to leave the Temple before passing the Final Rite." He stood and refilled our suddenly empty mugs.

"Do you mind if I ask what the Final Rite is, or are you allowed to tell me?" I asked, intrigued by his story.

"Perhaps, perhaps not, but I'm going to tell you anyway, like I said, this may come to concern you." He peeked out the tent flap, and once satisfied there were no eavesdroppers, handed me my refilled mug and sat down. "Have you ever wondered why they cover their faces?" He saw me nod silently as I drank. "Where do I begin?" He thought about it for a moment, and then continued.

"Each Ren-Tigarian carries a vial of powder around their neck. This powder is actually the ash of their own spleens, removed and burned in the Fires of Purification. This is their Final Rite." He saw my confused expression. "Did you happen to notice the grey smoke rising from the Temple?"

"Yes, it was blowing west, above that strange flag." I explained, enthralled at being privy to their secrets.

He lowered his voice and continued. "Ren-Tigarians follow a Fighter's Codex, as deciphered from the Tome of Lore by the Primus Master Ghazanfar Ren-Tigar, hundreds of years ago. It decrees that no one can become a true disciple of the Codex until making an offering of oneself into the Fires of Purification." I noticed a slight wince as he settled back into his chair.

"As an initiate, your hair is shaved and thrown into the Fire, which represents the destruction of your past and a vow to follow the Codex." He absently ran his fingers through his short-cropped grey-laden hair. "Each initiate is assigned a mentor who assumes the responsibility for your training and from that point on, your mentor is honour-bound for your life and you are bound by honour for this sacrifice. You become a Finger in his Fist." He rubbed at a white scar on his wrist as his hand mimicked his words.

"After that, years will fly by while you hone ancient combat skills and learn the nuances of honour described in the Codex," he let out a long sigh, "until the Temple Master decides you are ready to become a Ren-Tigarian. That's when you are asked to make The Offering of your spleen into the Fire." He paused in his reverie.

"You never made The Offering?" I asked into the silence.

"No, I left when I received the news of my father's imminent death. I broke my vow to the Temple and the vow to my mentor." He smiled at me. "It was the worst betrayal imaginable." His smile turned solemn. "My mentor was Barik N'Adir, the Temple Master dressed in grey who denied my existence today." He looked like a man defeated. "When I left, he needed to regain his honour and sent his Fist, led by my friend, Fen Gisar, to hunt me down and kill me. When he failed, it was a dishonour that both Barik and Fen had to wear." This confession still confused me.

"When a mentor loses a pupil, usually through death, they are honour-bound to tattoo that pupil's name on their face using the spleen-powder of the fallen. That way they both honour the sacrifice and acknowledge their failure to protect." He paused again, hoping I understood this strange ritual. "My name is etched on both their faces, but they had to use their *own* spleen-powder. It was the only way they could keep honour in the eyes of Thayer. I am the only lost pupil who still lives, and as long as I do live, I am a constant reminder of their disgrace. So they hide that disgrace behind those veils." He sniffed the air, satisfied with his description.

"I experienced unimaginable horrors during my flight home, and after all of that, I was still too late." He looked mad. "My father died three days before I returned." Loss played across his features as he remembered that day. "I despise those bloody Ren-Tigarians and was against Arian coming here."

"Lord Trevor, I'm confused," I asked hesitantly, "You said that this will concern *me* in the days to come. What did you mean by that?"

"I'm sorry, I'm trying to get there, but the path of my story is curved. My worst fears materialized when Fen showed up in Tyre with his Hand and pledged their service to my brother, who had just been crowned." After tapping the wattle from his pipe, he placed it back into his pipe rack. "I think he was trying to gain honour by serving my brother,

47

insisting I was dead, but it also gave him an opportunity to slip a knife in my back." He sat back again in his chair.

"This is my warning to you Thomas, don't trust them. Despite their twisted versions of honour, they would want nothing more than to reclaim the Sword of Prophecy." He let out a long sigh. "They probably think it will regain the honour lost in their failed 'Great War' a hundred years ago." He smirked at the thought. "You should get some sleep." He led me to the entrance of his tent. "It was good talking with you Thomas. Be mindful of your sword but rest assured, they'll have to go through a dead man to get it."

The next morning dawned grey. The wind continued its chilly embrace down the mountainside as Kay and I made our way to the training grounds that were set up near the horse pickets. We both had our swords and I carried my spear. A tent sat at one end of a fenced area where other knights, squires and trainees like us battled each other in various combat styles and weaponry. We stepped inside the tent and were passed by Graham, Geoffrey and Jared who were all dressed in light leather shoulder and chest armour and each carried a long poleaxe. We exchanged greetings as they made their way to the training compound outside and we approached the Training Master's table. He had a series of scrolls with lines and names scratched, underlined and circled so that it resembled a painting I once saw in our Mayor's house that he claimed was a famous artist's original copy of a work-in-progress of another painter's rendering of

48

a great battle. All it looked like was chicken scratch, but I never told him that as I nodded in agreement.

"You two are just in time." Master Dirk said as he consulted his charts. "Let's see, you'll be wearing light plate, spears and on horseback." He started laughing. "You ever face a Dirty Dirk?" We just stared and smiled at him. "Well then, let's get you two carps suited."

We made our way to the back of the tent where two older men, both squires by their badges, removed our swords, took my spear and started bundling us into light plate mail. We wore vambraces on each arm, pauldrons over our shoulders that resembled the leather armour the other three we wearing, a thin breastplate and backplate, helmet and gauntlets. We went over to the Master-of-Arms where he handed us two spears from a rack of weapons.

I examined my spear and handed it back. "If you don't mind I'd like to use my own." I went back to where it rested on the ground and picked it up.

"Just a minute, don't want you killing yourself." The Master-of-Arms, Gianno was his name, grabbed my spear and examined it. He checked the shaft and head making sure it was all secure, and held it at arm's length to check its length and trueness. "Perfect. Did you know this was forged in Torcal?" His light accent betrayed his home to the south. "This mark here, the double V," he pointed at the base of the head, "means that it was made by Vasselli Vasselli. A master weapons smith." He pulled out a dagger that hung at his side and held it hilt-end to me. The same

49

rust colour of my spear shaft matched the hilt of his dagger.
"This too was made by him." He twirled it in his fingers.
"This cost me nearly a year's wages." The dagger
disappeared back into the matching coloured sheath. "Talk
to me after your practice. If the spear remains intact, I
would like you to consider a trade." He smiled a toothy
grin, pulled out an oiled cloth and returned to his weapons.

We approached the assigned paddock and were helped to
mount two large horses. Master Dirk approached us
followed by Gianno, who had a pipe tucked into his smiling
teeth. Dirk pointed to the end of the fence. "Do you see that
device mounted to the post?" He indicated a swivelling
device with a shield on one side and a ball and chain in the
other with what resembled a mounted knight in the middle.
"The idea is to hit the shield with your spear, and not get
knocked off of your mount from the backswing of that
mace." His sudden whistle startled our mounts. "Jonathan!"
He yelled into the paddock. A young knight mounted on a
horse similar to ours approached. "Sir Jonathan here will
show you whelps what to do."

The young knight spurred his horse into a gallop and
levelled his spear at the shield. The smack of the joust was
loud and the device was left swinging in a circle as the
knight slowed his horse and returned to us. Someone below
the device stopped its swing and reset it. Jonathan stopped
just shy and lifted his visor. "The trick is to hit it hard and
fast and to stay low on your mount."

"Thomas! You're up first!" Dirk backed away to watch. Gianno just smiled, puffing away at his pipe and crossed his arms over his chest. He made a gesture of something breaking in half and then twitched his finger no.

I heeled my horse forward and then kicked my spurs into its sides. It flinched forward and galloped toward the 'Dirty Dirk'. As it approached quickly, I tucked the spear under my arm as I simultaneously held it forward. I thrust it hard into the shield, but to my horror, the point stuck and twisted from my grip. I turned my head to follow the spear when I saw the ball and chain levelled at my head. The ball clanged into the side of my helmet, sending me flying from the saddle head over heels. The grey sky quickly went black and the sounds around me disappeared.

I slowly awoke and watched dancing shadows on the striped underside of a tent. "He's awake!" Gianno smiled down as he blew out some pipe smoke. "That wasn't so bad, no?" I tried to smile back but my throbbing head made me want to puke. Gianno helped me sit up as Dirk grabbed my head.

"Look up. Look down." Dirk's red rimmed eyes examined my own. "You'll live." He let go of my head and returned to his table. I looked around the tent and noticed that besides us, we were all alone. "You're lucky we weren't using the iron-weighted ball. The ball that hit you was hollow steel." He sat at his table and continued scratching and underlining names. I could see outside the tent flaps and noticed that it was dark outside.

51

"How long was I out for?" I stood unsteadily, bracing myself on the edge of the table. Gianno came up and handed me a mug of water. Feeling extremely parched, I drained it easily. My stomach grumbled with hunger.

"You were out for most of the day." Gianno leaned against the edge of the table and drank deeply of a heavily spiced wine that reminded me of winter. "I brought you a plate of cheese and bread in case you were hungry." I noticed it behind me and began devouring it, savouring the aroma of the freshly baked bread. "Now, about our little deal." He crooked an eyebrow at me. "I am willing to make a deal for you. I will relieve you of your spear, the source of your current headache, and in trade I will give you a nice dagger." He held out the weapon to me.

The dagger was beautiful. The grip was black leather inlaid with metal silver wire. The blade gleamed in the dull light and fit snugly into the matching black leather sheath. "I'm sorry Master Gianno, but I can't." I handed it back to him. "My father gave me that spear and I believe it was my grandfather's as well."

"You're good." He put his glass of wine down and returned to his table. After sorting through the weapons, he returned carrying a round shield. "But you didn't let me finish. I'll give you that dagger and this shield. See, this is a very good shield." He held it up across his shoulder where I could make out the workmanship on the beaten leather that covered the shield and formed a pattern around the edge. It appeared to be some form of script that repeated again and again.

"What does this say?" I asked as my finger traced the pattern.

"It calls upon the gods for protection and strength and death to your enemies." He handed me the shield and retrieved his glass of wine. "Very nice don't you think?"

My stomach jumped as I knew that I would never be able to afford these, but I still felt loyalty to my father and grandfather. I gently handed it back. "I'm sorry." I felt terrible. "But as I said, it's an heirloom that connects me to my father and grandfather. He apparently fought and survived in a war as a young man and this spear saved his life. I hope it will do the same for me one day." I picked up my spear and sword and headed for the tent opening.

"Enough!" He went back to his table. "You'll make me a beggar!" He picked up something else and came back to the table where the dagger and shield sat together. "I will also give you this. It is my last and final offer." He put a helmet on the table. I noticed it was the same one I wore earlier in the day. It had a noticeable dent in the side where the ball hit me. "Last offer!" He drained the cup of wine and eyed me again.

I picked up the helmet and felt the dent with my calloused fingers. "I guess you could say this will be my heirloom as it has already saved my life once." I smiled at him.

"Yes! I see you are a very wise man." He spit into his hand and held it out to me. I spit into my own and shook hands with him. "There, it is sealed! And now we will drink to celebrate our deal!" He filled our glasses and we drained them in good cheer. "Lord Trevor has already told me about your strange sword, so I won't even ask you about trading that." He paused and eyed me to see if he could persuade me into negotiations, but when I just sat there he continued. "Now tell me again as much history you can recall about my new Vasselli spear."

I returned to our camp with my new shield, helmet and dagger. They all stared at me as I appeared out of the darkness, smelling the aroma of the stew they were sharing around the fire.

"I hope there's some of that left." I said as I took off my new helmet. "So what happened after I was dismounted?"

"Are those your rewards for not killing yourself?" Kay suggested as I settled in beside him. "I suppose I should have played the fool instead of breaking that bloody Dirty Dirk." He smiled at me. "That's right. After your performance, I had my turn and hit that thing on the breastplate instead of the shield breaking it clean off the post." He quickly lost his smile. "That's when I got the pleasure of Dirk's anger and Gianno's tongue for breaking my spear as well. Not to mention the evil looks from every man on the field for breaking that damned thing." He looked into the fire.

Graham, Jared and Geoffrey exchanged worried looks as I ate a bowl full of hot rabbit stew. "How do you feel?" Geoffrey asked across the fire.

"Better." I eyed each one of them. "How did you three fare today?"

"Well after we had the pleasure of beating the crap out of each other, we had the crap beaten out of us. Then we broke for lunch." Jared said as he scraped the remains of his meal into the fire. "After lunch we got to clean the stables and the latrines." He sat back down and offered the jug of beer to Graham. "A little different than your day I imagine."

"My back is bruised, my arms are sore, and my hands smell of dung, human and otherwise." Graham sat forward of the log and pressed the small of his back. "Other than that, it was a wonderful day." He handed the mug to Geoffrey. "I could have done with a nice sleep as well."

"King Arian returned just before dark. Alone." Geoffrey drank deeply and then handed the jug to me. "I heard a rumour that your name was mentioned when he met Lord Trevor and actually asked after you when he heard you had been hurt." I grabbed the mug, but passed it on to Kay. "The King knows you by name?"

Kay drank the remainder and stood up. "Lord Trevor asked after me too, but only because he wanted to know which numbskull broke the Dirty Dirk." He proffered the jug. "Does anyone want more? Your highness?" Kay disappeared toward the canteen before getting an answer.

Later, I crawled into my bedroll claiming a headache still, but I couldn't help feeling a gap opening between me and my friends because of my growing friendly relationship with Lord Trevor and the King. It didn't seem like a conscious decision to abandon them or to elevate myself above them in their eyes, but I got the distinct impression that they were beginning to resent me. Cradling my new dagger under the blanket, I tried to relax by running through the days' events. I saw the Dirty Dirk's steel ball flying toward my head but it bothered me why I hadn't taken Sir Jonathan's advice and ducked down to avoid getting hit. Why had the King asked after me when he returned? Were the Ren-Tigarians planning on stealing my sword?

Before falling asleep I vowed to reclaim my waning friendships starting tomorrow.

FIVE

The Chase Begins

I will curdle thy blood
And gnaw on thy bones.
Do not awaken me.
~Book of Eth

We awoke again early the next day with implicit instructions to strike camp quickly. We went about our work methodically deconstructing the camp and loading everything into a barrage of carts that would follow behind the army. I took over the worst chores given to my friends in hopes of smoothing over their ruffled feathers and it seemed to work. By mid morning we found ourselves on the march west and my friends had given me the nickname Shitewright, as they had enjoyed watching me dismantle the latrines. Being a soldier in Lord Trevor's contingent found us at the head of the army just behind King Arian's veteran soldiers from Tyre. As we marched, I tried to reason out why the King chose to rule all of this land from his castle on the island, instead of from the mainland and during a break in our march late in the afternoon I found Lord Trevor and asked him about it.

"You aren't the first one to ponder this, and I'm sure not the last." He bit into a shrivelled apple and made a sour face. "I've known a few Kings and Queens in my time as you can well imagine and the majority of them rule through fear by planting themselves squarely in the middle of everything, constantly monitoring and measuring each man and ready to stomp down any detractor." He threw the core into the bushes behind him. "Arian, like my father before him decided that the best way to effectively rule is to remove yourself from the middle and place yourself on the edge along with the rest of your Lords and Ladies." I looked at him in bewilderment. "Do you know where Lord Fiongall is?"

"No, we haven't heard from him since he left in the middle of winter." I munched on a handful of nuts.

"Men like Lord Fiongall are a rare commodity and their worth is more than their weight in gold. I'm sure you'll meet such men in your lifetime. Fiongall is married to my younger sister Lillian, thus he is bound to the throne by blood. But he also served under my father and thus is bound to the throne by loyalty. He was knighted in Tyre and gave both Arian and I bloody noses more than once growing up and thus is bound by friendship." He pulled out his pipe and stretched his legs. "He is also one of the finest bards I've ever heard. It's said he got his voice from his mother, who was the Clan Chief of Upper Doros. His father was a huge mountain of a man and a skilled fighter who vanished mysteriously one day in the Northron Climbs."

"I still don't understand what this has to do with ruling land from afar." I pulled out my own pipe which I had traded with one of the cooks for cleaning the worst pots and joined him for a smoke.

"You are only as strong as your weakest link and you need a man like Fiongall to test the chain and make sure it won't break when you need it most. He has the King's utmost trust and has been sent out to raise the local garrisons and to try and track down this Queen Mordeth. The men he is raising feel that same trust to their Lords that rule this land as those Lords in turn trust Arian." He puffed a blue ring up into the blue sky. "As you will learn, trust is the most valuable commodity you can have, and trust is not bought through bribes or promises, it must be earned, and the strongest are earned by sharing spilled blood."

"Well, Lord Scat would need to bleed quite a bit before he earned my trust." My comment raised Trevor's eyebrows.

"Yes, Lord Scat, now there's a rusty link. He is newly raised and his mettle has not yet been put to the test." He looked at me askew. "What is your impression of the man?"

"He seems suspicious of everyone and everything. And scheming, always scheming." I shrugged my shoulders noncommittally.

"He seemed to like your girl if I remember correctly?" He smiled back at me.

"Maura would never go for him. He's too old. He must be at least forty!" I felt embarrassed as Lord Trevor leaned forward choking on his quickly inhaled pipe.

"Well, forty or no, Fiongall hand-picked him and made sure he knew his duty is to protect our homes while we bleed out our lives here. Don't you go worrying too much about him Thomas; Arian trusts Fiongall and so should you." He clicked his teeth with his pipe and sat back folding his arms behind his head. "He tries to rule equally with all his Lords and Ladies. He believes that on a level field it is easier to watch one another. If you try to rule from above, you are vulnerable to attack from below."

We both stood as a horse galloped up and stopped abruptly. "Lord Trevor, you are commanded to the King." He pointed behind us before turning and disappearing up the road. We both looked to where he had been pointing and noticed a small group of armed men quickly gaining on us.

"Look lively!" Lord Trevor ran forward to find Arian as I rejoined my companions. I told them about the group behind us as we were brought back into formation by Dirk who rode a large black warhorse that whinnied and side stepped down the long line of men. Our entire front rank had been turned and now faced the group of men behind us. We were guessing that this might be the vanguard of Queen Mordeth's army. King Arian and his Lords sat their mounts as the running men suddenly crested a hill and we all breathed a sigh of relief. They were Ren-Tigarian priests, and more than the four that had stayed behind at the Temple. They halted in a triangular array before the King.

The lead priest stepped forward and held a fist over his heart. I noticed the golden eye on his forehead. It was Fen

Gisar. He wore a belt strapped across his chest that was dyed a deep burgundy while his three scions who formed his Hand wore dark blue, and the nine behind them wore brown belts. The remaining twenty seven behind them all had black belts that blended into their clothing. Each belt held a sword on their backs and each sword had a similar hilt to the one I carried at my waist. There were forty priests in total and even though they looked insignificant beside the mounted knights and men-at-arms, their combined presence seethed with a deadly confidence that hinted at their fighting acumen. Each man's forehead cloth had a similar eye as Fen's sewn into it with the colour of their belt.

"Sire, may I present my Tricaste. Gisar!" He turned and yelled at the priest-warriors. They simultaneously drew their swords, brandished them above their heads in a shimmer of reflected light and presented them across their left wrist on bended knee, faces studying the ground.

"Rise and be welcome!" Arian's voice carried across the now-quiet field. The priests moved as one as they stood and replaced their blades in one smooth motion. They stood once more with clenched left fist in open right palm and as one bent at their waist to acknowledge the King.

"Sire, as we approached we noticed thin grey smoke rising from the west." Fen's clipped tones didn't betray the fact that they had just run all the way from their Temple.

Everyone within hearing distance turned to see where Fen pointed and sure enough what had been dismissed as low drifting mist above the far tree line proved to be smoke coming from the forest in the distant west. It was at that time while everyone's attention was fixed on the smoke that I looked up at Lord Trevor. He wasn't looking at the smoke but instead was grimly watching the priests. I followed his gaze and to my surprise, saw that they were searching our troops until one by one their eyes settled first at my sword, then onto my face. I imagined what instructions had been relayed behind their impregnable walls, and unconsciously my right hand strayed to my hilt.

"Trevor, recall your scouts! Where the hell is Fiongall?" Arian said behind him as he spurred his horse forward. Lord Trevor relayed some quick commands and a group of three riders quickly sped off to the west, north and south. We began marching toward the smoke at Dirk's command. The priests fell in behind the main body of the army maintaining their strange triangular formation. The carts as always trundled slowly in the rear behind the new additions.

Lord Trevor edged his horse closer to me and leaned over. "Vigilance Thomas." He flicked his eyes to my sword, and then kicked his horse ahead to catch up to the King.

"What now Shitewright?" Jared asked running beside me. "Does he need his horse's balls scrubbed down?" He laughed back to Graham who was running behind us.

"You there, shut your gob!" Master Dirk spurred beside us and clubbed Jared on the head with the end of his riding crop. His eyes constantly searched the young recruits looking for any excuse to maintain discipline.

We continued our forced march for more than two hours until we were suddenly called to a halt. Thanking the break, we got a chance to rest and drank from a small creek that ran on the north side of us. Kay walked up and sat down beside me. "The riders Lord Trevor sent out have returned but only them. There's no sign of our lead scouts." He pulled out a heel of bread that he ripped in half. As I shared his bread with my meagre wedge of cheese, we saw a group of Ren-Tigarian priests break formation and approach the head of the column. Kay elbowed me to follow, so we wolfed our food down and walked slowly up to where a small group of soldiers had formed and stood deep in discussion.

"What do you mean no sign?" King Arian questioned the men who had returned, looking displeased with his arms on his hips.

"The scouts are gone. If Lord Fiongall came this way, he must have walked. There are no tracks or manure. Perhaps they took the southern route after all, but the scouts would know more if we could find them." The man drank again from the skin he carried. His clothing would blend into any forest and appeared light and supple. His black hair stuck to his forehead. The other two riders shook their heads in agreement.

"Brian, could you see anything of Jahad's Rest?" Arian asked the other man.

"No Sire, like Robert, I was concentrating on finding the other scouts or any signs of Lord Fiongall's troops, but like him, I found nothing." He wiped the beading sweat on his forehead with a cloth. "As I approached the north crossroads from Jahad's Rest, my horse got spooked. He started snorting and acting up, so I quickly backtracked so as not to give away my position."

"Aye Sire, same thing happened to me. As I approached from the south, my horse also got spooked, and then I smelt it. Awful stench carried on the north wind. My horse started backing away and it was all I could do to keep him under control." The last rider said as he stood with his hands tucked across his chest.

"Out with it Nigel, what did it smell like?" This time Lord Trevor asked the question.

"Death." He spat on the ground to ward off any spirits and signed a ward of protection.

"Sire, if you would permit us?" Fen Gisar asked at Arian's elbow. "I will take my Tricaste to Jahad's Rest and find what has happened."

"No." This time Lord Trevor protested to his brother. "I'll take a group of my own men and surround the village before the rest of you arrive." Standing side by side, their sizes were almost a perfect match.

"Trevor I need you for something else. Fen, go now and we'll follow close behind. We should be there before nightfall." Arian led his brother away by the shoulder. The priests bowed and started west at a fast run. They looked like a murder of crows in search of carrion. Arian held his brother close and whispered something to him. Trevor nodded and left the group. As we walked away Master Dirk barked orders at the remaining men to begin arming themselves.

"Come with me you two." Lord Trevor noticed us listening on the fringe and we followed in his wake making our way back to our group. As we approached, Masters Dirk and Gianno appeared behind us. "Gentlemen, gather round so I don't have to repeat myself." Lord Trevor sat on a log as we fanned out in front of him.

"We have been given the task of finding Lord Fiongall and his men." He picked up a stick and quickly drew a map into the dirt at his feet. "We are here on the outskirts of Manath Samal approaching Jahad's Rest. There has been no sign of Fiongall since we marched north to Ren-Tigar and then west to where we are now. It is our opinion that he has travelled south from Seacliffe to Beltar's Cove and followed Coldstream northwest through K'Larn in the hopes of approaching Jahad's Rest from the south while we approached from the north after our pleasant visit to Ren-Tigar." He looked at all of us slowly and in turn. "From here, we will go straight south between Jahad's Rest and K'Larn. If they've been through there it should soon become evident. If not, we'll start looking for bodies."

He issued orders to Dirk and Gianno to assemble a group of one hundred of the best new recruits and seasoned soldiers and to make sure they were armed and horsed for a fast ride south. He ordered us to assemble a wagon with the supplies required by this group for a month. We grabbed Graham, Jared and Geoffrey to help us and by the end of the first hour we had commandeered enough supplies and had the wagon assembled and waiting to the south of the main army.

We watched as Lord Trevor and King Arian spoke quietly to each other and embraced. Then Lord Trevor mounted and led our men away to the south.

Thinking back on it now, the moment we split as a group became a defining point in time where all men's view of the world would change. It was precisely at that moment when we went from being recruits to becoming soldiers in our own right. There would be no more time for training. Our next exchange of blows would be against armed men who wanted us dead.

It took us all day to reach the edge of the forest and the road that led north to Jahad's Rest and south to K'Larn. We stood in the waning afternoon light squinting into the dark trees that stretched endlessly in both directions. To the south we could just make out the still snow covered tip of Mount Kali above the tree tops, sunlight glinting from its peak.

One of our scouts that had been dispatched earlier in the day approached quickly from the north. The one dispatched to the south had not returned yet. As orders were issued to set up camp the man approached Lord Trevor and they both walked away from the group in discussion. We set about erecting tents, horse lines and the food wagon and helped in the preparation of the evening meal of a rabbit stew that had been caught on the ride south. Masters Dirk and Gianno had stayed with King Arian and the main army. Our Commander was Master Dirk's twin brother Lyas. Their resemblance was uncanny except for the eye patch and puckered scar starting over his right eye and ending on his cheek.

Rumour had it that Dirk had been the one to remove the arrow from his brother's eye and stopped the bleeding during a skirmish with poachers in their youth. It was said that even though he hadn't been hit, Dirk had bled from his eye the same as his brother. Some made a warding sign behind their backs as they retold the story claiming that the brothers had been marked by the Goddess at birth and shared more than just the same womb.

Lyas stood at the edge of firelight and stared north. Someone heard him cry out, "By the Gods!", and watched him crumple to the ground unconscious. Lord Trevor had returned by then and gently slapped the Commander's cheek trying to wake him.

"Lyas! Lyas!" There was no reaction so he directed Kay to grab his legs and both of them lifted the lifeless Commander into his tent. "Get me some cold water!"

After laying him on a cot, Trevor loosened the clothing around Lyas' neck and patted a damp cloth on his head that I had handed to him. Lyas' one eye slowly fluttered open. "What?" His eye focused on the faces around him. "Trevor, it's not good. Jahad's Rest," he gathered his thoughts, "it's lost to us."

"He's returned," Graham's head popped into the tent, "the scout from K'Larn. But he's not alone."

SIX

Devastation

Maddening desire consumes.
Want and need.
Bar me at your peril.
~Book of Bashal

I sat in Lord Trevor's tent with Kay and Lyas who now appeared fully recovered from his experience, but not from what his mind's eye had witnessed. Standing patiently inside the tent opening, the returned scout studied the strange stick-thin old man who nervously twisted an old cap over and over again in his dirty hands under the watchful eyes of all assembled. Dust covered both of their clothing evidencing the hurried ride back, but it was nothing compared to the other man's filthy condition and unbearable stench.

"Begging your pardon Lord Trevor, but as I approached the outskirts of K'Larn I was waylaid by a group of men." He coughed and nervously eyed Lyas, trying not to sound as feeble as the thought of being caught unaware by the likes of the filthy stranger. "His name is Wadja, and he led a small group of men who are the only survivors of an attack on K'Larn, the likes of which only he can describe. I would like to add that I witnessed some of what they have experienced and," he trailed off unable to finish his thought.

"Thank you Pieter. Please, have something to eat and drink." Lord Trevor motioned to Kay and he handed both men bowls of stew and some day-old bread while I handed them mugs of beer. "Please sit down, Wadja was it, and tell us what we need to hear."

"Thank you Sir, you're most kind." He settled onto a small chair and swallowed the beer in one motion, letting out a deep belch. "It'll be nigh on three months since the life that I knew came to an end. My wife, my kids, my house, and my village are all gone. We did nothing to deserve this Sir, nothing! We were peaceful and paid our taxes to King Arian as what was right and due. Lord Tal, the Gods bless his soul, was a great man and held our trust in all things but he died defending our homes. There was just too many of them you see." He lifted his eyes from the ground in front of him and looked at each one of us. "They," he paused and swallowed, "they ate them, Sir." His incredulous look seemed lost between disbelief and horror.

"Ate them?" Lord Trevor asked into the silence. "Was it Queen Mordeth?"

"Aye, I believe so, her and those men. They wore robes, but we thought them were Priests! Priests don't do the things they did!" He started rocking back and forth. "They rounded us up like so much cattle and went about picking off the more plump ones first, and then the babies, and then," he trailed off again as tears streaked down his dirty cheeks.

"Please Wadja, we need to hear this." Lord Trevor asked patiently.

"Aye Sir, well they began eating them while they were still alive. The screams, the blood, and once it started all chaos broke loose." He seemed to be lost in thought. "We couldn't save 'em." He began to sob softly. "Me and some others managed to escape when no one was looking and we disappeared into the forest. I looked and looked, but I couldn't find my wife and children." He wiped tears on his dirty sleeves which already bore the evidence of previous treatment. "I don't know how we survived the winter. We lost some to despair, others to hunger, and then some went mad and tried to kill us." He ate some of the stew. "About two months ago another group on horse appeared, so we hid deeper in the forest thinking that they'd returned to finish us off. They didn't stay long, then headed north." He cleaned the bowl with the last of his bread and sat back in the chair. His eyes glazed absently. "We decided that we'd stop the next rider we saw, and he turned out to be your man, Pieter. There are less than a dozen of us left and we don't know what to do or where to go. We keep thinking, what if some of our families survived and what if they return looking for us and can't find us?" Even he seemed aware of the hollow hope in those words.

"You have been through too much Wadja and deserve at least one night of restful sleep. Let us discuss this among ourselves tonight and we'll have an answer for you in the morning." Lord Trevor advised as he led the older man to

71

the tent flap. Trevor issued orders to a soldier outside to see to the man's lodging (and a quick wash-up) and led the dispirited man away.

"I knew Tal as a younger man." Lord Trevor sat down and sipped his beer. "This is damned foul business." He looked at Lyas. "Do you think Arian's finding the same thing up in Jahad's Rest?"

"I wouldn't doubt it. The feeling was," Lyas clicked his teeth with his tongue, "It felt like absolute and terrible devastation."

"It's obvious to me that we need to head back north. I don't believe there is anything left for us in K'Larn. I just hope it was Lord Fiongall and his men who headed north and they're not digesting in some Priest's stomach." He sighed and looked at Kay and me. "I'm sorry for dragging you boys into this. Perhaps I should have left you on the island."

"These bastards will bleed like any other." Kay responded.

"Them and us both." Lord Trevor stated. He looked at Lyas, reading something in his face. "I believe we'll need the Lore Masters to fight this Queen. If they were in fact Priests, you can bet they're from Chafet Temple and are using something evil they've found in the bowels of that cursed mountain they live in." That garnered confused looks from both of us. "Where have I lost you?" He smiled knowingly. "Was it when I mentioned the Lore Masters?"

"We've heard the bedtime stories, but I've always assumed that's all they were." I looked back and forth between the two older men. "Wizened old men living under the mountains, casting charms to steal your soul?" The older men just drank their beer and smiled. "Fighting dragons and all that?" I asked incredulously.

"Babes." Lyas smiled over the edge of his mug. "Where did you say you scraped these two arse-lumps from?" He asked Lord Trevor.

"Lillydale." He smiled widely back at Lyas.

Lyas nodded in some unsaid agreement on the people originating from that area. "Fiongall own land there? Yes, I thought so. East Islanders." He rolled his eye as he returned to the ewer and refilled his mug. "We'll need to get authority from Arian before involving the Lore Masters. I just hope he's managed to capture this evil bitch. Where in the name of Petra's arse is *King* Mordeth? Trevor, didn't they send their son to us last year for training?"

"Dermot." The acid was clear in his voice. "He lasted all of a week and I sent him packing back to where he came from." Trevor spilled the remaining drips from his mug onto the ground. "He was caught raping one of Fiongall's daughters, my own niece." He gave Lyas a sobering look. "He was lucky that I sent him home with only some dark bruising on that pasty white flesh of his. Perhaps his mother is reaping some form of revenge on us for that beating, but you boys now know why Fiongall is so keen to find his mother."

Before sunrise we were mounted and on our way north along the well-worn road that bordered the forest. The wagon rumbled along loudly behind us. Wadja had been left behind with instructions to return to his people and make straight for Beltar's Cove. He had been given one of the spare horses and enough provisions for himself and the men that remained for their long journey east. Lord Trevor gave him a stamped and signed letter to give to the Mayor of Beltar's Cove instructing him to take the survivors in and give them lodgings and food for as long as they needed, and to leave directions in K'Larn for any possible survivors.

It was impossible to miss the bones littering the forest side of the road, sporadically appearing as if a skeleton had taken miles to fall apart. It was approaching mid-morning on our second day back when a black figure suddenly stepped from the edge of the forest and halted us. We slowed to regroup and followed the Ren-Tigarian into the forest along a beaten-down deer trail. We trotted single-file through the dense tree cover until we passed the canopy and emerged into bright sunlight. I can only imagine the breathtaking vista revealed to a road-weary traveller approaching the village nestled at the base of the mountain from our route.

My breath held in my throat, but for a different reason as I searched the black ruins for some semblance of what must have been. Our horses whinnied uncomfortably at the stench of death, still strong after so many days. Our eyes could discern bustling activity below as soldiers busied themselves with the removal of burnt wood and charred remains from every point in the ruined village.

Kicking his horse forward, Lord Trevor made his way over to the striped pavilions set up south and east of the devastated village that was once Jahad's Rest. I looked around for our Ren-Tigarian guide but he had already returned to his guard post in the forest behind us. We followed Lord Trevor and picketed our horses amongst the others, quickly grooming and feeding them as we made our way over to our camp, always situated in the fifth rank to the east. We dropped off our provisions and made our way over to Master Dirk's tent for instructions. He sat at his table, but the familiar scrolls were gone, replaced with a map held down with rocks on all four corners.

He looked up from his study of the map. "Have you been briefed?" When we answered no, he told us to gather up everyone that had been in our contingent to K'Larn and wait for him in the tent until he returned.

Master Gianno took advantage of having that many men in one place and asked them to help him clean his weapons until Dirk returned. He took me aside as we cleaned some daggers.

"It is good to see you returned unharmed Thomas." He looked around to make sure we were out of earshot. "There has been a terrible tragedy here, but Master Dirk will tell you all about it when he gets back." We were now in a corner away from the rest of the men. "Listen Thomas, I

75

have overheard some strange tales about you from an unlikely source." He looked around again before leaning in even closer. "It seems that our Ren-Tigarian friends are very interested in your sword." He leaned back and gave me his best greasy smile. "You never showed it to me last time you were in here. May I?" He held out a gloved hand.

I looked around anxiously but nobody paid us any attention as they busied themselves cleaning the weapons. I drew my sword quietly and handed it to him hilt first. He clucked his teeth as he perused the hilt. He looked down at my scabbard and then returned his attention back to the hilt. "I've seen this sort of workmanship before. It is made from the skin of a large ocean fish called a sharke." He clucked his teeth again. "It is rare, mind you, but not completely unknown." His eyes moved then to the blade itself. "This is strange." His gloved finger ran down the blade. "Strange and yet to all appearances, inconsequential." He smiled at me. "The blade looks completely common. And yet, is it sharp?" He asked me.

"I've seen Lord Trevor hack a table leg cleanly in half. But that's about all it's been used for." I shrugged noncommittally.

"The Ren-Tigarians believe this is the fabled *Sword of Prophecy*." His words hung in the air.

"What exactly does that mean?" I asked him completely baffled.

"Have you ever heard of Al-Shidath, no, well the Ren-Tigarians believe that this is his mark and therefore, his sword." He indicated the little mark that Fen Gisar had pointed out months ago. "But he neither made this mark nor this sword. It is much older than a mere hundred years. I know a little about weapons, but a Lore Master could tell you more of its history." He handed the sword back to me and I re-sheathed the blade. "Needless to say, this is more valuable than anything I could ever offer you. Keep it close and keep it safe. The Weapons Guild has an old saying, 'Owners don't find their weapons, weapons find their owners'."

The tent flaps were thrown aside as King Arian, Lord Trevor, Master Dirk, Lyas and another man made their way to the other end of the tent. "Men, please be seated!" Dirk yelled as we put the weapons down and seated ourselves on the ground. Master Gianno made his way over to the older men who arranged themselves around Dirk's large table with the map.

Lord Trevor looked around and waited until everyone was settled. "Many of you men know Lord Fiongall here, but some of you do not." He indicated the seated man at his right elbow. I felt my mouth gape open in disbelief. The man sitting before us with the ashen complexion and cropped grey hair did not resemble the fair-haired jovial benefactor I remembered walking into my father's shop last autumn after the harvest festival. I could clearly remember him singing and playing a song he'd composed on his blonde-wood lute before the feasting began that night. He had caroused and laughed late with all of us before returning to his stately manor home.

The Lord everyone was looking for had been found, but the man sitting before us looked old and his sunken, furtive eyes enhanced the new skull-like look of his face.

"I would speak for him, but he's insisted on telling his story himself." Lord Trevor looked around the room again at the faces staring back at him and nodded to himself. "Just so," he concluded and backed away from the table pulling out his pipe and tobacco.

"The Gods have seen fit to let me survive to tell you a tale that will freeze your very soul." Lord Fiongall began and I found my throat catching as his sonorous voice had at least not changed since last autumn. "It starts at the beginning of winter last year when I left my home and my family safely back on the Isle, home to many of you that I recognize here today, with a group of men not much bigger than all of you seated here today." His eyes searched the crowd. They settled on me briefly then continued their measure of the crowd. "The crossing was especially cold, but my men and I were ready and anxious to reap the King's vengeance from this Queen for the unholy atrocities we'd heard rumour of. We landed safely in Seacliffe and made our way south to Beltar's Cove, following the trail of rumours whispered in taverns by scared villagers and carried across the sea to Tyre." He shifted slightly in his chair. "We heard nightmares breathed in the light of day about an army eating their way through the villages of our province.

78

Tales that sent an icy finger of fear into the pit of each man's stomach. These phantom stories soon became realized truth as we entered the outskirts of K'Larn, stuck in the middle of winter's grip." He drank deeply of the steaming spiced wine sitting before him.

He pulled back his sleeve and held up the bandaged stump of his left arm, ending just below the elbow. "A common enough sight to seasoned soldiers baptised in the blood and stench of battle, a confirmation of loyal service and a talisman to share with your sacred brothers-in-arms." He put his maimed arm down and let the sleeve fall. "Soldiers expect death when they stand toe to toe with an enemy." He stood and slowly walked through the crowd, drawing all eyes to the remnant of his arm. "Soldiers don't expect to find a wasteland of human bodies brutalized beyond any moral understanding." He pointed to his side. "Naked babes found with their sides ripped open, their blood crusted around the mouths of their lifeless mothers." He pointed at his neck. "Flesh and muscle torn from the necks and faces of unarmed men who were obviously trying to protect their loved ones." He stood in the midst of our group as tears flowed freely down his gaunt cheeks.

"This was the murderous scene that greeted us back in K'Larn." He let out a long sigh. "We did not stay long as the devastation was complete and the carrion eaters had already begun their unholy feast." He moved back to the table. "Fury, disgust and revenge now filled our minds more completely as we followed their gruesome trek north. We

79

came across the discarded remains of their grisly travel rations tossed unceremoniously, cruel treatment for those unlucky enough to have survived the desecration in K'Larn." He sat once more beside King Arian.

"You men travelled along the same route, so you have born witness to the evidence of which I speak." He placed his right hand on the table and clenched the goblet of wine. "We surprised them as we crested the hill coming down here into Jahad's Rest. They had already begun unleashing their carnal depredations and the screams of the villagers filled our ears with dread." He drained the last of the wine and set the empty goblet down. Gianno quickly filled it over his right shoulder, and offered more to King Arian who shooed him away.

"Our attack was swift and deadly. We broke their flimsy perimeter and searched for the instigator of these brutal crimes and found her, there at the centre of it all." He stared at the table in front of him. "They were feeding her." He looked up once more. "She sat upon a throne constructed of bleached bones, naked as the day she was born, tanned of skin and beautiful to behold." He stopped as the men imagined seeing her for themselves. "Her priests, wearing their blood-soaked robes of office, methodically held each struggling villager before her." He absently caressed his forehead. "On her head she wore what I can only describe as a golden skull, but not that of any creature I've ever seen. By the Gods, but it looked like a dragon's skull." He whispered that last line. "The eye sockets were glowing red, the colour of fresh blood, as she supped the offered lifeblood from the bodies offered before her." His confused look encompassed the group of men that began to shift uncomfortably.

"A priest stood behind her, chanting incomprehensibly, reading from a large leather-bound book. He wore the robes of office of the Head Priest of Chafet Temple and I saw clearly with my own eyes that it was indeed Jal-Tabor." Fiongall sated his thirst again from the goblet of wine as men mumbled denials. "We began killing the depraved priests and tried freeing some of the villagers, but we had to stop." His face took on a vacant expression as his memories came flooding back. "The freed villagers smiled at us, but not with relief on their faces. They had the look of madness. As I looked around me, I saw what had happened in K'Larn happening all around us." Unbidden tears ran down his cheeks. "I saw a mother eating her baby as it squirmed pitifully to escape." He began to sob quietly and couldn't continue, the memory overwhelming him with remorse.

"Unfortunately that is where Lord Fiongall's memory draws to a close." King Arian stood and placed a comforting hand on his brother-in-law's shoulder. "When we arrived in Jahad's Rest, we only found the still-smouldering remains of the houses, and like you, the gruesome testimony of human remains already being picked clean by the ravens and crows." He looked at the soldiers seated before him. "We found Lord Fiongall lying in a pit amongst other half-eaten bodies and thought he was dead,

81

but when we pulled him out, we discovered that he was still very much alive." He looked uncomfortably down at him. "I'm sorry to have to tell them this Fin, but when we found him, he was gnawing on his own arm." That drew startled gasps from the crowd.

"I only tell you this so that you are made aware that we are dealing with more than just an army with swords and arrows that we can fight." Arian moved around the table to stand in front. "We are dealing with an enemy that can turn our swords against ourselves, and make us do it willingly." He folded his arms across his chest and leaned against the table. "I cannot and will not risk another man's life in this venture until I know exactly what we are dealing with. As it stands, Fiongall's remaining soldiers and the survivors of K'Larn and Jahad's Rest appear to have been taken by Queen Mordeth's army, whether by force or willingly we'll never know now." He looked at his brother for some unspoken confirmation and received an affirmative nod in response. "On the morrow we'll head to Upper Doros and then hopefully up to the Temple of the Sky to plead our case to the Lore Masters." He stood again. "For now, you can join your compatriots out there to bury the dead and purge the evidence of these poor murdered souls."

Lord Trevor gathered Lord Fiongall under one arm and helped him to the tent flaps. As I joined the procession out, I heard Lord Fiongall confess quietly to his other brother-in-law, "I will never play music again Trevor, for me the song has ended."

As I made my way outside into the bright afternoon sun, I assumed that he had said that because of the loss of his left arm, but as I walked slowly down into the remains of the village with the rest of the soldiers, I understood that he meant his soul had died here along with the many villagers and soldiers.

SEVEN

Bleneth

Toss the stone.
Observe the ripples.
Action and reaction.
~Book of Thayer

A week had passed since we left the ruins of Jahad's Rest behind us. I had assumed that Lord Fiongall would have been sent home with a protective force like the survivors of K'Larn, but he chose to accompany us. He rode at the front of the column with King Arian and Lord Trevor, the three brought closer through shared loss, but the bard remained silent and aloof, lost in his own dark thoughts. There was only so much we could do to cover the mess left behind in that village. The night after our arrival we had a bonfire that lit the entire valley. The healers that travelled with our group consecrated the pyre and danced around the blaze incanting their blessing on the souls they claimed would return to the Creator, bones to ash and blood to smoke.

As we followed the forest road west a constant stream of riders were sent out and returned gesticulating in whichever direction they had come from, and by the looks of the tired men it appeared that Queen Mordeth and her followers had completely disappeared from our trail. Eventually the riders sent ahead didn't return, so King Arian recalled all the scouts and put the army on alert.

We crested a hill and found ourselves looking down into a verdant valley busily dotted with sheep being quickly herded by ululating shepherds and an army spread out across the road preventing any further passage. Our scouts were bound and staked ahead of their front line, but appeared unhurt. I quickly counted upwards of one thousand men, none of them mounted. Half held upraised bows and as one, released a warning over our heads, sending birds screeching into panic from the forest behind us.

They were more than two hundred yards away and could have killed us if they had wanted to. It was clearly a warning to retreat back to where we came from.

Immediately Lord Fiongall raised a white kerchief above his head and circled his horse while warning Arian and Trevor behind him. He kicked his horse down toward the assembled army shouting something and was allowed to pass through. The quickly regrouped line reminded me of a bird eating a worm.

Master Dirk shouted commands to form up across the ridge as we had in our many practice skirmishes. I ended up beside Kay who scanned the enemy ahead for any visible weaknesses. I nervously stepped from left to right foot. My sword felt feather-light in my right hand, offsetting the heavy weight of my shield in my left.

"There." He pointed to a shorter man carrying a large square shield. "You take him on the left which will open his other side to my sword thrust."

"Why don't I just cut under his shield and when he drops it, you stab him in the face?" My blood lust surprised even me. Kay just smiled. "What?" I asked confused by his mirth.

"You are a cruel bastard aren't you? Very well, we'll do it your way." He slapped his shield with his sword then squatted into his usual fighting stance.

Their front line began singing a war chant, rocking from front foot to back. Dirk and Lyas both trotted the line trying to calm us down while pushing us back with their horse flesh. Some men broke forward to jeer at the enemy as they pointed to their groins and asses.

Lord Fiongall appeared from the enemy's front line with two other men mounted on horseback. They approached slowly and from our point of view it looked like they were sharing in a jest as they passed a deerskin of some liquor back and forth. Lord Fiongall said something reassuring to our tied-up scouts as he passed them and they nodded their heads in answer to whatever he told them.

"Arian!" One of the men separated from the trio and approached the King on horseback. From our vantage point you could see that he wore some sort of skirt that ended at his knee. His upper body was clothed in a loose patchwork pattern cloth draped over one shoulder. The tunic worn underneath was dark brown and inset with fist sized flat pieces of metal. Both of his shins and forearms had metal armour and a silver looking band encircled his head and bound his arse-length black hair into place.

Arian dismounted and exchanged a bear hug, eventually kissing the other man on both cheeks. It was at that moment while the other man surveyed our assembled army that I realized that this was no man. The undeniable form of breasts was visible through the metal sewn tunic and when her eyes finally fell on me, I couldn't believe I actually mistook her for a man minutes earlier. Her wild beauty stopped my breath. High cheekbones in a deep tanned face offset her full lips. Like the rest of the men lined at the front, we looked at the ground, the sky, then back to her in the hopes of catching her eyeing us again.

"Calm down you dirty bastards!" Lyas yelled as he ordered us to break rank and form up for the march down into the valley. The assembled army did the same, folding in on itself to form an honour guard for King Arian, Lord Trevor and Lord Fiongall as they walked side by side with the woman-warrior. The army clapped sword to shield as the quartet passed before them, ululating a cry of welcome.

We were brought to the far side of the village where we once more set up camp. Slowly the afternoon faded into twilight and the valley settled into evening. We could hear haunting music being played on the outskirts of the village and when I asked one of the local men what it meant he laughed.

"We are beckoning our lost souls home. And for those that are truly lost, comfort in the coming darkness." He continued on with a song of lament as Kay appeared out of the darkness.

"Once again Thomas, we have been summoned." He looked rather dismayed and I commented on it. "These people are happy Thom, it reminds me of home that's all." We wished our friends a good night as they returned to their dicing and drinking.

"These people are truly remarkable Thom." Kay said as we walked toward a big house in the center of the village where smoked poured out through several large holes in the thatched roof and muffled laughter carried softly on the night breeze. The same yearning music could be heard coming from inside.

We entered through the front and were stopped by guardsmen who clapped us on the shoulder and handed each of us dripping antler horns from a vat of mead sitting just inside the main entry. It tasted of warm honey, bitter-sweet and potent. I choked on it at first then drained the antler and handed it back for a refill.

"Ho! So we've got ourselves a *real* Martin!" One of the men handed it back to me laughing. I laughed along with him but had no idea what he was talking about and followed Kay into the large house. Smoke drifted up to the rafters from several large fires that burned in the open space welcoming us. I followed the smoke up and was surprised to see the large round beams supported by even larger posts around the room. These were some of the largest trees I had ever seen in my life. Six men standing arm to arm would barely touch around their middle. My mouth gaped in admiration. At the cross-points between post and beam hung large white skulls. I recognized a bear skull and a bull skull due to the pointed horns, but the others fascinated me as they defied description. My eyes stopped on a large skull that looked terrifyingly familiar, as the definite human shape betrayed the fact that it would take at least three men's heads to fill it.

"Terrok." The velvety voice shook me from my appraisal of the skulls and I found my eyes captured in the dark reflecting pools of the woman-warrior's eyes. "I killed it." She said matter-of-factly, tossing her black hair over one shoulder as the circlet of silver on her brow tried to hold it in place.

I dropped to one knee realizing that Kay had already done the same as we had suddenly come face-to-face with our host and as we had found out earlier, their Clan Chief.

"And what are your names?" She asked. My eyes settled on her sandaled feet where I noticed that her toenails had been painted a dark red.

"Thomas and Kay, both Cartwrights." Lord Trevor offered from behind her. He appeared unruffled as I quickly looked up and then back down at her feet. "They are my men and have finally arrived to my summons." He laughed easily. "Thomas and Kay I would like to introduce you to my sister-in-law and Clan Chief of Upper Doros, Heather

89

dan Kalon." We both kissed her proffered ringed fingers. "Her lovely sister Clarissa dan Kalon is my other sister-in-law and your Queen. Don't let her beauty fool you boys, she's a cold-hearted bitch." That received a hard slap across the face.

"I'll not have you tarnish my reputation or my sister's you hairy over-sexed beast!" She laughed easily at him over her shoulder. "Just because my husband is dead these past five years doesn't mean you can waltz into my bedroom like a Pandrosian Dreamweaver during Festivale."

Utterly stunned, we both watched her feminine guile in mute admiration. Her easy grace belied the strength evident in her muscled arms and thighs just visible under her skirt from our lowered position.

"You two had better get up before she gets any ideas." Lord Trevor remarked and received another slap on his smiling face.

We were led to the other end of the room where Arian chatted with a group of Bleneth's elders. Fiongall, Lyas, Dirk and Gianno made up the rest of the group and by their sombre faces we could tell what they were talking about. Fiongall talked animatedly with the men in their own language, the dialect sounding easy on his tongue. His left stump waved up and down, as his invisible left hand mirrored the solid right. We stopped short as the Clan Chief turned to Lord Trevor.

"My younger brother seems much changed Trevor." Her large black eyes regarded the older man's questioningly.

"Mischief has left his face and in its stead is pain." Her concern dragged at my feeling of guilt. "The spark that once danced in his eyes has been extinguished."

"Aye," Lord Trevor grabbed her hands into his, "Fin has experienced an atrocity that we can only imagine." He kissed her fingers. "Only time can heal his wounds. Time and love." Absently he pushed a lock of hair back that had fallen across her face. "But I believe the song will come back to his heart. Dorosians can't be kept down."

"Upper Dorosians! Upper!" She quipped back at him. "Lower Dorosians are naturally down."

They were both smiling as we joined the group. We seated ourselves by Masters Dirk and Gianno as the Clan Chief and Lord Trevor sat on the cushioned benches beside King Arian. We were introduced to the elders who quizzically took our measure before returning their attentions back to Lord Fiongall.

"Thomas, we have learned from my brothers that you may be carrying something unlooked for, but sorely needed in our uncertain time. If it is indeed the Sword of Prophecy then events are unfolding as predicted long before our lifetimes and none but the Lore Masters can give us guidance now." The firelight reflected brightly from Lord Fiongall's eyes. "A piece of advice, as the Sword tests your strength, rely on your kith and kin, for in the end, blood always proves stronger than steel."

Murmurs of assent cascaded around the group until a man sitting outside our circle raised his antler horn and yelled 'Kalon' up into the rafters. This was matched by all and was followed by the draining of drinks.

Lord Fiongall continued, "We have agreed to leave tomorrow to seek the Lore Masters in their Temple. My sister will help outfit our group for the journey and our remaining troops will combine to scour this land for any signs of Queen Mordeth and her", his voice failed while he unconsciously touched his stump, "followers." He clenched his teeth. "It is going to be of the utmost importance to protect the Lore Masters from that rabid army."

"On that note," King Arian addressed the group, "if any of our men comes into contact with them they are to fall back and warn Bleneth. You must flee from them and take to the mountains or forests."

"We do not flee!" One of the elders blustered. "We have never run from an enemy! Upper Dorosians chase others away!" Spittle ran down his white beard.

"Seamus, from what I've heard from my brother, we wouldn't stand a chance." Heather dan Kalon spoke softly after his outburst. I looked around behind me as the room's sudden silence was interrupted by sporadic outbursts of bravado. She stood and surveyed the people before her. "There is no shame in protecting our people. My brother is living proof that this evil Queen and her army are more than they appear and are not to be approached lightly." Her anger suffused her speech and once again I felt awestruck by her beauty in the flickering fire light. "We travel to the Lore

Masters tomorrow and only with their knowledge will we defeat and ground our enemies underfoot."

Voices rose up among the crowd followed by more drinking and toasting. She sat again to more cheers of 'Kalon'.

"I am going to leave Masters Dirk and Gianno in charge of our remaining army. We will take the Ren-Tigarians with us. They will be ample protection and are used to fighting in the mountains." Arian spoke elegantly to the elders, calming them with his reassurances. "I will take Master Lyas, Thomas, Kay and Lord Trevor."

"And me." The Clan Chief announced. "I know the way better than any other and will guide you there." The elders began shaking their heads in protest again. "Fin, will you please stay with our people?" She asked of Lord Fiongall. When he also began to protest she spoke up again. "Brother, they know and trust you. Your experience with Mordeth will be better suited here than on a visit to some cloistered old men." She smiled then, after seeing his nod. "The Goddess knows the last time they've seen a real woman. It'll be enjoyable to see if their tongues loll as much as our two young pups here." My cheeks betrayed me so I studied the beams again.

"You should have been the bard, my sister." He laughed and threw his arm around her. "Aye, but I've missed you these past years." He kissed her on the forehead. "You have my word that I'll become temporary Clan Chief and protect them as well as you. But you must promise me that you won't break too many hearts up there or cause some to fly their roost."

She poked him in the ribs. "Don't flatter yourself brother, our Clan hasn't had a male Chieftain in over a hundred years, and the Goddess alone knows it isn't because of our abilities in lovemaking." She winked at Lord Trevor. "It's because of our coolheaded abilities in diplomacy." She stood up and smoothed her skirts drawing all the men's eyes to her. "If we're to get an early start tomorrow, then we should get some much needed rest." She emphasised the word rest. "And the mountains are tiring even for the halest man." She smiled as the group stood. "Gentlemen, if you'll excuse me." She made her way to the entrance with one last look behind.

We excused ourselves and left King Arian, Lord Fiongall, Masters Lyas and Dirk conversing with the elders. Lord Trevor followed behind us. As we passed the guardsmen, Lord Trevor stretched his arms in an exaggerated movement, said he wanted to get some fresh air before retiring and then made his way to the large house situated behind the meeting hall where the waiting Clan Chief smacked him on the cheek before disappearing together inside.

We exchanged smiles and made our way back to our camp. As we passed by a house with a faded sign of a sheep, Kay also excused himself, and said that he had to check in on something. After knocking quietly on the door, a smiling woman grabbed Kay and closed the door quickly behind him.

I shrugged my shoulders and looked around, but couldn't find any beautiful women summoning me. I reached inside my tunic and felt the reassuring weight of Maura's lock gently pressing against my skin. I sighed and made my way back to an uneventful, but well needed night's sleep.

EIGHT

Temple of the Sky

Trembling on bended knee
We prostrate willingly.
Silent prayers
Replace arrogant threats.
~Book of Man, 2nd Century

After two weeks in the saddle, I was beginning to hate the tiny trotting steps of the shaggy pony I rode. My legs almost touched the ground, and in fact I had walked most of the way through the surrounding forest until we reached the base of the mountain where the pony's sure footing was preferred to my boots that couldn't get a grip on the slick stones. We rode closely grouped up the winding mountain trail. The Clan Chief led, followed by Lord Trevor, King Arian, Kay, myself and then Master Lyas whose single eye continually scanned the forests on either side for a sign of the black clad warriors that invisibly surrounded us. I could barely hear his mumbled protests through the thick fog about not trusting a Ren-Tigarian as far as he could spit. The sound of unshod hooves clacking on the hard stones was muffled by the fog that managed to penetrate my light cloak, making me feel like a damp, cold and useless toadstool clinging to the back of a moving log.

My new lined helmet provided some warmth for my head and the shield on my left arm added some measure of protection, but from exactly what, I was uncertain. A sudden drip down my neck made me shiver in trepidation of the hidden dangers cloaked in the dark forest. My mind and the swirling mist conjured images of lumbering Terroks, to match the enormous skull I remembered clearly hanging from the meeting hall beam. I couldn't fathom Heather dan Kalon facing a creature so terrifying (as told by Lord Trevor over this morning's early repast), alone, carrying just a hunting bow. Before we mounted she confirmed his details and lifted her skirt to reveal the lurid purple scar marking her upper thigh and the desperate fight with the creature, to my chagrin and Trevor's big-toothed smile. After another playful slap on his bearded face she pulled a leather thong from beneath her tunic and produced the large black claw that had given her the scar.

Remembering the size of that claw, I panicked and looked around for evidence of my companions. As they slowly appeared and disappeared in the encompassing whiteness, I signed the Eye of Thayer behind my shield while gripping the reins in my right hand a little tighter, mouthing a silent prayer for protection. We reined in to a stop as the Clan Chief dismounted and approached a large rock monument that loomed largely on the side of the mountain trail, appearing first as a dark smear. It resembled a large stone finger with a carved eye at the top as a fingernail. I recognized Thayer's symbol but the remaining marks were in an unintelligible script. She reached into her scrip and placed some coins into a slot carved into the monument at chest level, then removed a thin stick of incense from an unseen cache, lit it and stuck it into a small hole above the slot. The charred remnants of other incense sticks stippled the ridge above the slot reminding me of the moustache Geoffrey was trying to grow.

The Clan Chief bowed once and was turning back to her pony when she reached for her sword, startled by something she saw in the fog. Fen Gisar melted from the miasma and held up a palm in greeting as he approached King Arian. The King leaned over and they conversed silently. He nodded once and the warrior disappeared again into the mist.

"There is a spot up ahead that will allow us to set up camp for the night and rest the ponies." Arian looked like he wanted to say more but instead clucked his horse on ahead of the group.

Lord Trevor looked at the Clan Chief but she only shrugged her shoulders in mute consternation. She remounted and our group continued on more quickly than before. As we rode further, the Ren-Tigarian priests slowly emerged from the thinning tree line as the sloping sides of the trail became steeper and the fog dispersed allowing the late afternoon sunshine to break through. Eventually the warrior-priests ran beside us betraying not the least sign of tiring or exertion of any kind. I grew a new appreciation for Lord Trevor recalling his flight from these warriors through similar territories miles away in the east. To be troubling to these silent killers, he must have been quite daunting in his youth. Even now I could see the disdain plainly on his face as he watched the men shadowing us.

The ground to our right broke suddenly into a harbour shaped area that was grassy and appeared man-made. Heather dan Kalon noticed our surprised looks and commented that the Lore Masters built this refuge for travellers caught in the sudden storms that always came mid-winter. She said it also marked two days remaining to reach the Temple. Our group settled into the area once the ponies were left to roam the thick verdant grass and Lyas lit a fire to make a pot of tea and cook the bird he'd shot in the morning.

We hungrily ate the juicy meat, dried bread, cheese and drank deeply from the wineskins we each carried, full of Bleneth mead, and began a discussion about the Temple of the Sky.

King Arian began with a history soon after the original provinces had been established, some five hundred years ago when only three provinces made up the known territories; Pandros, which encompassed the entire south coast, Kali, which sat in the middle and included Rheal and Torcal, and finally Dorosia which spread from Mount Kali to the Northron Climbs to the sea. He started with the names of rulers that defended their borders and the ensuing wars but after a time I felt confused and overwhelmed and he still hadn't begun the history of the Temple of the Lore Masters. I excused myself and tucked into my bedroll. The chill night air at this altitude crept in, but I was exhausted and fell asleep at once.

We all awoke early the next morning surrounded by mist again and packed the camp quickly. Kay and I retrieved the ponies that were huddled together and then approached the others who were sitting around the small morning fire enjoying a hot cup of tea before the day's continuing trek.

Together, the Ren-Tigarians rose to attention and scanned the mist, sensing something we couldn't see. Lord Trevor was standing and staring up at the ridge behind us.

"Quickly, gather your belongings." He issued the terse command. "Lyas, gather the ponies, forget about the fire." That's when I noticed they all had their swords drawn. Following suit, Kay and I drew our weapons and followed Lord Trevor's gaze. We slowly walked backwards as the Ren-Tigarians formed a black wall with Lord Trevor standing in their midst beside Fen Gisar.

Lyas handed the reins of the ponies to Kay as we tried pulling them back toward the mountain path and away from the harbour camp. The pony legs stiffened and they defecated as a soul-piercing howl emanated from the ridge behind us.

"Terroks." Heather dan Kalon whispered.

"I guess we're not the only ones to know about this place." King Arian said into the silence.

"Flee! Now!" Lord Trevor commanded.

The mist prevented us from seeing much, but I had the impression of the sheer cliff wall and swore we were being watched by something up there. The sun, which had risen slightly behind the cliff face, produced shadows of the creatures lining the ridge, no doubt studying us from above. I saw the middle creature, larger than the rest, stride forward from the other shadows and then I heard a pounding of fists, like on a solid drum, as it let out another deep-throated roar.

We began running up the mountain path, dragging the ponies behind us. Arian, Lyas and Heather stood side by side, weapons drawn as they slowly followed us, eyes never leaving the ridge. Arian's broadsword glinted dully in the muted light as he carefully tested his footing blindly behind him. Heather dan Kalon's bow had an arrow knocked and the full quiver on her hip was the only bright yellow color against the grey mist and rock. Lyas' spear waved menacingly from side to side, unable to ascertain from which direction we would be attacked.

I turned my head just as we gained the higher ground and heard large boulders being flung from the top of the ridge, smashing on the path behind us. Both Kay and I stopped to watch as the creatures rained terror onto the Ren-Tigarian priests who nimbly avoided the projectiles. The warrior priests were slowly arcing their way back out of the safe harbour in a single curved line that changed into a wedge shape. Surprisingly Lord Trevor stood side by side with Fen Gisar whose burgundy belt stood out clearly against his black clothing.

The warriors turned as one and ran up the mountain behind us. Arian, Lyas and Heather turned as well and started running up toward us. As we had the advantage of height, I watched as a large Terrok with blackish-silver chest hair and two other smaller versions flung themselves down the ridge and began running on all fours, howling as the hunt had begun. They were covered from head to foot in a white shaggy fur except for their black faces and claws that contrasted sharply. Beady eyes shone fury from their wrinkled and toothy faces.

I pointed down the path with my sword in warning as I was simultaneously yanked up the path, finding my hand wrapped in the reins of my pony. Kay was furiously trying to pull the others up the mountain, but for some reason, my pony spooked and turned up the sloping ridge on my right side. I watched in horrified disbelief as one of the creatures diverted its charge in my direction. The other Terroks were attacking the Ren-Tigarian warriors from behind. The priests stopped their retreat and turned their deadly attentions to the creatures. Blades spun and suddenly the dirty white fur was spotted with bright red blood. Whether it was the creatures' or the priests' I didn't know and didn't have time to figure it out.

My pony suddenly stopped as the incline prevented it from running any higher and stood there shaking in fear, its eyes showing white. The creature was closing in on me fast. I had to let go of my shield to release my hand from the reins. The loud clang of the shield boss on the rocks spooked the pony again, causing it to turn and run away from the noise and directly toward the Terrok charging up the slope behind me. My precious shield slid away, back down the slope.

Never losing speed or slowing its stride, the Terrok picked up the small pony in one large clawed paw, chewed its head off and flung the dying body beside it. Time seemed to slow down. My mind suddenly calmed and my training, unlooked for, took control of my body. As the Terrok approached from below and to my left, I backed down the slope to my right. The Terrok, sensing my attempt to run, swerved its charge and suddenly found itself attacking from higher ground. It hunched its rear legs and leapt at my head. I slowly dipped my body as I brought up the lithe blade in both hands. I could feel the sword slip completely into the Terrok as its weight pushed me backwards, sending our entwined bodies rolling head-over-heels down the slope. As we came to a stop back on the path, I found myself lying on top of the hairy body, staring into the blood-stained mouth and smelling its final putrid breath. As I pushed myself away from it, my helmet was yanked free, still gripped in its dead black claws. My sword slid easily from the creature's body.

I looked around and saw Kay running back down the mountain path toward me, the ponies now under the control of Lyas who shooed them into submission. Heather dan Kalon stood beside me grinning from ear to ear.

"Hopefully that little move of yours didn't break all of my arrows." She quipped while rolling the creature over onto its side. "Petra's arse!" She swore as the creature settled onto its stomach. The creature's back had three yellow fletched shafts penetrating from it, all of them snapped in half.

"Is everyone okay here?" Lord Trevor asked coming up beside us. His face was smeared in blood and his left arm sported a large slash through his leather armour. Blood dripped down and stained the path where he stood.

"By the Goddess what were you thinking?" The Clan Chief chided the older man as she examined his open wound. He grunted as she pulled out a large black claw from his wound. "That's convenient, now you'll have a scar and a claw bigger than mine." She smiled as she laid it into his open palm.

His face betrayed no mirth however. "We lost three of the Ren-Tigarians before that large bugger got to me." He pocketed the claw and looked back down the hill where King Arian spoke with Fen Gisar and the remaining warrior-priests. "Hopefully the Lore Masters can accommodate their funeral rites." He glanced back at the ridge. "I believe we won't be bothered by those Terroks again since it looks like we took down their alpha male."

"Thomas!" Kay grabbed my face and examined it. "Are you okay?" He checked my arms. "That was some move. I thought it had killed you." He looked at the body. "It's bigger than I thought." He bent over the Terrok and rolled it back to expose its face. "Gods! It looks like my Aunt." He smiled up at me. "Not your mother Thomas, although, I do see a slight family resemblance."

"That one he killed is just a baby." Lord Trevor said. "Follow me." He led us back down the path, past the warriors who eyed me suspiciously and stopped at the other two dead creatures. My breath caught in my throat as I finally understood what Lord Trevor and the Ren-Tigarians were up against. The alpha male was more than three times the size of the creature I had killed and the other was about twice its size. "I believe they must have been father and sons, the prime bloodline of those Terroks. The King and Princes of these mountains."

I noticed black clothing under the massive bodies which I discerned were the arms of the fallen warriors twisted at too-wrong angles, their weapons protruding from the matted and bloody fur. I turned away from the carnage as the King and priests approached.

"You are uninjured?" Fen Gisar asked first. I gaped as his face cloth had been ripped off revealing a single tattoo which I knew was Lord Trevor's name in an odd script. He sensed his exposure and clumsily tried to mend the cloth, but it hung down awkwardly once more.

"Yes, I think so. I'm sorry about your men." I offered in sympathy.

"Do not dwell on it. We live to fight and fight to live. Dying is inevitable to either. There is honour to die in combat." He reached out his hand as he eyed Lord Trevor sideways. "May I see the Sword of Prophecy?"

I looked over to Lord Trevor questioningly. He nodded slightly so I handed my weapon over to the tall leader of these deadly fighters whose demeanour belied no sorrow for his fallen comrades.

`"Have you noticed any difference?" Fen Gisar held up his own weapon beside mine. They were nearly identical, except for the colour of my hilt with its scaly skin and his with the twisted leather binding dyed burgundy to match his belt. The blade of my sword was still unremarkably flat black whereas his had the dull sheen of steel covered in drying blood. "Nothing at all?" He offered again.

"Thom's blade isn't covered in blood." Kay interjected. "Are you sure you stabbed that thing?" He asked.

"Of course I'm sure!" I said incredulously. I lifted my hands to show the blood on them.

"I don't understand Fen, what does this mean?" It was King Arian who asked the question of his bodyguard.

"The Sword of Prophecy cannot be marred, even with the blood of its victims." Fen studied my face for understanding.

Lord Trevor wiped his wound with a gloved finger and smeared the blood on the blade. We watched in amazement as the blood appeared to suck itself into the metal, leaving the surface as unremarkable as before. The warrior-priests signed the Eye of Thayer symbol in the air and fell to their knees, face prostrate on the rocky trail chanting 'Thayer' in unison.

Fen Gisar handed the sword back to me and I re-sheathed it, trying to hide the evidence from questioning eyes. He barked an order for his men to rise. Lyas had organized ropes tied around the ponies and rolled the large creatures off of the ruined bodies of the slain warriors. The priests retrieved their fallen comrades and rolled them in their bedrolls, not before removing the spleen-powder vials from around their necks and handing them to Fen. We helped sling their bodies over three ponies that Arian directed them to use instead of carrying them up the slippery slope.

We headed back up the mountain path where I retrieved my shield and my helmet from the creature's dead grasp. It turned out that I had my own black claw as well which had snapped off, still embedded in my helmet. I realized belatedly that my helmet had now saved my life twice. The dent from the Dirty Dirk was still apparent on the right lobe and now a puncture hole offset it on the left. I tucked the claw into my leather thong and followed the company on foot. I turned one last time to look back at the destruction. The three white-furred bodies still filled me with wonder and awe until my eyes settled on the small body of my headless pony. I blamed myself for its death and had to turn away, feeling guilt and sadness rise in my throat.

The sun had settled hours ago but we dared not stop again until we had reached the Temple. Lyas had handed out torches for front and rear positions that flickered against the rocky walls. Owls screeched from out of the darkness, causing me to curse and flinch each time. Earlier we had donned our heavy cloaks to ward off the chill but the cold still penetrated our tired and weary bodies. Only the Ren-

Tigarians appeared unaffected by the night chill or the hours of travel. We rotated riding the ponies, and I noticed the men allowed the Clan Chief more time in the saddle as the remaining pony was overburdened with the majority of the equipment we carried and she was lighter than the rest of us.

"We are here." Fen Gisar spoke out of the darkness as we finally crested the top of the mountain. He had managed to fix his face-cloth on the march. Settled below us in a natural valley, moonlight outlined the walls of the Temple which sat on the closer side of a large lake that reflected the starlight back to the heavens from its dark unruffled waters. Torchlight could be seen in many of the windows throughout the structure which resembled more of a castle than a place of learning.

"I believe we may have arrived just in time." King Arian said from the darkness. "If I'm not mistaken, tomorrow is the Spring Equinox, marking the Lore Master's Initiation Ceremony when their acolytes gain the Mantle of Knowledge."

"Is there anything you don't know?" Master Lyas sneered at him.

"Well, I haven't been here in a long time, but if I'm not mistaken their preparations for tomorrow's festivities will continue long through the night. We might even be able to get a hot meal and a taste of their famous Crystal Wine." Those words caused more than my stomach to rumble in response as the last meal we ate had been interrupted by the Terrok attack.

"Well then, let's make haste and hopefully we won't interfere too much with their preparations." Heather dan Kalon added. "I hope my room hasn't been commandeered by any unwanted visitors." She winked at Lord Trevor.

"Hopefully they have a healer as I believe I'm going to need all of my strength." He smiled weakly and started down the path after her.

As I followed after him, I passed between the priests who blended easily into the night and I noticed that each one nodded their heads slightly in acknowledgement. I nodded back uncomfortably, but I wasn't sure if it was meant for me or for the sword I carried.

NINE

Lore Masters

Heat and blood,
These I crave.
Destruction and Death.
~Book of Eth

"What?" An old man peered through the silvery crack in the door. His bespectacled round face looked tired and not at all ready to deal with unexpected strangers.

"*You* are the Master of Offices?" The Clan Chief asked in her most regal voice, the lilt in her tone more pronounced as she questioned the mole, hands clenched on hips.

"What?" He asked again. "No!" he sputtered, "No! I was just passing by when I heard that intolerable pounding." He pushed his glasses back onto his small pug-nose. "The *Master of Offices* is in the Main Chamber organizing tomorrow's events, exactly where *he* should be." The small man smiled wantonly as he appraised the sudden-discovered female figure, licking his already-moistened lips. "Might I ask *who* is bothering him at this late hour? The entertainment arrived two days ago." Three long straight white hairs fluttered from his neck (just out of reach of his razor no doubt).

No longer amused, the Clan Chief pushed the door open and forced her way inside, knocking the small man onto his arse, the rest of us following in her wake. Fen Gisar closed the door silently behind his Hand of three, locking the remainder of his men outside with a quick hand gesture to wait patiently. The old man's eyes went from face to face in shock and terror, taking in the travel-worn clothes and the blood-stained faces. His fish-eyes fell on the shrouded warrior-priests standing behind us, and they grew impossibly larger. He threw his arms in the air, rolled over onto his stomach and pushed himself upright, and then shuffled down the hallway crying "Alarm! Alarm! We're under attack! Protect the books!"

He rounded the far corner and pulled a hidden bell cord, which started a gong to peal loudly through the quiet corridors. Young and old men spilled into the corridor at either end, disturbed from whatever chores they had been busy at. They pointed and blinked at us in confusion, confirmed that intruders had indeed entered their Temple, then joined the already-raised voices in warning the remaining cloistered men within of their imminent peril.

"Follow me, and whatever you do, do *not* draw your weapons." She pointed to a boy whose cracking voice was the most annoying. "You there," she held him in place with her finger, "We have left our ponies outside of this door. See them to your stables and have them fed." She flipped a silver coin that he caught in the goblet he held before him.

"Those men dressed in black will see to the disposal of the bodies." His eyes shot up from the coin.

"Bodies?" The pimple-faced boy gulped as Fen led him by the arm back out the main door. His Hand remained behind to his silent command.

We made our way slowly along the bright and remarkably clean corridors until, after a few meandering turns, I was utterly lost. Heather dan Kalon continued unperturbed and once again I found myself marvelling at her memory despite the fact that it had been years since her last visit. Blood flushed my cheeks when she turned and caught me staring at her bottom, but she just smiled and continued on ahead. As we rounded another corner, we were met by a large group of unsmiling older men. Each wore a different coloured robe, like rocks along the seashore. They blocked the doubled-door entrance to a massive room behind them, lit by a multitude of candles and braziers that reflected down from an immense round-domed ceiling above.

"STOP!" One of them yelled, holding up both an admonishing palm and a wooden staff to bar our progress and to protect his brethren crowding in behind him. "You have broken into our Sacred Temple! Turn and leave now or face the consequences!" He wore a silver circlet on his brow that announced some position of importance. An amber gem that was embedded into the end of his staff began to glow menacingly. A small white beard hung from his chin, giving him the look of a maddened goat.

"Forgive us, Lore Masters." The Clan Chief said, bowing from the waist. "We have arrived late, but we are in dire need of your sustenance and care." She straightened. "I am Heather dan Kalon, Clan Chief of Upper Doros." The old man didn't register her comment. "This Temple resides within Upper Doros, which means that it falls within my jurisdiction and protection." There was still no reaction from him. The amber gem levelled at us still glowed with power. "Therefore, we did not *break* in." Her regal posture heightened her diminutive stature.

"You are not *our* Chief, my dear lady." He puckered his mouth, making the word look distasteful. "Our *Lord* is the God Thayer, who rules *here* and I should dare hope, in Upper Doros as well." His mockery hung in the echoing corridor. The men behind him nodded their heads in agreement. I could sense that she was losing ground here.

"I am ruled by no *man* be them human or God!" She said loudly. "Do not presume to lecture me on the Gods!" She lowered her voice and walked closer to him. "For all of your vast knowledge hidden within this mountain, your *memory* seems to have stopped at the front door. Have you so-soon forgotten that it was my Grandmother who stopped the attempted invasion from Mount Kali when they tried laying claim to the Soul of the Earth?" Her voice rose steadily with each accusation. Arian touched her arm, which she shook off angrily, as he stood beside her.

"Lore Master Laban, please excuse our untimely visit but we were attacked by a group of Terroks, and have travelled

113

all day and night to get behind your protective walls." He smiled at the Clan Chief, which seemed to relax her, but her fists still remained clenched on her hips.

"Terroks?" The gape in his mouth seemed to grow longer until the glow from the amber gemstone finally extinguished. "Did they follow you here?" The group of men exchanged worried looks and comments at our revelation. "That would be too much to deal with in one day!" He rubbed his hands together. "Arian my boy, I didn't recognize you behind that beard." The old Lore Master laughed. "The mud and the blood didn't help my old eyes either." He clapped his hands loudly. "Pizzle!" He searched around questioningly.

The mole-man we had met at the door appeared at his elbow. "Master?" He pushed his glasses back and snuffled his pug-nose.

"Yes! What?" The old Lore Master glared down at Pizzle. "What are you doing creeping up on me?! These are honoured guests, Pizzle." The small man continued staring up at him apprehensively. "Well? Snap to it man!" The Lore Master snapped his fingers. "Quickly! Open some of the West Wing rooms. Five, no six rooms should be sufficient." He scanned our group again. "Chief dan Kalon, you shall want your regular accommodations I presume?" He nodded, not waiting for an answer as Pizzle grabbed his sleeve and whispered something in his ear. "Yes Pizzle, put our brethren from Ren-Tigar in the *common* dormitory." He sniffed in slight disapproval at the smaller man's reticence.

"You are more than generous Lore Master Laban." King Arian addressed the older man as the gawking crowd dispersed quickly down the corridor, squabbling over the bedding, water, candles and which one of them would have the honour of preparing the Clan Chief's room.

The Lore Master bowed slightly and shook his head. "Apologies my boy, but things have been so busy these last few weeks preparing for tomorrow's ceremony, that I've barely had time to read." He led us into the room they had barred, which turned out to be the Banquet Hall, and described the preparations taking place, and the work that still needed to be done before dawn. Tables ran the length of the room, covered with white linens, goblets, pitchers and the many candelabras that had created the golden aura visible from the hallway.

Tapestries dominated the walls in a miasma of colour and fabrics, displaying the known and unknown history of the lands. Some of the exotic creatures depicted stirred childhood memories up of whispered bedtime stories and late-night fireside chats. My eyes caught on one in particular, displaying the unmistakable black claws and white fur of a Terrok. It reared up on hind legs as it was attacked by a group of spear-wielding armoured warriors. A small man, obviously a Lore Master, stood behind the knights, wielding a staff with a shiny red gem depicted in shimmering cloth. The black claws and fangs looked bigger than I remembered.

115

I scanned the other tapestries with amusement, and as I did, something sent butterflies fluttering away in my stomach. If a creature, thought to have been a myth only days ago, was clearly depicted here, then what about the other creatures on these tapestries? My humour died down as I examined another tapestry detailing the shimmering skin of a red-and-gold scaled dragon. Candlelit reflections danced along the myriad shimmering golden scales climbing up the dragon's back and ruby eyes stared down, appearing to simmer knowingly at this unwanted visitor.

"Don't worry Thomas, dragons haven't been seen in these parts for some time." Lord Trevor said behind me, startling me out of my reverie. Kay stood opposite, examining the tapestries as closely as I had. "Most of these creatures do exist, but are seldom seen by the eyes of men who return to tell the tale. We were extremely lucky and should make an offering to the Gods while we are here. If we had come any earlier in the year, or if we'd had too few in our party, we might have been sleeping in the belly of those foul beasts tonight instead of soft beds."

"Some are softer than others." Kay said absently, a smile playing across his face.

Lord Trevor rubbed his arm unconsciously; the crudely made bandages were black with crusted blood. "Yes, well, it looks like your days spent beating each other senseless have finally paid off." He smiled and lowered his voice. "And don't let her hear you talking like that, or you'll wish you had been eaten by that bloody Terrok."

"Luck against beasts is one thing, but in the heat of battle, when you're facing against a living man, well, that's something different altogether." Lyas spoke from our other side. He had seemed aloof since missing his chance to fight the Terroks. "Still, that was an amusing bit of tumbling you did." His yellow teeth flashed a smile. "It reminded me of a tumbler I saw on the Isle of Holbrook, during Festivale. A man, dressed as a Terrok, cart-wheeled around the crowd for money. It was very amusing, but now that I've seen one in the flesh, I know Terroks *hide* their genitalia. Speaking of which," He winked at Lord Trevor as Heather dan Kalon walked up with King Arian and Lore Master Laban.

"Your rooms have been prepared." The stately Master of Offices said as he smiled and pointed to Pizzle who waited hunch-shouldered in the doorway like a disgruntled cat. "Please refresh yourselves. Lord Trevor, our healers await you in your room." He looked at each of us in turn. "Afterwards we will gather for a small meal to fill your empty stomachs. Perhaps then you can reiterate the *real* reason for your visit, to the Master of the Temple himself." He snapped his finger. "Pizzle!" The small man jumped and rushed ahead of us down the corridor.

We each had a separate room assigned and the thought of sleeping on a stuffed bed filled my head with dreamy anticipation. After putting my weapons and armour on the dressing tree, I peeled off my dirty clothes and washed my face and body with the soap and warm water left on the small table. It was an unlooked-for luxury, and after drying

117

my face, I slipped into a brown robe and slippers I found lying on the bed. I lay down on the bed and absently took the claw from my thong along with the lock of Maura's hair and the small carved Thayer amulet. I felt myself slowly sinking away into sleep.

There was a quick rap on the door as Pizzle burst in.

"You're dressed! Good, follow me." He backed into the hallway where the others were waiting. As I stood up, I slipped the objects back into the thong, and hung it around my neck. Kay was dressed in the same coloured robe I was wearing, but Lyas, Lord Trevor and King Arian wore white robes. My breath caught at the sight of the Clan Chief. She was wearing a plush red robe, inlaid with exotic birds, and where ours stopped just above the ankles, hers stopped mid-thigh, letting the purple scar peek out. The matching red boots stopped just below her knees. I examined the floor, trying not to stare too hard at her ample bosom that threatened to fall out of the plunging neckline at any moment.

Pizzle had started licking his lips again. "Very nice, I mean, very well, you are now refreshed." He rubbed his hands under invisible water. "Please follow me. The Master of the Temple has requested your presence in his private dining chamber." He offered ladies first, but when she slipped her arm into Trevor's and told him to lead the way, he snorted and wobbled ahead of us like an abashed badger. We passed back by the doors opening into the Banquet Hall as men continued dressing the hall, reminding me of a bee's hive on a warm summer's day. The Temple dwellers methodically swept the floors, arranged vases of flowers, polished silverware or simply walked in pairs down the corridors, engaged in animated conversation.

We stopped in front of a large polished-wood door where the Eye of Thayer had been cleverly etched within the dark woodwork. Upon closer examination, I was amazed to discover that the eye was actually part of the wood, a naturally occurring darker vein that gave the impression of the all-seeing, lidless eye. Pizzle knocked once and then twice again in quick succession. He didn't wait for a response, but opened the door and swept us inside. He sniffed the air in mock disdain as the Clan Chief sauntered past, thanking the small man for holding the door for her.

A long table filled the room with foods of all kind decorated on plates of various sizes and colours. As we walked in, seated men rose from the table. Lore Master Laban greeted us first and introduced his colleagues. Each of them wore a circlet on their brow, similar to Laban's, but where his was silver, theirs were bronze. The richly-robed group began with Lore Master Laird, who told us that he heralded from the sea-swept Filmount Castle in Lower Doros. His fluffy white beard reminded me of the Terrok's fur (without the blood of course). Lore Master Quinn Korid came from the harbour city of Perg on the Isle of Holbrook and his large, strong hands encompassed mine completely. His red beard was streaked with white on either side of his mouth giving him the impression of someone caught drinking fresh milk from the pail. Lore Master Mai-Hon had travelled from Yearth in the province of Torcal, his handshake felt cold and bony. He didn't wear a beard, but his long, waxed and curved moustaches made up splendidly for that. I imagined that birds could perch on either end quite easily without bending it. Lore Master Donato came from Castle Cragthorne in Pandros and was completely devoid of any facial hair, in fact, his cheeks had a slightly reddish hue as if scraped with a dull razor. His round face shone as he absently patted at the sweat trickling down from his bald pate (a fringe of short dark hair nested his egg). He appeared to be the youngest of the group and was the only one wearing spectacles besides Pizzle who had disappeared from the doorway. A door opened at the back of the room as a man dressed in rich blue robes worked with silver thread entered the room drying his hands on a towel that he deposited on a side table. He had a golden circlet on his brow, announcing him as the Master of the Temple. He had a white beard, neatly trimmed, that flowed around his mouth. Where Mai-Hon's moustache over-awed the viewer, this man's gave the impression that it might fly away at the slightest breeze, like a single cloud in a clear blue sky.

"You are welcome to our Temple of the Sky. I am Meda, Master of the Temple, and Keeper of the Tome." He scanned our small group, but instead of the usual quick glance, I imagined his deep-set blue eyes took the full measure of each person's character and had solved our histories by the time he got to Arian. "By the Gods, Arian, it's good to see you again. How soon the son becomes the father." The older man crossed the room and hugged the King, putting one hand on his shoulder. "Has it taken us so long? What has it been twenty, twenty five years?" He smiled warmly at the younger man. "How quickly the world spins outside these learned walls! What may I ask brings you here, besides checking up on your father's old counsellor?"

"Meda, I thought you may have heard." The King paused, thinking where to begin. "Queen Mordeth has declared war in Manath Samal." He took the offered chair as we were all seated around the food-laden table. "I need to fill you in on what's happening in the outside world, before it finds you hiding in these mountains." We dug into the food and made idle conversation as the King and Meda caught up on their shared past and more current events.

I ended up sitting between Lore Master Mai-Hon with his impressive moustache and Quinn Korid with his streaked red beard. During the meal they described to us how each had arrived months ago in anticipation of tomorrow's ceremony, and were completely unaware of this troubling news. They explained their individual roles as witnesses to the events and also as officers during the Acolyte's Raising Ceremony. Their words swam in one ear and fell out the other as my mind was completely focused on eating the splendid repast laid out before us. Most of the food was unfamiliar, but there was no avoiding it as the Lore Masters piled my plate with everything they could reach.

121

The food disappeared from the painted plates quickly and the wine drained from the sweating ewers even faster. I exchanged smiles with Kay who seemed lost between satisfying his hunger and quietly releasing his belches from across the table. I surprised the Lore Masters with the tale of the Terrok attack, which seemed to both unsettle and excite them. They tried to determine exactly when we planned on leaving so that we could all coordinate our travel from the mountains together. Their retinues didn't comprise of any military personnel, just men of learning. Books, they surmised, wouldn't replace meat if they were set upon by the beasts and were forced to defend themselves.

Heather dan Kalon had been sandwiched between Donato on her left, who casually tried to leer down the front of her robe at each mistakenly dropped utensil, and Laban on her right who deferred to her continually because of their earlier disagreement. She adopted murderous looks aimed at Lord Trevor, who sat amicably across from her, pondering aloud a question about the sexual organs of Terroks, and where they might possibly be hiding them. He jumped in pain when she kicked him under the table, after he pretended to drop his knife on the floor like the young Lore Master.

I looked away, hiding my laughter at Donato's face flushing a brighter red when he realized his ruse had been discovered. Looking down the table, I found myself caught in the eyes of Lore Master Meda who was staring at me from the end of the table while Arian spoke quietly into his left ear. He shook his head gravely behind steepled fingers, as the King's story was relayed. The candlelight reflecting from his deep-set eyes, gave me the impression of a mischievous cat who considered whether to eat the mouse in its paws, or to continue playing with it.

Surprising me, Meda stood and dismissed himself. He assured us that he would dedicate more of his time to each of us in the next couple of days, but that tomorrow's events demanded his immediate attention tonight. He levelled his gaze at me again and crooked a finger to summon me where he waited (the mouse swallowed nervously). I pushed back the cushioned chair and walked over to where he waited by the rear door he had originally entered through. As I approached, he turned so that he faced the back door, away from the table and the seated people's eyes and ears.

"Your King tells me that you have come into possession of a rather unique artefact." He smiled down at me. I thought I was tall, but he towered a head above me. Being this close, I surmised his age was closer to the King's, despite the white hair, as his skin was free of the tiny wrinkles sported by the other Lore Masters. He smelled of lavender and musty books.

"Yes, the Ren-Tigarians believe it's their Sword of Prophecy." I offered meekly.

"Prophecy? Bah!" He laughed. "What would *they* know of Prophecy?" His smile disappeared. "They *know* how to kill people. Death from a thousand cuts, points of pressure to render paralysis, powders, weapons. But Prophecy? Leave that to Lore Masters. Our library fills this mountain, but as any recently-raised Acolyte will learn, Prophecy is based on *history*, not the mutterings of mad men who only know how to kill." He opened the door and stepped inside, but did not offer me passage. "We will talk of this tomorrow. Sleep well Mr. Cartwright." He closed the door slowly behind his smiling face.

The others continued with their conversations, but didn't ask of my talk with the Master of the Temple, despite eyeing me sideways. Laban finally stood and asked that we end our meal as the servants needed time to clear it away before their other tasks forbade them from returning to this room. Our group shook hands once more with the Lore Masters in the corridor outside, wishing each a good night's sleep.

Donato offered his services to Heather dan Kalon, explaining how he had tinctures and ointments in his possession that would help alleviate any sleeping disorders or muscle pains she might be suffering from her long journey. When Lord Trevor coughed quietly, Donato recovered and quickly added that anyone was welcome to use them if needed. She politely refused and took Lord Trevor's offered arm. Flushing again, Donato excused himself, telling us he needed his own tinctures to help him fall asleep.

We walked back down the corridors and found our way to our rooms as the busy night continued all around us. As we left each other's company King Arian reminded us that we'd meet in the hallway before the festivities began, at dawn.

Dawn!

I was already exhausted and the wine at dinner played heavily on my eyelids. I quickly ducked into my room, blew out the candle and collapsed onto the bed. Sleep came quickly. If I hadn't been so tired I would have noticed that my sword had disappeared along with all of my clothes.

TEN

Awakening

Blind seeking,
Aim true.
Heart's desire,
Arrow flew.
~Book of Bashal

"**G**et up Shitewright!" Someone whispered into my ear after poking me hard in the ribs. My blood-shot eyes slammed open. I tried to get up but my body and arms refused to move. They lie beneath my body and refused to acknowledge being attached to me. I sat up slowly, and watched Kay buckle on his belt, sword swaying at his hip. My eyes adjusted to the dim room. His clothes looked clean.

"Where did you get those?" I asked, licking my dry lips and tasting the sourness within my mouth.

"They're mine you goat's turd. Why aren't you dressed?" Kay seemed upset. Why was he so upset? Feelings were slowly returning to my arms, sending the sensation of stinging nettles brushing up and down them. I swore and stood up, swaying and yawning slightly.

"What time is it?" I asked, searching blindly along the dressing tree for my own clothes. "Where are my clothes?" I looked around confused. "And where in Petra's arse is my sword?" My drowsiness melted away. All that sat on the tree were my battered helmet and scraped shield.

"Here!" Pizzle appeared in the doorway and threw a pile of clothes at me. "You two had best hurry if you want to be there in time!" He continued down the hallway in a flurry of blue-fringed robes, his breathing laboured and loud. My clothing had been cleaned and dried like Kay's. I pulled the robe over my head and dunked my face into the cold water to try and wake up.

"Aren't you two ready yet?" Heather dan Kalon asked from the door. "Oh my, that water must be very cold." I pulled my head out and noticed where her gaze rested.

Covering my nakedness, I felt the heat return to my cheeks. I turned away from the door as I quickly got dressed, fumbling into my clothes. I found my belt, but again there was no sword. "Have either of you seen my sword?" I asked as we ducked into the corridor where the others were waiting.

"What!? Your sword is missing?" Lord Trevor asked scanning my room, then pushed himself back into the busy corridor. "Arian, have you seen Fen or any of his Tricaste?" His intense look worried me.

"They're probably already down at the river's edge with everyone else. We've got to go right now, it'll be dawn shortly." He folded into the flow of running people and we fell in behind him. "Why? What's wrong?" He asked over his shoulder.

"Thomas' sword has been taken." Lord Trevor barked behind him. "Don't you worry Thomas, we'll find it. It couldn't have gone that far." He looked at my waist. "Do you still have your dagger?"

"Yes, and my helmet and shield were still there." I felt the reassuring hilt at the small of my back.

"Fen and the others were up all night seeing to their dead." King Arian said. "He may not be in the best of moods today so please, let me talk to him." He asked his younger brother.

"You're welcome to it." He grinned. "But if they have it, I'll wring his bloody neck and they'll be up all night again burning him as well."

Lyas eyed him warily. "Surely you must be feeling tired as well? I thought I heard you grunting in pain last night." He grinned knowingly. "That scrape on your arm was it?"

"Aye!" Lord Trevor said as he looked guiltily at the Clan Chief. "I kept bumping it. Not easy falling asleep when you're in pain."

"Easy for some," she said icily, "harder for others." She ran a finger under his grizzled chin.

I felt the morning chill as we stepped out through a portico and found ourselves walking along a well-worn mountain path. The dark forest encroached on both sides and high above the treetops stars still winked in their final moments before dawn. Torches gutted in iron brackets set at intervals that marked the snaking path ahead and behind. As we passed through the quiet forest, my mind kept wandering back to the night before and the bizarre creatures depicted in the tapestries. My hand tried to settle reassuringly on my sword hilt before I remembered that it was missing.

I traced through the previous night's events, trying to remember the faces, people and any possible leering looks that would have betrayed a yearning for my sword. I thought about Pizzle, but couldn't imagine him carrying anything heavier than a book. I thought about Meda, the Master of the Temple. He was the only other person outside of our party that knew about its significance, but why would he choose to steal it if he wanted to talk to me about it later today?

We exited the forest into a large clearing at the edge of a river where its mouth spilled into a large placid lake. Peering out across the water, I was once again amazed at the calm black surface sprinkled with reflecting starlight. A large disk floated on the water and as I looked up at it, I realized belatedly that it must have been a full moon last night, although I couldn't remember it illuminating our path to the Temple. Today was the beginning of the Spring Equinox and there was a full moon. I was idly wondering how often that happened when we were ushered to a location designated for outsiders. Surprisingly, we weren't the only ones, but as we waited, I could hear the nervous anticipation of parents who pointed out their child, pride swelling their voices.

I noticed that the path we had walked down continued up across the river to where a large wooden bridge straddled the river, decorated with coloured tapestries and flickering torches. There was a large crowd of people gathered in the middle that included the Lore Masters, who were seated in large chairs on a raised dais draped in various colours and symbols.

I wanted to know more about what was going on, so I began pushing my way over to Lord Trevor. As I approached I could hear him reassuring the Clan Chief that right after the ceremony, Arian and himself would push their appeal to the Lore Masters into helping their people. She stopped her argument when she saw me and indicated him to silence on the subject.

Grateful for the distraction, he began by explaining that all of the Lore Masters from each province had gathered and were in attendance, all except Rheal. Joran was the Lore Master from that province, and his conspicuous absence was being tied to Queen Mordeth's campaign of terror. After our meeting last night, they had removed his banners and a consensus had been taken among the Lore Masters. They had decided not to be complacent in removing responsibility for his actions as her advisor, and a replacement would be sought after today's ceremony for a new Lore Master from Rheal.

When Meda sat down in the chair hung with the banners of Manath Samal, Lord Trevor explained to me that Meda was still the Lore Master of Manath Samal, and counsellor to the King, even though he had not attended at Court for the past twenty five years, ever since his father had died. The

previous Master of the Temple had died that same year and
Meda had been chosen as 'Keeper of the Tome'. He never
had the heart to give up responsibility as counsellor to the
court and continued to send letters of encouragement and
wisdom by proxy.

"There's something foul going on with Lore Master
Joran's disappearance. Apparently, after we sent Dermot and
Joran packing from Tyre, Dermot made his way here to the
Temple and declared himself Lore Master of Rheal. He told
Meda that Joran had died during their journey, but had
bestowed the Mantle to him before he died." He looked
incredulous. "Arian told me this last night." He cocked his
eyebrow. "He blamed Arian for the old Lore Master's death,
saying that they were thrown off the Isle for no good reason
and the treatment played heavily on the old man's heart until
he died on the way back to the Temple. He carried the staff
of Lore Master Joran as proof." He looked around and then
whispered to me. "We said our goodbyes to Joran when he
escorted Dermot from Tyre. After apologizing for his
ward's behaviour, he promised to rectify the boy's attitude
on their way back to *Lanera*, not the Temple of the Sky."
He studied my face for understanding. "How did the boy
arrive here alone, and what ever happened to Joran?" He
gestured toward the bridge. "When they asked Dermot to
perform the Rites of Initiation to authenticate his claim as a
Lore Master, he feigned an illness and then disappeared into
the night, never to be seen again." He squinted his eyes in
anger. "And then his mother appears at the head of an

131

unstoppable army? Is Dermot or is Joran somehow involved?" His shoulders hunched at the unanswerable question. "Nobody knows that answer."

I began to see more clearly, realizing it was due to the sun beginning to rise. Dawn had arrived at the shore of the lake known as the Soul of the Earth. The crowd hushed as Meda rose, standing at the apex of the bridge. His upraised staff circled the crowd, the large blue stone at the end sparkled in the reflected torchlight.

"Distinguished guests, Lore Masters, Acolytes and Initiates, the Temple of the Sky welcomes you and is honoured to have so many witnesses on this, the Four Hundredth Initiation Ceremony on record." Silence answered his words of introduction. "Behold Thayer's Glory!" He stamped the staff three times. "Let the Initiates approach."

One by one a group of older boys dressed in plain black robes approached the edge of the bridge, removed their robes and then walked up the stairs, naked as the Gods had made them. The first boy knelt before Meda who sketched the Eye of Thayer above his supplicated head, then held the staff's stone to the boy's forehead and spoke the single word, "Awaken."

The boy stood and made his way to a platform that jutted out from the middle of the bridge where he bowed his head once, and then dove into the dark river water churning below. Each of the boys followed the first in succession. There were seven boys in all, and one by one they resurfaced and swam over to the other side of the river to a decorated platform where a group of seven Acolytes, waited wearing blue-coloured robes. As each boy came out, they held aloft a stone and pronounced loudly, "My eyes have been opened. I am awake."

With each pronunciation, an Acolyte walked forward, pulled a green robe over the boy's head, and spoke loudly to the crowd, "I am your witness, arise," and spoke the boy's name. After the final name was spoken, and recorded by Meda in a large brass-bound book, each pair of Acolyte and Initiate walked reverently up onto the bridge from the far side and they fanned themselves out from shore to shore alternating blue and green, man and boy, teacher and student.

Meda joined them in the middle of the bridge once more and faced out to the lake, the Soul of the Earth, and held up his staff. "Thayer, God of Knowledge, your Initiates have found their Heartstone from the depths of your baptismal water. Their pledges have been made to your Acolytes and the sacred task of Apprenticeship has been accepted. The Books of Lore may be opened and their sacred knowledge revealed!" He tapped his staff three times on the wooden bridge, then lifted it hand over hand until only the tip remained in his shaking, upraised right hand. As the staff wobbled tenuously at the apex of his reach, the sun broke over the mountains, east from across the lake, and sent the first rays of sunshine across the Soul of the Earth and into the clear blue stone embedded in the end of his staff. Sparks radiated from the stone, cascading its cerulean rays over the dark, churning water below.

I rubbed my eyes in disbelief and wonder. The Initiates, standing proudly, held up their newly-found stones in unison. Meda's blue staff-stone flashed brightly with its pulsing light, and like a match to kindling, its power flowed into the smaller river stones, throwing up a myriad of colours above the bridge. In turn, each Lore Master stood up behind the group and held up their staffs, igniting their multi-coloured gemstones from Meda's still-pulsing stone. They reached into their robes and exposed their own Heartstone, and each flared to life and pulsed in rhythm to their staff-stones. Every member of the Temple repeated the act until I lost count of the number of stones filling the area with pulsing light.

The dazzling play of coloured light mesmerized and excited each smiling face as we gazed silently up at the evidence of the God Thayer's power. I noticed tears running down Heather dan Kalon's cheeks as her face lit-up with joy. Lyas and Lord Trevor stood, mouths agape, wonder plainly written on the veteran soldiers faces. Only King Arian appeared unaffected by what he saw. Perhaps he was hoping for more than a dazzling light show to fight the Cannibal-Queen.

That's when I heard something. Something quiet, but then more pronounced.

It was a strange humming sound, like bees searching for nectar in my ears.

I looked around for the source of the noise and that's when I saw the Ren-Tigarians, at the edge of the clearing, whirling their strange devices above their heads. We had watched them do this before at Ren-Tigar, but from our distance at the time, the noise had sounded muffled. Now that we were surrounded by thirty-seven priests from only twenty feet away, the air was being pummelled in a barrage of light and sound and it was affecting my mind. I was overwhelmed.

The noise penetrated my head, even after covering my ears.

The lights blinded me, even after squeezing them shut.

Something uncoiled within my mind.

It felt like a curtain being drawn back in a dark room.

A voice, distant, called inside my head, muffled and indistinct.

I felt my body walking uncontrollably to the edge of the river.

Somewhere in the black depths, a voice called me.

It beckoned me, urgent and desperate.

Before I could stop, my body dove into the water.

The cold water stabbed my skin, but I continued downward, ignoring the pain.

The underwater current pushed me back, trying to force me out into the lake, but my strong arms pulled me down, deeper and deeper.

The voice called, just out of reach.

"Thomas, it is time to awaken."

I reached out to touch the voice, but instead picked up a stone, and was surprised as sudden warmth drove the stabbing cold from my body.

I caressed the smooth stone as it pulsed softly in my head, like a heartbeat.

Like my heartbeat, now loud in my ears.

My lungs burned for air. Panic set in as I realized where I was. I used my feet to push up on the bedrock, and sent my body shooting up through the smothering water.

I heard people shouting all around as my head broke the surface. People on both sides of the river were yelling and pointing, holding branches out for me to grab. I felt hands seize my shoulders and haul me up bodily out of the water, laying me on my back. Kay and Lord Trevor stared down at me, concern plainly written on their faces as Trevor slapped my face.

"What in the name of Petra's withered teats were you thinking boy?!" Lord Trevor's anger reminded me of our days of training.

"There are better ways of making an ass out of yourself." Kay's concern could be heard through his admonishing tone. "I think the Lore Masters are sorely pissed at you, not to mention every other person here today." He looked over his shoulder as Meda loomed behind him, a scowl screwing up his gentle features. The feeling of warmth washed out of me and I began shivering in the chill morning air.

"Get up!" He raised his eyebrows angrily. "Do you think that was amusing Mr. Cartwright? Ruining our sacred ceremony? In four hundred years, nothing like this has ever happened! And during my tenure, by the Gods, I'll be recorded as an imbecile for letting you attend! What do you have there?" He asked pointing at my clenched fist.

I unrolled my fingers and showed him the stone.

He gasped as it flashed a brilliant blue and then lay still in my wet palm. Kay and Lord Trevor helped me to my feet as Heather dan Kalon wrapped her cloak around my soggy shoulders.

"However did you," he trailed off, trying to compose himself. He picked the stone up gently. It looked like a shard of broken glass. He fingered it apprehensively and then hesitantly placed it against his now-quiet staff-stone. It slipped into an unseen mar in the staff-stone, fitting perfectly.

The Master of the Temple's hands started shaking uncontrollably and he removed the shard once more, lest he drop it back into the water.

The assembled community of the Temple swore and began speaking to each other animatedly. I heard them say "Impossible", "Prophecy" and "End of days." The robed assemblage started walking and then running back toward the Temple in a panic.

"HOLD!" Meda's voice echoed across the clearing. "Stand and bear witness to the Glory of Thayer!" He surveyed the crowd as they slowly returned, unsure of what was happening. Once he had their attention, he lowered his arms. "This is a day of celebration, not of panic!" His bushy eyebrows lifted and then fell. "This is a day dedicated to the God Thayer!" His voice was calming them down. "For four hundred years have we borne witness to the Power of Thayer on this, his most sacred day, but little did we know that it was incomplete. Today, we bear witness to the true glory of the God." He held up both staff and shard. "Today, the Eye of Thayer has been opened. The Stone of Knowledge has been made whole! The Tome of Lore will be revealed at last!" His voice rose to a shrill and the crowd exploded into cheers and uncontrolled weeping, either in joy or fear.

I felt awkward as people approached and shook my hands, thanking me. They patted my shoulders or my back and began to sing praises to Thayer and some even added my name, to my embarrassment. We walked together back to the Temple like a school of fish, colours flashing in the early morning light and the feeling of joy overtook everyone, even the dour Arian. I laughed and smiled with the general feeling of goodwill that had infected the group. I had no idea what the Temple Master had meant with his cryptic words, but in my mind's eye I could turn and point directly at the location of the shard that had spoken to me, and was now in his possession. It pulled at my mind and I could feel it pulsing in my heart.

I had the beginnings of anger and greed forming – why had he taken it from me? Did each of them not have their own Heartstone? It was a part of me just as much as my sword was.

Thinking of my sword, I looked over my shoulder and saw King Arian speaking with Fen Gisar. The Ren-Tigarian black clothing, which had seemed so menacing before, now seemed out of place in the sea of colours. The pattern of their groupings suddenly stood out plainly to me. I noticed that they were bunched into small groups of three. Then I remembered the mountain trail and the Terroks. Three men had died, not two or four. There was something to the pattern that tickled at the back of my mind, like the shard still calling out to me.

"Mr. Cartwright seems to have a knack for causing disturbances." Lyas quipped to Lord Trevor who now flanked me. "Like poking a stick into a bloody hornets' nest." He squinted at the bright morning sunlight with his single eye. "The last time I was neck-deep in water like that, my wife tried giving me a bath." He looked up the trail to where Donato was trying to help Heather back to the Temple, his hand caressing her lower back. "You might want to hurry up Trevor or you'll be neck-deep in hot water." Lord Trevor left my side and skipped ahead up the mountain path, pushing the Lore Master aside and slipping his arm around Heather's waist.

King Arian appeared by my side, an older version of the man who had just left. "How do you feel Thomas, hopefully not any worse for the wear?" His smile brightened his usually sardonic face.

139

"I'm fine Sire." I lied. My wet clothing chaffed my thighs and my boots sloshed with every step. I felt miserable and angry.

"You'll be glad to hear that the Ren-Tigarians do not have your sword." He offered. "They are very concerned that it has gone missing and have vowed to scour the Temple." His bright blue eyes reminded me of the shard. "Perhaps we can talk of this later and you can tell me exactly what happened back there?" He moved ahead without waiting for an answer and made his way up to Meda's side. Did he sense my mistrust of the Temple Master?

Kay appeared beside me and slipped another robe around my shoulders. "This might help you dry off a bit faster." A smile split his face as well. "Won't Pizzle be happy to know that he washed your clothes last night for no reason?"

"Very funny." I said, tugging the robe closer as I tried cutting out the cool breeze coming off the lake. "Kay, that water was cold but when I picked up that stone, it made me feel warm all over." We entered the portico into the Temple and my boots began to squeak and squish loudly.

"Are you sure you weren't just thinking about her?" Kay elbowed me in the ribs.

I shushed him as we met up with Heather dan Kalon and Lord Trevor who were waiting for us in the hallway by a table set with mugs and a large bowl of a clear steaming liquid.

"I hope you boys are hungry because this day is dedicated to feasting and drinking." Lord Trevor handed me a mug brimming over with the slightly-amber liquid. "This should shake off that river-chill."

As I sipped it, my mouth exploded with a sensation of flavours that reminded me of the riverbank swimming in colours. It warmed my throat as I drank it down and it slowly returned the heat to my body.

"Slowly boy, you don't want to be knee-walking by noon." The Clan Chief chided as she herself drank deeply. "By the Gods that's strong!" She waved a hand in front of her mouth. "At least we have some idea what they do with themselves up here in the middle of nowhere." That got a laugh from Trevor.

Lyas winked. "Not everything I suspect. Kind of weird for my liking, but then again, who am I to judge?" He drank his whole mug in one gulp. "Not bad," he snickered, "not bad at all." He said in again in a hoarse whisper while he refilled his mug.

We made our way back to our rooms to change into the robes we wore last night as directed by the Master of Offices for today's ceremonies. I handed my dripping clothes to Pizzle, whose mummified look told me exactly how unimpressed he was with my find as we entered the crowded Banquet Hall for a day of feasting, drinking and entertainment.

ELEVEN

Stone of Knowledge

Knowing all,
And yet ignorant.
Find the key.
Unlock the Tome.
~Book of Thayer

As we had been declared special guests by the Master of the Temple, I found myself seated at the head table with the other Lore Masters, the King, Lord Trevor the Clan Chief and Kay. I felt exposed and uncomfortable as the assemblage scrutinized my every move behind raised hands, whispered words and pointed fingers. After the absurdly-large morning meal which consisted of boiled eggs, cheese, dried fruit, nuts, fresh baked bread and fowl we were allowed to witness the Consecration Ceremony as the Initiates from the bridge were each brought forward, noted by name, and entered into another large book (how many records did they require?) by a small wizened man, whose toothless mouth, gummed the names to the point of mumbled misunderstanding. The older Acolytes announced their own name and the Apprenticeship course of study to which the Initiates would be committed, scribbling this information in the book beside the boy's name. The courses of study included Music and the Arts, History,

Serology and Tinctures, Engineering, Military Tactics and Political Sciences, and Ephemera. When I asked what the last course involved, Lore Master Laird sniffed loudly beside me.

"You should understand it better than any other after your little performance at the ceremony this morning." He didn't notice the bit of yellow egg that he'd just spat out, staining his pristine and fluffy white beard, and after his comment, I chose not to point it out to him.

For some reason the Lore Masters had taken an immediate dislike to me after the ceremony, saying that I had ruined it and mocked their beliefs, and deserved to be flogged from the Temple. I was shocked. After the joyous romp back to the Temple, I thought everyone had been overcome with hysteria and that 'A New Age' had dawned. I found out afterwards that the Lore Masters thought it was all hogwash and that Meda was mistaken. They didn't share his belief that I had found the mysterious missing shard because in their opinion, the Stone of Knowledge and the shard were still two separate pieces and since it had been sundered, it could never be mended. In fact, they went so far as to say that the Mindstone in Meda's staff was not really *the* Stone of Knowledge that Meda claimed it to be, just another Stone of Power, like the ones they possessed. They all believed this except for Meda, who winked knowingly from the center of the table, trying to reassure me that I belonged at the head table. I sank down lower in my seat, dejected and angry. I didn't dare tell them that I could feel the shard in my head.

"I'm sorry Master, Ephemera sounded more like something describing the manner of courtly ladies or foppish lords." I said sheepishly. He frowned down at me like he'd just discovered some stinking creature that had crawled out of a swamp and burped in his face.

"Things that are here and then gone. Transitory, like your presence here in the Temple." He stated it matter-of-factly, and then sighed when I didn't respond. He stuffed another hard-boiled egg into his wide mouth. "Frogs from tadpoles for example." He burped. I sprayed a mouthful of wine across the white linen in an attempt to cover my laugh, as his face had just reminded me of the frog he had just mentioned. My outburst had the effect of turning everyone's eyes to scrutinize and glare at me disapprovingly.

Pizzle walked up to the head table and began crying despondently about the stains that the wine would leave and how old the ceremonial cloth was. He cried out for help, and a group of scullions appeared from the kitchen carrying a bucket of steaming water and a cup of white powder. Egg still clung to his beard as Lore Master Laird began scrubbing at the purple stains himself, cursing outsiders and their disruptive presence in a place of learning.

I excused myself quickly and quietly as a group of tumblers and musicians entered the hall wearing bright spotted clothing, thanking the Gods for the distraction. I needed to stretch my legs away from those judging, pompous fools. If they worried about staining the damned cloth, why did they serve red wine in the first place? I made my way outside, relieved myself in the makeshift privy, and then strolled onto a large tiled terrace that commanded a view of the lake spreading out into the valley below. Eagles soared high above in their never-ending circles, rising higher and higher on the warm afternoon air currents. Dappled sunlight played across the surface of the lake, rippling as a slight breeze carried the scent of flowers up to my height. I started to feel calm and peaceful again, and understood why they called it The Soul of the Earth. It was a beautiful place that perfectly suited their solitary and studious practice.

I couldn't imagine it ever falling into ruin like Jahad's Rest or K'Larn. The thought brought back the reason why we were here in the first place. Images of charred and hacked-up bodies, some partially eaten, came back unbidden. Lord Fiongall's half-eaten arm and the lives of hundreds of those people utterly destroyed. Jahad's Rest must have been just as beautiful as this place before Queen Mordeth destroyed it. I could imagine the serenity the name implied looking across at the lake. And here we were drinking, dancing and forgetting. I felt nauseous. I missed Maura and began absently plucking at the thong around my neck, sending words out to Thayer to keep her safe.

"I don't mean to disturb your reverie Mr. Cartwright." The Master of the Temple stood beside me. "Few people view this beauty and have a look of horror on their face." He sat on the balustrade beside me, arms crossed on his chest. "Would you like to share what is troubling you?" He asked.

"I just remembered the reason why we're here." I copied his posture, sunlight warm on our faces. "How are we supposed to stop an army that can turn people against themselves and make them do such horrible things?" I could sense the shard on his person.

"A most curious predicament," he sighed, "but I believe there is more to Queen Mordeth than meets the eye." He stroked his feathery white beard, pondering his next words. "Her son stole things that were not his to take." They weren't the only one. "Now they have access to powers that are only deserved of the chosen, of a Lore Master, duly baptised and raised." Is that why he took it from me, because I'm not a Lore Master? A servant approached carrying a tray with two pipes. Lore Master Meda took the long, curved pipe and lit it. The servant offered the other to me which I accepted graciously. The taste was sweet and the smoke swirled up to the blue sky above us. It reminded me of strawberries and honey.

"If he wasn't truly a Lore Master, then how could he have access to these powers?" I asked, but I held back my real question.

"Dermot still needs to account for the whereabouts of Lore Master Joran. He's disappeared and nobody knows where he is." He puffed slowly. "But I know where he was going." His deep-set blue eyes looked at me. "Mount Kali. Chafet Temple to be exact. They have powers there to

146

unlock secrets, but some are best kept hidden." He stood and stretched. "Arian has told me that Queen Mordeth wore a golden helm in the shape of a dragon's skull." He sighed. "After your discovery this morning, it no longer shocks me. Events are unfolding around us rather quickly and time apparently is not on our side." He finished his pipe and tapped the wattle into his hands, ground the ashes into a powder, and then sprinkled them over the edge into the forest that spread out below us, muttering some words. "I believe the Gods are awakening," he smiled at me, "and I have something I need to show you." He held out his hand, and there it was, the piece of blue stone.

"I was going to ask you about this." I took it from him. "I don't know how to say this, but I can hear it in my head." The warmth returned briefly and joy surged through my body.

"And what is it saying?" He had an amused look on his face.

"Heal." It felt stupid saying it. How could a piece of stone talk?

"This isn't what I wanted to show you." His smile was contagious. "Follow me." He stood waiting to go. "Oh and Thomas, you aren't crazy, because I hear it as well. The only difference is that I know what it is trying to say."

He led me off the terrace and back into the Temple where we handed the pipes back to the waiting servant whose baleful look filled me with a sense of mirth at everyone's sense of place and purpose and how much I could never fit in here. I felt confused and heady from all the wine I had drunk since this morning and the noticeably loud protest from my belly was a reminder that I hadn't eaten for several hours. My curiosity was piqued and so I followed Meda down the mysterious corridors and down deeper through hallways that turned and split off until we ended up in front of the strange Eye-of-Thayer door leading to his private chamber. The Eye stared at me accusingly from within the wooden panel, as if the God was trying to measure my worth before I passed beyond His all-knowing seal. I assumed that I was deemed worthy as Meda opened the door and led me around the tables to the mysterious door at the back of the room where he had appeared from last night. Meda held a restraining hand against my chest.

"Beyond this door lie the greatest treasures of our age." He removed his hand and placed it onto the carved door handle. I almost laughed at this sudden formality, but found the strength to restrain myself, even as the image of a belching frog appeared in my mind. As if sensing my hidden humour, he looked again at me solemnly. "Thomas Cartwright, you must understand that you are the first person to bear witness to the history of our land who is *not* an Initiate, an Acolyte or a Lore Master. I am taking a great risk in doing so, but due to the recent event this morning, I feel that I must. You are more closely connected to all of this than most. I will try to explain further, but first, may I present to you our Library." He opened the door and ushered me in ahead of him.

Darkness enveloped us as the door sealed shut behind him. My imagination clawed at the walls pressing in on both sides and echoed off of the unseen ceiling high above. Meda uttered unintelligible words and a dim blue light blossomed from the end of his staff, he had retrieved from some niche in the wall. He squeezed ahead of me, crushing me against the rock wall behind as he passed and then headed quickly down the narrow corridor that looked like it had been carved out of the living earth. As I fell into his wake, I noticed the floor was banking down slightly, reminding me of the reeling deck of the *Merry Widow*. I regained my composure and strode steadily after him, not wanting to be left alone in the swallowing darkness behind us.

As we walked, I couldn't help but stare overhead at the shadows looming down garishly from various carved faces decorating the walls. When I asked about them, Meda laughed at my question, "This Temple has not always been dedicated to the teachings of Thayer." He shuffled on ahead of me. "The parts of the Temple we are entering now have deep roots in the mountain and once and awhile new figures like the ones above are unearthed as we need to expand our Library."

We arrived at another door, but this one was not as ornate as the one we had entered through his chamber and the iron hinges protested loudly as he pushed it open. We stood on a small steel balcony overlooking a large round chamber. Shelves of all sort stood at impossible angles radiating from a central core dais. Torches, carefully bracketed and shielded, hung from the walls around the perimeter, throwing their soft light throughout. I looked up and noticed the curved dome. I couldn't begin to fathom how someone could construct such a monument within the earth or how long it had existed here. Dotted around the circumference of the dome were the same ghoulish creatures, smiling their secret history down on us. Meda started down the metal staircase that spiralled down into the chamber along the edge of the curved wall. As I followed him, I noticed the dark maws of corridors that radiated out from the central chamber, supposedly going deeper within the mountain and some back under the Temple.

Hundreds and thousands of books littered every conceivable nook, cranny and shelf. The round chamber was segmented into six equal arcs, delineated by colour and each shelf had been coloured to match the arc it stood within. Each of the coloured shelves held books, and each book had numbers written on their spines, with a corresponding coloured tag.

Sitting on the central dais were several large oaken tables and on each table, books were being held open in place by the use of strange metal clamping devices and from each book, a string was secured to a particular spot and hung suspended over to my sword. There it was, held in one of those metal devices. My anger surged again at this old man and his presumption that he could take whatever he wanted from me. But once more, he read my emotions before I could say anything.

"You will undoubtedly have noticed that I borrowed your sword. Please accept my apology for not asking you earlier, but I was hoping to have it returned to you after the ceremony this morning, but your remarkable discovery changed all that. Thomas, I'm asking you this time, may I have the shard back, to study it further?" I handed it to him willingly this time as we mounted the dais and made our way over to the tables, ducking under several of the strings. "These," he plucked a string, "help us to identify and locate separate elements of objects throughout various subjects and courses of study." He thumbed a blue string held within a book in front of him. "This book is on symbology from the," he gently pried the book back and read the spine, "first century." He followed its length down to the sword. "You may not have noticed the marking here." He pointed to the mark that Fen Gisar had pointed out months ago. He picked up a large round piece of glass set into a brass ring. "Here, look through this." He handed it to me.

I held the glass up to the blade which brought the tiny detail into shocking clarity. It appeared to be a tiny coiled snake eating its own tail and I remarked upon this. Meda affirmed this and showed me the spot indicated in the book. Before turning away, I studied the blade and was surprised to see that it wasn't actually dull black, but was rather a dull dark-grey. The magnified surface appeared to be textured, almost a miniature version of the spiny skin adorning the hilt. I moved the glass over the cutting edge and was surprised to see that it actually had a honed edge like a normal sword, but even this was dull in colour.

"I have traced the symbol's first appearance back to this text. It's called an Auroboros and represents immortality and the perpetual movement of the universe. No beginning and no end." He traced the strange scripted words in the book. Beside the script was a large picture of the snake eating its tail. "The Ren-Tigarians believe that Al-Shidath was the last owner of this weapon and that he lost it during the last century." He moved to another book, this one with a white string. "According to this text, he was a formidable and competent leader but when faced by the hordes of Mount Kali, he retreated to the coast, close to where you claimed to have found this, and was never seen again. Man and sword were swept clean from the face of the earth. That is until you came along."

The picture of the man beside the script in this book looked somewhat familiar and tugged at the back of my mind. He was dressed as a Ren-Tigarian, but didn't have the face veil that they all wore and his cheeks didn't have any tattoos. I found that strange, for surely he had lost some men under him during his leadership? "Do any of your books say where the sword came from?" I asked as I surveyed the man-made web of strings tied to my sword. I noticed one string was attached to a book with a large fish creature drawn inside it with angled fins and pointy teeth. The cover of the book was the same material adorning my sheath and hilt.

"These texts here, here, and here all tell stories about the Sword of Prophecy." He pointed to another. "This one here talks of a 'Blade of Destiny', but this one I find the most interesting." He grabbed my elbow and led me to a stand holding open a bright colourfully painted page. A red string tied to the metal device hung limp from the page. "Tell me what you see here." He pointed to a small picture in the middle of the page as he turned and grabbed the loose red string.

I studied the tiny pictograph in black, red and blue inks. "It looks like someone holding up a sword." I held the brass circled glass to the page and the picture leaped to larger-than-normal size. "Yes, it looks similar to my sword and it looks like," I trailed off as I squinted closer at the picture, "it looks like he's wearing a necklace with a large blue stone." I turned around as Meda clamped his staff into another metal device beside my sword and tied the red piece of string to the clear blue stone in the end of his staff.

"Precisely, he is *wearing* the Stone of Knowledge. I believe he must have used it to find the Sword's strange metal buried somewhere within the bowels of Mount Kali and that he used the mountain's magma to actually forge the Sword." He smiled, reviewing his setup. "Where is the man standing?" He asked.

153

I turned back to the page and reviewed the picture again without the eye-glass. It suddenly came into sharp focus. I understood why the page was so colourful.

"You see? He stands upon the bridge, directly over the waters from where you retrieved this." He held up the small blue shard of stone. "There is only one object in the entire world that could have cut this shard from the Stone of Knowledge." It glinted faintly in the reflected torchlight as he touched it. "And these two marvels, the Sword of Prophecy, and the Stone of Knowledge are somehow connected in their shared past histories. Come." I placed the looking glass down next to the picture of an Initiation Ceremony as he beckoned me over.

He gently placed the shard against the Stone of Knowledge, like he did by the river, and I could clearly see where it had been cleanly shorn away.

The blue stone flared to life as it came into contact with the shard and my sword began humming in the metal clamping devices. It shook violently in the restraints. Meda swore and reached out with one hand to unclasp his staff, as his other appeared to be stuck to the Stone. My mind began reeling as the humming of the sword and the singing of the shard pervaded my thoughts. I reached out and grabbed my sword as it broke free from the metal bindings and slapped against the Stone with the flat of the blade, ringing a loud peal through the echoing chamber. The instant they touched, light burst from the Stone, temporarily blinding me. I gritted my teeth and tried pulling it free but the vibrating continued and coursed up my arms. As my sight slowly restored, I felt Meda pull his staff against me in a tug-of-war. His eyes had rolled back up into his head so that only the whites glowed back at me. His mouth hung agape in a silent scream matching the shard's urgent plea for healing. The strings tied to my sword and to his staff ignited in flames and burned their way back into the waiting open books.

I couldn't let go of the blade and watched in horror as the books burst into blue flames.

Like a living creature it leapt from book to book, igniting each as it landed on the dry paper. I looked up painfully and noticed the bracketed torches had burst their glass shields and rained heavenly blue fire down upon the shelves of waiting books below. Meda's silent gape unnerved me as the Stone's blue fire spread throughout the chamber from book to book and down the open corridors, and if it wasn't for the wonton destruction, I would have described it as beautiful.

Meda slumped forward and released his touch upon the Stone of Knowledge, crumpling into a pile of loose blue robes. The humming ceased and the shard's voice disappeared, but the flames and the heat remained. I looked around uselessly, realizing that I was going to be burned alive in minutes. I searched for a place of respite and my eyes settled on the winding stairs.

The *metal* staircase.

I bent down and scooped up Meda over one shoulder and the Stone of Knowledge cradled in his burned and bleeding fingers. I shook away the remnants of his staff, now turned to charred ash, and placed the now-quiet stone into a pocket in my robe. I retrieved my sword and made my way to the metal staircase, slicing a path through the burning shelving that blocked my escape. Slowly I walked up the stairs, feeling the heat of the metal on my feet as I had discarded the comfortable slippers on the dais, fearing that they would trip me up. The library was a swirling, choking inferno, and made me feel like being trapped inside a smithy, the old books providing a perfect kindling. I ducked through the open door at the top of the stairwell and made my way down the dark corridor, and back toward Meda's chambers.

The flickering fire sent ghostly shadows along the floor and the walls ahead of me. I couldn't look above to see if the ghoulish faces were laughing down at me. I reached the door and fumbled for the handle, trying not to drop my sword as I didn't know if I would be able to retrieve it again. Panic rose when I couldn't feel the handle and I didn't dare put down the Lore Master as there wasn't enough room to turn around. I began to pound on the door with the hilt of my sword and yelled in frustration, cursing every one of the miserable bastards that filled their faces, immune to the dangers below them. Impossibly I began to feel the heat on the back of my neck, flaming my fear of a fiery death, which led to even louder pounding and screaming pleas for help.

The door opened suddenly pushing me back down the corridor, back toward my death. Steadying my legs, I burst into the room and put the Lore Master down gently on the large dining table as Pizzle stood looking down the corridor, stammering incomprehensible nonsense.

"Don't just stand there gawking! Help me!" I yelled at the small man who just stood there pulling the remaining thin hair from his head.

"What have you done?" He turned at my voice and I could see in the muted light tears staining his cheeks. A sudden gush of warm air slammed the door closed and pushed Pizzle into the room, rolling him onto his back. He screamed in terror as the door started smouldering. Impossibly, some of the small glowing embers from the burning books had been blown into the room before the door had slammed shut, and settled quietly on the carpet, the wall hangings and the book-laden shelving lining the walls.

"Pizzle! Get up man!" I reached down and pulled the little man to his feet, hauled Meda back onto my shoulder and led us from the room as it began burning as well.

Pizzle recovered and ran ahead of me screaming, "Fire!", but this part of the Temple was empty as everyone was attending the ceremonies in the main Banquet Chamber. I followed him blindly down the myriad passages, his scream echoing down the empty corridors ahead of us. I didn't have time to fathom how and why he happened to be there at the exact time when I needed him to open the door, but later I would learn that he'd come looking for the Temple Master to reside over the Raising Ceremony when the new Lore Masters would be named and recognized. He had watched me leave the terrace with Meda and as we scrambled through the Temple he admitted that he was the one that had taken my damnable sword to Meda, and he shouldn't have listened and now it was his fault for admitting us into the Temple in the first place.

Chaos erupted in the Banquet Chamber as they saw us appear at the doors. King Arian was at my side instantly and shouldered the weight of his unconscious mentor. We followed the flow of people again down the corridors, away from the Temple and found ourselves going through the same Portico we had come through that morning. We stopped at the river's edge, where Arian placed Meda gently on the ground. He studied the old man's face and called his name, but there was no response. His eyes were still lolled back in his head and his breathing sounded ragged.

People pushed me to the ground and cut away the robe from me. I looked to see what they were doing and was aghast to see that my skin was blackened and red along my arms and chest. My feet were pulsing in dull pain as others splashed water over the burnt flesh. I slowly lost consciousness after drinking an offered draught of some pain-killing potion by one of the Ren-Tigarians. The last thing I remembered seeing was a group of men and boys running with buckets of water from the river back to the Temple crying "End of times" and "Prophecy" over and over again, as they glared at me and shook their heads in abject fear.

I dreamt I was swimming underwater, slowly trying to get away from a large snake that had bright-red glowing eyes. It chased me deeper and deeper away from the surface of the water as it continuously ate its own tail over and over again.

TWELVE

Trial by Fire

Holy Fight,
Sacred Rite,
God's Might,
Death Tonight.
~Book of Man, 3rd Century

I awoke to the gentle and familiar bumping sounds of a cart traversing a mountain path, sending my mind down the familiar memories of childhood when I would ride in the back of my father's cart, sunning my face as we slowly made our way back home after a successful day of trading in the town market. The feel of the wood, the creak of the wheel, the clinking of the horse's bridle lulled me in a false sense of security. The sky above me was clear blue, not a cloud in sight. My reverie clotted in my mind. The sky was blue.

The air was blue with fire.

More recent memories flooded back when I closed my eyes. *"What have you done?"* The reproach in Pizzle's voice filled me with guilt. If I hadn't been at the Temple, if I hadn't brought that accursed sword with me, if I hadn't left home and Maura, none of that would have happened. If I closed my eyes tighter, I could imagine that I was still back at home in my father's cart. My hand moved up to feel the reassuring weight of the thong and Maura's lock of hair but my fingers refused to feel anything as the bandages wrapped around them bound them tightly in place.

"Easy Thomas, I don't want to have to rewrap those again." I opened my eyes and saw Kay looking down at me from the back of his small pony. I tried to lift myself up, but he leaned over and pushed me back down. "For the God's sake man, rest." When I finally subsided, he let go of my shoulder. "We're on our way back down the mountain." He leaned in slightly. "Thomas, can you tell me what happened?"

"Fire," Was all that I could manage.

"You don't say," He smiled again. "Pizzle's been telling everyone that you were solely responsible for it."

"I am." I said despondently. "If I hadn't been there, it would never have happened."

"Well if I were you I'd keep that opinion to myself. The lot of them want to finish off what the fire tried to do." He looked behind him. "Heather has kept them busy and away from you. She's promised to geld any man that lays a hand on you." He looked ahead. "Meda is still out cold." He looked down at me, concern written on his features. "Did you try and kill him?"

"What!?" I asked incredulously, which started me to cough spasmodically. My lungs burned and my body ached. The coughing caused concerned looks again from Kay who apologized for asking. He kicked his pony forward and left my field of view. My position in the cart forced me to face

161

backwards, up the mountain face where I could see the billowing plume of grey smoke from the burning Temple, rising hundreds of feet into the air.

Lord Trevor suddenly appeared where Kay had just been and looked down at me. "Get your rest while you can Mr. Cartwright, it's a long way down." He moved out of view, leaving me to witness the horrible evidence of my destruction. A millennia of history recorded into all of those books were burned and gone for good. If I had been a Ren-Tigarian, and those books had been my Tricaste, my face would be swollen blue for the next year from the tattooing required.

The rocking cart lulled me back into fitful slumber. I dreamt of Meda, eyes bulging white, hands clawing at me, flesh melting from his face, and the accusing words crying from his mouth over and over again, "What have you done?"

I awoke again under a star-filled night-sky feeling famished. Trying to avoid being noticed, I rose up slowly on one bandaged elbow and peeked over the lip of the cart. The cool mountain air felt brisk on my burned face. My heart sank when I realized we were camping in the same place the Terroks had attacked us only days before. I felt sick to my stomach thinking how my fortune had changed so much in a such a short span of time.

Since I destroyed the Temple.

I searched around for a friendly face. The harbour was full of people milling about aimlessly, trying to keep busy with the most menial of tasks. The main area of activity seemed to be at the entrance where flickering torches outlined acolytes who arrived and were directed over to respective areas where they would unload objects recovered from the Temple. The hollowed-out rock wall reflected the light of many fires and my mouth watered at the smell of roasting meat. As if sensing my thoughts, Kay's head popped up by the closest fire and he walked over carrying a plate of steaming food.

"Here, eat up, you must be hungry." We sat in silence as I wolfed the food down. As I ate Kay examined my arms and face. "Well, you don't have any eyebrows and you've singed your hair, but there's nothing at all I can do for that sour look on your face." He smiled. "How are you feeling cousin?"

"Better, now that I've eaten something." He offered me some water which I drained quickly, but my throat still felt sensitive. "How's Meda?" I asked worriedly.

"Well, there's good news and bad news." He pulled out a wineskin that was lodged between my leg and the cart that I hadn't noticed earlier. "Here, have some of this." I drank deeply, and was thankful the mead didn't burn my throat. "He would probably thank you for saving his life, if he could talk." He looked at me, trying to read my expression. "What exactly happened Thom? Meda won't wake up. His eyes are peeled back into his skull and his breathing is extremely shallow." He saw the worry in my face. "He's barely alive but not badly burned thanks to you."

"I don't know what happened Kay. I'm still confused."
I decided to tell him of the events leading up to the fire.
"All I know is that it has something to do with my bloody
sword and that bloody stone I found in the river!" The
frustration in my voice caused men's heads to turn in our
direction. I noticed shadows approaching and out of the
darkness King Arian and Lord Trevor appeared.

"If you're well enough to argue then perhaps you could
do the honour of accompanying us." Lord Trevor asked
coolly. "You have been placed under trial, Thomas
Cartwright, and we are here to act as your advocate." He
looked at Kay. "Please help your cousin to the tent."

Abashed and ashamed, I didn't know what to say to
them. Kay bent into the cart and looped his arm under mine,
dragging me out. I tried standing, but fell limply into his
arms as pains shot up from my feet. I wondered how much
flesh I had left on the metal staircase. I remembered my
plunge into the river and regretted that I hadn't just worn my
wet clothes or my boots. Kay helped me limp slowly
through the clearing past the fires where men's severe looks
accused me without the need of a trial. I could see the blue
and white lined tent now and the shadows reflected on its
illuminated walls. It was large and protected by the sheer
rock wall behind it. I looked up the cliff wall above the tent
and noticed black-clad human shadows against the purplish-
blue sky. The Ren-Tigarians would not be caught unaware
by the Terroks again.

"Thomas, just tell them what you told me. You're not to blame for this." Kay smiled and nodded to Lyas who stood guard outside the tent. His sneer was marred by the scar running under his eye patch. He didn't say anything as he opened the flap and allowed us inside. A large wooden table was sitting by the back wall and each of the Lore Masters sat behind it, all except Meda of course. Clan Chief Heather dan Kalon was speaking quietly to King Arian and Lord Trevor as I came in behind them. Acolytes and other robed men flitted back and forth from the main table to minor tables set with food and drink laid out for the Masters. They were trying to maintain the festive atmosphere from the Temple, but their dour faces betrayed their true feelings at being relocated to a mere tent. Their grim looks reminded me of the stone carvings from the passageway leading down into the hidden Library.

"On your knees Mr. Cartwright!" Lore Master Donato yelled at me. "You are on trial for the wanton destruction of the Temple of the Sky and for eradicating the written histories of this land. Walls may be rebuilt, but ashen pages cannot be unburned!" Even in the high cool mountain air his face dripped with sweat and his reflecting spectacles gave him the appearance of an owl that had just cornered a mouse. Candlelight caught the silver circlet on his shaking brow, proclaiming his new status as Master of Offices.

"Forgive him Lore Master Donato, but his legs have been badly burned." Kay offered on my behalf.

165

The Master of Offices pointed at Kay, "Who are you to address this council? Leave." His ringed finger moved from Kay to the door behind us.

Kay bowed slowly to the long table, gave me a pat on my shoulder and then left me alone to face the group of vultures. I knelt before the assemblage, grunting painfully as the burns on my knees reopened and abased myself on the cold rock floor.

"Please, get this man a chair." Lore Master Laban ordered a servant. He wore the golden circlet proclaiming himself as the new Master of the Temple. Did this mean that Meda was never going to reclaim his position? "Mr. Cartwright, would you please do us the courtesy of retelling the events leading up to the fire?" He looked over at his fellow Lore Masters. "Guilt has yet to be determined, despite the pressure from my peers."

"This is intolerable!" Donato screamed. "He is guilty and must be brought to justice for our loss!" Spittle ran down his chin as his words received nods from the others.

"Gentlemen, please!" The new Master of the Temple rose to his full foreboding height. "If you are not willing to listen without prejudice, then I must ask you to leave these proceedings." He glared at each person in the room, and I felt a trifle victory that Laban hadn't called it a trial. The memories I had of trials back home usually ended up with someone swinging from the end of a rope. I cleared my throat, but it wasn't because it was still raw. When satisfied with their silence he sat back down again. "King Arian and

166

Lord Trevor both stand as your advocate, and their reputations alone are beyond reproach." He cleared his throat. "Therefore, we will allow Mr. Cartwright to explain his actions, and on his advocate's honour, we will take his account as unequivocal truth." Once more he surveyed the group and when he felt satisfied with what he saw, he indicated me to continue.

Staring at my bandaged hands in my lap, I retold my story exactly as the events had unfolded. During my recitation I looked up and noticed that Fen Gisar had entered and stood behind King Arian listening intently for hints of the sword's legacy. The room settled into quietude as my story was digested by all. They asked me to retell certain aspects of it, detailing exactly what I had felt and what I had been shown. A cup of water was offered and when I looked up, I was surprised to see it held by Fen. I accepted it with gratitude and sated my parched throat which felt more sensitive after my long speech.

"Well, this puts everything into a different perspective." Lore Master Mai-Hon pronounced, absently twirling his waxed moustaches. "Clearly this boy is not guilty of doing anything other than saving the life of Master Meda." He gave me a reassuring nod.

"Agreed," Laird concurred as he fluffed up his white beard, "the boy is not guilty of the crimes laid at his burned feet."

"I am also in agreement." Quinn Korid nodded as he ran fingers through his streaked red beard. "He is not responsible for the destruction of the Temple or the records."

"But he brought that damnable sword here in the first place!" Donato yelled. "If it wasn't for him, we would all be sleeping in our own beds tonight instead of fleeing for our lives through the mountains!" He stood and walked around to the front of the table. "*He* brought it here! *He* is the direct cause of the bloody fire! *He* found that God-Forsaken shard!" He pointed accusingly down at me. "Thomas Cartwright is guilty and shall pay for his crimes!"

"Then we are all guilty." Lord Trevor spoke up. "I brought him from the Isle of the Red Oak because King Arian summoned him to fight against Queen Mordeth. Heather dan Kalon allowed us passage through Upper Doros to gain access to the Temple." He walked over to Donato and stood toe to toe with him. "Laban granted access to the Temple and Meda *took* the sword." The younger Lore Master stared back defiantly. "All Thomas did was to find the missing piece of the Eye of Thayer and save Meda's life."

"Donato, please take your seat. Your argument has been duly noted." Laban asked the new Master of Offices. "Mr. Cartwright is not to blame." He let out a long sigh. "Meda is to blame." This garnered exasperated pleas from the others. "Quiet!" He demanded. "Lord Trevor is correct. If Meda's damned curiosity hadn't got the better of him, this might never have happened." He stood. "But that's who he

168

was, who he *is* I should say." His bushy white eyebrows fluttered. "Please accept our apologies Mr. Cartwright. Our healers will now attend upon you. You are all dismissed." He raised a hand to indicate the tent flap.

I stood and attempted a slight bow. Heather dan Kalon put her arm into mine and helped me limp from the tent. I looked at her and smiled my thanks.

"Now don't go trying to charm me too Thomas." Her eyes twinkled. "I couldn't possibly sit in there all night arguing with those frustrated old men." She winked at Lyas as we left the tent. He didn't seem to notice as his face was stretched with concern. "Lyas, surely you heard he's not guilty." She asked again. "Lyas! What is it?" He didn't respond at first.

"It's happening." He said in an almost whisper.

"What's happening?" She asked more stringently. Tears flowed down his cheeks. "Lyas!" Her scream brought Arian and Trevor from the tent.

"What's wrong?" Arian asked. He grabbed Lyas by the shoulders. "What do you see?" He asked of his one-eyed Captain.

"Death," his eye focused on the King, "She's attacking Bleneth."
"NO!" The Clan Chief's wail of terror and sorrow reverberated off of the stark cliff walls.

I found myself once again in the back of the cart, speeding down the mountain path in the early predawn

169

hours. Kay was leading the cart from a saddled pony, and the Lore Master Quinn Korid sat beside me, grumbling about how bumpy the trail was, what an unearthly hour it was, and would he ever again get a proper night's sleep. After Lyas had had his prophetic vision from his twin brother Dirk, the Clan Chief had tried to leave immediately but was held back by Lord Trevor, who nimbly avoided her thrown punches and kicks. He shook her back into sense, convincing her that we needed to have a plan of action and we couldn't just fly off to face the unknown.

The questions we had about Queen Mordeth's power had still not been addressed by the Lore Masters, our reason for travelling to the Temple in the first place, which then lead to an all-night forum by the remaining Lore Masters who tried desperately to recall any clues written in forgotten texts that might have been of some help to us.

This led to even more crying and hand wringing as the reality of their lost histories settled in again and again. Quinn Korid finally volunteered to accompany us because he claimed that with his green Mindstone and the Lore he had mastered, he could invoke a dampening effect on men's minds rendering them unconscious and open to manipulation. They all agreed that if he got close enough, he might be able to render the Queen unconscious long enough to remove the golden skull, which they saw as the source of her power. At the least, he could try and negate any affects she might try and influence on our men.

In the following weeks, the remainder of the Lore Masters and residents of the Temple planned to carefully make their way down the mountain and back to Bleneth where we would await them, in whatever remained of the village.

The Clan Chief, frustrated by our hampered party and the added population of the Temple, sped away shortly after midnight pursued by Lord Trevor, King Arian, Lyas and the Ren-Tigarian priests. I briefly had the urge to ignore my pain and follow them, but I could barely grasp the sides of the cart, how did I expect to grip reins and sit a pony down a twisting mountain path?

As we trundled down the mountain path, I studied the older Lore Master's face as he was lost in thought. The white-streaked hair on either side of his mouth reminded me of a travelling puppet show I saw as a child. Being overly curious, I had snuck into the caravan and that's where I discovered that the puppets had been controlled through hidden contrivances which allowed their mouths to open and close through a hidden means of levers and pulleys. I was imagining them again when I was slapped in the face.

"Are you listening to me?" Quinn Korid asked, looking rather perturbed. "For the last time, what was your father's name?"

"Thomas." I answered sheepishly, rubbing my stinging cheek. "My grandfather's name as well. Actually, my father's name was Thomas Vincent, but he went by the name Vincent as he didn't like being compared to my grandfather, but then he gave the name to me, so he must have had some feelings towards him." I imagined the red in his beard was partly due to chewing raw meat as he goggled wide-eyed at my inane ramblings.

"Thomas the Third?" He looked down the mountain path. Sunlight lit the treetops in the valley below to reflect the abundant variations of greens and yellow. It reminded me of the dazzling lights that had played through the clearing below the Temple yesterday morning. "Triads everywhere, the Holy Triptych pattern repeating itself through all things." He said to himself absently.

"Master, is there a relationship between light and sound?" My mind was on yesterday morning.

"Are you planning on entering the Temple Mr. Cartwright?" He looked amused, "What am I saying? What Temple?" I felt uncomfortable after last night's 'trial', and sensing that he continued on, "I'm not an expert, but I know they talk about the resonances of sound and light, about harmonics and wave patterns in the study of Ephemera. Perhaps that would interest you?"

"No Master, it's the fighting life for me." I smiled weakly and held up my bandaged hands. "During the Initiation Ceremony, I could actually hear the shard calling to me, but only after the Ren-Tigarians began using their devices and created that strange humming noise."

"Young man, it is my belief that your sword has loosened something inside you. It has allowed your mind to perceive things around you in a matter not unlike attuning yourself with something like," he pointed at the stone in his staff, "like this stone." He reached within his robe and pulled out his Heartstone. "My Heartstone is attuned to my soul, that is how I retrieved it from the river, but it is also attuned to my Mindstone. All three are connected, heart, mind and soul. The Holy Triptych." He peered at the smaller stone and it began to glow and pulse to the slow rhythmic beating of his heart. He held the smaller Heartstone nearer to the larger green crystalline Mindstone in his staff and it began to glow in response.

My sword picked up on the rhythm and began to hum in unison.

"Stop!" I shouted, desperate not to have a repeat of the Library. The glowing faded and Kay turned around at my outburst. When he saw that I was okay, he turned back to his study of the mountain trail ahead of us.

"What's wrong?" The Lore Master questioned, studying my face for clues.

"I could feel it again." I looked in the cart and found my sheathed sword behind my back near my legs. "But I wasn't even holding my sword this time."

"Incredible." Quinn hid his Heartstone within his robe and placed his staff into the bed of the cart. "Tell me what you felt." He placed an inquisitive hand on my forehead.

"It was the same feeling as yesterday at the river and in the Library." I tried explaining it to the best of my ability. "When your stones are activated, I think the Sword is being triggered in some way." I shrugged my shoulders. "It's like driving a cart, you feel each bump in the road despite the fact that you aren't even touching the ground, the wheels are." I searched again for some relevant meaning. "You may burn your tongue on hot soup, even though the soup hasn't been in direct contact with the fire, the pot you cooked it in was." I felt confused the more I tried to explain it. How do you describe love or pain? Isn't it relative to the one who experiences it?

"Could it be possible," the older man trailed off as his sight focused on the distant horizon. He didn't say anymore to my repeated pleadings for an explanation over the next week as we slowly managed our way down the mountain. My bandages were gone, but my hands face and feet were still sensitive.

"Whoa!" Kay said loudly as the ground suddenly levelled out. We had finally left the downward slope of the mountain and had reached the valley floor and there assembled before us stood the broken armies of Manath Samal and Bleneth that we had left behind. I looked around and noted to myself that indeed here were the fighting men of Upper Doros and Manath Samal, but where were all the elders, wives and children we had left in Bleneth? Lyas saw us approaching and diverted us before we reached the main encampment.

"Took your bloody time," his smirk confused us, "apologies Lore Master, the Clan Chief needs you right away. She's been unstable since we arrived three days ago. Arian was hoping you could use your Lore to help her

174

sleep." He shook his head in disgust. "I don't know where to begin," he paused, "apparently Bleneth resembles Jahad's Rest, only fresher. Arian has held us back until you arrived, so at least we've got some protection if she's still there." He helped the Lore Master down and showed him over to a large tent, after telling us to meet up with Dirk and our detachment from the Isle.

The same fiery destruction and bloody ruin we had experienced in Jahad's Rest met us as we approached the outskirts of Bleneth days later. We slowed to a stop and Kay untied the ponies from the cart we pulled behind. We had been left in charge of returning the ponies from our mountain expedition. They nickered and ran over to join the other animals feeding in a field some distance away from the carnage. The other animals looked up at us, ears twitching, and then resumed their meal unconcerned in the affairs of man, though some twitched and shook their heads in the familiar behaviour when an animal smelled death.

We saw the same charred buildings, toppled walls, blood and body parts and felt the deep overwhelming sense of loss that pervaded everything. The returning survivors split into two groups. One began searching the ruins for bodies and the other began the demanding process of rebuilding the protective barriers around the remains of the village. The number of bodies weren't adding up. There were too many people missing to account for the detritus we found. It appeared that once again, Queen Mordeth had swollen her own army's size with the missing villagers, but had they been coerced or enslaved? Kay and I promised that whoever found out first would share the news privately with Lord Trevor, and it would be up to him to break the news to the Clan Chief.

Before we arrived in Bleneth my feet and hands had healed and my eyebrows had grown back. What I had suffered was nothing in comparison to the poor people that had died or the warriors who combed through the remains. Grown men cradled objects that had either once belonged to a loved one or were the gruesome part of someone they had loved. Some men simply walked around inside the ruins of their home, talking to themselves about what to do now. I saw Lord Trevor surveying the ruins of the Chief's Longhouse with Dirk and Lyas while Arian hovered by the side of Heather dan Kalon, providing comfort and suggestions for the refortifications.

Kay and I cornered our friends Jared, Graham and Geoffrey and pleaded with them to explain what had happened while we had gone up to the Temple, but after hearing it from them I began to understand their hesitation and haunted looks. A week after we had left for the Temple, things were running smoothly in Bleneth. The combined armies shared the task of sweeping the surrounding countryside for any signs of Queen Mordeth's army. On one of these sweeps, the Clan Chief's scouts had been captured, and altered. We didn't understand what they meant, and after furtive looks between themselves, Jared continued.

The scouts returned to Bleneth, but it wasn't obvious to the gate-keeper that they were under the control of the Queen, until it was too late. They began to attack their friends and family and the effect was immediate and chaotic. Rumours flared within the walls, confusing all as to who had gone out, who had been affected and who they could trust, but it was too late. As the village began to rip itself apart, the Queen's army walked in through the now-abandoned gates. Panic set in and those who could flee ran into the forest under the explicit direction of Lord Fiongall. They were told to abandon everything and everyone without a moment's hesitation and run as far and as fast as they could. Our friends had managed to stay together along with a majority of the army from Manath Samal.

By the time everyone had calmed down, regrouped and reorganized into the semblance of a fighting force, they could see the village burning uncontrollably, and hear the screams of those being slaughtered. It took all of Lord Fiongall's authority and strength to stop some of the men from running back blindly into Bleneth where he agreed they might save a few people, but they might also be turned against their will and face the survivors here under the forest canopy. They surveyed their friends and agreed to remain outside Bleneth, but put the souls of the dying on Lord Fiongall's conscience. He gathered a small group of archers and soldiers to approach the village, and these few he had watched from the forest with the strict orders to fire upon anyone that appeared to attack each other. Cautiously, they marched back into sight of the village and found the Queen's army spilling back into the open fields. They dragged animals and people away, the plunder and currency of war.

Fiongall ordered close ranks, shields were raised, and arrows aimed at the foremost stragglers that weren't aware of their imminent deaths from above. Tense strings slackened and bows were lowered as archers recognized some of the people forming the front ranks.

These weren't seasoned warriors they faced.

Fathers, brothers, mothers and children looking distorted, bloody and insane quivered spasmodically in the falling afternoon light. They carried bloodied swords and axes. They carried pieces of meat. The meat had fingers, toes, hair.

How could they be asked to kill their friends, or their wives, or their own children?

Lord Fiongall ushered everyone back slowly, trying not to catch the attention of the Queen's forces. That's when they heard the laughter, mocking and taunting, rise above the noise of the assembled armies and the burning village. Petra, Queen of the Underworld appeared, naked and drenched in blood among her wicked army of followers. She had returned among the living to sow hate from love, despair from hope, and belief from the unbelievers, but she didn't order her army to attack, that would have been too easy, instead she used them as a cowardly shield to cover her escape.

Our army could do nothing except slowly retreat back into the forest, and watch helplessly as smiling, insane mothers picked up children and began eating them alive, or offered them to the Queen to satisfy her insatiable appetite. Husbands pleaded and called out as their sons restrained them, pulling them back to safety. Some went mad with grief and took their own lives as the mocking laughter of the blood-soaked Queen continued, standing proud among the unfolding carnage around her. Others loosed arrows at their loved ones, killing them before they could defile themselves or be defiled. Some men broke free and tried to attack, only to fall under her control and disembowel themselves before the Queen, presenting their own intestines to her as an offering, which she ate appreciatively, before collapsing in bloody ruin.

Lord Fiongall recognized the Queen's son who appeared beside her, in his pasty-white skin and bald head, a stark contrast to the dirt and blood all around him. He stood smiling beside her as sycophantic red-robed priests chanted their mind-control powers over the masses, salivating in apoplectic frenzy around the mother and son. Dermot, false Lore Master, spawn of the evil Queen, waved his staff in mocking holy benediction to the atrocities around him, kicked over the helpless and used his staff to poke at the fallen, leaving behind bloody faces and ruptured bowels.

As suddenly as the Queen's army had appeared, they disappeared again just before dawn. The men didn't return to the village, instead deciding to wait for their King and

179

Clan Chief at the bottom of the mountain, hoping for a swift return and a method to seek vengeance using the unknown powers of the Lore Masters. The Gods and Goddesses were overwhelmed that night with silent and not so silent prayers for retribution and vows of justice.

After I had returned with Master Quinn Korid, more than one look of murder fell on me, as people learned the truth about the Temple burning to the ground, stranding the desperately looked-for help from the Lore Masters. Some swore that I was in allegiance with the Queen and others spat on the ground when they saw me, invoking the Eye of Thayer in protection. The Ren-Tigarians increased their watch over me, at the bequest of Lord Trevor, which surprised me after their previous animosity.

"So what do we do now?" Kay asked Lord Trevor as we approached him after burying the last of the bodies we had found. Others were busy pounding posts into the soft earth, forming a new palisade around the village.

"We await the Lore Masters and see them set up safely here." He had scrolls tucked under his arms, plans for the village and the rosters of the remaining men. The stress was plainly written on his face as we both knew he wanted to be out chasing the Queen and avenging Heather dan Kalon, but instead he was being held back here while we waited on the slow moving progress of the Lore Masters and the community from the Temple of the Sky.

"And then?" Kay asked again.

"We go hunting," he had a fierce look in his eyes, "in Rheal. It's time we had a face to face talk with *King* Mordeth about his fucking wife and son." Since the day we had returned, Lord Trevor had been seen at the smithy, fixing his weaponry, and training hard with Fen Gisar. He was preparing for the upcoming confrontation in the best way he knew how, with a sharpened sword.

THIRTEEN

Mordeth

Stiff legged,
Shadow looming,
Death from above,
I hunt.
~Book of Eth

Our new army (as I called it) travelled slowly away from the memories of Bleneth as we followed the well-worn trail leading south toward the province of Rheal. We had kept only a single pony-and-cart from our trip to the Temple, and now it carried both Lore Masters Quinn Korid and Donato, who scowled at me under his cowl with a hatred of being denied justice for the destruction of the Temple. Lying in the middle of the cart, Meda was bundled and strapped in and around our provisions to prevent him from unintentionally hurting himself. During our breaks, the Lore Masters poured broth and water past the old man's chapped lips. He let out the occasional moan reminding us that he wasn't dead, but still lost in the trap of his own mind. Despite the care he received, he looked like he was growing more gaunt and frail with each passing day. I overheard Donato whispering to Quinn that if his mind wasn't unlocked soon, they would lose him for good. He augured his eyes over Quinn's shoulder when he saw that I had heard his dire prediction. I hung my head lower with guilt and went back to my regiment.

Bloody and half-eaten body parts littered the trail at intervals that were neither regular nor expected. We tied soaked cloths around our noses and mouths in an attempt to stop the sickening smell that leeched out of the bloated corpses that we found and buried. Heather dan Kalon oversaw each burial, and if she didn't recognize the body, she would consecrate the body 'Paladin of Upper Doros'. The bodies of the fallen men were easiest to bury. The bodies of the women and children had many a man wiping back tears not only for the death of their loved ones, but for the loss of a whole generation who would never see Bleneth restored or Upper Doros made whole once again. The forlorn sound of pipes followed us like a death knell as they played over the graves, helping the lost souls find their way home. I heard in secret that her cousins had been taken, but that their bodies had yet to be found.

Before we had left Bleneth, a council had been held after the Lore Masters and their acolytes had finally appeared from the mist-soaked mountains. The new Master of the Temple proposed to remain in Bleneth and rebuild the village with the Temple populace and any villagers that remained. There were too many old and young men that wouldn't survive a long trek and as Laban put it, "We are men of learning, not fighters, despite the urge for retribution." The remaining Lore Masters would put forth the call for paper and would begin the impossible task of rewriting the histories to rebuild their Library. Laban had finished the council meeting with, "Like the legendary Phoenix, from the ashes of death, we will breathe meaning back into our lives."

Lord Fiongall decided to stay behind and help rebuild the village. He had looked sick when we had found him in Jahad's Rest, now he just looked lost and said that he felt like he had betrayed his sister when he hadn't been able to prevent the attack or to protect her people. The task of rebuilding would give him a purpose to live and a direction to give the other survivors of Bleneth and the Temple, and he gave his sister his solemn oath to spend his last breath in rebuilding their village and her trust. He would begin the rebuilding of Upper Doros by fortifying the palisade wall with a ditch ten feet deep and twenty five feet wide filled with water to repel any future invaders, but also to prevent any survivors from joining the Queen's army, as the deserters could be shot from the ramparts. He would send word back to the Isle of the Red Oak for his wife and daughters to sell his ventures there and travel back to Upper Doros with the first available armed escort or merchant train. Bleneth would become their home once more.

Donato, as new Master of Offices revealed that he didn't want to stay and write but that he needed to fight and tried unsuccessfully to convince more of his peers to join him and Quinn Korid. He claimed that with his green Mindstone he could call upon the forces of nature itself, specifically the weather, and he believed that he might be of some use to us when next we faced off against the Queen's army. More importantly, he volunteered to play the part of nurse-maid to Meda until we reached the Priestesses on the Isle of the Crescent Moon. It was agreed by the Lore Masters that the Priestess' healing abilities with the minds of the sick might help bring Meda back from his comatose condition.

That revelation took me aback.

The younger bespectacled Lore Master didn't look like someone who could fight, and his constantly-sweating face made me think that he might die at any moment due to the stresses of his own body. How could he last a thousand-mile journey and then face off against a blood-thirsty cannibalistic horde? He was adamant about his decision and wanted to hear nothing about the possible dangers ahead. I thought he was besotted with the Clan Chief, but her demeanour had become dark and brooding since losing her people and village, and his innocent-seeming ministrations had been reprimanded severely by her in public. When she stalked away, leaving him red-faced and embarrassed, he saw me watching and unleashed another torrent of abuse and blame on me for the Temple, and now for the destruction of Bleneth, before slinking off to his darkened tent. I wondered what was in the ribbon-wrapped package he tried to hide behind his back.

The road headed due west first and then slowly turned southwest and after that, it led into another old forest, the perfect place for an ambush. The Clan Chief chided us into vigilance as we began heading south through what she called

'Terrok's Pass'. The forest stretched out before us as we entered the canopy and looking up the trunks of some of the tallest trees I'd ever seen, the sky seemed impossibly out of reach overhead. I could finally understand how they had built the massive meeting hall in Bleneth if they had used these trees, the smallest dwarfing anything that grew back home on my island. I tried to imagine how many carts my father could have built out of a single tree, and with the thought of my own family, I sobered up and remained alert for any signs of ambush. The sunlight never truly entered in to warm us and small clumps of choking bushes prevented movement off of the well-worn path.

The scouts had been warned to pace themselves apart to avoid falling into the trap set before by the Queen. They pulled sticks to determine who took point. It was rumoured they carried within their gloves a paperweight of poison and a vow not to be caught unawares like their predecessors in Bleneth. Mile after mile passed without incident or noise except for the occasional indistinct roar of a Terrok somewhere off in the mountains high above us, but they never approached our army directly as our size proved to be a deterrent to any sign of wildlife. Being in the middle of such a dense forest also had the benefit of allowing fires for cooking and keeping the strange animals at bay. When changing shifts for sentry duty, I was amazed that the forest had the ability to swallow the light from our fires at less than a hundred paces, which kept the location of our army in relative secrecy from the prying eyes of the Queen's scouts, or at least that's what I hoped as I took up position along the main trail south of our party. Along with the light, the ordinary noises of a traveling army were absorbed by the foliage. It proved to be a long shift as I tenuously stared south, waiting to see or feel an attack that never happened. My fellow sentry, a man from Bleneth named Connor, remained silent for our shift despite my attempts at conversation.

During our second week inside the forest the Terroks made their presence known. They must possess some little form of intelligence as it wasn't a direct attack on our troops, but instead they weeded away the solitary men they could find. One night, when our rear scouts didn't return from their regular sweep, we went into instant alert thinking that the Queen had circled around us and was preparing to attack us from the rear. The Lore Masters, Quinn Korid and Donato placed themselves in our middle, staffs glowing and wards of Lore placed, but these were removed once one of the Ren-Tigarians returned with the tattered raiment of one of our scouts discovered hanging from a branch twenty feet above the ground. The other scout's body wasn't found, leaving less evidence with only a single boot. We scoured the area in ever widening circles until we found the steaming remains of their horses which bore the distinct claw and fang marks of a Terrok. It was shocking, but also a relief to know that it wasn't an ambush.

The Ren-Tigarians began a vigil and I started to believe that they actually never did sleep. When I asked this of Lord

Trevor he laughed and explained that the priests could enter a state of hyper-consciousness that allowed their bodies to rest while their minds remained active. He even suggested that some could mind-walk, leaving their sleeping bodies behind while their spirits roamed high above the forest floor. I slept restlessly that night imagining mist-like forms flitting heedlessly around the furry Terroks, causing them to howl in frustration at the taunting wraiths.

Three weeks after leaving Bleneth we approached the southern edge of the forest without any further incidents. Everyone was aware of the fact that the bloody evidence strewn away by the Queen's Army had stopped somewhere in the middle of the forest, just around the area where we had lost our own scouts to the Terroks. It had been argued over whether they were aware that we followed behind and perhaps were circling around behind us, or perhaps they had been eaten by the Terroks. The Ren-Tigarians confirmed that the Queen's army had not been dispatched by the Terroks as there was no evidence of that. It still baffled me how over two thousand armed men could remain as quiet as we had in that final week of progress through the forest. The Ren-Tigarians had been ordered to lag a day behind to ensure of no rear ambush.

Below us, set into the picturesque background of rolling fields and lush farmland lay the source of all our grief and anger. The city of Lanera was at least another two day march down into the valley ahead. A large stone marker to our left indicated the border of this province's farmland and by bringing their armies together here, Arian and Heather dan Kalon were announcing war on this bucolic community. As we exited the forest, the army was barked into fighting formations across the road and then we began the formal bloodless conquest of the innocent-looking land. Lone farmers ran back into their houses grabbing children and animals, knowing what an army brought and what an army took. I couldn't help but think of the villages we'd found, and our people fleeing in the same manner, but where we allowed them to flee, ours had been slaughtered without pity or mercy.

Two days later, we laid siege to the city of Lanera, sending officials into a flurry of acquiescence and gifts that were summarily refused and sent back. The emissaries claimed that King Mordeth had emptied his castle of everyone, including his own Chamberlain (who stood amongst them) and had refused to let anyone back in. The streets had been emptied of all civilian life, except for the same officials and their local militia of tradesmen who tried to block our siege of the castle that stood west of town. In a wise move, they quickly disbanded, and seemed genuinely interested in how we were going to gain access to the castle as the doors had been closed and barred from the inside and the portcullis had been dropped. They denied knowledge of any rear access doors, but that didn't seem to trouble the King or Lord Trevor.

Arian spoke with the Ren-Tigarians and gave them explicit orders to open the gates, but without causing any harm to the structure. Without fire or siege engines we didn't have a chance of breaking our way through the fortified rock walls, solid wooden door or the portcullis that lay on the other side. The red tiled roofs and white banners were misleading in their cheerful emblemise, compared with what the townsfolk told us. We watched in stupefied disbelief as the warrior-priests appeared to climb up the outer walls like careful spiders, finding hand and foot holds in the smallest of rock formations. As they disappeared over the parapet, I held my breath for the telltale sounds of swordplay or raised alarm.

No sounds could be heard and in a relatively short amount of time, the drawbridge was lowered and the portcullis lifted to reveal the black-clad fighters, swords drawn and unsullied. An advance group was sent into the castle and when it was secured, the remainder of our army poured through the opening to the protestations of the officials who demanded that we stop in the name of the King and Queen, which drew angry looks from Arian and the express command that her name was not to be mentioned in his presence. I ran in beside Lord Trevor's horse, carrying my shield, wearing my helmet and carrying my mystical sword with my dagger sheathed at my side. It felt good to be useful again and I was itching for a good fight. I touched my amulet and prayed silently for an encounter with the army that had ravaged our lands.

The castle appeared to be deserted. I formed part of the advance guard with King Arian as we foxed our way through the castle and into the main throne room. I had to hold my breath as we encountered the stench of rotting meat pervading the air, making it feel thick and sticky. The tapestries covering the windows were quickly thrown back and the closed shutters were forced open, allowing fresh air to circulate back into the stale room. As our eyes adjusted to the ruin all around us, a story began to emerge of this pitiful King's downfall. A corpse sat on the throne, ruined beyond recognition, headless and pinned into place by several daggers which held it upright. Only the coat-of-arms on the tattered clothing proclaimed its former owner. Tables, littered with discarded foodstuffs and soiled linens appeared to have been disturbed mid-celebration. It reminded me of how the Temple must have looked just before it had burned.

Arian spoke with Master Dirk and asked him to bring the Laneran officials inside. He sent his other men to scout the entire fortress to find any signs of the living. Lord Trevor sent me, Kay, Geoffrey, Graham and Jared into the castle to scout for any usable weaponry. After being separated during our time at the Temple and because of their experience in Bleneth, my friends had grown in maturity and capability. Every room we entered looked to be in disarray and the floors were covered in either broken glass and ripped books, or torn clothing and faeces. We couldn't find anything that might be used as a weapon, and anything of value had long since been taken, but by whom?

We began making our way down into the lower levels in the hopes of exploring the storage rooms when we ran across some soldiers coming up the stairs quickly, shouldering an older man between them who swore and yelled profanity at their man-handling. His thinning white hair was pasted down with caked bloody spots across his balding pate and his naked skin looked filthy and smeared with dried blood. His eyes were red-rimmed and wild, like a caught animal. We decided to cease our investigation and followed the men back up into the throne room to find out who this mystery man was and hopefully hear some answers as to the state of the castle and how King Mordeth had died.

"By the Gods! It's Joran!" Donato announced as we entered into the room. The young Lore Master was in shock and exchanged horrified looks with Quinn Korid who was on the verge of tears. They found an extra cloak in their belongings and covered the older man's nakedness, taking him into their care. Quinn Korid used his staff and spoke words of Lore to put their peer to sleep, to the anger of Arian who wanted to question him right away. His high-pitched ranting stopped as he collapsed into a heap of cloth on the hard stone floor. They picked him up and placed him gently on a cleared table, laying him on his back. King Arian, Lord Trevor and Clan Chief Heather flanked the table. Arian wanted the Lore Masters to wake him again, but Quinn told him that their friend would be in no condition to talk until he had a chance to sleep and calm his mind. I peered over their shoulders as the two Lore Masters studied their colleague closely. His cheeks were gaunt and his lips loose as his teeth had been removed. Scars covered his torso, the evidence of torture, and the tell-tale bite marks of rats covered his arms, head and feet.

They asked for and received clean water and cloths to begin cleaning the lost Lore Master, believed to be dead this past year. The men had found him locked in the dungeon, alone, with the scattered bodies of partially eaten rats strewn about him. They had also found evidence of newly prepared foods and skins of water just beyond his reach outside the dungeon cell and when they unlocked the door, the old man had attacked them, blindly scratching and biting, to claim the food before the rats got it. Here was another Master of Lore lost within his own learned mind. They promised to watch over him and would warn us when he awoke again, though they said that wouldn't be for awhile.

The Mayor of Lanera and the Chamberlain entered the throne room, uttering curses and swearing revenge upon the usurpers, expecting to find their King being held ransom. As their eyes surveyed the room and fell upon the decapitated body pinned to the throne, they both fell to their knees in shocked disbelief. The Chamberlain rocked back and forth and shook his head in denial. "This, this, this is not happening," he sputtered.

"By Petra's withered teats!" The Mayor repeated the sentiments. "What has happened here?" He asked of the assembled people, and then looked to the Chamberlain beside him for guidance. "What do we do now?"

Prostrate on the cold throne room floor, the Mayor and Chamberlain alternately filled in the holes of the tale they told King Arian, who stood above them in stern judgement, arms folded, face a thunderhead, before he ordered us out of the castle and into the town while he listened to the ghastly history unfold. The castle was emptied of our soldiers who flooded the local rooming houses and Inns. The castle gates were ordered open and the city dwellers were allowed to wander in but usually ran out signing protective wards against Petra, and vanished into the nearest chapel. Some buried amulets at the base of the castle walls while others broke prayer tablets and buried the pieces in fields or under elm trees.

The castle had become a crypt for their missing King.

We took refuge in an Inn called *The Smiling Sow*, which was pleasant in atmosphere and bristling with activity, and for a single silver coin (bitten and hidden within his grease-stained apron) the owner, Mr. Flatule, retold the same events that the Mayor and Chamberlain were explaining to King Arian in the castle.

Apparently, the Province of Rheal had been degrading slowly under King Cadarn Mordeth's reign, a slap in the face to their former King Sagar, Cadarn's aged father who had built the kingdom up in wealth and status until the day he died at the ripe old age of sixty two. Rheal's decent began with the birth of Cadarn's only son Dermot, who had been born prematurely, during a rare solar eclipse. The King

194

had blamed the ominous event for the unnatural transparency of his son's skin and his smaller-than-normal birth weight. The mother, Queen Hadiya, had disparaged over the unsightly condition of her son and the outright rejection by the King for her and his newborn baby. She didn't accede the formal demands of a drowning by the Omen-Reader of Lanera, who was gaining the support of the townsfolk, as these were the very same townsfolk who had shown her nothing but disdain, hatred and suspicion ever since her arrival in Lanera the year before. Instead of drowning the child as they demanded, she withdrew into the castle and smothered him with the love and affection that only a lonely mother could give.

Mr. Flatule, swallowing the last of his mug of beer, began the tale of Queen Hadiya's arrival in Rheal, a story, he promised, was worth another coin. After it disappeared into his apron pocket, he motioned for his serving girls to bring another jug of his best bitter, which he helped himself to. Upon signed and witnessed agreements between the aging and single King Sagar and the strange silk-clad Ambassador Abbas from the Kingdom of Shadazar located beyond the Wasted Lands, his Caliph (as their King was called), would present the hand of his most beautiful daughter Hadiya in marriage, along with six trunks of gold coins, four barrels of the best scimitars (a rare *curved* sword) and a casket of valuable incense called Eaglewood, in exchange for the exclusive trading rites with Rheal and the chance of opening all of this land to the goods and trade of

Shadazar, of which King Sagar, now related by marriage to the Caliph, would receive an annual percentage of any profits.

How could he say no? These foreigners didn't know that King Sagar had the smallest province in the land and that his relationship with the neighbouring provinces was tense at best. This agreement would change all that and Rheal would become the richest province in the land with a steady supply of gold and arms from an outside source. King Sagar was a happy man and looked hungrily at the prospect of creating more heirs as soon as his mysterious bride arrived. After a night of feasting and desires sated, Ambassador Abbas withdrew to his sand-swept lands atop his beautiful and sleek horse, happy and excited by the agreements that had been forged between their nations and promised that the Princess and her goods would arrive from Shadazar on the same mid-summer day, next year, the Creator be praised.

Lanera was abuzz with speculations about the strange man in his bright silks and what the mysterious Princess from another land would look like. The townsfolk had a royal wedding to look forward to in the coming year, and thus preparations were made, rooms expanded and decorated for the bride and future Queen, taxes were raised and every house in town was painted and cleaned upon orders from the King who rode through the town and greeted his subjects with a smile and words of encouragement. Wherever King Sagar rode, Lore Master Laban, his friend and advisor, rode with him. Rumors surrounded the Lore Master that he was using incantations and ancient Lore to prepare the aging King for his future bride. Some said the King rode straighter in his saddle, that his hair was growing back, and that his appetite for the local whores betrayed his age. Amid all of this excitement and rumor, King Sagar died suddenly, just before the mid-winter festival.

The atmosphere in town deflated faster than a piper's bladder and blame for the untimely death of their beloved King was aimed at Ambassador Abbas, Lore Master Laban and the local whores, of which some had disappeared under mysterious circumstances, leaving behind their clothes, money and even their children. The official cause was put down to old age and the undue excitement of the upcoming nuptials, but the Innkeeper (whose sister had worked in the castle) had heard that someone had seen Prince Cadarn enter and leave the King's suites *alone* just before Sagar was reported dead. Mr.Flatule couldn't remember the informant's name, but he swore they were beyond repute.

The following mid-spring, Cadarn Mordeth was crowned and as many people celebrated their new King, many more whispered in dark corners about regicide and about how their new King had only craved the promise of gold and swords, not to mention the young and beautiful bride. Where the father had been bright and cheerful, this new King was dark and moody. He raised the taxes even higher, despite the fact that the preparations for the wedding were nearly complete, and where his father had practiced for his wedding night among the local whores, this new King inflicted his darkest desires upon them, knowing that he would not get the opportunity after he was married and under surveillance by his wife's and Caliph's advisors. The disappearance of the whores after Sagar's death took on a whole new meaning, though still only whispered in those same dark corners. As mid-summer approached, the King grew more angry and violent towards his staff, possibly feeling that his father's death and his ascension would have somehow jeopardized the agreements signed by his father, perhaps because the whores had refused their services to him and had either changed their profession or got married (to all outward appearances).

Mid-summer came and went and the people became confused and angered at the false promises made by the perfumed Ambassador Abbas. King Mordeth rode into the mountains with his army in search of the wedding party, but returned weeks later with no news. His anger had been terrible before, but now people avoided him at all cost. He raised taxes again and the people surmised it was to replace all of the gold that wouldn't be arriving. The soldiers that had returned with the King reported of a premature winter arriving in the mountains and they dismissed the idea of a wedding party arriving this year as the only route through the mountain was becoming impassable. Autumn came and went, and during the first snowfall of that year, she arrived.

There was no wedding party, no trunks of gold or barrels of swords, only the half-frozen body of Princess Hadiya and her brother Hassan, Prince and future Caliph of Shadazar.

She barely clung to life when her brother had stumbled down into Lanera from the mountains, carrying her unconscious body, delivered her into the hands of King Mordeth, and then promptly collapsed and died at his feet. Days later, half-crazed with despair on hearing of her brother's death, she told Cadarn of her doomed journey from Shadazar.

Two months journey from her father's palace, at the base of the Westron Mountains on the desert side, their caravan was set upon by an army of bandits who took everything of value, including her men and women who would be sold as slaves. All but five of her personal armed guards and brother escaped under cover of darkness and headed into the forest and then up into the mountain range. They didn't dare return to Shadazar to face shame and certain death for their failure and loss of so much wealth. The only hope they had was to reach Rheal alive, marry her new husband, and then send an army back over the mountains to attack the bandits and reclaim the treasures and their people. With that plan in mind, they set off into the unknown and for the next six months they experienced a living hell made up of starvation, attacks by strange creatures, drowning in torrential river crossings and then the unending trudge through the snows of an early winter. It was a miracle of survival that any of them had actually made it, and Hadiya cried continuously for the sacrifice her brother made in carrying her the final days until reaching Lanera.

Cold hearted and unmoved by her tale, King Cadarn actually laughed at her misery. He mocked her supposed beauty which was now marred by starvation, the affects of exposing her tanned skin to the freezing weather and the scars on her left cheek left by an attack from a creature she had described as a bear. He lamented the loss of wealth he was promised and the cost of having to bury her brother in the middle of winter in frozen ground. The only promise he did give her was that he would never send a rescue party back through the mountains on the slim chance of catching a group of bandits that had more than likely dispersed in the last six months. He agreed to marry her, but swore that if she didn't give him a son, he'd make her the first Queen to become a common whore, strike that, an uncommon whore seeing that she was "the exotic beauty from another land".

The royal wedding that everyone was hoping to celebrate never happened. Lore Master Laban married them late one winter night, and her screams echoed through the castle as he consummated the marriage with lust-filled hatred. Winter lasted longer than usual that year, the taxes were never lowered, and the people of Lanera felt upset and embarrassed by their King's unseemly behaviour. A sordid, foul feeling entrenched itself into the land until news of the Queen's pregnancy reached the public's ears, and hope returned once more. Candles were lit, prayer tablets purchased and small smiles were exchanged in doorways as people hoped a son would improve the mood of their King. As the snows melted and life returned to the land, the King left the confines of his castle and rode the land, still angry, but some could see him smile once and awhile as the thoughts of an heir improved his mood slightly.

Petra's shadow must have fallen over that family when it covered the sun at midday in the middle of summer, causing people to panic and the Queen to give birth three months prematurely. Some blamed the early birth on the solar eclipse, others blamed the constant beatings the King visited upon his young bride, and still others (after seeing the babe) blamed the early birth on the unnatural-looking child himself, cursing his name with inscriptions to the Gods in the air for protection.

Former castle servants reported that the King felt no compassion for his disfigured son, but instead treated him with the same unabashed hostility that he showed his wife. King Mordeth ruled his son and his subjects with an iron fist. Those same servants found themselves rushing to find meaningless tasks to avoid hearing the cries of pain when the vengeful father appeared at his son's chamber to administer punishment for the boy's least offence. Only the mother stood between her son and certain death, absorbing some of her husband's blows with her own body in defiance and hatred of the man she had faced death to marry. She threw guilty reprimands in his face, inflaming his volatile anger, about the loss of the gold, the loss of the weapons, the death of her brother and the impotence he called love. His anger sated, Cadarn would stumble drunkenly from the room, and yell at the servants to leave them to care for themselves. It was heard more than once, "That bastard and bitch can rot for all I care! She's brought me nothing but misery and he's a pasty-faced imbecile!"

Three years after Hadiya's arrival in Rheal, Ambassador Abbas had returned with a hundred armed guards during an unseasonably hot summer. He was greeted by King Cadarn with suspicion, as the Ambassador proffered apologies for the unavoidable delay in the arrival of the princess and her retinue, and offered his deepest sympathies on hearing of the death of King Sagar. The Ambassador asked several candid questions, hinting about the caravan's ambush, but never made any suggestions that the money, swords or princess were never coming, merely that they had been delayed. When the Ambassador reminded the King of his promise and duty with the Caliph of Shadazar, Cadarn laughed in his face and told him that those false promises had died along with his father. If the Ambassador had arrived with the gold or the swords that had been promised, he might have reconsidered. King Mordeth dismissed Abbas and told him to return to his Caliph with the news that Rheal's allegiance could not be bought with promises or false hopes. The King personally escorted the Ambassador and his troops to the edge of the mountains, careful to avoid the strange pile of stones that hid the bones of the future Caliph of Shadazar.

Over the years, despite the regular beatings, the boy grew stronger and more defiant. Eventually Cadarn ordered his Captains of the Guard to administer the boy's punishment, as he no longer affected Dermot, and just as the drink had made him physically weaker, it had turned his verbal abuses more virulent, rejecting and isolating his wife and son from all others, driving them closer together than he could have imagined. Rumours of their secret love spread like weeds between the castle's failing mortar and rock walls. Tales of their unnatural and incestuous relationship grew and changed as the boy became a man and his tastes in women, like his father before him, leaned towards the violent.

Dermot became adept at sneaking into and out of the castle. He knew who to bribe and who not to trust, and during this time in his adolescence, more than one whore had left town, beaten and bleeding, vowing never to return, after spending time in the hands of a mysterious and pale boy. After an appeal from a man who discovered the prince fleeing his house, and his wife dying from a ruptured abdomen, King Cadarn consulted with Joran, his Lore Master, who agreed to take Dermot to the Isle of the Red Oak for their disciplined military training program. It was the farthest place they could send him away from the angry citizens of Lanera who demanded retribution for his crimes, and although Cadarn didn't care a whit for his son, he was still his only heir.

Weeks later, Queen Hadiya, furious upon learning of her husband's deceitful plan, burst into the packed throne room, vowed revenge for having Dermot sent away without her knowledge, then left in tears, chasing after her son (and lover), but after months failing to catch up to him, she stopped at Chafet Temple for sanctuary. King Cadarn learned of her final refuge as the soldiers he had sent with her to ensure that she didn't try to escape back over the mountains and bring the might of the Caliph's army down on his head, were sent back to him with strict instructions that she and her son would never return to Rheal, and King Cadarn would die without an heir.

They were not seen or heard from within the borders of Rheal again, until the mid-winter festival last year, when they had both suddenly appeared before the aging King and his assembled court of sycophants. Dermot, wearing the full dress regalia of a Lore Master and Hadiya, wearing the robes of the High Priestess of Chafet Temple were flanked by a retinue of red-robed priests and the High Priest of Chafet Temple himself, Jal Tabor. Where she had left skinny, haggard, and broken, she now returned voluptuous, powerful and confident.

"Husband, you find me once again in the middle of winter, but this time, it is not I who hangs on the brink of death." After shocking the nervous ensemble into silence, they ordered the King's guests and the entire castle population into the winter night and after the priests shooed the last disgruntled person across the drawbridge, the portcullis was dropped and the drawbridge was raised.

The Chamberlain hurled his insults at the wooden structure and scanned the parapets for the King's soldiers who had been allowed to remain inside and strangely hadn't interceded in the Queen's bizarre command. When no one appeared to rebut his insults, the Chamberlain apologized to the assembled guests standing in the snow and along with the Mayor, they had ushered everyone into the town where lodgings were found for all.

It was reported later by a farmer who had been keeping vigil with a birthing cow throughout the night, that the drawbridge had been lowered quietly and the garrison had ridden around town and headed east. Someone had raised it up again after their departure but it hadn't been opened again until today, half a year later. The people had expected the soldiers to return home to their families, or for the King to appear and apologize to his guests, or for the Queen to assume the throne, anything, but the grind of daily life resumed and the townsfolk continued on with their lives, hoarding or spending their share of the taxes that were no longer being collected.

Life continued. People simply avoided going anywhere near the castle and some didn't even dare look at it. Mothers warned their children to be good or they'd be sent within its walls and everyone offered nightly prayers to the Gods for some sign or knowledge of what had happened that fateful winter night. Mr. Flatule finished his story with the question, "What happened that night and where were the soldiers?"

I told him, and then went to find Kay.

Long into the same night Arian, Trevor and Heather dan Kalon retold the brutal tale of Queen Mordeth's campaign of horror to the disbelieving faces of the Mayor and

Chamberlain. Each shook their heads, wrung their hands, and denied that such things could have been done by their Queen. In the end, it was agreed that the townsfolk needed to be warned and a militia formed to begin regular patrols, starting with the outer farms. The Mayor suggested that horse-drawn carts be prepared at each of the four entrances to Lanera to whisk away the women, children and elderly when and if the Queen's army decided to attack.

It was agreed that the castle would be purged and cleansed of all remnants of King Mordeth's last meal. King Arian and the Clan Chief would use the castle as a staging area with their soldiers taking up temporary residence until the militia was assembled and prepared for a siege.

The Lore Masters began to scour the remaining evidence for any clues to the Queen and Dermot's intentions while still playing nurse-maid to Meda and their broken friend. Joran's ravings stopped when he came to the realization that he was no longer going to be locked up in the dungeon. He would break into crying fits, but after his first peaceful night sleep in almost a year, he awoke in a better frame of mind, if still fragile. The next morning he asked for a mirror, letting out a long sigh when he saw his condition, but a steady flow of warm food and wine changed his pallor, brightened his mood and gave him the strength to tell his story, which caught everyone off guard.

Lore Master Joran's story began a year ago when King Mordeth ordered him to accompany Dermot to the Isle of the

Red Oak and to help mentor the abusive youth's tendencies. He agreed that the boy was unruly and disparaged at his unsettling enjoyment of inflicting pain on others, but he knew who was to blame for the child's behaviour, though he never said it to the King's face. He had hoped that once the boy was removed from the negative influence of his father, he would be able to infuse some healing Lore techniques he had learned at the Temple of the Sky. Thus they disembarked, Master and Acolyte on their long overland trip. It had taken over three long months in the saddle to reach the Isle of the Red Oak, and by that time the Lore Master was ready to throw his uncooperative student into the ocean and rid the world of his sadistic tendencies.

They had to scurry out of more than one village in an attempt to escape the mob justice that would have ensued once the battered and bruised girls Dermot had left behind were discovered by angry husbands or vengeful fathers. Joran prayed nightly to Bashal to change the boy's character or to at least make him feel some form of remorse for his actions. Punishing him had absolutely no effect, and Joran was convinced that the boy actually enjoyed the pain.

Less than two weeks after their last harrowing escape from Filmount Castle in Lower Doros, they found themselves being thrown out of Tyre after Dermot had been caught raping someone's daughter in the kitchen. When they eventually arrived back on the mainland in Beltar's Cove, Joran washed his hands of the boy and told him that in his estimation, he had more than completed his moral sense of duty, but now he wanted nothing more to do with Dermot, his warped father or his incestuous mother. He would not have any further responsibility for the boy's actions from here on out. As he turned to leave, Dermot hit him from behind, and he lost consciousness. When he awoke, he found one end of a rope had been tied about his neck and the other end was tied to the back of a horse. He was completely naked and his vestments of office were being worn by Dermot, who sat mounted in the saddle, grinning down in horrible anticipation of the living hell he was about to inflict on his former master.

For the next two months they travelled slowly from town to town throughout Lower Doros, like a cat playing with a dying mouse. Dermot whipped and branded Joran, claiming to anyone that they met that he was a murderer and a rapist being returned to Chafet Temple for judgement. Joran was jeered at, spit upon and stoned by the crowds that turned out to watch the criminal pass, and in every town they stopped in for the night, Dermot continued his cruel rapacious treatment of young girls, who he would then blame on the old man and say that he had escaped from his bonds during the night. Dermot would punish him publicly, humiliating the protesting Lore Master, and then drag his naked and scarred body onto the next town behind the slow-walking horse.

When they eventually arrived at the gates of Chafet Temple, mother and son were finally reunited, making no secret of their incestuous relationship in front of the depraved priests. Joran was handed over to the kitchens and forced into slavery. He thanked the Gods to be released from the boy and took to his new work gratefully, feigning platitudes to the angry Head Cook who hit him and all of the other scullions with his thick-handled wooden spoon. Days turned into weeks and weeks into months, but the kitchens were warm and he could always find a scrap of food or an errant rat.

Chafet Temple was preparing for a very special mid-summer ceremony and rumours found their way down to even the lowest of ears that Jal Tabor was preparing to crown the first-ever High Priestess of Chafet Temple. The former Queen Hadiya Mordeth of Lanera was becoming High Priestess, Queen of Mount Kali, living vessel of the God Eth and where once she was tortured and rejected, the people of this land would wail at her approach, bend to her will, and give their lives freely to her.

For months the Temple had combed the surrounding land for every scrap of human detritus, from diseased lepers to bawdy prostitutes until the bowels of the Temple bulged with hundreds of people who had no idea where they were or why, but few complained when they were given a place to sleep and regular meals for a few hours of forced slavery a day.

The day of the ceremony began deep inside the bowels of Mount Kali as the slaves were herded with excitement into a large underground cavern lined with bracketed torches, stripped of their clothing, and chained to the wall.

Joran felt something wrong and knew it wasn't the suffocating heat pressing upon his naked skin from a large hole in the center of the room. It steamed and shimmered from the intense heat rising up from the orange magma flowing below the room, fed from the never-ending source in the mountain's core. Priests, masked and wearing blood-red vestments stood to either side of a large dais sitting just beyond the glowing maw, and there sitting proudly, was their newly invested High Priestess, splayed upon a throne made of bleached bones. The High Priest opened a large book and began chanting forbidden words of Lore, words that had been banned for millennia, and although they were foreign-sounding to Joran's ears, the meaning was evident and the effect upon the slaves was immediate.

At this point in the retelling of his tale, Lore Master Joran stopped and began to sob into the shoulder of Donato. Composing himself, he continued, and detailed the same scenes of cannibalism that Lord Fiongall had described to us in Jahad's Rest, except that as the chaos unfolded, the High Priestess's power magnified and grew. After feeding on a slave, she threw the body into the mountain's hot belly, whether they were dead or not, and as she fed, the Skull of Power sitting on her head appeared to come to life. Intelligent malevolence manifested through its ruby-red eyes. Joran recoiled in horror as the last body was thrown into the liquid fire, and tried to hide against the rocks from the rabid, blood-soaked priests. It was Dermot who reached down and yanked the old man to his feet by what remained of his hair.

He stopped again and looked at his peers, Donato and Quinn Korid. "I was spared." His face became serene, but on the point of madness. "Dermot promised to spare my life, but only if I divulged the Lore I had mastered and the secret power of my Mindstone." His guilty look confirmed his actions as he raised his hands in supplication. "Once I had agreed to his demands, his mother *stepped* into the magma." His eyes opened wider. "I saw her body *transform*. It seemed to shimmer, like polished gold, and when she stepped out, standing naked before us, I felt the very earth tremor. I could have sworn she grew larger. Her skin somehow reformed itself, like a candle melting in reverse." He stared at his feet. "I witnessed the rebirth of a God."

"By the Gods, but I'm sure I felt that same tremor on the Isle of Holbrook." Quinn Korid went pale.

"And I in Cragthorne." Whispered Donato.

Lord Trevor spoke quietly. "Lore Master Joran, we need to know what we are dealing with in order to fight it." He coughed gently. "We have seen what this Queen, what this reborn God, is capable of doing, but exactly what kind of power have you given Dermot?"

"Travelling." The withered old man seemed to shrink into himself, lowering his chin to his chest after whispering the answer. "After the ceremony, I was forced to teach him how to use my Lore, and after many long, frustrating months, he figured out that I was hiding some vital information from him. The God forced me to reveal the fact that he couldn't complete the Lore without his own Heartstone." He let out a long sigh.

"How could she force you to reveal such a thing?" Donato asked, sounding incredulous that the Lore Master could reveal the very core of their teachings.

"She took my testicles." His sad expression added weight to his answer. Donato looked at Quinn Korid and shook his head, tsking as he sat down once more. "Dermot forced me to Travel to the Temple of the Sky, last autumn, where he retrieved a Heartstone from the river in secret." He looked up once more, seeking forgiveness from his fellow Lore Masters. "He told me that he claimed to be the new Lore Master of Rheal, and that I was dead, but when Meda confronted him for proof, he panicked and fled, and brought us back to Chafet Temple. He wanted to show off my Lore to his mother, so he brought us back to Lanera, where he locked me in the dungeons." He looked tired at reliving his experiences. "He Travelled back regularly to feed me, to torture me, and to gain more insights into the intricacies of my Lore. Most of it was speculative and what-ifs."

"What *kind* of speculation Joran?" Quinn Korid pressed his friend more insistently.

"How someone might use the power of the Skull to enhance the powers of the Mindstone and create a larger gateway, so that more than just a few people could Travel at a time," he turned his eyes away in shame from the shocked faces, "but doing so would come at a high price. The Skull requires blood, and the more virgin the blood used, the more stable a gateway would result, and the more quantity of blood used could result in a much bigger gateway." The room was suddenly quiet. "But of course, that was just idle speculation."

FOURTEEN

Ambush

Succour and Release.
Placate and Comfort.
A Mother's touch,
A Lover's Promise
~Book of Bashal

W e gathered again the next night for a dinner hosted by the Mayor who we learned was the owner of the Smiling Sow, named after a rather affectionate pig that used to walk the streets of Lanera, greeting passersby with welcoming grunts. I wondered if the ham I was covering in honeyed gravy was any relation. Gathered around the table were King Arian, Lord Trevor, Clan Chief Heather, Masters Lyas, Dirk, and Gianno, Lore Masters Quinn Korid, Donato, and Joran, Chamberlain Cud Throup, the Mayor Oppedia Thresher, Kay and myself. Fen Gisar refused the offer to join us, preferring instead to stand watch outside and keep any nosy townsfolk at bay. An old man sat by himself in a corner quietly plucking away at a tune on his lyre that was burnished a deep-golden hue, the colour of honey in sunlight. He would look up once and awhile, smiling to himself, content to entertain the old cat nestled at his side.

The food was delicious and the beer and wine flowed freely. The Mayor went into great detail about the deteriorating conditions in Lanera during King Mordeth's reign after gesturing a Ward against speaking ill of the dead. The taxes had risen greatly, distressing the common people, but even more distressing were the reports of the prince's craven behaviour and the unannounced and frequent visits by the red-robed priests from Chafet Temple. This, he said, was the most frustrating aspect, because they took what they wanted with impunity, never paying for lodgings, food, or whores and demanded respect from all as special envoys to the Queen. The Mayor eventually found out through the Chamberlain that the increasing taxes were in-fact being collected to build a new Temple for the Priests at the edge of town under the Queen's consent. During this time period, there were also disturbing reports of young girls and boys who went missing on almost a daily basis, until families were forced to lock up their children day and night for their own protection. Whispers of dark powers surrounded the Queen and her Priests so much so that the citizens created a group of men called "herders" who followed the priests on their daily routines so that no fewer than three sets of eyes were on each priest from when they left the castle at dawn to their return at dusk, and all for naught. Impossibly, the disappearances continued.

The impertinence of their behaviour drove the Mayor and citizens mad with rage until he demanded a meeting with the King, but the Chamberlain claimed that the King had nothing to do with it and that if the Mayor didn't like it, he could take up his grievances with the Queen. When he tried to, he was charged with insubordination of duty, stripped of his office, his house was given to the Priests and his family was forced out onto the street, even though he had been duly elected by the people and not appointed by the King or Queen. Oppedia moved to his brother's farm and continued his life in silent fury. As the Queen had asked, "Would you rather be removed from office, or from life?" Nobody else opposed her decisions after that day and all paid the inflated taxes and obeyed the Priests lest they were made an example of like their former Mayor and friend.

Then one day, all of the Priests disappeared from Lanera and abandoned construction on their new Temple. What remains of the Temple now sits vacant, facing east, having been looted by the local population to reclaim anything of value, including the brick walls and tiled floors. With no visible opposition, Oppedia quietly moved back into his house and at the urging of the town council, resumed his office as Mayor. Taxes continued to be collected, but when no excise officers appeared from the dormant castle, the money was distributed back into neglected projects throughout the city.

"Sounds like you narrowly missed that arrow." Donato remarked while sipping a glass of dark red wine. "I only met the High Priest once, but that was all it took to grow an instant dislike to Jal-Tabor's arrogant face." He drained the remaining wine and put his glass down, steepling his fingers below his ample chin. "A couple of years back, I was staying with Master Laird one summer at Filmount Castle when he got the idea to introduce me to the painful burr in his side known as Jal-Tabor. So we packed lightly and travelled to Chafet Temple, and as was within his rights as Lore Master of Lower Doros, Laird asked for lodgings for the both of us for a fortnight. We never made it past the main gates as Jal-Tabor and his cronies denied us entry telling us that we had no lawful rights over the *Disciples of Eth* as they called themselves." His incredulous look told us exactly how he must have felt. "We decided not to press our case, but as a reminder of who were the *true* Masters of Lore in Lower Doros, Laird and I created a maelstrom of wind and snow over their Temple that must have lasted a couple of weeks judging by the size of it when we left." He laughed as he refilled his glass.

Lore Master Joran, who appeared to be recovering quickly, had a distant hooded look to his eyes at the mention of the Temple and Jal-Tabor. Picking up on his darkening mood, Lord Trevor quickly changed the subject.

"The time has come for us to divide our forces." He sipped on the same red wine, and after tasting its berry-wood flavour, nodded his head in approval and sat back within his over-stuffed chair. "Arian and I have a mind to the future of our endeavour that we would like to share with all of you."

The King bowed his head and put his mug of beer down. "We have two clear problems that need immediate resolution. The first is Lore Master Meda and the second is

Queen Mordeth." He looked around the table trying to gauge people's faces and their reactions to his comment. "Meda needs to get to the Isle of the Crescent Moon, we've already decided how imperative that is, but our quarry lies in the opposite direction and I fear that need grows more dire by the minute than Meda's." He looked impatient. "I fear we may be losing the advantage of surprise by staying here in Rheal. According to Lore Master Joran, Dermot is due for a visit soon. If he finds the Lore Master missing, I'm afraid his actions will become vindictive." He looked at the Mayor. "Your people will be targeted and abused once more."

"We could subdue him and reclaim my staff." Joran spoke quietly. The entire table went quiet as all eyes fell on him, wondering if he was raving once again. The old man had stopped playing his lyre cocking his ear over at our conversation as he started to adjust the perfect-sounding strings. "You could lock me in my cell, and when he appears you could subdue him." He smiled a gummy, sunken-cheeked grin.

"By the Gods it might just work." Dirk offered into the still room. "But how could we ever subdue him if he's grown more powerful and if his mother's involved..." The unfinished question hung in the air.

"I'll do it." Quinn Korid spoke up. "That's why I'm here isn't it?"

"Does he usually travel alone?" This was from Lord Trevor.

218

"Yes. He rather...enjoyed our time together." He winced. "He liked to watch me squirm and enjoyed...punishing me." He picked up his beer and drained it hastily.

"Do you know how to catch a mother bear?" Lyas asked.

"You take her cub." The Clan Chief finished the thought, smiling at the one-eyed man.

"This changes everything." Arian exchanged looks with Trevor. "Our timing will have to be flawless." He eyed the Mayor and Chamberlain. "Of course this also means that you'll have to evacuate the town." He judged their looks. "Mother bears can be vicious when deprived of their young. She'll level this town looking for him." He looked again at Joran. "How long were his visits?"

The Lore Master looked sheepishly at the table top. "Depended on what he needed to know, or wanted to do."

Arian tapped the table top with his dagger. "Let's begin preparations."

The lyre player eventually stopped when his sleeping cat perked up, stretched and sat by the door cleaning its paws. He packed his beautiful instrument away, said goodnight to our host, and followed the cat out the front door. Our meeting went long into the night, but by the end, a weary group went to bed cognizant of the fact that our lives were about to get even more complicated.

219

How Lore Master Joran survived down here for so long eluded me. I couldn't imagine waiting an hour, let alone weeks by myself in the oppressive dark and damp cold, listening to the constant skittering of fighting rats going about their nocturnal lives deep down in the bowels of the castle. There was no light, and I could feel the immense weight of the world above my head. Kay's steady breathing to my right and the occasional clink of metal weapon on rock as soldiers shifted their weight were the only sounds I could hear besides the rats, while we waited for Prince Dermot to appear. We were four hours into the second day where we all sat patiently waiting for the dread Prince to arrive. I steadied my nerves by thinking about the nice soft bed waiting for me, a nice hot meal and mugs of cold beer. Lord Trevor's occasional words of encouragement helped mark the time as I tried to ignore the always-hungry rats.

Across the darkened corridor I knew Quinn Korid continued to prepare himself, but I still worried that his planned effect wouldn't work on the Prince, and the rest of us would be rendered useless. I felt the reassuring sticky grip of my sword and prayed silently to Thayer, feeling the familiar shape of my amulet in the bag hanging around my neck. I prayed that my sword wouldn't interfere in our dealings with the Prince today, and this worry left my nerves feeling frayed to the point of snapping. I started thinking of names for my sword, as Gianno had a name for every weapon he owned. *Sword of Prophecy* was too wordy and

Blade of Destiny sounded presumptuous. It needed a better name, smaller, scarier.

My eyes picked up a brief flash of light, like a small red spark shot from a sap-filled burning faggot. I could hear everyone tense in the dark as Lord Trevor culled our idle thoughts and called us to attention. Another spark shot out, and then another. A gradual increase in light began in the middle of the hallway creating what looked like an eye of light, swirling from a single point above the floor, which continued until a large hole appeared. I could clearly see through the hole into what appeared to be a comfortable library or drawing room.

A person stepped through the opening, levelling a staff before them that sparked the red lightning outwards, and seemed to push the hole wider. They wore a flowing red cloak, which completely covered their form and around the collar, black feathers fluttered from a hot gust of heat from the room they had appeared from, and sitting in the middle of the black feathers I could see a white-skinned scalp, looking like a giant egg resting in a nest. So this was the prodigal son Dermot returned. He held the staff at hip level and the red stone in its end, arced red flecks of lightning outwards, keeping the hole open.

I felt my sword begin to hum in response to the close proximity of power. *Hummer*? Was that an apt name?

He was not alone.

Another man walked through the opening, taller than Dermot. He was careful not to touch the edges of the sparkling opening, dipping his head while he held the small flat-topped cap in place with a hand that sparkled with numerous gemmed rings.

"Ah, so this is where you've been keeping him." The taller man said in a deeply sonorous voice that echoed in the dark chamber. Light from beyond the hole filled the hallway, illuminating the pathetic naked form of Lore Master Joran curled up inside his cell. "How low the mighty have fallen." He clicked his teeth in a stifled laugh. "A pity, but then again you proud Lore Masters have always denied your true Master. Eth will show you what power is. We will teach you the meaning of *true* Lore." He let out a long sigh. "Your mother, the High Priestess, will enjoy consuming this one, although by the look of him he won't make much of a meal."

Dermot produced a key from his belt. "Hold this." He handed the staff to the taller man who now held open the sparkling doorway. Dermot moved forward and unlocked the cell door. "Get up you stinking vermin." His reedy voice sent shivers down my spine. "You're finally getting your wish today old man. It's time to die." The creaking metal door clanged open fully. "I said get up you miserable sack of shit!" He kicked the prone older man.

I felt Kay restrain me as my sword arm quivered uncontrollably. My forearm muscles were cording trying to stop it from flying from my grasp. We were waiting for Lore Master Quinn Korid to take the lead, but what on earth was he waiting for? Eager? That might make a suitable name.

I shouldn't have come; my sword was going to give us away. I should name it Trickster.

"What is so funny you pathetic piece of shit?" Dermot asked as we all began to hear weak laughter coming from Joran.

"Pathetic indeed." The taller man said in mock disdain. Concern crossed his features as the staff he held began to bend towards where I crouched in the dark. He coaxed it back into position and urged Dermot to make haste.

"Two for the price of one!" Joran laughed aloud.

"What?!" The younger man asked incredulously. "I said get up!" He reached down to pick up the old Lore Master, but before he could grab him, several things happened at the same time.

Quinn Korid began intoning his Lore, raising himself up from the floor opposite, the green glow from his staff throwing more light into the corridor.

The taller man turned, his mouth gaping in surprise and horror.

Dermot turned at the same time and was thrown into the metal cell grating by Joran from behind.

The sparkling doorway began to lose its voracity and visibly began to shrink as Dermot's eyes rolled back into his head as he lost consciousness.

The taller man, realizing too late what was happening, tried to return back through the gateway while still holding the staff at arm length. I was up and across the floor before I could control myself. I only had enough strength left in my arm to deflect my sword from the red stone in Dermot's staff at the last moment, cleaving the staff and the taller man's hand in one smooth motion. The gateway winked out of existence with a loud snap.

Dermot fell to the ground in a heap of red robes and feathers as Joran began to punch him, yelling "bastard" and "rapist" over and over.

I stared dumbfounded at the severed corpse lying in the hallway. The taller man's body had been cleanly sliced in half. Blood and gore slowly oozed from the remaining half as it slumped into lifelessness. Beside the half-body lay the man's hand, still clutching the top end of the severed staff and the now-quiet red Mindstone.

The hallway flared to life as Kay lit a torch.

"That's enough Joran!" Arian ordered as he pushed open the gate again and stopped the older man's assault. Lord Trevor followed behind and handed the naked Lore Master his robes of office.

"Who was that?" I asked, pointing at the half body with my now-quiet sword.

"That *was* Jal-Tabor, High Priest of Chafet Temple." Lore Master Donato spoke up, disgust evident in his voice. "Won't she get a lovely surprise?" He began to laugh slowly. "I bet she'll blame her son for his unfortunate demise." He swallowed loudly. "I wonder if she'll eat the other half, being denied a Lore Master for dinner. Thank the

Gods we didn't end up with his arrogant face." He looked quizzically at me. "How did you know how to close the gateway?"

"Let's get out of here." Lord Trevor said as he walked past Quinn Korid with the unconscious Prince slung between him and the King.

As we left the dark dungeon behind, I could hear the scramble of fighting rats swarming over their fresh and unlooked-for feast.

We stood in the throne room where we had found the decapitated King Mordeth, and watched as the tied-up Prince slowly regained consciousness. His skin was not only pale white, but translucent as well, like onion skin, enabling me to distinguish the individual veins treeing up into his head from somewhere beneath his feather-shrouded neck. I couldn't determine his age as he had no hair, but was told by Joran that he was around eighteen.

His eyes fluttered open and he swayed slightly, shock registering in his face as he discovered his arms were tied behind him. He looked around the room slowly, studying each of us in turn as smug satisfaction played across his features, curling his lips back over yellowed teeth. He had larger than normal canine teeth which gave him the look of a man-creature embroidered on one of the tapestries in the Temple of the Sky called a Wampür.

"Looks like I'm not the only whose been busy." His eyes settled on Arian. He smiled and was struck across the cheek by Gianno who was wearing a nasty looking leather glove, studded across the knuckles with knobby steel studs.

"A remarkable weapon don't you think, son of a whore? It's very light, pliable, and yet very effective. I've heard tales that it can break bones." The Master-at-Arms flexed his fingers.

A rivulet of bright red blood dripped from the torn corner of the prince's mouth, marring his pale skin. "I didn't know you had met my mother you Samalian goat-fucker." He spit blood onto the ground and smiled again. "What have you done with my father's body?" He looked around the room. "I liked him the way I left him. A province without a King and a King without a head." He smiled again. "Have you found it yet? No? Well, soon Rheal won't be the only Province without a King." He trailed off laughing to himself.

"Why have you and your mother attacked Manath Samal?" This was from King Arian who sat casually in a chair opposite the Prince. When the young man didn't respond, Arian nodded and Gianno hit him again. "I'll ask you again nicely, why did you attack Manath Samal?"

A bruise appeared quickly on that white face.

And a smile.

"You can't hurt me you pathetic puppet!" He spat again. "My mother will suck the marrow from your bones and shit in your skull!" He smiled once more, "Although she does prefer them younger than you," he licked his lips, "they're so much more sweeter."

This time Arian arose, fury playing across his normally stoic features, and punched the young man squarely in the face, breaking his nose and sending him flying backwards across the stone floor still tied to the chair. Gianno and Dirk picked the chair up and sat him upright again. Arian didn't ask another question, he just turned and left the room to the gurgling laughter of the pale prince. The rest of our group followed the King out of the throne room and Dirk followed, closing the door behind as he smiled. As the door closed we could heard the Prince curse as Gianno punched him in the face once again.

"Augur." I said to Kay.

"What?" We had separated from the group and were headed back to the Smiling Sow.

"My sword, I was thinking of a name for it and Augur came to mind. Just as the sword has two sharp edges, and two uses, its name must have two meanings. Augur because it seems to know or predict when danger is about to happen, and Auger like the tool my father uses when boring holes in wood. This blade can bore holes in men." I smiled, proud at my sword's new name.

"An apt name indeed." He wasn't smiling anymore. "But can your sword deduce when the Queen will arrive with her army to rescue that little white bastard?" He waited for an answer that wouldn't come. "I didn't think so." We kept walking in silence. "I prefer not knowing. It helps me sleep."

FIFTEEN

Priestess

Knowledge begets power.
Maintaining power
Is true knowledge.
~Book of Thayer

The late afternoon sun was setting in the west, but a blanket of stifling heat still hung thickly in the air, depriving all thoughts of relief of a cool nights sleep. The buzz of flies and the constant bite of mosquitoes forced me to cover my face with a soaked cloth to keep them at bay but that only ended up stifling me even more as I tried unsuccessfully to nap. We were weeks south of Lanera and had taken roost in a remote mountainous camp that was called Tanner's Lodge. It was really just a collection of empty shacks that were precariously clinging to the edge of a mountain, trying not to fall into the forest below. The Mayor had explained to us how the Kings of old had used it as a hunting lodge for generations, but as we surveyed the crumbling structures it soon became apparent that they hadn't been in use for ages.

We left strict orders for the Mayor and Chamberlain to organize a retreat of their townsfolk up into the highlands north and west of the town for at least until the end of the year. They were leaving their homes and harvests behind to too much clamour and outrage, but after the Clan Chief described the events from her own lands to the irate farmers, some decided to leave Rheal altogether and headed north to help with the rebuilding efforts in Bleneth, promising to return by the end of the growing season to reap as much as they could from their own lands in secret. All of the animals were herded north, and those that were too old for the trek were slaughtered and the meat prepared for the journey, or simply let loose to survive on their own. Lord Trevor made it absolutely clear to the townsfolk that they try to leave no trace of their passing behind that the Queen's scouts might be able to follow. He taught them about circled sweeps and how to use forward and rear scouting parties to clear the path ahead and hide the path behind.

Gianno and our armourers helped the local blacksmith with acquisitions, mending and sharpening of anything that could be used as a weapon. On my way through town I saw him showing the blacksmith my grandfather's spear and when he spotted me watching, he waved and hefted it in a mock defensive pose. The blacksmith nodded and eyed the strange sword at my hip, but even as he formed a question, Gianno turned him back to the forge with another story of our adventures.

Dermot did not relent under the Weapon Master's attentions during his time in the castle and had been left to sit tight-lipped by himself during the final days leading up to our departure. No one was allowed to be alone with him or to talk with him. We came and went in pairs to feed and guard him. He soiled himself repeatedly, but King Arian didn't care when asked if we should wash or change him. The Prince continued his crude and demeaning discourse and promised everything from killing us to leading us to hidden hordes of treasure in the castle. The three Lore Masters eventually took over care of the Prince themselves and alternated in techniques to try and illicit information about the Queen and the Priests at Chafet Temple, and their ultimate motives in declaring war on all.

We heard the story later about how Lore Master Donato had to physically remove Joran from Dermot as he walked in on the older man trying to remove Dermot's teeth with a pair of blacksmiths tools. He had succeeded in removing the enlarged canines, but that was enough to satisfy the Lore Master, who decided to wear them around his neck as a trophy. I thought it weird until I remembered the Terrok claw nestled within my thong. A different kind of creature, but no less deadly than the pale-looking Prince. The younger man's grin was even more terrifying with his teeth removed, like a wounded animal, and he promised all kinds of pain on the older Lore Master who only laughed and shook his trophy necklace at the de-fanged Prince.

The forest spread out below us, dark and forbidding, as we skirted its western edge. At night we could hear all forms of bestial grunting and snuffling sounds coming from somewhere below and couldn't imagine what the old Kings of Rheal would have wanted to hunt so badly. In the end, the last King had become prey to his own son, and soon the last heir would share his father's fate, but not until after Arian had some answers.

Mount Kali could been seen far off in the distance, giving us some semblance of relief knowing that *she* was so far away, and the fact that we had removed her ability to Travel brought a sense of accomplishment, even though we had not yet come face to face with her army. The red Mindstone from Joran's staff that had fallen uselessly to the floor in the dungeon when Jal-Tabor had been cut in half by the closing gateway had been retrieved by its rightful owner, removed from the shattered remains of his old staff, and now was worn around his neck in a beautifully-wrought necklace made by a Laneran silversmith (the teeth offsetting it gruesomely).

He used his Mindstone to Travel back to Bleneth to inform the council of Lore Masters about our course of action. He wasn't yet strong enough to take any others with him, but he returned later that night with news that the rebuilding was coming along nicely, and that Lord Fiongall had sent messengers to all of the known villages and towns about their plight. He said that Bleneth was blossoming, despite their predicament, and that there had been no further attacks. This put Heather dan Kalon's mind at ease and her mood changed visibly for the better.

That evening when Lore Master Joran returned to our camp from Bleneth, I found myself on guard duty with Jared over our Royal prisoner. After the attack on Bleneth, my friend had shorn his hair to stubble and shaved off his beard.

He now looked younger than I was, but his eyes had that sullen haunted appearance of someone much older and I knew that it was due to what he had witnessed. He had told me one night over drinks, weeks later, how utterly useless he had felt turning his back on those poor mothers and children. His training burned within him and it took all of his strength, and those of the soldiers restraining him, from unleashing his killing frenzy on the Queen's army. He blamed himself for his inaction and vowed that he would never stand idly by again and let it happen. If he did, he vowed to drive a dagger up through his own heart because as he claimed, "It will be less painful."

As we relieved our friends Graham and Geoffrey from guarding the prisoner, we exchanged pleasantries and promised to throw dice later after our duty ended. They promised to stay up and Geoffrey agreed not to win too many of the measly coins we had left. For some reason the young man had Petra's own luck dicing. As they walked away, I noticed the Prince was sleeping, still tied to the same chair, and still wearing his fouled clothing. The pungent aroma was heightened by the still air within the room. I had thought the flies outside were annoying, but they swirled around his legs and the stain under his chair in their frenzied dance. Looking at his skin gave me the creeps and I still hadn't heard a good reason why it looked the way it did. He stirred as we entered and sat down in the chairs flanking the doorway. I had to cover my mouth and nose with a cloth to keep from gagging. He looked defeated and pathetic to me now, a far cry from when we had first captured him. Only a single feather remained hanging from his collar, the remaining plumage having fallen off during our flight.

I turned my head slightly to avoid the Prince's hate-filled gaze and watched as Jared's mask of companionship that he wore between friends changed into that of a man preparing to kill. He stood and picked up a cup sitting beside a jug of water on a table, filled it, drank it slowly, and eyed the prisoner over the rim. Jared clenched his jaw and threw the remaining water into the Prince's face, who sputtered, shaking his head and let out low, hoarse laughter.

"Thank you, that was refreshing." He mocked as the water soaked his clothing. "It *was* getting rather hot in here. Be a good woman and give me some more."

"Shut it." Jared said through clenched teeth as he put the cup back. He ran a calloused hand over his shorn hair.

"Yes master shit-licker." Dermot said in mock ceremony. "Where's my dinner woman? I'm famished!" He licked his lips. "And still thirsty!"

Jared backhanded him. I stood and grabbed him by the upper arm, forestalling another attack on the helpless prisoner. "That's enough." I said to my friend. I looked around but I couldn't see any food. The remnants of his last meal littered the floor under his chair and fed the swarm of flies. "I'll find someone to replace me as guard and get his food." I spoke quietly into Jared's ear. "Remember, we're not supposed to talk to him."

233

"Reprieved!" Dermot announced happily. "Now there's a good wife! Remember girl, I like my meat rare!" I heard him slurp his lips as I poked my head out of the door looking for someone to replace me. I saw Lore Master Joran approaching up the path, surprised that he had returned so soon from his trip to Bleneth, and that he wasn't being interrogated by Arian or Trevor.

"Master!" I surprised him as he looked up from the path. "Can you sit with Jared and watch the prisoner while I go get him some food?" He smiled at me.

"Of course young Master Cartwright", he looked pleased with himself. "I was planning on seeing him anyway." He put a finger beside his nose, "I believe I have learned a new way to get information from our uncooperative prisoner." He smiled and went into the room. I could hear Dermot exude with mock delight as his old Master entered the room.

I walked back down to the camp and found the cook just cleaning up. He handed me a plate of leftovers and a mug of watered wine and made me promise that I'd return the plate and mug clean before turning in for the night. I promised and turned to make my way back. I found myself face-to-face with Kay who was bringing back some dirty plates to be cleaned.

"Cousin! What's new with the nobility?" I asked pleasantly.

He harrumphed and hefted the plates. "Just running around at Lord Trevor's beck and call," he smiled, "but I suppose it's better than guarding that stinky bastard."

"We're playing dice later if you can make it." I told him as I continued on my way.

"What, and lose more of my hard-earned coin?" He laughed. "I can't afford to play against Geoffrey anymore, but I tell you what, I'll sneak some of Lord Trevor's beer if you lend me some coin?" He winked and we parted ways, agreeing to meet later under his conditions. After today's heat, I looked forward to enjoying Lord Trevor's beer as it was some of the best I had ever tasted.

I made my way back up the steep cliff path, making sure to watch my footing along the winding trail and trying hard not to spill any of the food or watered wine. Dermot had been isolated from the rest of the main army in a tiny cabin that clung high up on the cliff face. I knocked on the door with my foot as my hands were full. There was no response so I kicked it harder and was met with silence once again. Panic set in so I put the plate and mug down and tried the door. It had been barred on the inside. I pounded and screamed at Jared to open the door. I pressed my ear to the wood and could hear muffled screams inside. I put my large shoulder to the door and heaved on the old wood. The rotting wood gave way suddenly and the iron bar that had blocked my entry skipped loudly across the stone floor, coming to rest beneath the impossible, as I stumbled into a scene repeated from the dungeons of Lanera.

The gaping maw of a gateway swirled silently in the middle of the room as Dermot stood laughing over the wrestling bodies of Jared and the Lore Master Joran. The

Prince held one end of the Lore Master's necklace wrapped around his wrist while the other end quivered mere inches from the gateway's opening, the Mindstone spitting angry red sparks across his white forearm and over the combatants sprawled at his feet. He looked at me briefly, dismissed me as a nuisance, and then continued haranguing Jared into finishing off the old bastard. My sword began to hum against my leg as my eyes were drawn slowly back to the gateway.

She stood there staring at me from within a room that appeared through the gateway and seeing her in person, she appeared larger than life. Despite being naked, she didn't exude vulnerability, but rather raw confidence and power. She was surrounded by priests wearing blood-red robes who chanted unnatural words of power that buffeted the room, and sitting atop her head of black hair, sat a golden skull. It demanded my attention and bent my will towards it.

Both mother and son laughed as my friend, possessed by unseen powers, picked the old man up and bit deeply into his neck. Joran flailed and pounded uselessly as his bright lifeblood spilled down his body to stain the dirty flagstones.

I wanted to react, to save the old Lore Master, but my body wouldn't respond. Somehow, my fingers managed to crawl the small distance across my leg to reach the metal hilt of my sword which broke the spell holding me in place.

I slowly drew Augur even as my arm strained between the unseen powers holding it in place and the powers demanding to be released.

I managed to point its quivering tip towards the Queen, and as it did, my mind filled with pain and fear. I forced my eyes open and watched as my friend threw Joran's spent body to the floor, and then turn his deadened eyes toward me. Blood stained his mouth, his neck and his torso so that the only white showing was his teeth, pulled back in a rictus that reminded me of the Terrok as he closed the distance between us. I slashed out once and severed his head from his shoulders. Blood fountained from the neck as his body slumped forward with a meaty thud. Augur smoked as the blood was consumed into the hot metal. Jared's head landed beside the gateway, and stared back up at the women who had taken control over his mind and body.

I turned my gaze back to mother and son, anger playing across my features. Dermot was laughing hysterically as he stepped carefully back through the opening. I lunged forward and grabbed the necklace just above the Mindstone as he stepped through into the room beside his mother.

The Queen stared down at me murderously. She was only inches away. I could smell her sickly-sweet sweat mixed with a heady perfume and I could see the old scars on her left cheek. The ruby-red eyes set within the golden skull flared to life but her eyes widened in surprise as she realized her powers were having no affect on me. Dermot would not release his end of the necklace and we both continued pulling at it from either side of the gateway. Queen Mordeth howled with fury as she tried exerting her powers once more, her face contorting in bestial rage as the flesh around

237

her features quivered uncontrollably. We both climbed a hand down the necklace until we each grasped the Mindstone over the precipice of the opening.

Augur vibrated more fiercely in response to her renewed assault and began to glow white-hot in my grasp. I could feel the heat of the blade on my hands and face, but didn't dare raise it toward the Mindstone, cognizant of the inferno it had caused back in the Temple of the Sky. I could feel my resolve melting under her flaming gaze. My resistance was faltering. I felt an urge forming in the back of my mind to gnaw the offending hand off that held my sword. I wanted to stop the pain, feed my hunger, give myself to her and obey the God's will.

"Thomas!" Someone screamed from behind me. I felt air brush past my face as an arrow appeared in the Queen's breast, yellow fletching against bright red blood.

"NO!" Dermot yelled in horror as the portal began to collapse out of existence.

My eyes compressed shut as searing pain shot up my left arm, crippling me, and sending me crashing to the hard stone floor. My right hand released its grip on my suddenly-quiet sword and searched gently for the source of pain. I expected to feel the shaft of another arrow protruding from my palm, but something about my hand felt terribly wrong. I forced an eye open, which sent the dancing white lights away but then had to adjust to the suddenly-dim room.

I could see that half of my left hand was missing. I searched the floor for the missing half and saw the cleanly severed Mindstone, the remnants of the necklace that had once held it and half of a white hand that once belonged to Dermot.

As I toppled back from the crippling pain, I could see in my mind's eye the glowing red eyes of that golden skull and the overwhelming feeling of pure, unadulterated rage. I could see her laughing and holding the other half of my hand. I could see her licking my dead fingers, and then slowly biting off the pinkie finger. My promise-making finger that I had given Maura that afternoon, promising that I would return to marry her, and my ring finger next, where I was going to wear a gold band until the day I died. The God Eth's malice entered my thoughts then, driving out the memory of Maura lying next to me. The ruby-red eyes bore holes into my soul, laughing, menacing, promising to find the other half of me and finish what it had started.

I awoke sometime during the night, still holding my hand as it continued its outrage in pain, my shirt was sweat-soaked and clinging, sending sudden chills through my body. I heard voices then, all around me, calm and reassuring, but I fought back pitifully, my strength sapped. I thought I saw the red-robed priests, smiling, trying to bite off the remainder of my hand. I raged back, denying them their feast, when I heard a clear voice calming me back from my panic. I felt a cooling touch on my heated forehead and heard more soft words, gently spoken, caressing my ear. I slowly relented, lying back down in response to gentle pressure applied to my chest. My eyes swam with watery images that coalesced between the naked sensual body of Queen Mordeth who mocked me with throaty laughter at my lust and the dark-haired beauty of Maura, calling me back to our bed that afternoon. I cried out to her image, apologizing for leaving her when she needed me the most. I asked her for forgiveness for breaking my promise as I sank back down into mind-numbing blackness.

"Bravely done, Thomas." I heard as my eyes flickered open. I was looking up into an unfamiliar face. She was beautiful. Her light blue eyes were offset by blonde hair that framed her smiling, oval face. "You should sleep longer as your mind is not yet fully recovered."

"Where am I?" I asked; confused as I felt gentle swaying back and forth. Horror crept back as I recalled the movement of the cart coming down the mountain from the Temple of the Sky. Had all of those days been a dream? Was I back on my way down to Bleneth? Was Jared still alive?

"A good question for someone that has been lost within his own mind for over a month." Her laughter reminded me of the dinner chimes from the Temple of the Sky. "You are on a boat sailing to the Temple of Bashal that sits on the Isle of the Crescent Moon." She placed a cool cloth on my furrowed brow and shushed me back into the bottom of the boat, cooing a song that cradled my troubled mind slowly back down into gentle slumber.

SIXTEEN

Isle of the Crescent Moon

Gods and Goddesses,
One, All-Knowing.
One, All-Loving.
One, All-Reaping.
Let us Pray.
~Book of Man, 4th Century

A scream woke me.
Disoriented, I pulled back the warm down-filled covers and slowly twisted my legs over the edge of the bed into a sitting position, resting them on a stone floor that bore the evidence of a recent sweeping. I noticed that some sand had refused to dislodge itself from the cracks between the stones. I heard the scream again, but now that I was awake, I realized it was the call of a hungry seagull perched somewhere on the roof over my head. I inched myself slowly forward, one cheek at a time, and tried to stand. I ignored the pins-and-needles shooting through my legs and shuffled over to grip the frame of a window where the vista of ocean stretched as far as the eye could see. A warm breeze blew into the room, filling my nose with a mix of the tell-tale scent of brine and a delicate floral aroma. I watched some people at the edge of the surf who were skipping rocks out across the light-blue water then

disappeared into the white foamy waves that broke up and down the beach. The seagull screeched again from its perch above me and when it noticed my menacing glare, it flew away awkwardly, protesting at my sudden intrusion.

Pain thundered into my head from somewhere behind my eyes, forcing me to search blindly for the bed to lie down once more. I tried to open my eyes again but felt the room lurch sideways in protest. I needed to vomit. I had to breathe in and out slowly, shaking the feeling from my head, but the sound of the crashing waves augmented the rushing sound in my ears. I tried opening my eyes again, but more slowly this time, only managing tiny white-washed slits. I forced my nausea down, my stubbornness at being subdued so easily outweighing any reason to remain prostrate. A memory flashed back of old Mr. Partridge swerving down the road after a night of drinking, hand waving in farewell, manoeuvring out the door of Maura's Inn and down the road towards his house without stumbling once. If an old drunk could do it, then I'd be damned if I couldn't.

I used the wall this time to push myself up and fought back the urge to yell as the pins-and-needles were replaced with painful leg spasms. I closed my eyes again and pressed my forehead against the cool wall. I took a deep breath. I pushed the pain away while flexing the muscles in each leg. I had no memory of this place or how I got here but the sound of the breaking surf felt comforting. My face felt irritated and as my left hand felt for the stubble, a bandaged stump hit my chin. Memories of that day in the cabin came flooding back. I looked at the white lump where my left hand used to be, and noticed a pitcher sitting on the floor by the door, beaded with condensation. Suddenly feeling parched, I stood with determination this time and drew the attention of someone on the beach who began walking toward me.

It was heavily watered wine. I downed the first mug quickly, sating my parched throat, and after the third, I slowed down. The fingers of my right hand caressed the shape of a crescent moon that formed the handle on the mug and the last words I heard echoed in my thoughts, *"You are on a boat sailing to the Temple of Bashal that sits on the Isle of the Crescent Moon."*

Bile rose up into my throat as the image of Jared appeared unbidden, blood staining his face and chest, arms outstretched as he came at me. Slowly my arm came up, heated blade in hand, and I watched helplessly as it severed his head from his shoulders. Blood spewed up, like some gruesome fountain as my thirsty blade drank deeply of it.

I sat once more on the edge of my bed as Kay walked in through the door and stared down at the puddle of wretched-up, watered wine staining the cleanly swept tiled floor at my feet.

"Thomas," he moved to sit beside me, "it gladdens me to see you awake once more." He was wearing a white robe that matched the same I wore. Lord Trevor walked in behind him.

"By the Gods, he's awake!" His grin split his face. "Well that's a relief, and it looks like your thirst has returned as well." He helped himself to the wine. "No wonder you were sick, this stuff has been too-watered down." He put the pitcher back down on the table. "You've been in slumber land for the past month my boy." He moved to stand by the window to avoid the smell I'd left on the floor. "We rushed here transporting *two* unconscious bodies that flopped about in that bloody cart, but you'll be glad to hear that Meda has come around as well, although he's not seeing anyone at the moment." He reconsidered the watered wine again, and then decided against it. "Between both of your death-like states and that severed hand, I'm surprised either one of you woke up, let alone survived the journey here."

"I don't know how much you remember Thomas, but it was Lord Trevor that shot the Queen." Kay looked admiringly at the older man. "We heard your shouting at Tanner's Lodge, but Lord Trevor was the first through the door." He looked at me for understanding. "She's dead Thomas. The war is over and we have Lord Trevor to thank for it."

I laughed weakly, "She's not dead." They looked at each other confused, and then back at me.

"What makes you think otherwise?" Lord Trevor asked seriously.

"Because I can feel her!" I pointed at my head. "Here." I looked at both of them, but it was clear they didn't understand. "She tried to control me. That, skull, was alive,

244

I could feel its malevolence, but somehow, I think my sword was protecting me from it." I looked down at my bandaged hand. "She ate the other half of my hand, making me a part of her." I pointed back at my head. "But she's also now a part of me, and she is definitely *not* dead."

They studied each other in silence, judging my words and no doubt wondering if I had lost my mind along with the other half of my hand.

"Thomas, there was blood everywhere. Can you tell us exactly what happened before we arrived?" Lord Trevor asked.

I told them all that I could remember of that horrible day, and as I did, the pain in my hand flared up with the memory of it being sliced in half by the closing gateway.

"I failed." I said dejectedly. "I should have killed them both when I had the chance."

"If anybody else had arrived in that cabin, besides you, the Gods alone know what would have happened to the rest of us. Let me assure you that it would not have ended with the death of only two of our men." Lord Trevor said reassuringly. "I can only assume that they weren't expecting to be stopped so suddenly. I don't know if you realize this Thomas, but you single-handedly managed to destroy their only means of moving their army." He paused and spoke gently with his hand on my shoulder. "There will be no more surprise attacks on unsuspecting villages because of what you managed to do. You are being lauded a hero by everyone, and thus our hurried flight here to save the person who has saved so many by his selfless actions."

"I had to *kill* my friend!" I yelled vehemently, the anger seething in my mind as I couldn't erase the image of Jared dying. "I had to cut his head off." Tears ran down my cheeks. "What kind of a hero kills his friends?"

"Son, I understand what it has cost you, believe me, but you've saved hundreds, if not thousands of lives at the cost of a single life. If you hadn't had your sword, Augur as Kay has told me, if you hadn't had reacted the way you did, it would have fallen on me to fill you full of arrows," Lord Trevor said calmly, "and for that mercy, I have thanked the Gods." I understood the implication of his words. I could have been possessed like Jared and he would have had to kill us both. I might have attacked my other friends. I may have ripped their throats out.

"Are you troubling Mr. Cartwright?" A woman said from the doorway. It was the same dream-woman from before. "You have been expressly warned by the High Priestess not to distress him in any way. He still requires healing." She moved to the bedside and leaned over, pushing Lord Trevor aside. The scent of lavender was overwhelming as my eyes hungrily devoured her feminine beauty. "Are you hungry Thomas?" She asked through perfect smiling teeth, after surveying the remains of the watered wine on the floor.

"Yes," I said sheepishly, "famished." I took her offered arm and was led out of the room, followed by the two other men. She steered me into the bright morning sunshine and down a path that wound its way around driftwood and wild flowers. Bees moved drunkenly from head to head, pollinating the flowers that had smelled so strong from the room. "Breathtaking." I said, catching a sidelong look from her.

"Yes, Bashal resides here in every flower, in every breeze, in every scent. The Goddess' bounty knows no limits." She smiled again. "My name is Elise and I'll be your Attendant during your stay here on the Isle."

She was leading us over to a large building that was as white as the sandy beaches and appeared to have rounded windows carved out of the smooth structure. The shape of the building resembled a large shell, abandoned by an even larger sea creature. The interior was light and airy, a complete opposite to the castle in Lanera which had been domineering, dark and filled with the stench of misery. Light-coloured fabrics hanging from the support beams fluttered in the ocean breeze as conversations buzzed around the room while soldiers ate their meals surrounded by the pleasing women who inhabited the island.

"Pull your eyes back into your head *Lord* Trevor or I'll push them back for you." The Clan Chief chided as she walked up to the building joining us before we entered. "How *are* you feeling Thomas?" She asked looping her arm through Lord Trevor's to claim him as her own.

"I don't quite know." I smiled at her. "It almost feels like I'm awake inside a dream. Maybe I'll feel better after I eat."

"I'm sure Elise here will have you feeling better in no time at all." She eyed the younger woman appraisingly before heading off to a table where her fellow clansmen were seated.

Elise led me slowly into the center of the room. That's when I took notice of the strange seating arrangements. In the middle of the room a large oblong table sat below a larger opening in the roof and snaking out in wavy arms, the tables radiated out from this central table. From any seat at any table you would be able to see everyone else in the room. I smiled at familiar faces as I followed Elise, my legs feeling stronger the more I continued to walk. She sat me at the middle table and then disappeared behind a periphery staging area where I could see other women preparing food. Kay sat on my right. I was greeted by my fellow diners seated at the table, King Arian, Lore Masters Quinn Korid and Donato, three elderly women who judged me with stern appraisal and one stunningly beautiful woman, who commanded the attention of all. She radiated calm assurance, and a loving acceptance that mirrored the layout of the tables in the room.

Her eyes were a bright sea-green and her wavy red-blonde hair cascaded down her bare shoulders. She accepted plates of food on her right side, and then passed the remains to the person sitting on her left. She wore what appeared to be a crown, embedded in her hair, made of sea-shells and reflective gemstones. I concluded that this must be the High Priestess Elise had spoken of. She looked to be around the same age as the Clan Chief, but her skin was tanned a light brown. King Arian introduced us to the table and indeed she was the High Priestess, named Sarha de Cent.

The conversation in the room dimmed suddenly as the two Lore Masters rose to their feet. I turned around to see what they were looking at and saw two people standing in the entryway, shadowed by the bright light behind them. They entered slowly and resolved into another of the young priestesses leading an older man by the arm around the twisting rows of tables.

It was Meda and he looked so much older than the last time I remembered him awake, months ago at the Temple of the Sky. His young Attendant steered him over to our table and helped him to sit between Lore Masters Donato and Quinn Korid. He appeared to be looking around the room for someone when his gaze stopped on me.

"Thomas." He said with a comforting smile. Sympathy overwhelmed me as I saw the old Lore Master's eyes. Where once, bright-blue eyes shone out from under his white fluffy brows, they were now replaced by milky-white orbs.

He had been blinded.

Guilt filled me as I knew I was the one to blame, because of the fire.

"Meda, I'm so sorry," I choked on the words.

"Nonsense! You aren't to blame, and don't let anyone tell you otherwise!" He said more forcefully than I expected a vision of his former-self. "We will speak of this later, but now let us eat in peace." He trailed off as women appeared at our table, presenting splendorous plates of food.

We ate in relative silence for the meal, exchanging only small pleasantries with soldiers that welcomed me back among the living. I had to ask Kay to help cut my food until Elise appeared and slapped his hand away. She sat down on my left side and proceeded to cut my food into small pieces and place them in my mouth. She named each item I ate it and I was surprised at the variety of seafood they caught here on the island. She rose, taking away my empty plate and disappeared back into the serving area. As she left, I noticed another red-haired girl removing Kay's plate who winked knowingly at him.

"Kay, have I missed something? What's going on here?" I asked incredulously.

"What do you mean?" He asked, grinning from ear to ear. "Do you mean, what is with all the beautiful girls here on this island?" He drained his cup. "I hadn't noticed my dear cousin, but now that you've mentioned it..." They were returning back to the tables, but this time each carried a large sweating pitcher in each hand. Once placed on the tables, the women poured each seated guest a glass of the clear-blue, cool liquid.

Sarha de Cent stood and raised her glass, commanding silence once more from all assembled. "We Maidens of

Bashal welcome our visitors to the island and to our Temple." She drank and we copied her in response. "We Maidens of Bashal salute the honour of your Quest." Again she drank and we copied. "We Maidens of Bashal honour your commitment to the Consecration Ceremony. Tomorrow, The Holy Crescent, *Silya*, will rise. Tomorrow is also mid-summer's eve, and so, we shall consecrate ourselves, once more, to the Goddess." She drained her cup and sat down.

Confused, I looked to Kay who only smiled and drained his own cup. "Drink up Thomas; you don't want to insult our host."

"What does she mean 'Consecrate ourselves once more to the Goddess'?" I whispered, placing my empty cup down.

"I've only just found this out Thomas, but during the mid-summer solstice here, when the moon happens to be a crescent, which apparently doesn't happen too often, the Attendant Priestesses must," he hesitated and looked around lowering his voice, "copulate as part of their 'Consecration' to the Goddess Bashal." He smiled at the Attendant who refilled his cup and then moved on. "Each Attendant has already picked their Consecration Mate, that's why Elise is so happy that you're finally awake. I can't imagine doing it asleep and missing everything." He jabbed me in the ribs.

"What!" I said too-loudly, and gained the glaring looks of everyone seated at our table. I leaned in close to Kay.

"But I can't! I've committed myself already to Maura, I mean *consecrated* myself to her, if you get my meaning."

"Would you insult the Goddess?" Elise asked, appearing suddenly behind me. "Would you insult the Priestesses of Bashal after we've tended your wounds and healed your mind?"

I stuttered and made denying comments, trying to defend my position, but she just stood there, arms folded beneath her breasts, and I slowly felt the colour rise in my cheeks at my pathetic stammering. Defeated, I stopped and dropped my chin to my chest.

"If you want to enjoy the delights of food, drink and hospitable care," she pointed at my bandaged hand, "then you must honour the Goddess, and our Rites."

"Thomas, can you help me back to my room?" Meda asked, appearing at my side.

I jumped at the opportunity to avoid the questions jousted by Elise, so I apologized, rose and took his proffered arm, leading him out of the building. We walked down the path, but I had no idea which direction I was going and told him as much.

"Contrary to what the others believe, I'm not totally blind." He explained.

"But your eyes," I said awkwardly, "I thought I had blinded you."

"Thomas, do you remember that day, months ago, in the Library?" He asked while he expertly led me along the sandy path.

"Of course I do, I could never erase those images from my mind. I had burns that took months to heal." I was confused. "Meda, you seemed relatively untouched by the fire, except for your eyes." We came to a small building, similar to the one I had woken up in.

"Hardly untouched, Thomas." He asked me to get two chairs from inside which I set up outside, facing the ocean. As we sat, Meda offered a pipe, reminding me of that day on the terrace at the Temple of the Sky. "Now this tobacco is special, cultivated here on the island." We both puffed away, enjoying the beautiful sunshine and the warm breeze. "Thomas, The Eye of Thayer was made whole that day in the Library, and Sight has finally been restored. Do you remember me telling you about the Tome of Lore? Yes, well it has been revealed to me at last." He puffed away mysteriously.

"I don't understand." I said, lost in his logic. "I thought most of the books had been lost in the fire, burned beyond all hope."

"Thomas, when you dived into those waters, you didn't just find *your* Heartstone, you found *The* Heartstone, the lost shard buried in the Soul of the Earth and severed centuries ago from the Stone of Knowledge. It seems so obvious now, but the Sword of Prophecy, your sword, the *Blade of Destiny*, was the missing catalyst needed to restore the Stone of Knowledge. You see, the Stone is the key to the Eye of Thayer, the iris. They are one and the same, not separate as we've always understood." He looked at me, and I was startled to see the milky whiteness in his eyes moving, like clouds across a sky. He said quietly, the words loud in my ears, "Thomas, *I* am The Tome of Lore."

"What?" My mouth hung open. I didn't understand what he was telling me, but I could see that the old man I had met all those months ago had become more than just a Lore Master.

"The knowledge contained within all of those books in the Library has not been destroyed. It is safe. The Stone of knowledge has absorbed it all, corrected it, and written the corrected version within me." He tapped the spent wattle on the ground, re-pocketed the pipe and tobacco within the folds of his robe and smiled at me. "I have become the Tome of Lore by absorbing within my mind, nay, within my very being, the entire written histories of the Land. Like the crude strings we used to connect separate pieces of information from many sources, I have awoken with the unshakable knowledge that everything has been linked and connected throughout time." He reached into his robe and produced the Stone of Knowledge, now set within a golden necklace, and held it up to the sunlight. I could see the same sparkling-milky substance that floated across his eyes now flowing within the heart of the blue crystal. "The Stone of Knowledge is a part of me. Its completed crystalline structure holds limitless knowledge." An unnoticed tear flowed from his eye. "I can *see* history. I can *hear* time." He looked at me again, and his eyes appeared to glow with the same blue colour as the Stone. "Thomas, I am Thayer incarnate."

I fell to my knees before him, perplexed, at finding myself in the presence of a living God. My forehead pressed to the sand before him in obeisance.

"Thomas, please. I'm still Meda, the same old man and Lore Master that you knew before." He held out his hand, helping me up. "I just happen to be the living embodiment of the God Thayer. If anyone can convince you of my normalcy, please let it be me." He smiled, holding both my hands in his. "Thomas, enjoy the tranquility that this place offers and allow Elise to complete her Consecration Ceremony, despite your reluctance. It is very important to her and of all the men assembled here on this island, she has chosen you." He tried reassuring me, but his eyes were unsettling to look at for too long. "Thomas, life is short, and when you approach the end of it, believe me, you don't want to be looking back, regretting missed opportunities." He smiled benignly. "Besides, even a blind man can see that she's a beautiful young woman!"

SEVENTEEN

Bashal

Destroyer of Hope.
Disembowelling Peace.
Quashing Love
Between blood-soaked Claws.
~Book of Eth

The next day passed rather quickly in anticipation of the coming night's ceremony. We were all forced to bathe, whether we needed to or not, and that was when I saw the remains of my left hand for the first time. Elise helped to remove the bandages and examined my hand closely for any sign of infection before she let me see it, and as she pushed and poked at it, she detailed her history of tending the wounded, from childbirth to broken bones to massive head trauma on the battlefield where the only cure for that was a quick prayer to the Goddess to guide their confused soul. By the time she finished and released my hand, I imagined the worse, and slowly opened my eyes expecting to see the pus-filled bloody ruin that was once my left hand.

My third and fourth fingers as well as half my hand were missing. The two remaining fingers and thumb reminded me of a bird's claw. The wound had become a purplish-pink line of scarred flesh, appearing to have been cut, burned and cauterized all at the same time. She asked me to recount the story of how I wounded my hand and when I got to the part about the gateway, she reached under my cot and pulled out a satchel that was lying on the floor.

"Is this the stone that opened the gateway and caused you such pain?" She held out Joran's red Mindstone, which was cleanly severed in half, just like my hand. "Why would you keep such a thing that has caused you so much pain? Was the sacrifice worth it?"

I nodded my head to the first part of her question and then shook it in denial at the second half, surprised that the Lore Masters had not taken it back. "I didn't choose to keep it. I told you how I lost consciousness shortly after losing my hand." I picked up the half-stone hesitantly, hefting it in the remains of my left hand, the smooth texture feeling weird against my sensitive palm and remaining fingers. I wondered if the stone still held any power, so I stood and shuffled over to my sword that stood in a corner behind the door, waving the half-stone around in the air in slowly decreasing arcs.

Nothing happened.

There was no tell-tale humming from my sword, and no sparks of red lightning shooting from the stone. Both appeared to be inert and I concluded to Elise that the Lore Masters must have let me keep it because it had been rendered useless and no longer posed a danger to me or anyone else. I breathed a loud sigh of relief. I could still see, in my mind's eye, the stone's previous owner bleeding to death on the floor, looking in desperation at his Mindstone being dangled in front of his face by Dermot. What did the Lore Master do? Just before his death he had smiled at me outside and said, "*I believe I have learned a new way to get information from our uncooperative prisoner*", and minutes later he was dead. How did things change so badly?

"And now it's time to disrobe Mr. Cartwright." Elise smiled at me, seeing my concern for the dead Lore Master as something else. "Don't worry Thomas it's nothing I haven't seen before." She walked over to the table where a steaming pail of water waited. "Remember that while you were unconscious, I needed to tend to all of your needs during that time, which included keeping you clean after all of your bodily functions." She held up a dripping soapy sponge. "I have done the same for infants and the elderly." Why did she have to smile then?

I complied and slowly disrobed, remembering the words of Meda, and stood there in my stark nakedness as she slowly washed me. I studied every crack in the plaster around and above me and wondered how old this cabin was. I prayed silently that my arousal wasn't too obvious, thanking the Gods that the water wasn't cold. Once finished she rinsed out the sponge in the pail and then to my abashment, removed her own clothing.

"And now, it is your solemn duty to wash me, in the name and in the sight of the Goddess to prove my worth." She held the sponge at arm's length. "This is a vital part of our ritual Thomas, and I must be seen by the Goddess to be worthy before contemplating tonight's coupling. There must be no hindrances between us." Her concern was genuine.

Embarrassed at my hesitation, I grabbed the sponge and re-soaked it in the pail, several times, until the lather covered my hands up to the wrist, and my nerves had settled. I turned and methodically began to wash her body, starting with the shoulders and back. Her skin was tanned and smooth and I had to concentrate on a small mole on her lower back, not on the goose pimples rising across her perfect skin.

"Thomas, I believe my back has been cleaned enough." She turned around. "Please don't miss a spot as I need to present myself in honour to the Goddess tonight." She held out her arms from her sides, so I washed them carefully and caught her eyes straying down to mine. I ran the sponge around her breasts, noticing the arousal, but maintained an impassionate look to my face. I continued on down her body across her naval. "Have you ever seen a naked woman before Thomas?" She asked as I stopped and hesitated, just above her womanhood. I swallowed loudly, and closed my eyes.

"Yes, of course I have, I mean, Maura and I...we coupled, before I left home." I stammered uselessly, still hovering above the spot, sounding so much like a scared boy. I stood up and looked her in the eye. "We...I can't remember much from that day, but, yes of course I've seen a woman naked before." I swallowed again. "Yes."

She grabbed my face and kissed me full on the lips. I dropped the sponge and tried to pull her closer, feeling myself engorge with arousal, but she pushed me away.

"Not now Thomas, it's not the right time." She picked up the sponge and returned it to the pail, rinsing it out. "You had best get dressed, I can finish washing myself." I turned around, ashamed, and picked up the new blue robe with a red sash lying on the cot, trying to hide my erection. I quickly shrugged into the robe and was tying the sash as I turned around. Elise had already finished washing and was redressing herself as well, in a blue robe with a white sash.

"Good, you look presentable at last." She picked up the pail and sponge. "You should go now and find your friends who will be gathering for refreshments before the Ceremony begins." Her eyes gauged my full measure. "Don't worry Thomas, I'll find my rose among the thorns." She opened the door, spilling orange-red light from the setting sun across my confused face, and walked away as I tried to understand her last cryptic comment.

I followed her out onto the sandy path and noticed other men standing around dressed in robes similar to the one I wore. They smiled at me as they watched Elise walk away. Graham walked up, shaking his head and smiling.

"We had to wash up in the group bathhouse." When I didn't react, "By ourselves!" He punched me in the shoulder. "How come you get special treatment Shitewright?" He began to laugh as Geoffrey and Kay joined us.

"Pinch me, but I think I'm dreaming." Geoffrey winked, seeming too-small in the large coloured robe. He had started growing a moustache after Bleneth, but it still wasn't filled in and looked more like dirty fuzz on his face that he forgot to wash off.

I was suddenly reminded of Jared and his clean-shaven face. He was the only one of us to have worn a full beard before. *His head flung from his shoulders, dead, staring eyes intent on eating me, blood spraying across my face.* I had killed him. He would have liked this place.

"What's wrong Shitewright? You'd think he didn't like naked women clinging to him like moss to a tree." Graham said as we walked together into the large Temple that dwarfed all of the other buildings on the island. "What's been going on in that mind of yours for the past month?" I dismissed his question quickly and reassured him that I was fine.

We passed through an outer ring of columns that circled the entire Temple. Stairs descended down between row-on-row seating that appeared to be cut from the native sandstone. Torches flickered around the perimeter and two large coal urns burned on the raised dais below. We could smell strange herbs burning over the coals and the sweet, heady aroma of incense that filled the arena. Before descending the stairs we were each offered a large mug of warm, spiced wine from masked women who flanked the Temple entry, and this time, thankfully, it was not watered. If that sponge bath was any indication of how I might react later, I needed any source of courage that I could find. We made our way down the slowly-filling arena and found an empty row that we all filed into. As we drank the strong-tasting liquor, I found myself staring at the open sky above that was turning a dark, purplish-blue along the horizon. Stars began littering the darkening sky with their uncountable, sparkling bounty.

Just over the top edge of the Temple columns, I could see the crescent moon rising, huge and scythe-like, its dark-half appearing purple and indistinct. The buzz of conversation around the Temple quieted as a dozen purple-masked and robed women walked out onto the dais from each side, fanning out across its length and stopping at measured distances from each other. They each wore a blue sash over their purple robes. They raised their arms, forming a crescent-shape above their heads, and began to sing holy words devoting themselves to Bashal, words that spoke of sorrow and loss, words that tugged at the heart and reminded us of the people we loved, and the sacrifices we've made to preserve and to protect them.

The song changed, becoming more desperate, as it told of Bashal's unbridled avarice in the search for love across the rolling lands and the turbulent seas of this world, but in the end, she realized the source of her sadness lay in her barrenness and the want of a child. She yearned for this offspring and begged her Holy Mother, Creator of all, for the gift of the sacred seed she needed for reproduction.

In response to the words and tone of the song, a woman, dressed all in white, appeared in the middle of the dais, walking up from an unseen set of stairs, giving the impression that she had been spewed up from the depths of the earth. Despite the white crescent-shaped mask she wore, her wavy red hair marked her clearly as the High Priestess, Sarha de Cent.

It was at this point in the song that a parade of young women filed into the arena below us, garbed in blue robes sashed with white, Elise among them somewhere. Each wore a blue mask, carved in sorrow, with gemmed tears glinting in the torchlight from each eye. They stood before the dais and swayed back and forth to the cadence of the song, carrying the haunting melody in their movements. It was at this point that the High Priestess turned and reached into the depths of the earth from which she appeared, pulling something out from within blue material that represented the ocean. The purple-robed priestesses released their arms from their upward curve as the crescent moon now stood dominant above and behind them, centered above the dais.

Sarha de Cent held aloft the object in both arms and we saw that it was a hunting bow of unbridled beauty and craftsmanship. It was white in colour, curved elegantly like the crescent moon, and had gold etched along its length. Still holding it above her head, she turned slowly so that all present could see it and marvel at its unearthly beauty and power, and then walked to the end of the line of Attendant Priestesses and handed it ceremoniously over to the first in the line. The woman accepted it with both hands, bowed, and then stroked the gilt runes along its edge and spoke unheard, powerful words into the bow. She held it at arm's length, drew the invisible bowstring back to her masked cheek, and then released her unheard wish into the crowd of spectators.

A soldier, sitting silent-witness like us all, stood as if struck by an unseen arrow from his chest, and walked down the stairs to the foot of the dais. The Attendant turned and handed the bow back to the High Priestess who accepted it back, then handed it gently to the next Attendant Priestess. As the first man was joined by the woman at the foot of the stairs, the couple held their clasped hands up to the High Priestess who touched them and bowed her head. The couple turned and ascended the stairs, leaving the Temple and all of us behind. As I watched the couple leave the Temple, I felt something hit me in the chest and stood in response to the unheeded call.

Unable to control my actions, I made my way down the stairs and stopped at the base of the dais. The Attendant Priestess, whom I knew now to be Elise, gently grasped my maimed half-hand and held both up to the High Priestess who touched them and said for our ears only, "Bashal, consecrate this union and raise your Attendant Priestess to the glory of Dedicated Servant", then bowed her head and released our hands. We turned and made our way up the stairs, passing through the outer Temple columns into the crisp night air. When did it become so dark? Elise led me silently back down the sandy path to my cabin, our shadows running ahead of us in anticipation. As we entered the room, I was surprised to discover a single candle burning on the table, illuminating a tray heavily laden with food and drink.

She sat me on the bed, closed the door, and filled a clay mug with some liquid that she handed to me. I smelled it, wary of what I might be drinking, but found it had a pleasing fruity aroma that proved to be warm and satisfying. She perused the food and put together a plate containing a variety of foodstuffs, then sat beside me on the small cot, and offered the food my stomach so loudly cried out for. It was some kind of seafood that tasted slimy and smoky, that I realized was heavily-spiced oyster. I ate grapes, cheeses, hardened breads and another kind of herbed seafood that was sweet and salty at the same time.

Elise was lightly perfumed with something alluring and floral that I inhaled deeply, and the feel of her thigh against mine, along with the knowledge of what was about to happen, caused my indiscreet arousal that the robe could not hide. Sensing this, she stood and moved slowly, deliberately, and as she did, her exact movements enhanced her candle-lit figure to its best viewing from my position on the cot. She ate and drank as well, never uttering a single word. Our eyes met constantly but I didn't want to break the spell by saying something stupid or awkward.

Sated of thirst and hunger, she held out her hand, which I took in my left, and was raised to my feet. She gently untied the red sash holding my robe closed and her soft hands pushed the robe back over my shoulders, revealing my erect manhood. She removed her own robe, dropping it around her ankles, but not the mask.

"Thomas Cartwright, do you give yourself willingly to the Goddess?" She asked, the only words breaking our silence.

"I do." I responded quickly and embraced her, smothering her lips with mine in a needful kiss, her mouth tasting of the food and drink.

She took back control, pushing me gently back onto the cot, and mounted me from above. We made love that way until finally collapsing together on the small bed, satisfied and sweaty. I cradled her in my arms, holding her close, and listened to her breathing slowly recover. However, the smell of her skin brought back to arousal, and we coupled again. Sated once more, we lay side-by-side and I cradled her head in the crook of my arm.

"Do we get married now?" I asked tracing a finger down her small arm.

She rolled over and looked at me quizzically. "Thomas, I am a Dedicated Servant to the Goddess now and can never marry." She regarded me with concern. "I thought you understood that."

I felt confused and embarrassed. "But what happens if you should become pregnant with my child?" She finally removed the mask and I could see her bright eyes smiling down at me. "What?" I asked, wanting to know what she had found so amusing in what I said.

"You truly don't know?" She asked, looking into my face for honesty. "Thomas, all of the women on this island are barren, like the Goddess herself, and knowing this, we've dedicated our lives in service to her." She traced my jaw line with her finger.

"I'm sorry, I didn't know." I felt stupid and searched her face for any feelings of loss. "Are you *sure* you can't have children?"

"I may look young Thomas, but I was once married before coming to this island. My husband and I tried to have children." She looked sad at the memories of her former life. "After two years of trying, he decided that I was barren and had our marriage annulled. He also arranged for me to come to the island as he had already chosen his next wife." She paused and looked away. "It was my younger sister Aurelia, and they have four beautiful children. A boy and three girls."

"I'm sorry." I said, not knowing what to say and feeling out of my depth at her loss. "Are you happy here?" I asked.

"Being barren has its benefits." She smiled knowingly as her fingers traced their way down my body. My desire stirred. "Besides, I have found great pleasure in serving the Goddess." Her eyes added a double-meaning to her words.

I cradled her face, kissed her lips gently, and this time I took control.

I awoke in the middle of the night, hearing something familiar in the back of my head. The humming had returned. I quietly left Elise asleep in my bed, put on the robe and strapped on Augur which, curiously, was not the source of the humming. I closed the door silently and stepped into the night. The waves continued their crashing noise but no other person could be seen this late as the moon had set long ago. I turned my head, and like a divining rod, I felt the source of the hum coming from the direction of the Temple. I made my way along the sandy path toward the Temple and as I reached the first building, a shadow detached itself from the wall and joined me. It was one of the Ren-Tigarian priests.

"I don't mean to startle you Thomas Cartwright, but after Tanner's Lodge, we have vowed to keep vigil over your person and the Sword of Prophecy." He had his face covered with the black veil. "At King Arian's behest, of course." I wondered how many tattoos this priest wore on his face.

"You've been watching me?" I looked back to where I had left Elise sleeping, embarrassed at having been watched by others. "You should have asked first." But then these warrior-priests had taken a vow of chastity and perhaps didn't care.

"Please take no offence. We will always maintain your privacy, unless you are threatened." He bowed slightly. "Where are you going this late?" His concern was magnified when he placed a hand on the hilt of his sword poking over his shoulder.

"I don't know. I can feel...something, coming from the direction of the Temple." I continued walking along the path and the priest followed beside me, his hands clenched into fists by his side. His eyes scanned the roofline constantly, and the dark recesses in each building, and the path behind us.

"Should I get others?" He finally asked, seeing my concern at his vigilance.

I laughed nervously. "No, I think you are more than enough protection from any woman that might fling herself from the rooftop."

We approached the Temple cautiously, hearing a man and woman's voice coming from somewhere within it. I waved the Ren-Tigarian to disappear into the shadows on the opposite side of the entry as we both moved between the columns, removing our swords in preparation of the unknown. I peered around a column and was surprised to see a single torch flickering gently in the warm night breeze above the dais. The High Priestess and Meda both stood on the now-empty dais facing each other. She gently handed him the white bow and he raised it above his head, uttering unintelligible words of Lore. I gasped when I saw Meda's eyes begin to pulse with the same blue-light I had witnessed yesterday and knew for certain that something important must be happening if the God, Thayer had become involved.

The Stone of Knowledge that hung around his neck on its golden chain flared to life, radiating blue light throughout the empty arena. Loud, unknown words of power reverberated in the air, echoing off the stone columns and vibrated within my chest where my held breath anguished to be released. A breeze, smelling like the sea, blew into the arena to gutter and then extinguish the single torch, which plunged the arena into sudden darkness, lit only by the pulsing blue light of the Stone and Meda's eyes. The breeze swirled around the arena faster and I could have sworn I heard wailing from unseen women. My sword, quiet up to that point, began to vibrate in unison with the wailing. In response, I pulled it from the scabbard, holding it firmly in my right hand and watched as the tiny symbol etched into the blade flared to life with a green light, strangely offsetting the flashing blue coming from within the arena.

Pulling against my tightening grip, the sword dragged me physically into the Temple. As I stepped into the arena, my held breath was sucked out of my lungs to join the swirling torrent as I was lifted bodily off of the ground. I felt like I was drowning amidst the current of swirling air, remembering the river, months ago, when I found the shard, but nearly lost my life. My body was being pulled down toward the centre of the Temple within the deafening whirlwind. I thought that my head might be dashed upon a column or that my foot would be ripped off on the edge of the carved seating as I was pulled into the eye of the storm. My lungs burned for air, even though I was drowning in it.

Meda stood firmly untouched, the anchor in the middle of the storm, but to his side Sarha de Cent arched her back in muted rage. I couldn't tell if the wind was being forced into her mouth, or if she was sucking it all in, but I felt myself being pulled toward her. The bow being upheld in the old man's hands sparkled with a white and gold light along the gilt ruins that reflected the Stone of Knowledge's blue-flaring light. My sword pulled me closer to the High Priestess. Would I kill her unintentionally? The High Priestess stood upright, suddenly recovered from her arched back, and took the bow from Meda's grasp as my sword narrowly missed her head and I came crashing to the dais at their feet.

Sarha de Cent held the bow *Silya* up to the heavens.

Meda held up the Stone of Knowledge and I held up the Sword of Prophecy as the storm raged on around us.

As all three items contacted each other, the whirlwind came to an abrupt stop.

The blue-flaring light from the Stone of Knowledge sucked back within the gemstone.

The green light from my sword's emblem did the same and stopped its vibration.

But the bow still pulsed with a soft white-and-gold light.

I recovered quickly, sucking air into my burning lungs and stood questioningly at Meda whose eyes still had the shifting white clouds flowing across them.

I turned to the High Priestess and saw that her eyes now had the same odd look, but where the old man's had glowed with a blue light to match the Stone, hers were glowing with the same green light that had sprung up from my sword. The shifting whiteness reminded me of foam surging on the waves of an ocean.

"Thayer," her voice sounded far away and seductive, "why have you summoned me?"

"Bashal, our legacy is being unmade," his voice echoed and hummed eerily, "by Eth." Where Sarha's voice was light and melodious, Meda's was dark and looming. "Somehow *they* have summoned Eth. Hopefully we are not too late."

They became aware of me standing beside them. "You ply the Creator's gift?" They spoke as one. "You have been summoned also." Unspoken words passed between them. "We must find Eth and then you can return us from whence we came." It wasn't a request. I stood in the presence of a God and Goddess, but for some reason, did not feel intimidated.

How could I survive being confronted by all three Gods?

I had witnessed the fury of Eth within the Queen before losing my hand.

Now she knew who I was and what I carried.

With each person she consumed, Eth's power grew.

How soon would it be before the God's power was restored and it cast off her body?

How do you stop a God?

What would be the cost?

272

"Where do we begin?" I regretted the question as soon as the words left my lips.

EIGHTEEN

Revelation

The winds blow,
The seas rock,
My destiny falls,
Mother, I come.
~Book of Bashal

We arrived on the mainland in an armada of ships piloted by the women of the Island, and regrouped with the remainder of our army that had stayed behind on the outskirts of the port city, Harding. The bustling harbour reminded me of our landing in Seacliffe and was run just as efficiently, having us all unloaded and ready to go in less than half a day. Our army now comprised of King Arian's men, the Ren-Tigarian warrior-priests, the fighting Clansmen of Upper Doros, the Lore Masters, and now a contingent of *Maidens of Bashal*. Masters Dirk and Lyas made it implicitly clear to all the fighting men that the Maidens were not to be trifled with, and that the night on the island was to be forgotten and buried in the past. Any violators would be forced to march back to Manath Samal in chains. The Priestesses were almost unrecognizable from their flowing robes and polished appearances. Armed with curved bows and brimming quivers of white-fletched arrows, the women were sturdily clad in hammered leather cuirasses, bracers, greaves and helmets that were curved into shell-like shapes that held their hair in the round bell-like shape at the back of their heads. Our army was a formidable force to behold, and hopefully, would be enough to stop Queen Mordeth and her army of raving cannibals.

I reminded myself, not for the first time, that this was *not* the Queen, *not* the princess Hadiya, the foreign daughter of the Caliph of Shadazar, but rather the twisted and warped being that held the evil God Eth. We were facing the God of Destruction and Death, *not* the mother who had defiantly protected her only son from being beaten to death. After that night on the Isle when the Goddess Bashal had entered into Sarha de Cent, Meda had been quite thorough in his lecture of everything I needed to know of the God Eth, but after a week of travel, only a fraction of that information stuck within my thick skull.

My nauseous stomach wasn't due to the sea-crossing this time.

I was heartened to learn that Elise was travelling with us, but after the Consecration Ceremony, and Master Dirk's warning, she had remained distant and focused on her duties as a Dedicated Servant of Bashal. The women of the Temple were overcome with ecstasy when they had discovered that their High Priestess had become the living embodiment of the Goddess. Some were delighted and had rejoiced, some were despondent and frightened and still others had been found floating face down in the ocean, trying to flee the implications that this was an omen of the end of days.

Nobody had made note of Meda, the embodiment of Thayer, as being responsible for summoning the Goddess and neither myself, nor the Ren-Tigarian Priest had revealed to the others what we had witnessed, afraid of being responsible in some way for those that had taken their own lives. Regardless, I would not have been able to distinguish the Ren-Tigarian if forced to. The dead women's lives had been spent honouring the Goddess and in return she had accepted each sacrifice as honourable, if not a waste, with the winds of war being blown across the land.

That was the hardest thing to comprehend and accept. Meda and Sarha were still the people we knew, Lore Master and High Priestess, and yet knowing that the Gods spoke through them filled everyone with trepidation. I hesitantly asked Meda about this, trying not to offend the God, and he tried to explain it to me by using an analogy of a cup, saying that it can hold many liquids but in the end it is still a cup. He said that most men's cups are filled with water, most soldiers' with beer, and some learned men's with wine. He explained that his own cup was now filled with a strong wine, with an equal mix of ethereal essence, not satisfying to the drinker, but present nonetheless.

I asked him if I was full of water or beer and he just laughed.

"You my friend are more like a cup of mead. Sweet if you sip it, strong if you swallow it. Distilled from honey, but still containing the sting of the bee." I liked his allusion, but didn't understand what he meant. I imagined the sting was my sword, but I preferred Augur for its name.

Once organized and assembled by strength, we made our way east along the coast of Pandros, towards its capitol, Castle Cragthorne, in an attempt to further inflate the size of our army before we turned north to infiltrate and lay siege to Chafet Temple. We were going to starve the maggots out of that rotting corpse and capture us a God in the process. Lore Master Donato promised the help of King Gavin in Cragthorne, claiming bound loyalties and a just cause, and being its resident Lore Master, he hoped would help his plea. Quinn Korid claimed that the Isle of Holbrook's shipping fleet would be donated to our cause and that he would personally attest and vouch our plea bargain to the Countess Deanine of Perg, after we secured King Gavin's help of course, as she would not pledge help without Pandros' support and recompense.

It took us another two weeks of hugging the southern coastline to finally approach the outskirts of Gilmouth, the next town of any reasonable size before Cragthorne. Waiting for us on a hill overlooking the town, we found Oppedia Thresher, the Mayor of Lanera, leading a small group of two hundred armed men. He was sweating profusely in the afternoon sun, but it wasn't due to the heat.

"I had hoped to meet you heading this way, but months ago! What in the name of the Gods took you so long? We were just getting ready to pack up and head back home." He opened his arms in greeting and was welcomed by the leaders of our group once more. He pulled off his felt cap and patted down his few remaining hairs as he bowed low to the High Priestess and the Maidens of Bashal. He had nothing but wolfish eyes for her and for the armoured women that followed. It was obvious that Oppedia and his men had been on the road for quite some time, and by the sight of their dreary camp, they had been waiting outside of the town's walls since their arrival.

"That yon bleeding excuse for a Mayor in Gilmouth, FAT STINKING SWINE!", he yelled his insult at the town, "only allows the *townsfolk* out for trade and such, but won't allow *us* in, to stay within the walls of that bloody town." His unshaven and sunken cheeks gave him the look of a man wild with desperation. He yelled at the town again, "BASTARDS! I believe it's because of that bloody Queen Mordeth!" He looked anxiously at King Arian. "Did *everyone* know about her bloody army, *except* us?" His exasperation was evident on his face. "Tainted! '*Tainted by association*' – he said! This is unacceptable! If *they* had come to us in Lanera, we would have shown them full hospitality, but this," he waved his hand around in a circular motion, "well I suppose *you* lot must be used to travelling like this, yes? Sleeping on the ground. Smelling all of the time." He shook his head in disgust. "The stench of the latrines?" He pulled out a dirty handkerchief from the end of one of his sleeves and held it to his nose. "It's too much for an old heart I tell you. Too much." He composed himself again. "It's a good thing I don't complain and have been able to take it all in good stride." He fanned his face with a well-worn and rumpled scroll of paper. "Ahh! I forgot My Lady, this arrived for you. A messenger had arrived in Lanera looking for you just before we left." He smoothed the flattened scroll as best as he could, and handed it to the Clan Chief. "I promised that I would personally hand it to you. It's too much for one person to take with a bad heart, honestly." He finished by pulling out a small flask from his vest pocket, upending its contents in two swallows, a sharp intake of breath and a puckered wince to suit.

She quickly scanned the document. "It's from my brother." She read the entire script in silence before deciding to share its contents. "He writes about Lore Master Joran visiting Bleneth and being disturbed at his brusque demeanour. He says that Joran seemed distracted and unfocused and got into a heated argument with Temple Master Laban, resulting in Joran clubbing him in the head with his staff. Joran left as mysteriously as he had come, so Fiongall questioned the Temple Master about their argument. Laban claimed it was private Temple business and that it was no concern of others, despite the deep gash and bruise to his head." She looked up from the text. "Curious." She looked at Meda, Quinn Korid and Donato. "He says that the Lore Masters left Bleneth and headed south the next day, taking their Acolytes with them and refused any military escort." She looked incredulously to

Arian and Trevor. "He's deeply concerned about their behaviour and their sudden flight. They left all of their partially started books behind." She handed the scroll to Meda who read it quickly and then handed it back to her. She handed it to Arian who also perused the strange message. "What could have caused this?" She asked Meda, who just shrugged his shoulders and walked away, mumbling something about inept fools and craven lunatics. "He had them followed to the borders of Upper Doros, but they continued south without a second thought."

King Arian decided to hold a council later that night to discuss this new information and how it may affect their assault on Chafet Temple, but first he needed to approach the Mayor of Gilmouth for some much-needed supplies. That garnered a knowing smile from Oppedia Thresher. Lord Trevor persuaded his brother that he would go in his stead and that he would take only Kay and me to accompany him, claiming that a small foraging party would have better luck than a large army. As we left the encampment, I spotted three Ren-Tigarians shadowing us from a distance. I was certain that the small walls of this town wouldn't prove too hindering to men that could scale vertical rock walls.

We approached the timber-walled city slowly, nearing the south gate as instructed by Oppedia Thresher, but stopped and traded with several peddlers as they were either leaving or entering the town, buying small foodstuffs and gathering information on what we faced to gain entrance. At the south gate Lord Trevor asked for Pester Grim, the man apparently in charge of defending the town, and the name gained from the last merchant for a silver piece. A wiry old man peered out through the face-peep in the wooden door, spitting some brown dunge into the mud at our feet.

"Who're you and waddya want?" He asked, eyeing our weapons and clothing suspiciously, then spat again, narrowly missing Lord Trevor's polished leather boot. He had only one good eye, and where Lyas wore an eyepatch to ease the viewer's gaze, this old man sported his empty eye socket without any remorse. It looked like a dog's arse-hole.

"I am Lord Trevor, brother to Arian, King of Manath Samal, brother-in-law to Clan Chief Heather dan Kalon of Upper Doros, representative of the Lore Masters Meda, Donato, Quinn Korid and the High Priestess Sarha de Cent of the Isle of the Crescent Moon. We request passage into Gilmouth for the purposes of purchasing supplies." The clink of Lord Trevor's horse's bridle could be heard breaking the silence that slowly passed as it sniffed the same foul air coming from the walled town that blew through the face-peep and assaulted our noses.

The old man eyed us suspiciously, chewed his brown cud that stained his lips, harrumphed in distaste and spat again. "You *three* can come in, but your horses'll have to stay outside these walls." He spat. "We don't take kindly to strangers trackin' their horse shit all over our streets." He closed the face-peep and slid the bolt aside. Lord Trevor, normally a patient man, began to show colour in his cheeks.

Even the most ill-informed person would recognize the noble breeding and temperament evident in his war-horse.

"Do you think they'd really notice?" Kay said as we dismounted and handed our reins to the old man as he stepped into the fresh outside air.

"Petra's Teats, I don't want to touch yer walking shite bags!" The old man actually looked offended. "CHEESE!" He yelled backed through the open door. A young man, large in size but dim in appearance walked out through the man-door behind the old man and grabbed the reins we handed over to him. He smiled at the horses and uttered some comforting gutturals as he walked them over to a spot in the outside wall where he hitched and watered them. "Thick as cheese he is. Gets it from his mother." He said, spitting another round of brown goo on the ground.

"If I find a hair out of place on my horse, I'll take it from your hide, and then from your son's." Lord Trevor threatened.

"No need to fume at me m'lord, Cheese'll take care of your damned horses. He's half-horse hi'self," he laughed, "but he gets that from me, don't he?" He elbowed Lord Trevor knowingly then waved us inside. We followed close behind through the small door and into the muddy street beyond. It was the middle of summer, and yet the streets were slick with mud. I remembered that it had rained last week, but surely it would have dried up the streets by now. For all his seeming hatred of horses, his waddling bow-legged stride spoke of years in the saddle. When I asked him about the mud, he gave me a dirty look with his one good eye while he rubbed the puckered hole where his other eye used to be. I imagined that if he ever opened that eye, I'd be able to see right into his small brain.

"What in the name of sweet Petra's teats yer barkin' on 'bout?" I didn't understand his retort as he turned around and stared at me dumbfoundedly, both of his feet were plainly covered in muck from the shins down. "Do I look like a bloody Lore Master? Do I have answers t'all life's stupid questions, like does yer mother spit or swallow after she's done?" He laughed at his own joke and continued on his way. Kay laid a restraining hand on my chest and shook his head.

He didn't have to offer an answer as it came flying from a second-story window, splashing wetly onto the muddy street behind us, barely missing our heads. The putrid smell of human waste was overwhelming in the summer heat. I couldn't imagine how our horses could have made the streets any worse. People crammed the street, filthy as they were, and those that knew Pester Grim offered a curt salutation, which was rewarded with a comment in their local dialect, a brown thumb pointed over his shoulder at me, and shared laughter.

I suddenly felt wary, like he was leading us into a trap. Why had he allowed us access, and not the Mayor of Lanera? Before we had entered the town, Lord Trevor had decided against lying about our identities as he thought it would lend our cause credence if the townsfolk knew royalty wanted entrance, not just the Mayor from another town. I thought it had been a mistake, but then I remembered the Ren-Tigarians. I quickly scanned the rooftops but of course, couldn't see any evidence of them. My hand rested casually on my sword hilt as did Kay's.

Kay had picked up on the same foreboding feeling as it looked like he was about to thump the old man on the back of the head when Lord Trevor stopped his arm and shook his head. We eventually made our way into the middle of the town to a ramshackle building that leaned precariously to the right. This, apparently, was the Mayor of Gilmouth's house. Pester Grim spat more of his unending brown juice onto the ground at our feet, swept his hand elegantly toward the decrepit house, laughed and then sauntered back the way we had come.

"I want you boys to hold your tongues. If we're met with the same incivility, I'll burn this damned house to the ground." He looked up at the precarious tilt. "It might be an improvement." He put his hand on the door and pushed it open gently, not bothering to knock or warn the inhabitants that we had arrived.

As we entered the building, I was surprised to find it as dark as night and as humid as a swamp. Pots of all sizes cluttered the entry and from each pot grew a separate species of plant that choked the space with their intertwining cobweb-strung branches that spilled dead leaves across the broken floorboards where some plants had managed to escape and had rooted themselves in the dirt hiding below.

Lord Trevor ordered us to keep the door open for the light and a quick escape. He called out a brief greeting, which was answered with silence. A slight breeze from the street behind us sent the gossamer strings of the cobwebs fluttering. We could hear birds calling from somewhere further into the house and strangely, the sound of chamber music could be heard filtering through the thick jungle. As one we drew our swords, sensing once more, that we were walking into an ambush. Rasping voices could be heard coming from somewhere upstairs. I felt a strange tingling running up and down my spine and shook uncontrollably, imaging that a spider had made its way down my neck.

We looked at Lord Trevor for instruction, but he just held up a finger to his lips and cautiously crept forward, using his sword to push the branches and cobwebs out of his way. The remaining floorboards protested loudly at our progress, causing us to stop and start at each sound, wary of an alarm being raised at our intrusion. I prayed silently that the sensations I felt across my flesh weren't the spiders I espied staring blankly from within their lairs, and thanked the Gods that my hands were full, else I'd be stripping my tunic to find the source of my discomfort.

We found a set of stairs at the end of the hallway and ascended them slowly, one step at a time, listening acutely to the heated debate going on somewhere above us. It was plainly obvious that we were intruding on someone's private conversation, but Lord Trevor didn't cry out another warning, sensing something malicious in the tone of the arguing voices, and the lack of a formal greeting.

Kay caught my arm and pushed me back against the wall as I swayed forward. The strange tilt to the building made it feel like you were falling forward, toward the middle opening in the stairwell. I couldn't fathom why the building hadn't fallen over by now, but perhaps the plants were the only thing holding it together. As we reached the top landing, Lord Trevor froze and pointed back down the flights of stairs we'd just ascended and then pointed to his ear. Sure enough, we heard the tell-tale creak of the floorboards below, but they stopped their noise when we did. Perhaps the building was settling. Perhaps we were walking into a trap. Lord Trevor pointed at his eyes and then over the stairs. Kay nodded and leaned over to the handrail. He peeked over, waited a moment, leaned back and shook his head.

"Hello!" Across the landing, a colourful bird screeched and flapped its wings which were the same colour as the green foliage it hid amongst. My heart pounded loudly in my ears, and my brain reeled at the shock of discovery from the bird's warning. But nothing happened. We could clearly hear the conversation coming from the room opposite us, but the voices continued, unaware of our presence.

"I believe your friends have finally arrived in Gilmouth." The man's high-pitched voice said.

"They tried to kill my son! I want them dead. I need you to kill them." The woman's voice crooned seductively.

"How am I supposed to do that? They have *Lore Masters*." The coward mewed.

"Feckless lump of camel shit! Delay them, like you did that bastard Mayor! I am *very* hungry." As she laughed, her voice deepened in tone.

I touched Lord Trevor's arm and mouthed the words 'Queen Mordeth', but he had already recognized her voice.

She was here.

We had been led into a trap. We heard the floorboard creak again, but it was getting closer.

Sweat dripped down Lord Trevor's face in nervous anticipation and from the stifling humid air. We needed to act before the trap was sprung. He pointed to our swords, and then motioned toward the room. He held up his left hand showing three fingers, then two, and as the last one folded, we burst into the room, ready for a fight.

The Mayor of Gilmouth sat completely naked at a dressing table, his back to the door. He was a large, heavy man and sweat trickled down the folds of his hairy flesh, reflected by the light of two candles that sat on either side of a strange mirror he stared into. The image within the mirror was the woman whose voice had been overheard in the hallway, the woman I had seen once before through the portal in that cabin.

Queen Mordeth sat on a throne made of gleaming human bones, skulls resting under each hand, and the only thing she wore was the golden skull-crown atop her brow. Bright red blood dripped from the crown, staining her face and naked breasts. She rocked back and forth as if being carried on the throne. As we entered the room, she peered over the Mayor's shoulder and smiled, warning the Mayor of our sudden appearance.

For someone so large, he moved rather quickly. He protested loudly at having his privacy violated and as he turned, we could see his high-pitched voice was the result of being a eunuch. He screamed in outrage for his guards even as the evidence of a fresh murder dripped from his own hands, face and breasts. A young girl's body lay twisted on the floor by his feet with a dagger impaled into her open chest. Her half-digested heart sat on the table in front of the mirror.

The Queen laughed wickedly as she recognized us and began to mouth dark words of power.

The Mayor convulsed slightly, then reached down and tried to pull the knife from the dead girl's body. He heaved it back and forth as he tried to remove it from her chest bone, finally throwing her corpse to the floor as the knife slid free.

"Come now put the knife down Mr. Mayor." Lord Trevor tried to negotiate with him.

For some reason, this naked, vulnerable man appeared to be more menacing than the Terroks that had attacked us on the mountain. Perhaps it was the blood staining his face, or the fact that he was physically changing shape before our eyes. His eyes began to bulge from his skull as the bones in his face distorted. His chest seemed to be growing wider and his fingernails were growing longer, sharper and black. He was becoming a Terrok.

"Get out quickly!" Lord Trevor tried pushing us back through the door.

I tripped on something and landed on my back. A black shape flew over my head and landed before me, sword flashing in the candlelight, but faster than the warrior-priest, the man-terrok grabbed the Ren-Tigarian, sinking its black claws into the man's torso and ripped his veiled head from his shoulders. It spat the head out and threw the corpse at Lord Trevor, smashing him against the wall. Another black shape rolled into the room and swung its sword at the creature. Its leg fell wetly to the floor and the creature lurched forward onto its three remaining limbs. Kay, who stood over the prone body of Lord Trevor, swung his sword down and severed the creature's head. The Mayor's deformed body stiffened and then collapsed, covering the dead girl's body beneath him.

The Queen continued to summon her dark words of power through the mirror. The Ren-Tigarian who had removed the creature's leg shook his head, as if shaking thoughts from his mind, and then turned to face me. I could see only the whites of his eyes as they fluttered up into his skull.

"Thomas! Get up!" Kay yelled from the other side of the room.

I scrambled to my feet and moved backward, away from the Ren-Tigarian. He was moving slowly, fighting for control of his own mind. I backed into someone standing in the doorway.

Meda pushed his way into the room, putting me behind him.

He spoke a single word of Lore and pointed at the mirror. The sound vibrated louder and louder around the room until the mirror shattered.

Screaming in pain, the Queen's image still appeared within each of the broken shards littered across the floor.

The Ren-Tigarian turned his sword on himself, spilling his entrails across the already-bloodied floor, and collapsed into a quivering pile of black clothing beside the decapitated body of his brethren.

Meda spoke another word of Lore and a bubble of silence fell over my head and judging from Kay's surprised expression, he experienced the same deafening effect. Together we slung Lord Trevor's body between our shoulders and waited for Meda by the door. The Lore Master gently removed the veil from the last fallen Ren-Tigarian, exposing his non-tattooed face, and used it to gently pick up a piece of the broken mirror, and tuck it into his robe. He surveyed the room, picked up the remaining lit candle from the table and used its light to locate and remove the two ash-vials from the fallen warrior-priests. He nodded to us and we moved down the rickety stairwell ahead of him, past the spider-laden plants and out into the afternoon sunshine.

And into a nightmare come to life.

The third Ren-Tigarian (they were always grouped in thirds) was laying face down in the street strewn amongst the bloodied remains of more than forty people. The arc of destruction spread out about twenty feet from the building where the evidence revealed people had either been slaughtered by the Ren-Tigarian or had turned on each other. The remaining townsfolk stood staring down at the corpses, crying and pointing at the bodies. When we emerged into the light, they looked surprised and then angered at our presence. Lord Trevor stirred awake between us, but we continued to offer our support.

A woman started shouting angrily at us and pointed to the body of a small child laying beside the dead Ren-Tigarian, but the deafening effect still encompassed us and we couldn't understand what she was saying. Lord Trevor pushed us away and stood on his own. He became aware of the effect and tried shaking it off, to no avail. The woman, angry at being ignored, stepped past the invisible barrier, just as Meda tried to stop her with a verbal warning, but it was too late. As she stepped past the child's body, she began to shake and spit, overtaken by the invisible effects of Eth's dark power, spotted the fallen Ren-Tigarian's sword laying at her feet and came at us.

The townsfolk, seeing the effect on their neighbour, took a step back and pointed in shock. Meda tossed the candle back into the building's open door, spoke a word of power, and sent the dead leaves bursting to flaming life. The three of us drew our swords to repel the crazed attacker, but she stopped at the foot of the porch stairs, an arrow sprouting from her mouth, and fell facedown into the mud. The townsfolk turned as one and followed our line of sight. The Maidens of Bashal were angled out across the street behind them, bows at the ready, with The High Priestess leading them. She dropped her bow and motioned for us to come forward. The remaining Ren-Tigarians flanked them, swords at the ready and kept a watch to the rooftops and dark spots between the buildings.

Meda led us past the dead bodies, pausing to recover the ash-vial from the last fallen warrior-priest as Lord Trevor recovered the man's sword. We could feel the heat on our necks as the building was consumed in fire. Miraculously, as we stepped past the invisible barrier, our hearing returned and was bombarded with the confused shouts and screams of the terrified townsfolk. Loudest of them all, and spitting the most vile words, Pester Grim led the angry mob, accusing us of murder and more. We met Sarha de Cent and Fen Gisar in the middle of the street, backs turned deliberately at our accusers.

Meda handed Fen the ash-vials and apologized for his loss as Lord Trevor handed over the recovered sword. He explained that they died well and fulfilled their promises to protect and defend. The Lore Master looked at Sarha, whose eyes were moving with the same other-worldly clouds as his own. God spoke to Goddess.

"The Mayor used a *Mirratyce* to communicate with Queen Mordeth." Meda said it matter-of-factly as he handed her the wrapped shard, "I wonder where he got his hands on something like that." As she unwrapped the shard, I noticed the Queen's screaming image no longer appeared within it. It looked like an ordinary piece from a broken mirror. He turned to face the angry citizens of Gilmouth. His cloud-shifting eyes shocked them into silence, but urgent whispers continued to float through the angry crowd. Meda used the voice of Thayer.

"We are sorry for your loss, but it was inevitable. Your Mayor was negotiating with Queen Mordeth for the invasion of Pandros. He imagined himself as your new King no doubt, but death follows fast upon the heels of treason. 'When you make a deal with Eth, prepare to pay with your own blood.'" He quoted the well-known phrase from the Tome of Lore. "Your hostile approach to strangers is just as much to blame. If you had heeded the requests of Oppedia Thresher to gain entrance into Gilmouth, you would have been warned of the chaos that has impacted every other province lying beyond your wooden palisades." He turned away from the meek-looking and silent crowd, nodded his head, and led us back to the entry gate.

One by one, the Maidens and then the warriors stepped through the doorway and into the fresh air outside the walls. Pester Grim was the last person to step through and stood blocking the others from leaving, arms crossing his chest. He looked even more miserable than the first time we saw him. His son Cheese walked our horses back from the outlying fields, the only person unaware of what had just happened in town. He was explaining to Lord Trevor how he had cared for the animals when his father cut him off.

"Get back in here you stupid bastard!" The big man's grin disappeared and was replaced with a pained expression as he lowered his head and shuffled back slowly towards his father who spat at the ground by Lord Trevor's feet.

"Wait!" Lord Trevor called out. "For God's sake I can't go on calling my new groom Cheese can I? What's your name son?"

Cheese's face lit up. "Charles!" He walked back to Lord Trevor's horse, and rubbed its soft nose. "Yer new groom? D'ya means it, sir, m'lord?"

"Of course I do, look how happy he is." I didn't know if Lord Trevor was talking about his horse or Charles.

"What'cha thinks yer up to?! You can't just come in here and steal my son!" Pester was getting angry, striding forward and planting his hands on his hips.

"I'm not. He's been recruited." Lord Trevor mounted his horse and shifted it slowly towards the wiry little man.

"Well, good riddance to filthy rubbish!" Pester Grim spat towards Lord Trevor, but instead of hitting the ground, it landed on his horse's hoof.

Lord Trevor pushed his horse closer to the small man, and then turned it away from him where it swiftly lifted its braided tail and ejected a steaming pile of manure at Pester Grim's quickly backing-away feet. "That's what we both think of your filthy town. Good riddance indeed!" He laughed and led us back to our main encampment.

NINETEEN

Choices

Across the heavens,
A seed falls.
An answer.
My destiny.
~Book of Thayer

After the incident with Queen Mordeth, Meda instructed King Arian on how imperative it was that we head directly to Castle Cragthorne and hopefully not encounter her army in the open field. He described the image we saw of her in the *Mirratyce*, and the effect that she had had on the unsuspecting citizens of Gilmouth. We relayed the conversation we had overheard between the Queen and the Mayor, confirming that she was indeed mobilizing her forces and heading south. Time was against us. It was obvious that Meda and Sarha were struggling to come up with a strategy to protect us, but where did the human loyalty end and the God's begin? Was a God's life more valuable? The three of them were connected in some way and I prayed to the Creator that they would choose us over their sibling.

A week after we began the forced march toward Cragthorne, I was relieving myself behind a tree, leaf in hand, when a quiet harrumph interrupted my moment of solitude. One of the Maidens of Bashal told me that Meda was looking for me. I sighed and told her that I would attend on him presently. I hadn't spoken to him since we had left Gilmouth. An army on the march is much busier than an idle one, and the only time I had available for quiet contemplation was being cut short.

I found him sitting in a cart at the rear of the army and as I approached, I noticed he was holding the Goddess' bow, *Silya*, across his lap. Sarha de Cent sat serenely beside him. The Lore Masters waited patiently on the opposite bench and scolded me for being tardy to a summons. Meda asked for the sheared piece of Joran's red Mindstone. I found it within the satchel strung across my back and gently handed it to him, confused at the strange request. No one had mentioned the severed Mindstone since the Isle of the Crescent Moon, and I had assumed they had forgotten about it. Obviously I was wrong.

His fingers delicately searched the ruby surface of the Mindstone until he found a spot that satisfied him. He pressed the spot he'd found against a pointed end of the *Mirratyce* shard and both of these he placed against the wood of the bow. At an unspoken command, Sarha placed a hand against the bow and together they spoke ancient words of Lore. The Stone of Knowledge which hung around his neck sparked briefly and an image appeared within the *Mirratyce* shard.

Meda had created a working version of the *Mirratyce*, but this one didn't require the blood of an innocent. He began to explain to the Lore Masters how he had utilized the travelling abilities of the Mindstone, the visual capabilities of the shard, and the seeking power of *Silya* to discover the exact location of the Queen, whose taint still permeated the shard, but after his third word of Lore, I was lost.

"She is about to enter the township of Tilshire. They are preparing to unleash another wave of wanton slaughter." He sighed, pathos clear on his face. "There is no time to warn them."

Sarha de Cent stared blankly at him. "So soon? If I had a blood-arrow, I could use *Silya* to stop her and spare the town." She paused. "And release Eth."

"We are not ready. It is not yet time." He said. "We must to Cragthorne quickly."

Before Meda pulled his device apart, I saw a brief image of the brutal slaughter beginning on the unsuspecting people of Tilshire. I kept that information to myself that night, contemplating what I had witnessed while the rest of our army setup camp and prepared to sleep. I took the first watch and couldn't help but stare north, wondering how many people had died. It frustrated me that Meda and Sarha were doing nothing. They were Gods after all couldn't they just snap their fingers and rid us of that damned Queen and her army?

My watch ended two hours later, and I spent the next hour trying to fall asleep on the hard-packed earth. I dreamt

297

I was trapped inside the Mayor's house, being chased down maze-like hallways, but he looked different. His blood-soaked body wasn't made up of sweaty flesh, but instead was covered in gold-like scales. Just as he was about to catch me in his black-clawed grip, I tripped over a plant and landed face-first into a spider-filled cobweb.

I awoke with a start, sweating and confused, and searched under my bedroll for my sword. It felt warm, but it wasn't humming. I breathed a sigh of relief and settled back down, trying to still my racing heart. A rock was determined to work itself into my spine, so I rolled onto my left side to avoid the offending lump, and froze. Across the camp I could see two sets of glowing eyes staring at me. One was blue and the other green. They slowly turned away after they realized I knew they were watching me. Did they know what I had dreamt of? Did they implant that dream into my head? I turned over onto my right side and eventually fell asleep again. I didn't dream of anything else that I could remember, and was awakened just before dawn. I felt like a sack of wet oats, a sack of oats that hadn't slept in a week, and as we packed up and continued on our march, I caught a glimpse of the Gods heading back to their cart. They both smiled at the people as they passed, looking fresh and well rested. Was that another of the benefits to being possessed by a God? No sleep to go along with no guilt?

During the two week flight north to Castle Cragthorne, I got to know Elise and the Maidens of Bashal better and eventually convinced them to teach me some basic archery

298

skills, as Master Lyas and Dirk had decided that despite my large size, I didn't possess the necessary muscles to draw a longbow. I preferred being a foot soldier anyway and was becoming more adept during our nightly combat-skill fights. Out of the newer recruits, Kay was still the only man who could best me, but even those victories were hard-fought, and he had just as many bruises to show as I had.

The smaller bows the Maidens carried proved easier to draw and each night after our test-fights we found a quiet location a little away (but still within chaperon view) of the encampment and the critical eye of our archers, and would practice shooting arrows at a driven stake. I developed a greater understanding of the teachings of Bashal and not surprisingly, we became friends. I was never left alone with Elise as she always travelled with at least five other Maidens and my friends always managed to tag along to practice as well. In return for teaching us, we showed them some knife-fighting techniques, but they proved stronger and faster than they appeared which resulted in more than a few bruised shins and egos.

In fact, they proved to be better knife-fighters than we were archers. As I pulled the last arrow out of the marked stake (making sure not to bend or break the practice head as I had done before), Elise came up smiling largely, her white teeth matching her tunic and breeches which were highlighted with gold and blue thread. The blue matched her eyes and the gold was a shade darker than her hair. She looked radiant.

"That was a good shot, wouldn't you agree?" She said smiling. Her hair was held back with two white combs that were apparently from some sea creature's mouth called 'baleen'.

"Elise, my dear, you've had more practice," I finally pulled it loose, "but I suppose it wasn't that bad of a shot." I paused handing it back to her. "For a woman, that is." She placed the arrow back into the quiver at her hip, and then punched me in the shoulder. I feigned injury, and then had an idea. "Do you think you could hit this?" I pulled out my black-hilted dagger and carved a very small 'x' into the top of the wooden stake.

We walked back a hundred yards and as she handed me the bow, my friends began to make bets with the other Maidens. After all of the bets had been placed, I stood behind the drawn line, drew back the cord and took my shot. It hit the stake near the top, but from our distance I couldn't see if it hit the mark. Kay and Geoffrey clapped their hands, but Graham shook his head in disappointment, proving who had bet for or against me.

I handed the bow to Elise, but before she drew, she nodded to her friend Deanna, who approached and tied a black scarf around her eyes. Kay and Geoffrey baulked and claimed an unfair challenge and as they continued complaining, she drew and shot, striking the stake as well, but from our distance, it appeared to have buried itself below mine. Deanna quickly removed the scarf and as she raced down toward the stake, she was joined by Graham as neither one trusted the judgement of the other.

"Thomas, do you realize that it's been a whole month since that night on the Island?" Her voice was calm, measured, and too low for the others to hear.

Deanna announced loudly that Elise's arrow was closer to the target and that mine was too low. Kay and Geoffrey cheered and Graham feigned being shot through the heart with my arrow he removed.

"No, I didn't realize that it had been that long. Time passes so quickly when you're on a forced march." I looked at her in the dying light. "Meda thinks that we'll reach Cragthorne tomorrow." Deanna returned both arrows back to Elise and Graham congratulated my aim as in fact, he'd just won his bet as well. He had only feigned his disgust to make me feel better about my archery skills. They walked back to the camp together arm-in-arm ahead of us and the others joined them to talk about the benefits of archery versus knife-fighting.

"Do you remember our conversation that night?" She asked as I removed her bowstring and handed it back to her. She wound it around her hand and then placed it within a pouch on her quiver. I offered to carry the unstrung bow back for her, enjoying the feel of the smooth-carved wood.

"Elise, like you said, that was a month ago, and I did have quite a lot of that heady drink that night." My excuse sounded feeble, even to me, as every moment of that night had been etched into my mind forever.

"Thomas." She placed a restraining hand on my left arm, turning me back to look at her in the failing light. "Thomas, I'm pregnant."

My mouth fell open and closed shut like a dying fish.

I didn't know what to say. I didn't know what to think.

Maura came unbidden into my mind. That afternoon before I had left.

I stood there dumbfounded. "What? But I thought you said that you couldn't get pregnant? You said that you're barren." My mouth felt dry.

"I am, I mean, I *was* barren." She took her bow from my hand and sat me on the ground.

"Are you sure? Does anyone else know?" I asked, afraid of the consequences. Masters Lyas and Dirk were going to skewer me and then castrate me. She shook her head. I thought I had seen a tool for castration in Master Gianno's weaponry. I began to panic.

"Thomas, I *have* to tell the High Priestess." She looked at me, registering the look of shock on my face. "By the Goddess, I shouldn't even be here."

"Are you *absolutely* sure?" I asked again. Hope was there. My manhood still had a chance to grow old with me. But then a thought entered my mind, I wondered what it might feel like to be a father.

"Thomas, I'm sure." She looked both beautiful and terrified at the same time.

I still couldn't get the thought of Maura out of mind. What was I going to do?

"Do you want to go back to the Isle of the Crescent Moon?" I asked. I imagined the trip back, a month away, with my army heading in the opposite direction.

"I can't go back Thomas! I'll have to *leave* the Temple. I can no longer be a Servant of the Goddess." She said dejectedly and tears began to flow down her cheeks as she cried.

"Why can't you go back? That's ridiculous! You're a Servant of the Goddess now! You've been Raised! I was there." I didn't know why I was telling her this. I didn't want her to leave.

"I'm going to be a mother Thomas." She continued crying. "I thought I would never have a child. My world has been turned on its head!"

We sat together as she sobbed quietly into my shoulder. I held her hand in a pathetic attempt at comfort. My gaze wandered back down the hill where my friends and the Maidens waited discreetly at a distance for us. They were showing off their fighting skills, abandoning their knives for swords. I should be down there with them. The biggest fight of my life was about to begin and it scared me to death. I felt like a child. I was going to have a child.

"I won't leave you Elise." I promised. I touched her chin and raised her tear-stained face up to me. "After this war is over, we'll get married and raise our child together." It sounded strange coming from my mouth. "We have a lot of room at my family's house. My mother will be pleased to have another grandchild and another daughter."

"Thomas," was all she said. I held her head to my chest and after the second call from my friends we got up and headed back down to resume our lives. I held her hand back to the camp and kissed it, wishing her luck just before she peeled off to confront the High Priestess alone, as she had wanted.

I found my bedroll, but once again, I couldn't fall asleep.

I was going to be a father.

I remembered K'Larn, Jahad's Rest, Bleneth and now Tilshire.

What if our baby became a victim of the same destruction?

What if Queen Mordeth forced Elise to eat our child?

I vowed silently to kill the Queen myself.

I fell asleep and dreamt of fighting a golden-scaled serpent. I was naked, vulnerable, and losing the fight. It was slowly backing me into a cauldron of boiling magma and I couldn't find my sword. Where were my companions? Where were the Lore Masters? Where was my child?

TWENTY

Praxis Moors

I do it in the name of Thayer,
I do it in the name of Bashal,
Creator forgive me,
I do it, in the name of Eth.
~Book of Man, 5th Century

King Gavin could have been a long-lost brother to King Arian and Lord Trevor. He had the same stature and the same determined look of a man who had faced adversity and won, but at a great price. Lore Master Donato had arrived yesterday ahead of the main army in an attempt to avoid the same welcome we had received in Gilmouth, and the proof of the King's smiling presence at the main gates had reassured everyone that Donato had been successful in delivering our peaceful intentions. I wasn't the only one to notice shining spear heads reflecting in the afternoon sun atop the crenellated wall. It reminded me of something my grandfather had said once when we had driven our best cart to a spring fair, 'Beware the smiling merchant who extends one hand in greeting while the other rests atop his dagger'.

Our forces assembled in the fields outside the castle and immediately began setting up camp. It had already been discussed prior to Donato leaving that King Gavin would only agree to help us, if our combined forces agreed to help refortify his castle. Castle Cragthorne had seen better days and the relative peace between Pandros and Torcal had not required the maintaining of a fully operational and defensive castle. The imminent approach of an aggressive army changed all that and our work parties began working under Meda's frenzied instructions. A work detail was sent out to help pull in the harvests early, to the frustration of the local farmers who couldn't understand why they were being forced to ruin their best harvest they'd had in years just to satisfy the hunger of a host of strangers. When offered the choice of harvesting early or having them torched, they complied reluctantly.

Other work details included dredging and refilling the moat, digging trenches in front of the castle at 50 yard intervals to prevent a cavalry charge and the construction of additional living quarters and latrines to suit the soon-to-be bloated population. The castle faced north as every assault had come from Torcal and Meda confirmed to a sceptical King Gavin that indeed the next assault would unfortunately follow suit. A steady breeze blew from the south ocean which helped to waft away the stench that had slowly built up over the days since our arrival and sent its putrid welcome northward to greet the invading army, wherever they were.

It had been decided by the Lore Masters and agreed to by King Gavin that the castle's women, children and elderly would be sent northwest into Worthing to avoid the upcoming conflict and if the unthinkable happened and the castle fell, they could take refuge in the forests beyond and eventually make their way north to Upper Doros, where the Clan Chief gave her reassurances with a signed letter that they would be welcomed and cared for. We didn't want a repeat of Bleneth and once that tragedy had been described to King Gavin by Heather dan Kalon, he heartily agreed, co-signed the letter, and sent his subjects away escorted by a small group of armed soldiers who had retired years ago, but their flattened noses and scarred arms were proof enough of their ability.

Many of the merchants, who had arrived in Castle Cragthorne ahead of the autumn harvest festival that was happening in two weeks, hitched their carts and bolted southeast to the Isle of Holbrook believing that the seas would provide them with the necessary barrier from the Queen's army. If they couldn't take advantage of Cragthorne's festival, then they wanted to be on Holbrook for *Festivale*, a harvest celebration unlike any other, or so I was told. One fleeing merchant claimed that despite popular rumour, you couldn't make a profit in the middle of a war because you were expected to give away half of your wares as repayment for protection. I agreed with him but wondered how many soldiers he thought really needed a glass-shaped bird to survive the upcoming war.

The day after we had arrived at Cragthorne, Meda had asked for the severed Mindstone once again and constructed his version of the *Mirratyce*. He let out a long sigh and solemnly announced that Tilshire was now in ruins. King Gavin said to no one in particular that his wife had had family in Tilshire, a favourite aunt and uncle. The remaining castle garrison had bristled in impotent rage and had ridden off to confront the marauders and send them back into the pits of Mount Kali. Barring their way, Sarha de Cent, small beside their foaming mounts, eyes beaming green-light with the essence of the Goddess Bashal spoke to the mounted men of Cragthorne.

"Yes, Tilshire lies bleeding in ruin, but Cragthorne stands impervious and unbroken. Stay and stand with us! Prove to the people of this land that Pandrosians can accomplish that which others have tried and failed. Prove that your hearts are as strong as your oaken shields. Prove that your will is as unbreakable as your steel swords. Become the battle cry of the silent dead! Become the hammers of justice! Become the hand of the Gods!" The crowd erupted in ululations of indomitable fortitude, and then turned back into Cragthorne and drank the alehouses dry that night.

The next day, in an act that drew onlookers to the top of the walls, both Thayer and Bashal circled the perimeter of the castle touching each foundation stone while singing a deeply melodic rhythm. After completing their task, I found Meda describing what he had done to the Lore Masters, and showed them how to do it themselves using their Mindstones and words of ancient Lore. He claimed that he had made the walls unbreakable by convincing the stones that they were still part of the earth that they had been carved from and although they were no longer in the places where they had been born, they were still rooted within its loving embrace. He laughed at our incredulous looks and said that despite our disbelief, the stones of Cragthorne had believed him and would provide the protection we needed. The Gods' action made everyone feel safer and more optimistic about the upcoming confrontation with the God of Destruction.

After convincing us of our invulnerability behind the fortified walls, our confidence eroded when they announced we were going to confront the Queen's army by Praxis Moors at a place called Knothill Manor. It was a hunting lodge (not another hunting lodge) that King Gavin used to hunt in early spring and late autumn and was maintained by his brother and his family. After asking why King Gavin would have abandoned his brother to such a desolate place, Lord Trevor explained that the King's younger brother had the distinguished honour of blocking the only invasion route into Pandros from Torcal.

He may not have been able to stop the scouring of Tilshire, but by the Gods, he wouldn't abandon his brother to the same fate. We were to assess the size and the speed of the Queen's army, to evacuate his brother's family and their servants from Knothill Manor and then try and slow her progress into Pandros by using the moors' murky landscape to accomplish this. Once harried and delayed, we could easily retreat back to the reinforced protection of Castle Cragthorne and await the Queen's arrival.

The Gods made it sound so easy.

Much to my disappointment, it had been decided that the Maidens would remain at the castle along with the castle's garrison as the persistent hanging fog would not allow for accurate use of their valuable arrows, which would be needed to defend the walls of the castle, and if it came to a hurried retreat into the castle, the archers could defend better from the higher vantage point. Lord Trevor denied my request to join the garrison as he wanted me and my sword standing between King Arian and Queen Mordeth. He said that she knew me, and that I was valuable bait that he couldn't afford to leave behind. He convinced me after noticing my gaze lingering on Elise too long and said, "Would you rather the Queen's eyes fell on her, or on you?"

Elise met me in private before I left. She told me that she had confided our secret to the High Priestess, but surprisingly, Sarha de Cent had already known about the pregnancy. The Goddess told her that she could remain in service until the baby was actually born, but after that, she would dismiss her from service and allow her to live her life however she wanted. Elise said that she would come to the Isle of the Red Oak, but only as my wife. She handed me a ribbon-bound clipping of her blonde hair which I placed inside my leather thong along with Maura's dark hair, my Thayer amulet and the Terrok claw. I promised her that I would return, and that we would marry once I was back in

310

the castle. I kissed her goodbye and asked if she would continue with her archery practice, because if she saw me being chased by a cannibalistic army, I'd need her skills, blindfolded or not.

I set out for Praxis Moors scouting at the head of our army, waving goodbye to the remaining well-wishers that lined the road heading north. I wanted to be alone with my thoughts of Elise and the Queen but Kay, Geoffrey and Graham caught up to me and broke my introspective mood with stories of drinking with the garrison. Apparently a soldier named Joshua had lost a bet with Graham and ended up spending his watch completely naked and forced to mark the hour by crowing with a rooster's feather pinched between his buttocks. I asked what he'd won and Graham showed off a silver Thayer amulet hanging around his neck. Kay shook his head when I asked what the contest was. Joshua lost his dignity and the bet when he waged that Graham couldn't steal a kiss from one of the Maidens of Bashal. Graham found the woman he'd spent the night with on the Isle of the Crescent Moon and promptly, won the bet and a knee to the groin.

Once we had crested the valley floor, leaving any view of Castle Cragthorne behind, the mood became grim as we silently prepared ourselves for the upcoming confrontation. Arian rode beside Gavin and behind them rode Trevor, Heather dan Kalon, the Lore Masters, Masters Dirk, Lyas, Gianno, Oppedia Thresher and his Lanerans, and lastly our soldiers. The Ren-Tigarians were left to roam the land around, ahead and behind us, and only appeared when they wanted to be seen. We were over three thousand strong and itching for a fight that we had been preparing for ever since we had stepped off the boat in Seacliffe. Only the Ren-Tigarians appeared to be relaxed, if you could call stalking mountain lions relaxed.

It took less than a week to reach the edge of Praxis Moors and as we did, we were cautioned by King Gavin to remain on the main packed route and not to wander off into the fetid swamps where he said men had disappeared without warning, sucked down to their muddy grave. It took us an additional four days to claw our way through the choking bracken and reach Knothill Manor, losing only one horse and a rider that had wandered too far from the path. We were warned too late as the horse screamed in terror at the clawing muck pulling at its hooves, but the more it thrashed about trying to escape, the faster both horse and rider were being sucked down. In his final honourable act, the soldier plunged his sword through his horse's neck to speed its slow death. By the time he tried to extricate his legs from the saddle and reach for the thrown rope, he realized that he had travelled too far from the column of men and slowly resigned himself to the same death as his horse. No man begrudged Lord Trevor as he acted likewise and ended his man's suffering with an arrow through the skull. We searched for the spot where they'd gone off the road, but all we managed to find was a piece of his torn cape being held by a greedy thorn bush. We left it there as a warning and a grave marker.

King Gavin's shocked brother William greeted us and then hurriedly ordered his servants to prepare the rest of the house for their unannounced guests, and then invited the other royals and the Lore Masters to stay within the Manor House with his brother, the King. The rest of the army set up camp on the manicured grounds that had been reclaimed from the swamp. The bright flowers and clipped bushes looked out of place growing in the middle of the bleak and foggy landscape. We left a barrier between the horse pickets and the twisted bracken that marked the edge of the moors that they eyed nervously. I imagined a horse's memory was as good as a man's.

A thick mist clung to the eerie moors in the mornings and didn't completely burn off until the late afternoon sun would finally break through, only to return us into darkness an hour later when the sun began its decent, as it was doing now. A red hue surrounded the yellow orb, casting sickly shadows through the mist from the choked and dying remains of stumpy, parched trees and tangled shrubs, looking like emaciated corpses wandering the afterlife. Once and awhile the black mud could be heard gurgling up a belch from the depths of their cold bellies, sounding like a satisfied old man after a full meal. The image didn't serve well as I remembered the horse and rider now being digested by the swamp.

I turned my mind to more enjoyable memories of Elise and decided to puff away at my pipe, tasting the Crescent Moon cherry-hinted tobacco. The images of that night on the island disappeared in a puff of smoke when my reverie was interrupted when someone opened the door of the Manor House and spilled light and laughter out into the evening's gloom. I heard a soft belch, saw the the tell-tale spark of flame, the draw and puff of pipe smoke, and knew who had drifted away from the party. I wandered slowly over to the porch where Meda sat in an old wooden chair, peering brightly out from his bushy white eyebrows. I offered a pleasant nights greeting.

"Ah, Thomas, might I have a word with you?" He asked politely. "Perhaps in private would be best." He stood and walked down the stairs, away from the house and towards the dark maw in the thorny bushes that marked the entrance to the Manor grounds that we had entered through earlier in the day. He used a new walking stick, a gift offered by King Gavin after the Lore Master had fortified the castle walls. The King claimed that it was his Grandfather's and had been carved from one of the slow-growing, hardwood bog-bushes that grew here on Knothill's grounds. I grabbed a lantern from the nightwatch that guarded the entry to light our way along the too-dark trail.

There was a stump of some blackened wood jutting up on the side of the road where he eased himself down to sit. The noises of the men drifted away behind us as they settled in for the night but the familiar ring of the blacksmith's hammer pierced the thick fog that blanketed everything.

"Master, you seem worried. May I ask what is troubling you?" I sat on the ground beside him, careful of the mud. He produced a wineskin took a swig and handed it to me.

"Thomas, I fear we may have put you in undue peril." He paused. "You are aware that the Queen knows who you are since you have met twice." He took another swig of the wine. "Well, I'm under the impression that she not only knows *who* you are, but *where* you are as well." I felt a chill creep up my spine and it wasn't the fog.

"How can she know where I am?" I asked, confused.

"We know exactly where you are Thomas." A voice added from the void as Sarha de Cent appeared from the fog, and sat next to Meda. "Your sword shines even on a night like this." She looked at me sideways, eyes glinting green in the lantern light. "Do you know the tale of the Gods and their quest for the gift of creation?" I nodded in acknowledgement, "Good, it's important to know such things, however diluted they've become over time. Keep it in the back of your mind as Meda recounts the true history of your sword and why we have returned." She smiled at the older man. "He is a Lore Master after all, and used to storytelling." He smiled at her, acknowledging some private humour and then began to weave his story.

"We have been summoned back for a reason, and that reason shines at your hip. Like a thirsty horse drawn to water, your sword beckons us. We do not belong here on

315

earth, and neither does your sword, or more accurately, the metal your sword was forged from. It came to earth millennia ago, in its primal form, and its *wrongness*, its *presence* drew us as a lodestone, even as it caused us great pain to be near it." He winced at those last words, and as he did, I realized what I had been noticing in them since they had become living vessels for the Gods. They looked worn out, like they hadn't sleep in weeks, or like a soldier that continued to fight despite being wounded. I saw in their weary faces what the true cost of glimpsing omnipotence elicited.

"I had no idea. I'll throw it into the deepest part of the moors and rid the world of its taint." I began unbuckling the scabbard.

"Thomas, please sit back down and just listen." Meda begged, motioning me to sit. "Even if your sword sat at the bottom of the deepest ocean, we would be compelled to find it." He managed a smile, still puffing away at his pipe. "We have lingered in limbo, trapped within the Stone of Knowledge and *Silya*, until we were released once more by the very device that trapped us in the first place."

"Thomas, have you heard of Al-Shidath?" The High Priestess asked solemnly.

"Yes, Meda told me that he was the man who originally held this sword." I offered. "I saw an etching of him in one of the books back in the Temple before it was," I trailed off not saying the words 'burned to ash'.

"No, not originally, only the last man before you came along, and that was more than a century ago." Meda idly tapped the wattle from his pipe into the mud and cased it once more. He took up the wineskin again, tipped it back and then handed it to Sarha de Cent, who drained the remainder. "Al-Shidath resided within Chafet Temple and the Temple resides within Mount Kali. During his tenure there, he clawed deeply into the roots of the mountain and discovered the sword buried within the catacombs that had been sealed shut." He smiled, "Most people believe it was a coincidence, but what they don't understand is, just as we are drawn to the sword, the sword is drawn to its rightful descendants." He smiled again, "Well, not *its* descendants to be exact, more like its progenies, and not the sword itself, but the metal that it was forged from."

I was confused and looked perplexingly from one god to the other.

They stared at me thoughtfully, expecting me to follow their logic and finish the story.

"Like a bored potter, the Creator reached down to earth, picked up a lump of clay, formed it to resemble its children, us, and then spat life into it. That spittle was the object that fell to earth that day and it still resides within mankind to this day. Throughout the history of humankind, there remains within a few bloodlines, down through countless generations, that singular element absorbed during the great confluence, and within some humans, that element appears stronger, less diluted. Al-Shidath was one of those rare

317

humans where the element resided more robustly, and as we've all come to know, you are also one of those rare humans Thomas." Meda looked at me strangely, his blue eyes taking my full measure. "The moment you picked up that sword and touched the blade, the element lying dormant within your blood became active and attuned itself with the metal in the sword, together acting as one. Your sword, or more precisely, the element residing within it is now a part of your being and it has given you the ability to sense any Lore being manipulated around you, which is the true power of the Creator and can only be wielded by a Master of Lore. You complete the sword and by doing so it has given you the ability to either access Lore or negate it."

A silence drew between us as his words sunk in and the events of the past began to make some sense. That would explain the strange humming I felt around the Lore Masters when they wielded their Lore, or when the Queen drew her power from the Skull.

"It was you and your sword that activated the Stone of Knowledge, and the Bow of Destiny. Thomas, you helped to summon us. The Priests of Mount Kali have found the Skull of Power in the same catacombs that Al-Shidath found the sword and they have used their twisted Lore to activate some of the Skull's darker powers, but they still need you and your sword to bring about the full manifestation of Eth." His eyes began to glow blue. "And they need us."

I looked him in the eye feeling utterly frustrated. "I won't do it! I'll run away!" The words echoed uselessly in the mist as I knew I could never run far enough and I would be responsible for the deaths of all the people who tried stopping them from finding me. I steeled my nerves. "Please help me. What must I do?"

"You must become the bait in our trap." He didn't smile. "Eth can feel your presence and it wants the sword to send us back and to rule this land uncontested." He shared a glance with the High Priestess. "Thomas, just as you unwittingly brought us back from limbo, you can send us back. All of us."

"Thomas, you hold the key." Sarha de Cent spoke up. "Not only do you hold our lives in your hands, but the lives of everyone around you." Her eyes flowed with power. "If Eth manages to gain the sword, the Creature's manifested powers of destruction will be virtually limitless." No smile played across her face either. "Eth will not stop until mankind is wiped from the Earth. As it was in the beginning, so shall it return." She suddenly looked sad. "Eth will use man against man to destroy itself." She laid a hand on my arm. "We can stop her together, and with the help of the Lore Masters we can return mankind to its simple balance and help preserve the Creator's gift of life."

We sat together as the Gods divulged a scenario they believed would work to disable the Queen and prevent her from summoning Eth.

I didn't sleep that night knowing that it was going to be my last.

TWENTY ONE

Day of Reckoning

Golden lids shade the flames
As searing heat burns the offal
Staining its lips
~Book of Eth

A thick fog had rolled in from the sea during the night, adding to the always-present mist, and which sent chills daggering to the bone in the pre-dawn hour, but it also helped to hide and blanket the sounds of our waiting army. Praxis Moors would enhance its claim to more lives by the end of today either from the day's planned fighting, or due to another man's accidental footing. Warhorses shied away from the slopping muck, nervously remembering the fate of the lost horse and rider, snorting their dissatisfaction at being unable to either see or smell despite the calm reassuring weight of their handlers. The horses' reaction had the effect of unsettling even the staunchest warrior, who I spotted warding symbols of protection at the abyss around them, kissing amulets and re-applying rotes of protection they had purchased in Cragthorne before we had set out. A half-penny of protection against the power of a disgruntled God, what chance did they have? Only the Ren-Tigarians appeared nonplussed, them and the frogs that chirped their love songs away in the pre-dawn darkness.

A quick meeting had Meda confirm that Queen Mordeth's army was indeed coming in this direction and so the Captains spread the army out in preparation for the ensuing conflict, barking unnecessary warnings about the sucking mud pools, and due to the treacherous footing all riders were to be led to their waiting positions by foot soldiers. The army was nearly ready, but I certainly wasn't. I stood at the head of the army, flanked by Meda, Sarha, the Lore Masters and the Ren-Tigarian fighters who encircled us, a dark stain against the enveloping mist.

Donato tried to use his Lore to push the fog away, but the strange landscape proved overwhelming and the fog simply rolled back in, regardless of his efforts. His frustrated conjuring was forestalled by Meda who put a hand on his waving bicep and claimed that the fog would be as much to our advantage as to our disadvantage. He surmised that just because she knew where we were didn't mean that the army she controlled could see any better than we could, and our advantage in that regard was still in a shrouded surprise.

He reminded us that our purpose here was to delay their inevitable advance and to cripple them before falling back to Knothill Manor and then back to Cragthorne. King Gavin's brother, William, his wife and household staff had left Knothill Manor just after midnight and were heading back to Cragthorne, awaiting the outcome of our skirmish. Our plan, in theory, was to draw the Queen towards me, and when she appeared, Meda and Sarha, along with the Lore Masters, would immobilize her using their combined skills. The Ren-Tigarians would form a human barrier between us and her army while I skilfully removed the Skull of Power from her head or both, whichever was easier.

My stomach lurched as I recalled Tanner's Lodge, and Jared. Why did my first kill, have to be my friend? I looked down at my marred left hand, ruined on that same fateful day. The priestesses had healed it as best as they could, but I still felt the ghost-like appendages where my last two fingers once waved. Gianno had customized the hand-hold on my shield to compensate for my weakened grip, turning the strap into a device that snugly cupped my forearm.

He had spat in frustration when I had tried to refuse using my shield, claiming that my crippled hand was more of an impediment holding a shield. He chided me, "My uncle lost more of his arm than you my friend and he still uses a shield. No *real* man would willingly forego the use of a shield when facing an enemy. Perhaps I was wrong thinking you a man." He paused and pursed his lips. "Will you be a man and accept your hand for what it is, or become a hairless boy and have more of it hacked off in your next encounter?" He had asked in a mocking tone.

Thinking about my hand brought back memories of Elise and thoughts of our unborn child which in turn spun my mind back to Maura and my family back on the Isle of the Red Oak. I looked around at the faces I could see in the fog, and guessed that each man was doing the same thing, running through the days of their lives, here on the brink of uncertain death.

My sword hand wandered up to the thong at my neck containing the hair of the two women I loved, my amulet to the living god standing beside me (I guess I should throw it away), and a claw from a mystical creature that had nearly taken my life, if not for my shield. Any more excitement in my life and I'd need to get a larger thong.

The croaking stopped.

The following silence was louder than the frogs.

My eyes searched the choking fog in vain.

"They have arrived." Meda said quietly.

As one, the Ren-Tigarians unsheathed their swords in answer to a hand signal from Fen.

Sarha's eyes glowed with a soft green light. "There are others." Her brows creased with concern. "Your brethren, the Lore Masters from The Temple of the Sky." She looked at Donato and Quinn Korid. "I'm so sorry. They have been subjugated by the Creature." It was a matter of fact statement that shattered the stoic composure of the two Lore Masters.

"What?!" Donato's incredulous question was answered by Meda's calming hand.

"If the head of the Creature is severed, they will return to us and themselves." He addressed Fen Gisar. "The Lore Masters must not be harmed."

The black-clad leader of the warriors nodded his head slightly in acceptance and received a confirming nod by each of his men who stood solid and unmoving, eyes constantly searching the swirling fog.

"I can't believe Laban turned so easily." Quinn Korid broke the silence. "After his argument with Joran, he must have believed that he could complete what none of us could." He looked at me and my unasked question. "Laban's Mindstone has the ability to stop a man's heart or to start it. He probably believed that he could kill her from a distance." He shook his head in disbelief. "And now she controls that power as well. We should have sent word to them that Meda had been returned to us, and that hope was not lost." He looked to Donato and spoke quieter, "Perhaps they grew desperate after seeing what had been done to Joran."

"What about Lore Masters Laird and Mai-Hon? What can their Mindstones do?" I asked the red-bearded older man. He looked over at his be-spectacled younger peer and then back at me.

"As Donato told you before, Laird's Mindstone can control the elements, much like his own," he raised his eyebrows in exasperation, "But I'm not exactly sure what Mai-Hon's Mindstone could do. He always kept that to himself." Donato nodded his head in agreement.

"His Mindstone gave him the ability to travel, similar to Joran's. In fact, it has helped to move her entire army here quicker than she should have been able to." Meda answered despondently. "Where Joran's Mindstone gave him the ability to travel *through* points in space, Mai-Hon's Mindstone allows you to travel bodily *to* points in space." He smiled at me. "But perhaps Mai-Hon can tell you that for himself." Meda gestured into the greyness before us. The mist swirled suddenly as if a great wind had blown through it, and standing there before us was Mai-Hon.

His unkempt look betrayed my last memory of him with his perfectly combed and cared-for moustache with its waxed and twisted tips. It now hung loosely and frayed from his unshaven face. His cheeks were gaunt and his eyes searched around furtively, like someone being hunted. His robes were filthy and torn along the bottom hem, exposing his bloodied and bruised feet. Surprise showed in his face at finding us here so suddenly in the gloom of the bleak landscape, and as Quinn Korid rapidly began to mouth the words to shield his mind, Mai-Hon raised his staff and disappeared back into the mist as suddenly as he had appeared. The last look on his face replayed over in my mind and could only be described as maniacally excited.

The Ren-Tigarians swore silently and readjusted their stances into a more forward protective, flanking manoeuvre.

"And thus it begins." Meda said as Mai-Hon reappeared again suddenly with a group of enemy soldiers, or more properly, men who were once soldiers, men who we recognized and who wore the raiment of Upper Doros, Rheal, Manath Samal, Lanera and carrying all manner of weapons.

They reacted instinctively, ravaging their swords wildly at anyone they saw. In my slow reaction, I noticed the whites of their eyes appeared to be flushed red with blood, matching the stains on their armour and their weapons. The remnants of Tilshire's slaughter still adorned their bodies and the blood-lust of more carnage frenzied their attack. The Ren-Tigarians cut them down methodically as stoic warrior faced raving madman, only to leave a steaming pile of distinguishable body parts that continued to twitch and die before succumbing to the inevitable.

The humming began again in the hilt of my sword so I unsheathed it and tapped it lightly against my shield in preparation for the next onslaught. I pushed my helmet up to relieve the growing pressure on my brow and despite the cold air, a rivulet of sweat dripped down my face, stinging my eye.

We heard surprised shrieks and the sounds of warfare to our right and to our left as Mai-Hon continually delivered waves of enemy combatants along our flanks, the only indications were eddies in the swirling mist due to his swift approaches and retreats back and forth to the unseen advancing army. His movements appeared random, which frustrated Quinn Korid who desperately tried to direct his Mindstone in the expected direction of his next attack, only to be foiled each time.

"Damn! Someone needs to slow him down! Shoot him if needs be!" He shouted through the growing noise.

Sarha de Cent held her bow *Silya* at the ready, with a red-fletched arrow nocked. She looked at Meda. "They have a giant!" As she said those terrible words, I felt the ground tremble. My legs continued to shake but that was due to my growing fear. We heard a distant yowl as she loosed an arrow and it found its intended target.

"Donato!" I yelled at him as he stood behind us, confused into inaction. "We need to see!" The young Lore Master held up his staff with the green Mindstone and began to chant his words of Lore. The mists began to swirl around us and slowly he managed to funnel it straight up into the air above our heads. The trembling under our feet continued, but there was still no sight of the approaching giant.

The trembling wasn't due to a lumbering giant. Through the clearing mist I saw the faint glow of amber light raised at the end of a staff. The earth shook again, sending me to my knees as a geyser of hot mud spewed up from the earth beside me. A fountain of water and mud shot twenty feet into the air, coursing up and out, showering our army in sheets of hot wetness and into this confusion the frenzied enemy took advantage and attacked.

The Ren-Tigarians, amazingly still stood on their feet and took up defensive positions against the continued onslaught. They were slowly being pressed back by the raving horde, which in turn forced us back into the front lines of our middle ranks. Quinn Korid remained standing and shouted his defiant words of Lore at his former friend and colleague, Lore Master Laird, who was responsible for unleashing the steaming guts from the earth.

Donato took up a position beside Quinn Korid, adding his words of Lore and began to pull lightning down from the dark skies. The ground around the enemy exploded as the lightning threw up clumps of heated mud and stone in answer.

The earth stopped spewing up around us as Quinn Korid's Lore enveloped Laird and he slumped face-forward into the muddy swamp, suddenly cut-off from the Queen's control.

An enemy sword flickered past the Ren-Tigarians and stabbed Donato in his side, felling him like a sack of cloth. My sword swung back in retaliation and took off the attacker's arm at the elbow. One of the Ren-Tigarians pulled the attacker back, slit their throat, and threw them onto the growing pile of bodies.

Sarha de Cent was immediately at the side of the fallen Lore Master with words of comfort. She laid her bow down on the muddy ground beside him, its perfection standing out as an object of brightness and craft amongst the chaos of mud and blood. The Goddess commenced healing the small Lore Master, but I couldn't watch as my attention was drawn back to the battlefield where something roared a warning, and there, not fifty feet before us, appearing in the middle of the gloomy morning mist stood the giant, a red fletched arrow pricking its massively muscled neck.

The giant was the height of four men, was hugely muscled, and carried a broken tree trunk as a club. A smaller man, dressed only in a red loincloth, yanked a chain that was attached around the giant's neck, and helped to guide the brute across the battlefield towards us with words of encouragement. The only armour the giant wore was a tight fitting polished metal cap that appeared to be held onto the flesh of his skull with metal clamps and which gleamed dully in the muted light.

"Fen! Quickly!" Meda shouted, pointing at the fallen Lore Master Laird who was recovering too slowly from his power-induced stupor. He shook his head and wiped the mud from his face, unaware of the lumbering danger behind him.

"Hand to me!" The warrior-priest's quick command had three of his brethren in the dark-blue belts fold in beside him as they ran out onto the busy battlefield. Never before have I seen, and never again would I witness the flawless fighting ability of those four men focused on the impossible task of retrieving a man from being swallowed in the mouth of death. It made me feel slow and dim-witted as I watched them dance amongst and progress steadily through a sea of enemies bent solely on their destruction. They leapt over projected spears, rolled over men who clutched at their own bleeding throats, cut launched arrows from the air, pulled devices from their clothing and threw them into the faces of the snarling ravers and still managed to continue forward to Laird who now leaned against his staff, looking confused and shocked at the chaos unfolding around him. He was completely unaware of the towering giant that approached steadily behind him, club slowly rising. The smaller man yanked on the chain and spit flew from his mouth as he coaxed the giant toward Laird.

In one flowing movement, Fen Gisar sheathed his sword, bent down, shouldered the Lore Master, grabbed the fallen staff and turned to run. He didn't see the down-swinging arm of the giant as the tree-club slammed into the body of one of Fen's Captains who advanced to protect his liege-lord with his own body. Black clothed limbs flung up as the club ended his life, embedding the warrior-priest into the slimy mud. One of the Ren-Tigarians flung white powder into the face of the smaller man holding the neck chain of the giant. The smaller man screamed and raked at his now-bleeding eyes with dirty hands, and ran blindly to his left. That's when I noticed that he actually wasn't pulling the chain, but was in fact attached to the giant's chain around his own neck, and where the smaller man led, the giant blindly followed. The giant yanked the tree-club free, dropping bloody chunks into the mud and followed the screaming smaller man away to our right flank.

The remaining Ren-Tigarians surrounding us angled out into the battlefield to defend their brethren while their own positions around us were taken up by other armed soldiers. Fen's two remaining Captains scooped up the ruined body of their fallen comrade. One shouldered the body while the other took up a defensive position behind as they made their way quickly back to us. I could hear men yelling off to our right as the giant attacked.

Fen Gisar pushed his way through the soldiers and placed Lore Master Laird down on the wet ground beside the still form of Donato as Sarha de Cent continued running her hand over the young Lore Master's stab wound. Lacking the strength to get up, Laird turned his head and looked at the still body of Donato, and then guiltily turned his gaze away. As his eyes lit on Meda, he began to simper in a pathetic mewl.

"How did I get here?" He asked of no one in particular. He beseeched his former Master of the Temple sounding mad with anxiety, "We all thought that you were dead!" He continued his choked sobbing, mixed with a few ranting words of disbelief. "The things she made us do! We thought that you were dead."

Fen's Captains returned, pushed their way into the circle and placed their bloody comrade's body on the ground beside Sarha de Cent and Donato. She looked briefly at the ruined Ren-Tigarian's body and shook her head. "I'm sorry but there is nothing I can do." She removed her hands from Donato who suddenly blinked awake, and finally came to his senses. She retrieved her bow from the muddy ground and stood beside Meda. "The Creature is approaching."

Donato sat up and looked around while his hand searched for the wound in his side that was no longer there. When he realized that Laird was sitting beside him crying, he reached over to try and comfort his old friend but as he leaned over, his other hand touched the cold body of the Ren-Tigarian and he looked around questioningly. Quinn Korid continued louder with his Lore, strengthening his protection around the remainder of our army as Queen Mordeth and her priests materialized on the battlefield before us.

I watched enthralled as her gruesome throne was revealed through the thinning mist. Eight hugely-muscled men placed the throne down amongst the dead and squirming bodies of her own fallen soldiers we had left behind our slowly retreating ranks. Her nakedness was an affront to the armoured and bleeding men around her, as if she were impervious to any weapon or the cold. Her son materialized beside the throne on her left side, while on her right, the subjugated Lore Masters Laban and Mai-Hon were prodded forward by her priests who fanned out behind her wearing their blood-red robes, and chanted their guttural words of dark Lore.

I felt hope draining from me as my bladder released, briefly warming my feet. I began to shake with fear and turned to Meda and Sarha for guidance, surely the living Gods weren't afraid of their kin? They stood together, staring at the Eth-Queen, not speaking, focused beyond the world of dying men. Meda moved slowly to stand beside Quinn Korid and placed a hand on the staff, lending his godly-power to the other's Lore and as he did this, Laban and Mai-Hon appeared to awaken from the Queen's control. They swayed and looked around, confused by their surroundings. Frustrated by their failure, her priests doubled their efforts to regain control of the two Lore Masters, raising their voices with rank words that the Lore Masters recoiled from.

Queen Mordeth stared at the Lore Masters and spoke her first words of war. "Kill them." The Lore Masters tried to recover by holding up their staffs in defence but the priests overwhelmed them with drawn daggers and black murder.

"NO!" Lord Trevor roared, appearing suddenly on our left while his flank continued to fight without his leadership. "Why aren't you stopping them?" He yelled at Meda in frustration.

Two of the Queen's priests ebbed off of the murdered Lore Masters, handing one recovered staff to Dermot and the other to the Queen. The remaining carrion priests continued their feeding frenzy, ripping the old men's bodies into shreds and cannibalising their remains. One held aloft a disfigured head in triumph, gouged the eyes out and slurped them like a prized dessert.

I turned and puked on the ground, as tears spilled down my cheeks. I tried to conjure up their smiling faces as I last remembered them from the Temple of the Sky in an attempt to purge the bloody images burning into my mind. Now I knew what Jared, Lord Fiongall, and the survivors of K'Larn and Bleneth had witnessed. How would I have reacted watching Elise being eaten, Maura, my family? I couldn't stop my choking tears.

Shocked into reality, I stood and witnessed the same horrors happening up and down our line as the Queen's army attacked our troops and then fed on the freshly fallen soldiers, who desperately fought back with fist and boot. But her soldiers were relentless and maniacally fought on despite missing an arm or having a sword penetrate their torso and in one shocking example, one of her undead soldiers crawled across the battlefield, trailing its entrails as it tried to bite at the ankles of the men fighting above it.

Aghast in horror, I watched as one of our own fallen men rose and turned against their brethren, joining in the unholy slaughter.

People I knew were dying and being reborn to fight against their kith and kin.

My mind reeled with shock. Was this the horror the Gods knew but refused to tell me?

Where were Kay, Geoffrey and Graham? Were they fighting for us or against us?

My resolve solidified.

It had to end, now.

I gripped my sword tighter and pushed forward through the Ren-Tigarian defence line, and strode across the muddy field. I heard Lord Trevor calling my name, but I ignored him and continued forward. I burned with rage. Seethed with determination to kill the Queen and end our misery. Meda and Sarha had said as much the night before. Dermot smiled as he saw me approaching and sauntered away from the throne, carrying the Lore Master's staff like a prize of war, the black feathers around his white head fluttered in the breeze of his movement. As his mother turned her gaze on me, my sword began to hum, its vibrations giving me courage.

We met in the middle.

"There you are you little shit." He held out his left hand, clutching Laban's staff. "You owe me for my last Mindstone, and my bloody hand." He began to speak words of Dark Lore and I felt my chest constricting. I remembered Quinn Korid explaining Laban's Mindstone and its effect on a man's heart. I swung my sword downwards at Dermot, but he dodged back cunningly, and it glanced down the length of the staff. It shattered the wood and sliced into the leather satchel hanging across his chest.

The world exploded into light and piercing pain.

I finally managed to open my burning eyes and found myself staring up at a mountain that dominated my view. I rolled onto my side and began to cough, either from the breath that had been stolen from my lungs when the world exploded or from the smoke pluming up from a crack in the earth beside my head. Confused and disorientated I looked around and saw Dermot twitching on the ground beside me. He was holding his throat and his face was turning red as he gasped for a breath. I crawled over and watched as he clutched at his chest. His face was now turning a purplish-blue and his twitching movements were slowing.

I remembered Quinn Korid's words, *His Mindstone can stop a man's heart. Or start it.* Laban's ruined staff lay on the ground beside the remainder of Dermot's hand, where I must have severed the remainder from his body and the staff. I touched the tip of my sword to the Mindstone and rested my other hand on Dermot's chest. He sucked in air as his heart started beating once more. The lack of colour slowly returned to his face. I was filled with mild disbelief and wonder at what my sword seemed to do. It wasn't just a weapon.

Words spoken by the Goddess filled my mind, "*Thomas, you hold the key. You hold not only our lives within your hands, but the lives of everyone.*" My sword must have the ability to unlock the power of the Mindstones without speaking words of Lore. I looked at Dermot as his eyes slowly cleared and he realized where he was, or in truth, where he wasn't.

He grinned at me with muted red lips.

"Pathetic." He began to laugh as his wheezing breath slowly returned.

My sword still rested on the Mindstone.

Jared's dying face came back to me from Tanner's Lodge, just before I cut off his head. His death was due to this man. Lore Master Joran's face came back as well, terrified and wild, driven insane by this man's cruel ministrations. Laban's and Mai-Hon's came back, eaten alive because of this man and his mother.

Elise's face came back, perfect and untouched by either.

I could keep her safe.

I touched his chest.

He began to choke again. His right hand, his only one, grasped at my clothes. He clawed at me, as he tried to pull himself upright. He wasn't the one smiling now. I stood and pushed him away from me.

It didn't take long for him to die.

I picked up the broken staff and freed the amber-coloured Mindstone, then pulled the leather satchel from around Dermot's lifeless body and placed the Mindstone carefully within it. I noticed the slice through the leather where my sword had glanced off the staff and cut into it on the battlefield. Inside the satchel I found the other half of Lore Master Joran's red Mindstone, the one that had allowed him to travel through points in space, as Meda had explained to me earlier.

That was how we had travelled here, wherever here was. I looked around for any telltale landmarks and then back up at the mountain that dominated the landscape. My eyes moved up from the plains to a constructed Temple entrance set into the mountain about a hundred feet up.

Mount Kali. Chafet Temple.

We had travelled hundreds of miles north and east. But why was I brought here?

I turned away from the mountain and looked southwest. Somewhere in that direction the armies still fought and my friends were still dying. I had Laban's death-inducing Mindstone in my possession and a way to end the Queen's life and this war she'd started.

I pointed the remaining half of Joran's travelling Mindstone southwest, held my breath, and touched sword to stone.

My world exploded again.

I reeled from the effects of travelling and fell to my knees as breath returned. I felt drained but as the earth stopped swaying, a thought came to me. When the stone was whole, Joran had been able to open a hole in the air through which he could physically walk. That would have been easier than being ripped apart and put back together again, twice. My stomach heaved at the memory and I had to lean against the rock to steady myself and try not to puke again. It felt cool on my forehead.

The rock?

Looking up, I stumbled backward at the sight as I shielded my eyes from the bright morning sunlight. The rock I had been leaning against was enormous. It stood at least ten men high and was probably twelve men around. It looked like a giant's finger pointing up to the heavens. Confused at the unearthly monument, I looked around and noticed roads heading west and east and alternately north and south. The giant's finger sat in the crossroads of both routes and was carved with many names, dates and directions. I saw an arrow pointing south with the word "Knothill" carved above it.

I was travelling in the right direction! Southward, the land changed from rolling grassland into the choked landscape of Praxis Moors and from this distance I could see the low lying fog covering the landscape further south where the battle was still taking place.

I was definitely closer, but I was still days away from where I needed to be.

I held the Mindstone southwest again, closed my eyes and touched sword to stone.

This time I had to puke. Closing my eyes had made the feeling of vertigo worse and the air had been completely sucked from my lungs. Now they burned as I breathed in fresh air that was tinged with salt. I could feel cold rock beneath my fingers again as my wits and vision slowly returned.

"Take it easy my friend! The celebrations don't officially start until sundown!" Someone tapped me on the back. I stood up quickly in response, which made me stumble and fall back down on my ass. "Whoa! Whoa! My friend, why don't you sit down before you fall down?" The stranger handed me a cup. "Here, drink this." Thankfully it was water.

I thanked him and sucked it back quickly, quenching my thirst and burning throat. I handed it back and asked where I was, squinting at the shadowy figure haloed in sunshine.

He laughed. "Hey Ginzo, get a load of this guy! He doesn't even know where he is!" He continued to laugh as a bigger, more solid man appeared beside him wearing pants that looked like they were covered in white hair.

"Who is he supposed to be Wasil? A soldier? Pah, everyone does soldiers!" The larger man, Ginzo, asked the smaller man as he handed him a mug of beer.

"Cheers my friend!" Wasil drained the cup as his larger friend Ginzo completed his costume by placing a white hairy suit over his head. A misjudged version of a Terrok stared down at me.

"Welcome to Perg and Festivale!" Ginzo said as he extended a black clawed hand to me.

TWENTY TWO

Loss and Gain

The Creature is not singular,
In feelings of fury and hate.
Simply take away that which one needs.
~Book of Bashal

I stared north across the darkening seas from a balcony perched high above the bustling harbour city of Perg, trying to imagine the battle on Praxis Moors that continued to rage on without me. I hoped it still raged on. Tonight, miles away from blood and death on this Isle of Holbrook was Festivale, a night of inhibitions and inebriation and somewhere down below me my hosts were careening through the city streets singing and carousing amidst the colourful crowds that stumbled along lantern-lit cobblestone boulevards. They had left behind a large bottle of wine, already half empty, from which I tried to drown my guilty sorrows.

It was working faster than I imagined.

Wasil, the smaller man, had dressed as a holy zealot complete with sandals and loincloth with holy protective symbols painted across his chest and back. When I tried to explain to him that I had actually met the God Thayer and the Goddess Bashal, he rolled on the ground in hysterics. I even showed him the two partial Mindstones that I carried in the leather satchel. His eyes nearly fell out of his head, but he quickly regained his composure and shushed me into silence while darting his eyes left and right trying to espy some hidden thief.

"I don't know where you've, ahem, *found* these, but if you need some quick money, I know the best merchants in this city." He held up an out-turned palm to his mouth. "No questions asked." He smiled benignly, "for a modest finder's fee of course."

Ginzo, the larger man, and to my surprise the younger brother of Wasil, gaped open-mouthed when I produced a real Terrok claw from within the thong hanging around my neck. He caressed it lovingly and held it up to the light in apparent disbelief; he even tried biting it to confirm its authenticity. He handed it back to me religiously, as I retold the story of my encounter on the mountainside and how I had procured the claw. I left out the poignant part about my sword and after impressing him with my story he clapped me on the back and asked for my impression of his costume that he'd spent a month's wages on for tonight's festivities. I didn't have the heart to tell him that the creatures' eyes didn't actually bulge out from their heads, or that their teeth didn't curve down below their lower jaws, or that their chests weren't bare of hair or that their genitalia didn't protrude out like an eel escaping from between two oysters. I told him it was like confronting the beast again for the first time.

They had left full of spirits but only after I had promised to look for them in the streets before too long. As the door closed behind them I heard them betting on who would get lucky first. I looked down at my possessions laid out on the table before me and tried to figure how I could use them to get back to the mainland, back to the army, back to Elise. I put the broken Mindstones away as I knew I couldn't travel that way again, the effects were just too unreliable. I didn't fully appreciate the fact that I hadn't ended up in the middle of the ocean.

I rested my head in my hands as I felt utterly lost and without guidance. I held Maura's lock of hair within my fingers, closed my eyes and tried to bring back the image of her face in my mind's eye. Her bright smile in that angular face washed away and was replaced with Elise's. I put down the brown tresses and picked up the blonde. This time I didn't need to close my eyes. I could see her smiling and gently cradling our baby. I was desperate to get back and protect her from Queen Mordeth but I didn't know what to do. Before I could stop myself, I picked up the bottle of wine and smashed it against the wall with impotent fury. Red stained the white-washed walls. The imagery didn't escape me.

I heard a distant voice calling my name. I knew it wasn't in my mind even though I felt like I was going crazy. I searched through my objects littering the table and then heard it again. I looked into the broken travelling Mindstone thinking Meda had discovered some way to communicate, like when he found the location of the Queen's army in his half of Joran's Mindstone. I heard it again, but this time I realized it was coming from the street below, not from a reborn God. I looked over the ledge and saw my new friends waving up at me with two girls on each arm, and each of them wore less than the other. I told them I'd be right down, gathered my belongings and then made for the door. Just before I left, I grabbed my sword, shield and helmet thinking that this costume would look more authentic than any oversexed Terrok or emaciated zealot.

At street level Wasil and Ginzo handed me another bottle of red wine which I accepted heartily and drank deeply. They introduced me to the four women but I got lost in their foreign sounding names. Two were supposed to be priestesses from the Isle of the Crescent Moon and the other two were supposed to be exotic dancers. Their costumes were not that dissimilar and I didn't feel the need to correct them, enjoying the flashes of skin in the lamplight.

"He told us he's actually met the Gods!" Wasil laughed as he placed a messy kiss on one of the girl's cheek.

"Is it true?" She asked me through long lashes.

"Actually they were two people possessed by the God Thayer and the Goddess Bashal" I answered truthfully.

The group exploded with laughter, slapping knees and pointing at me humorously.

"And I thought I was the zealot!" Wasil laughed again.

"That reminds me, we met someone this morning that might be able to help you, and he'll be down where we want to be tonight." Ginzo's muffled speech through the large mask was barely intelligible.

"That's right, a merchant from Cragthorne who owns a big ship." Wasil said before drinking from a bottle offered by one of the half-dressed women. "He's down in the harbour. We'd better hurry before the skyflowers start or we'll never get close enough." He steered our group around and started us down the cobblestone street toward the harbour.

I had no idea what he was talking about, but my excitement piqued with the thought of a possible way home without using the Mindstone, even though each method of travel had the same effect on my stomach. Along the way, two women detached themselves from the growing flow of people and attached themselves to each of my arms. They loved my costume and asked where I had bought it from. They rambled off half a dozen different names of shops and merchants, but I just answered that they were my own which seemed to titillate them even further.

Being taller than most had the advantage of being able to swivel my head around and admire the sights, sounds and smells of this fascinating foreign city. Lanterns hung everywhere, colourful banners arched across the streets, vendors sold everything from food to jewellery to masks, and everywhere the costumed carousing crowds made their way slowly down to the harbour. At the entrance to the docks we were stopped by armed guards who pushed back the press of people with thick-shafted spears.

Ginzo, being even larger than me, leaned down to speak a name to one of the guards and pointed to a moored ship through the iron grating behind them. The guard turned and spoke the name to an older man on the opposite side. The older man nodded and relayed the name to a dirty-looking boy who ran down the docks, disappearing in the bustle of workers who were busy loading ships even at this hour of night. Wasil handed the guard a bottle of wine that was accepted appreciatively and drained quickly between the two bearded toughs. After the last drop, he swung the bottle overhead where it arched beautifully in the coloured lamplight, bounced off the hull of the closest ship and plopped into the dark ocean water.

The crowd, now assembled on the rotunda built around the main harbour quay began to sway and sing a song that defiantly proclaimed its independence and superiority over the other provinces and kings, and heralded the beauty and grace of their own Countess Deanine. I noticed a stage, centered in the rotunda where a man, dressed in foppery, tried to quiet down the crowd and gain their collective attention. He finally had to speak through a funnel and made large hand gestures but we could barely hear anything from where we stood. I deduced from his body language that it must have had to do with a woman in the audience who stood below him, and her rather large breasts, but instead of being embarrassed, she made her way up onto the stage and paraded her goods to the applause and rowdy cat calls from the crowd. The guard answered my unconscious question with a rather possessive response, "That's our Countess now isn't it, and a more beautiful woman can't be found." From this distance I couldn't argue with him.

Wasil tapped my arm as the dirty boy returned with a well-dressed man in tow. The women on our arms moaned in disappointment as they had to remain on the opposite side of the gate, but Wasil and Ginzo promised to return shortly before the skyflowers began. The guards smiled at the forlorn women as we unmoored ourselves from them and were allowed passage through the gate. The old man locked the gate behind us, muttered his displeasure at missing the sights happening up on stage and then climbed back up on the wooden cask. The boy messenger climbed up on a barrel to stand beside the older man and both produced pipes in their teeth, arms folded over their chests, appearing like past and future versions of the same person. The boy's cat-calls were picked up by the older man as we shifted our way past them.

"This had better be the young man you spoke of and not some shit-eating soldier from the Countess's court or you can kiss your Pandrosian wine supply gone and your arse's goodbye when I kick you off of this dock." The well-dressed merchant spoke harshly to Wasil and pointed a ringed finger at my face.

Wasil assured the man by comforting him with soothing words as we walked away from the crowds, down the dock and towards the ship. Ginzo was still waving goodbye to the women on the other side of the gate who were planting kisses on the guards when he tripped on a large coil of rope. I caught him before he fell into the water and pulled him upright as he swore loudly and finally took off his large hairy mask. He thanked me and tried to blow a kiss back to the women but they had forgotten all about us and the guards as well as some well-dressed young men walked by, teasing them away with full bottles of wine.

"So what's your business with Cragthorne, boy?" The merchant asked me bluntly.

I was taken aback by his gruffness, but then hesitantly told him the tale of my arrival on the island and about my need to get back to the mainland. He didn't look convinced so I named King Gavin, King Arian, Lord Trevor and the Lore Masters to give my tale credence. He looked from me to Wasil and then back with a look of incredulity. He sighed, shook his head in agreement, and invited us onboard his ship. Wasil's sigh of relief was audible as we climbed the gangplank and stood on the deck of the ship. Tables had been set up with food and drink for tonight's festivities and he offered us to take our fill. Famished, I ate my fill and downed a flagon of honey-coloured beer that was refreshing and demanded more.

"Gillian Peacock at your service, but my friends call me Gill." The merchant rolled an olive between two gem-encrusted ringed fingers. "Your timing is impeccable as the entertainment is about to begin." He clapped his hands and popped the olive down his throat.

Women clad in silk scarves appeared from under the wheeldeck. Coins hanging from tassels clinked against their olive-coloured skin as they flipped and spun to the fast hip gyrations. As the women danced around the deck, musicians appeared and began to play fast tunes to match the fleshy spectacle. We clapped in time and were rewarded with flashes of hidden delights and winks from dark-lined eyes.

Gill leaned forward and spoke quietly. "I am thinking King Gavin might reward someone for your return, am I right?" His grin split his face as he kept his sights between me and the dancers.

"I can't speak for King Gavin, but my liege-lord, King Arian would be most grateful." I hoped that didn't taint my value.

"One King to another, it makes no difference." He rolled his shoulders. "You're in luck my friend, for I sail to the mainland in two weeks." He had a black bit of olive stuck between his large white teeth. My hopes for a quick return began to sink. "I have some, um, unfinished business here." He placed a large ringed-finger against his nose. "Some private business with the Countess if you catch my meaning." He laughed out loud. "Now *she's* a dancer!"

"But I need to leave tonight." I stood to my full height. "There's a war happening right now! My friends, your countrymen are dying as you drink and celebrate. I can help end it, but I'm stuck here on this god-forsaken island!" I said that louder than I'd expected as heads all over the ship and down on the docks turned to see who had just insulted them.

An explosion went off above my head and I dove under the nearest table. I thought Queen Mordeth had found me until I saw coloured lights spilling overhead and heard the merchant laughing and clapping. The bright lights and explosions continued loudly as I crawled out to see what was happening and watched in fascination as skyflowers bloomed in the night sky. Myriad colours and formations continued to explode above as Wasil and Ginzo found themselves waltzing around the deck with the silk-clad dancers. Sailors joined them and passed the women back and forth in formation. It was too much for me.

"I'll find someone else who can take me." I said angrily, gathering my shield and helmet and made my way over to the gangplank through the dancers.

"Wait! Thomas, don't go!" Gill shouted behind me.

As I turned to leave I noticed a commotion coming from the centre stage area on the quay. The man dressed in foppery was stamping his feet on the stage which appeared to be catching on fire. The skyflowers were not being launched up into the air anymore, but instead were exploding directly into the stage from below. The apparatus being used to launch the skyflowers was located on a flat barge sitting just below the stage at water level, but the men who were lighting them off were panicking and screaming as they tried to fix the failing series of tubes. With a final lurch, the tubes fell forward and were left pointing in the direction of the docked boats like a wall of fire-breathing dragons.

I raised my shield as the skyflowers exploded and felt something bounce off of it. I peeked over the rim to see what it was and heard a fizzing sound from the docks below where a skyflower slowly died out in a stack of oiled sailcloth that burst into flames. Chaos ensued around the docks as the skyflowers lit sails and wood on fire. Voices cried out for the dock-watch and for more buckets. The ship lurched as oars struck the water in an attempt to pull away from the burning docks and adjacent ships. Captain Peacock yelled through a deck opening to the men below directing them to pull on one side and push on the other. The ship couldn't escape the clutches of the fire as a heavy chain and padlock firmly affixed it to the dock. One of Captain Peacock's sailors was sawing desperately at the chain and quickly looking over the rail after each attempt. He saw me approaching and asked me to keep an eye out for some fancy dressed men as he continued trying to cut through the chain. I asked him what they looked like and why didn't he just unlock the chain.

"These are the Countess's big idea aren't they? She locks us to the docks until we pay her excise men the taxes owed for doing trade with them." He kept hacking away at the wrist-sized chains, but was barely making a scratch.

"Why aren't we free yet?!" Captain Peacock yelled after the sailor. As the man looked back at the Captain to respond, the ship lurched sideways suddenly and he cried

351

out in pain. The slack chain tightened around his fingers, crushing them and sent blood dripping down his forearm as the Countess's chain claimed its unpaid tax. My sword was in my hands and with a single slice I cut through the chain, sending the still padlocked portion into the dark water below, releasing the sailor's mangled hand from its clutches. A smaller ship that was docked opposite us burst into flames and showered burning embers out in all directions.

"GET US OUT OF HERE!" Captain Peacock screamed above the chaos.

The ship turned slowly and nosed out into the harbour just as two men dressed in gold-looped coats shouted up at us from the still-floating dock, the padlock and chain the only evidence that we had been there.

"You there, come back!" One of them shouted.

"Look, it's a blue lock too! You are thieving scoundrels!" They were the Countess's excise men and were reading aloud a proclamation that Captain Peacock hadn't paid the tariffs on his loaded cargo and that his ship was now forfeit. The coloured locks were their way of keeping track of how much was owed and what kind of cargo the ship carried. They didn't notice the dock burning around them until the document they were waving at us caught fire along with the lace trimming their gold coats. They looked around in desperation and at the very last moment, held hands and jumped into the water to avoid being trapped at the end of the pier.

Captain Peacock appeared beside me and looked curiously at my sword and then back at the man who clutched his bleeding hand with the other. "You owe this man your life Kassim. Head below and have the women tend to your hand. You're to be back within the hour for first watch." I sheathed my sword from his gauging eyes. "How did you do that? That chain is designed to avoid anyone cutting loose prematurely." He grinned again. "That was my bit of unfinished business I spoke of, so it looks like you are in luck after all my friend. We'll make for the mainland tonight, not in two weeks as I said earlier."

"Thank you, but I can't possibly afford to pay you for this voyage, despite what Wasil or Ginzo may have said." His eyes widened with surprise at mention of payment.

"Young man don't be ridiculous, you've just paid for a round trip journey if you require it." He hesitated and made a screwed-up face, "Although, after she hears of this incident, the Countess will want my head, or perhaps something else more delicate." He smiled weakly and raised a glass of wine as his eyes wandered down.

I watched the inferno happening in the harbour and heard people screaming in terror as the flames began to leap across the docks and into the city. Chaos unfolded quickly bringing death to the unsuspecting revellers. Boats, engulfed in flame, slowly sank below the glittering water to their deaths still tied to the unbreakable tax chains, carrying their valuable cargo to a watery grave.

It seems we were the only ship to escape the destruction. Small rowboats hovered around the entrance to the harbour, picking up the sailors that had swum to safety.

Wasil and Ginzo stood at the rail beside me, tears streaking their faces. They mumbled their confusion at the terrible ending to their night. Festivale would be remembered this year as a tragedy, not a celebration of the year's success. The dancers approached and comforted the men with soothing words and glasses of wine, then showed them to the food tables as the men sobbed into their gauzy silks. Food rolled from the table when the sails picked up a strong wind as we cleared the coast.

The water was relatively calm as we sailed northwest and because of that, my stomach remained friendly. I moved forward and stood in the bow, scanning the horizon for any signs of land. My eyes were drawn down to the reflected moonlight when I noticed the maiden carved in wood decorating the prow, as she slowly dipped in and out of the dark water. Her hair was yellow, her upturned eyes blue and from her waist down the fish scaling was painted a light green. She reminded me of Elise, but the Elise from the Isle of the Crescent Moon on the night of our coupling, mysterious, naked and unknown, not the woman trapped behind castle walls, pregnant and vulnerable. I looked up from the reflected moon and prayed to the Goddess Bashal, to Sarha de Cent, to keep Elise safe until I returned.

I was returning to them, albeit slowly, but this time I wouldn't fail. My resolve was set and soon Queen Mordeth would join her son. My hand rested on the Mindstone within the satchel, the stone that would stop her heart and free us from the God Eth's tyranny. I would send the God back to its Creator.

Later that night, curled up alone in the prow, I was awakened by the familiar humming of my sword. It stopped shortly after it began and I soon drifted back to sleep. I dreamt of running down dark hallways and always close behind me, searching, chasing, the red eyes of the Skull of Power pursued me hungrily.

TWENTY THREE

Tears

Knowledge is useful;
To enlighten the dim,
To augment the lesser,
To decimate your enemies.
~Book of Thayer

A stick in the ribs awakened me, and as I adjusted to my forgotten surroundings and rolled over to stand up, the muscles in my lower back decided to protest. My fingers were clenched around the hilt of my sword which had become buried in the ships railing. The source of the pain in my back was a result from sleeping on my shield, boss side up. I swore from the pain and then realized I was being watched. All hands on deck were focused on me as the assembled crew scrutinized the strange swearing foreigner.

"Are you, okay, Thomas?" Wasil asked, holding the long pole that woke me. I couldn't help but notice that it ended in a long iron hook. He had hesitated, however briefly, when asking how I was. Did he think I was losing my mind?

"Other than my back, yes, I feel fine." I looked again at their engrossed looks. "Why? What's happened?"

"You were screaming in your sleep and flailing that sharp sword of yours around." He put the pole down gently. "Are you sure you're okay? It sounded like two people arguing, but there was only you."

"I'm fine." I couldn't tell them about Queen Mordeth and the fact that she had been possessed by the God Eth. "It must have been a nightmare." One of the women, now properly clothed handed me a cup of something steaming and pushed it into my protesting hands claiming that it would revive me, and dispel the evil still lurking about.

The bitter black liquid was hot and soon I felt the cobwebs in my mind clawed away. I pulled my sword from the railing and apologized to Captain Peacock for ruining the wood. He clicked his tongue and waved his hand in dismissal saying that it was nothing and if it hadn't been for that sharp sword, his vessel and everyone on board would be sitting at the bottom of the bay in Perg. He ushered me over to the tables that now held a banquet of various warm and cold foods. The women picked over the food and placed bits of it onto pewter plates that they placed in front of both of us coaxing us to try the food they had prepared. We sat silently, satisfying our hunger, but I couldn't help notice the measured looks the Captain levelled at me from across the table.

"Forgive me, but you are a very strange man, Mr. Cartwright. Are you running *from* someone or *to* someone?" He slurped an oyster back and flung the spent shell over the deck.

"Well, yes and no." I copied him and threw the empty shell over the rail. The oyster was spiced and pleasant. "I need to get back to Castle Cragthorne and eventually back to my kinsmen who are fighting on Praxis Moors." I didn't know how much to tell him. "There is a Priestess at Cragthorne that I have promised to marry, but I believe her life maybe in danger. Have you ever heard of Queen Mordeth?"

"Some merchants that travelled with me from Cragthorne spoke about some kind of destruction up north, led by a terrible Queen. I didn't know her name until you spoke it, but it suits her, don't you think?"

"I killed her son." I said matter-of-factly.

The silence was palpable as he held another shellfish halfway to his open mouth. "You…you killed her son?" The only noise to be heard was the whip of ropes and the creak of the ship beneath us as the deckhands overheard our conversation. "We had better continue this conversation in my cabin." He slurped back the oyster, threw the shell overboard, rose and walked to the door set under the wheel deck and waved me in. He whispered something to a small sailor and followed me in.

His private cabin was small but well decorated and his bed sat below coloured glass windows that looked back toward the Isle of Holbrook, which was a dark smear on the horizon. The Captain sat at a table that was bolted to the floor and grabbed a flat bottomed bottle of red wine from a cabinet and two red glasses etched with a logo that matched the emblem on his surcoat. He claimed that the wine came from a monastery near Filmount Castle in Lower Doros which apparently made the best red wines in the land. He explained it had something to do with Mount Kali erupting centuries ago, covering the lower province in a thick layer of ash and molten rock. The wine had a rich flavour with a slightly bitter aftertaste.

"Now please tell me, why did you kill her son?" He asked bluntly.

"It happened two days ago, during the battle at Praxis Moors. Actually I killed him at the base of Mount Kali, and then arrived accidently in Perg where I met Ginzo and Wasil." I could hear the stammering in my voice, but I tried to hide it with more wine.

"Do you take me for an imbecile Mr. Cartwright?" He smiled, and reached to his waist, where I knew he carried a dagger. "How in the name of the gods did you arrive in Perg from the mainland? It is at least a good three days sail from here and Knothill Manor is another two weeks by horse if you are wise enough to skirt around the Moors."

"What exactly *did* Wasil and Ginzo tell you about me?" I asked him pointedly.

"They told me that they knew someone who needed passage to the mainland quickly, no questions asked, and price was of no object." He pulled a pipe out from his coat and began stuffing it with a strong smelling tobacco. He offered some to me which I accepted and packed into my own bowl. "They claimed that you carried some valuable jewels that needed to be sold. I might be able to help you with them, but let me warn you son, I don't like to be taken for a fool." He passed me the burning switch. "Two days! Bah, that's impossible."

"They are not for sale." I blew it out and placed it into the ash bowl sitting on the table. "Do you know who the Lore Masters are? Well I've not just met the Lore Masters, I carry two of their Mindstones with me." I still felt nervous telling him so much and exposing myself to a watery funeral.

"Did you kill *them* as well?" He asked sneeringly, hand still resting on his dagger.

"No, Lore Master Joran was killed by Queen Mordeth's son. Well, actually he was killed by my friend Jared who was being controlled by the Skull of Power." I looked at this man with contempt. He appeared to be a man unaffected by anything; a man removed from conflict, a man who slipped through life like an eel through reed-filled waters. "Have you ever had to cut your friends head off as he tried to kill you? Have you ever watched someone you know being eaten alive, and you can't help them?" The colour drained from the Captain's face. "That's how Lore Masters Laban and Mai-Hon were killed." My stomach felt queasy as the image came back to me. "Believe me Captain these are not tales I care to repeat or to share with just anyone."

"Eaten alive?" He stammered. He refilled my glass with wine and tried to recover his composure. "So you've seen this Queen with your own eyes? And was she as terrible to look at as she sounds?"

"No." Tanner's Lodge, the portal, her naked body, the Skull of Power. "No, in fact she's quite beautiful, despite the scarring on her face."

For the next two hours I told him my entire tale, starting with my arrival in Seacliffe and ending with my arrival in Perg. I left out the personal parts about Elise on the Island of the Crescent Moon as I didn't want her image within his head.

He sat back and shook his head in disbelief, looking at me sideways through his squinting dark eyes while I drained the remainder of the third bottle of his famous Dorosian wine.

"My friend, I don't envy your life for one minute. It sounds to me like you are a marked man and that this Queen Mordeth will stop at nothing until either you are dead or she gains that sword of yours. Auger you called it. May I see it again?" He held out a calloused and ringed hand, then scrutinized the blade and hilt like only a merchant could.

Finally he asked to see the Mindstones. I placed them gently on the table, careful not to touch either of them to the sword blade as I sheathed it. He blew out a low whistle.

"Now these are worth more than this entire ship and her cargo." He pulled out an eyepiece like the one Meda had used in the Library and scrutinized first the whole stone and then the cut one. "You said this one was sliced by the gateway created by her son? The Gateway where you lost half your hand?" He questioned as he thumbed the edge, drawing blood. He cursed, then sucked his bleeding thumb. "I can see how, this damned thing is sharper than a whore's tongue. And *this* is the piece of Mindstone that brought you to the Isle of Holbrook?" I nodded. "Then tell me why is it glowing? Are you planning on leaving me?" He asked as he carefully handed it back to me, careful of the edges.

The stone appeared to be glittering on the inside.

"It's never done that before." As I turned it over I could suddenly hear a voice in my head.

It was Meda.

"Meda?" I spoke his name out loud.

"Is that you Thomas? If so, talk to me as a thought in your head." I did as instructed. "Thank the Creator! Where are you? I know that you are somewhere south of us, but that doesn't make any sense." He sounded worried.

"Yes, I'm on a ship right now headed back to the mainland, to a place called Wellspring I think." The feeling was surreal, as if his voice were inside my head.

"What happened and how did you get there?" He sounded panicked.

I explained it all to him quickly, describing everything that had happened since the battlefield, including killing Dermot on Mount Kali and my failed attempt at using the Mindstone to return. Instead of describing what had happened, Meda sent the images so that I saw the battle through his eyes.

I saw myself approaching Dermot on the field, could vaguely hear us arguing and then watched as I swung my sword, shattered the staff and then disappeared in a flash of light. I saw the queen stand up from her throne in confusion, scan the battlefield and then slowly turn her attention north. As her focus was drawn away from the battle, they appeared to wake up from their mind-control stupor and began to wander around aimlessly. Most showed alarm at the carnage lying around them and the bloody evidence in their hands. I could hear myself ordering the men to disarm and return to our ranks before she became aware of her mistake. I could feel myself extending power to Lore Master Quinn's shield, but she must have sensed her son's death at that moment as she loosed a blood-curdling scream that pulled at my soul. As she reeled from the shock, one of her priests reached out to help steady her, but whatever humanity had remained within the woman had fled when her son died. I watched in horror as she grabbed the priest and ripped out his throat with her teeth. The Creature regained control of the army and the second wave became deadlier than the first. The ensuing carnage receded from my thoughts as Meda's voice came back. "We are desperately trying to retreat back to the safety of Castle Cragthorne, but Eth has managed to use Mai-Hon's Mindstone to move its army ahead of us." His voice went silent. "Thomas, I'm sorry to have to tell you this, but Kay and Arian are dead." He was quiet for a heartbeat as the news hit me. "Half of our army is either dead or wounded, and those that have died within its control, are now being used against us."

I couldn't speak and began to cry.

"The Ren-Tigarians managed to save Kay and Arian's bodies and they remain within our power for now." Again I heard silence, but the pauses seemed to imply that he was running. "Thomas, King Trevor is with me and has just given orders to split from our group and will head directly south to Wellspring to look for you and escort you back to Cragthorne." Silence. "Damn, the Ren-Tigarians have joined him."

"Meda, I'm sorry." It was all that I could think of saying.

"Thomas, we need you to end this. May the Creator protect and deliver you to us. Hurry." And with that the voice ended. I buried my head in my arms and cried for my cousin Kay and King Arian.

I had failed them despite my promise.

Night was falling quickly as we sailed into the harbour town of Wellspring the next day. The docks were ablaze with lights and swarming with people in preparation for our landing. Wasil and Ginzo had decided to stay with Captain Gillian and return to Perg at their first opportunity. I offered them a place in our army, but they demurred telling me that artisans didn't know how to fight. Gillian took me aside and handed me a golden locket and chain.

"Please give this to Elise, on the day that you decide to marry." I hugged and thanked him. "It appears that you weren't lying after all. My deepest respect Thomas, and may the Creator protect you. I would have said the Gods, but I remembered they are personal friends of yours." He smiled at that. I thanked him again, wished everyone a safe journey back to the Isle, kissed each of the women on their tear-stained cheeks and walked down the gangplank to meet King Trevor and the Ren-Tigarians who stood behind him, veiled and deadly.

King Trevor embraced me warmly as we shared in each other's sorrow. He told me that Kay died saving his life, taking a sword thrust in the stomach that was meant for his back, whereas Arian was swarmed by a group of kinsmen he had tried to console as they found themselves suddenly released from the Queen's power. He had noticed them first, but when she exploded in rage again, they quickly turned on him and dragged him away from protection, too far for any to reach him in time.

They pulled his head off.

The Ren-Tigarians were brutal in their revenge and recovered both the King's body and head.

But they had been too late.

They had failed to uphold their vow to protect their King.

I noticed Fen Gisar and his priests bow their heads in shame as the story of their failure was retold. Fen would be the one to wear the new tattoo of shame on his face. I felt angry at them, but realized they would torture themselves worse than anyone for failing their King and breaking their vow. In a twist of irony, their allegiance and vow of protection would shift to Trevor, the man they had vowed to kill. Perhaps they had failed because they had been trying to protect the Gods and the Lore Masters as well. They were human after all, and how could a human predict the actions of a God?

We moved up the docks and onto dry land where his horse and another stood waiting to whisk us away. The Ren-Tigarians, as usual, fell into stride behind us, melting into the black city shadows. The few people we passed warded signs of protection when they saw the black-clad warriors run past. We moved out of the city quickly and were on the road heading north and west. As we rode, I realized that they must have travelled straight from the battle to meet me without stopping once and didn't appear to be tired. Perhaps that was part of their self-punishment, King Trevor included.

As we rode I told King Trevor about my sudden disappearance from the battlefield, and my subsequent travel to and from the Isle of Holbrook. He told me that they had searched the dead high and low in the vain attempt of trying to find my body before Meda explained that I wasn't there to be found, that I was in fact miles away to the north, and then to the south. That had only added to the confusion before the Queen's army ran amok.

He was glad to hear that I had killed her son and spat on the ground beside his horse, cursing his body into Petra's warm embrace.

We continued long into the night, but finally had to stop as our horses were winded and began to falter. We set up camp, ate a quick meal and I fell asleep fitfully on the ground beside the fire. It took another two long days, from sunup to sundown, to reach the outskirt of the lands surrounding Castle Cragthorne and as we approached, my heart stopped.

The Castle was under siege.

By our army.

Queen Mordeth's army must have arrived ahead of ours and remained locked behind the massive doors.

From our distance, I could make out naked bodies hanging from the battlements and as we rode closer, panic flooded my thoughts and made me want to vomit and cry at the same time.

They were the bodies of women.

TWENTY FOUR

Vengeance

Why do we abase ourselves before the Gods?
Why do we abscond in abject terror from their displeasure?
Are they not liable for our very lives?
How does one bewilder the divine?
~Book of Man, 6th Century (Heretical Text)

My mind reeled with the implications of what I had seen, but the cool water splashing over my head freshened and revived my wits long enough to sit down and survey my surroundings once again. I sat at a table under a tent facing the grey stone foundation walls of Castle Cragthorne. My eyes drifted up but the tent stopped along the walls less than halfway up. I couldn't see the bodies. I rinsed the taste of vomit from my mouth then refilled the goblet of wine from the dew-covered pitcher. I couldn't look at the bodies. I didn't want to know if she was there.

"Is she dead?" I asked the crowd of people sharing the tent space.

"No, she is not." It was Sarha de Cent, the living Goddess Bashal, and her face was dark with worry. "She still resides within the walls of the castle, but we've lost twelve brave women so far."

Her loss was greater than mine but I still felt relief flooding through my body with the same surge of pressure that the shock of seeing them had done to me before. I covered my eyes and face with my dirty hands. Thank the Creator! But I could still see her face behind my closed eyes. I could still remember the night on the island, her naked body above me, alive and warm, her laugh, the smell of her skin, the dimples in her cheeks.

"Queen Mordeth is demanding retribution for her son. She is demanding you, Thomas." King Trevor spoke quietly.

"She has taken her last victim, my love." Clan Chief Heather dan Kalon spoke. Her face looked haggard, as if she had been crying for days. "Arian will be avenged. I owe that much to him and to my sister." She looked down, the words sounding impotent in our situation.

"She knows she can't leave or we'll cut them to pieces." King Gavin spoke as he filled his goblet with wine. "Thank the Gods we sent our women and children away." He looked at the High Priestess, "I'm sorry, I didn't mean that." He trailed off as he covered his slip by drinking.

"Thomas, may I have Joran's Mindstone?" Meda held out a hand. As I handed it to him, he turned it over and then smiled. "Yes, I believe it can be done."

"What can be done?" King Trevor asked anxiously, his question asked before it could be repeated by all watching the Lore Master.

Meda's eyes began to glow a bright blue as he concentrated. "Well, since I did create the Mindstones, I believe that I can fix them as well." His eyes grew even brighter as he reached within his robe and produced the other severed half of Joran's Mindstone through which he had spoken to me on the ship.

The tent fell silent as we sat in wonder at the power of a living God working before us. His mouth moved silently as ancient words of Lore spewed forth with speed, fingers dextrously touching and pressing different points on the edges of both stones. The Lore Masters gaped in astonishment and surprise as they watched the God Thayer repair the broken Mindstone. Beads of sweat poured down the old Lore Master's face as the strain of channelling the power of a God began to show in his old features. I felt sorry for him because as I studied his face, I could see that he looked older than I last remembered. Being possessed by a God appeared to be more curse than blessing.

Masters Gianno and Lyas both held Meda under an arm and helped him into a chair as the glow faded from his eyes and he collapsed into a heap of loose robes. In his bony hands he held the Mindstone, complete and intact.

"This will be the key to our success." He sounded exhausted. "We will enter the castle under cover of night and surprise them." He smiled weakly with satisfaction. "Your arrival, once again, has proved providential Mr. Cartwright." He downed a glass of honeyed wine. "Now please, let me regain some of my strength before tonight.

370

Prepare yourselves." And with that he closed his eyes and went to sleep where he sat.

The Captains of war began to pour over the table where a diagram of Castle Cragthorne had been drawn to King Gavin's specifications. It was disconcerting to watch both Kings working together as Gavin could have been Trevor's dead brother. Orders began to be issued to the troops for them to muster as the plan was formulated, decided upon and then agreed to by both Kings. Kay had been replaced by two men, and they held their positions with honour. Graham and Geoffrey had both grown into knights in the real sense of the term, no longer untested, their mettle and fate decided upon Praxis Moors.

We heard a voice calling for the head of the murderer, and then a sound from the castle walls. Everyone stopped and looked at me. I felt faint and closed my eyes as Dirk ducked his head under the tent flap. He came in, shook his head and said quietly, "The lass had red hair." I opened my eyes in relief just as Sarha de Cent left the tent. Her loss was greater than any of us could comprehend. She had treated the women from the Isle of the Crescent Moon like her own daughters, and the latest casualty had red hair that matched her own.

I was searching the room looking for someone when I stopped myself, realizing that Kay was no longer with us. Lyas, seeing my movement, came over and offered to take me to see Kay's grave after he realized who I was looking for. As we stepped out into the daylight I couldn't help but

371

glance up at the final swaying movements of the red haired women as her body came to rest against the cold grey stone wall. Sarha de Cent put her bow down and went back into the tent. To save the women a slow hanging death, the High Priestess shot them in the head with one of her red-fletched arrows. It was the only small mercy she could show, but the torture marks stood out darkly against the white skin. The woman looked young, and familiar. I thought she might have been the one serving Kay on the Isle. The ongoing tragedy of broken relationships within my small group of friends tugged at my heart. At least she would be reunited with Kay.

East of the castle (I must have ridden right past it), was Cragthorne's graveyard. Mounds of grass-covered earth littered the slow rolling grasslands and staring at me were two wooden boxes, their lids held down with heavy rocks and were being guarded by two torches and an old soldier who walked with a heavy limp and eyed us warily. He saluted Lyas as we came closer, and then thanked the Captain when he handed him some food. He limped away to give us some privacy. The bandages around his left thigh were stained with dried blood.

"We were going to take them back to the Isle of the Red Oak, but King Trevor thought it better that they lay here until the war is over, and the Queen's power can't influence them. Once she's dead, their bones will be interred in Tyre." He smirked. "Your cousin will lie with the Kings and Squires of old." Lyas clapped me on the shoulder. "I'll let you say your goodbyes. Don't take too long as we've got a long night ahead of us." He turned back to the camp, leaving me to stare at the boxes that looked too small for the men I remembered.

Arian's was clearly identified by his name and the telltale carved crown. Kay's was less auspicious, and below his name someone had carved – 'Valiant and Brave'. Seven months had passed since I first met the King, but during that time I had grown to respect and even love him. Memories of Kay went much deeper. I remembered as a kid he had poked his smiling face through the door of my father's shop and pretended to be Mr. Scat, calling me and my father both lazy idiots and demanding something ridiculous. I spoke to each of them about the trials ahead of me and then apologized for not being there to protect them and for not killing the Queen when I had the chance. I prayed that they wouldn't judge me a coward and promised that tonight's plan would finally see them avenged.

"Don't make promises you can't keep." The disembodied voice startled me. I looked for the old soldier to see if he was toying with me, but he was sitting a short distance away, quietly enjoying his lunch. "I'm right here you great lummox." Kay slowly materialized in front of me.

I fell backwards onto the grass and stared up stupidly. "But, but, you're dead."

"Yes, and lying there in that wooden box." He sat beside me and appeared transparent, like a reflection on water. "Thomas, I've come to warn you. Don't listen to her."

"To whom?"

"Hadiya. The Queen." His face betrayed no emotion. "Eth has taken control over her spirit. When she talks, it speaks."

"Why would I listen to her? I want to kill her for what she did to you, to King Arian, for everything that's happened." I couldn't understand his warning as it didn't make any sense. Him *being* here didn't make any sense.

"Don't blame yourself for our deaths. Arian died defending the people that he loved and I died defending Trevor." He smiled at me. "Thomas, you are going to be a father."

"How would you know...," I trailed off, "Is it a boy or a girl?"

"You'll have to wait and see." He began to fade. "Heed my warning." And then he was gone.

"Wait! Tell me! Is Elise going to be okay? Kay! Kay! Is she going to die?" I was screaming into the air.

"Mister Cartwright?" The old soldier stood in front of me, hand on sword. "Is everything all right here?"

"Did you see him? He was right here! My cousin Kay was right here!" I felt like I was losing my mind. I started to cry, and then held my hand up to my face to hide my shame from the old soldier. I had so many questions I wanted to ask Kay, but he had disappeared just as mysteriously as he had appeared.

"Your cousin was a good man. He gave his life saving our King. There is no greater honour a soldier can ask for." He stood quietly as I tried to regain my composure. "Sir, a group approaches. They have swords." He warned me.

"First I find you emptying your guts, now I find you emptying your soul. Soon there will nothing left of you Thomas!" I looked up and saw the serious faces of Wasil and his younger brother standing beside him. Captain Gillian stood slightly behind them with his serving women, who had left their silk scarves behind and were now dressed in leather armour. Magnificent horses and a covered wagon stood behind them. "Did you know them?" Wasil asked as Ginzo helped me up from the ground. I explained the significance of both men which garnered their respectful comments and embraces of comfort.

"Then let us drink to their memory." Gill stepped forward, proffering a wineskin from which we all took a swig and finally splashed a small amount on each coffin. It was not wine. The amber liquid burned all the way down my throat and into my stomach. It felt wonderful and helped me to forget what I had just experienced. The old soldier, Ceowulf, as introduced to the women, held onto the wineskin and smiled appreciatively.

"Sorry, but what in the name of Petra's teats are you doing here?" I asked Captain Peacock.

"Nice to see you too Mister Cartwright," Gillian said with aplomb, "but, it has to do with my cargo," he waved at the wagon, "and your story. The night you rode from

Wellspring we all agreed to try and help you and your cause in whatever way we might, because as you said, the safety of all the provinces is at stake. If the Queen can attack Manath Samal, Upper Doros, Lower Doros, Torcal and now Pandros, what is to stop her from attacking the Isle of Holbrook?" He put his arm around my shoulder and led me to the cart where he pulled back the canvas cover. "Perhaps this may help."

The cargo explained the reinforced springs, heavy axle, steel rimmed wheels and the large draft horses pulling it. Weapons and armour filled the cart, enough to equip our army.

"There are also six barrels of beer, three barrels of wine and several large sacks of food in the other cart, but it is a day or two behind us." His smile was in answer to my stupefied look. "I've also got three of the best guardsmen I know." In answer, the women unsheathed their swords and flashed them in a show of skill and craft. "Guards*women* I should say." Ceowulf whistled with approval.

We made our way back to the camp where we were met by sentries and were shown to Master Gianno. King Gavin broke out of the meeting to meet the Captain, whom he apparently knew personally. The arriving party was greeted warmly and treated with respect when their cargo was revealed. Master Gianno's open mouth was the only answer Gillian needed to confirm the timing of his visit. He refused payment, his stipulation being that after the war he would be able to sell his goods once again in Tyre. He told us that the city's merchant guild had black-balled him over an incident of unpaid taxes a couple of years back. He eyed me cautiously when telling the tale, but I held my tongue. King Trevor accepted the weapons and armour as payment for the unpaid taxes. Gillian said that the Goddess worked in mysterious ways, and then swallowed his words as Sarha de Cent thanked him personally. As a sailor, Captain Peacock had spent his life praying to and offering sacrifices to the woman now standing before him. She helped him to his feet and dismissed his supplications.

Wasil and Ginzo were equally stupefied when I introduced them to Meda, whose eyes were glowing blue once again. They apologized for their disbelief and offered personal service as dog-bodies to the God, claiming they weren't fighters, but artisans. He held them to their offer and had them running around the camp doing his bidding in preparation for the night's assault, which would include them having to follow him into battle. After their faces regained colour, they took the task to heart and draped themselves in blue silk scarves offered by Gillian's fighting women.

As the sun settled, we noted the lack of soldiers along the upper battlements of Castle Cragthorne, and after night finally cloaked the land in darkness we could hear chanting coming from within the castle. I asked Dirk what the chanting meant and he told me that when they performed the ceremony at night the next day would see another tortured priestess hung from the walls.

My heart sunk. What if they were torturing Elise as we were waiting for nightfall?

We needed to infiltrate the castle now while they were distracted.

King Trevor gave the notice and Meda used the restored Mindstone to open a gateway.

Our small group found ourselves within a dark and abandoned storeroom in the bowels of the castle as directed and led by King Gavin and his remaining men. Lore Master Quinn Korid joined and protected our group with his words of Lore as we filed into the room behind the King. Torches were lit by Laird's words of Lore as we joined ranks, causing the rats to scurry away from the sudden brightness. Meda wished us luck and closed the gateway behind himself and Donato. Both of the Lore Masters were going to enter the castle through a different gateway with King Trevor and the remainder of our army.

Fen Gisar and six of his veiled black-belted warriors remained with us while the rest joined the main army. King Gavin searched our faces and got a reaffirming nod from each one of us before he took a deep breath to steady his nerves and opened the oaken storeroom door.

The doors had been locked from the outside.

The chains could be heard rattling against the wooden doors. He cursed silently. I stepped forward and slid Augur through the doors above the lock, quickly swiped the blade down, and heard the severed chain and lock crash to the stone floor, breaking the relative silence with the sounds of clanking metal. The men warded symbols in the air upon witnessing the power of my mysterious sword and I heard Lore Master Laird whisper "Nothing shall block the path of the Sword of Prophecy". He smiled in the faint light, "As prophesized in the Tome of Lore."

As I stepped back into the room, one of King Gavin's men opened the door and went out into the hallway, shoving his torch ahead of him. He swept it back and forth then put his head back into the room and gave the all clear. We spilled out into the large corridor and searched the unfamiliar surroundings. I saw the remnants of the chain and lock on the floor and was surprised to see that they were relatively new looking. King Gavin noted it as well and told us that Queen Mordeth must have put it on, but why here, in the bowels of the castle?

We heard stifled sobbing coming from down the dark corridor behind us. Fen Gisar nodded to his men who disappeared into the darkness, somehow seeing without the use of our torches. They were gone briefly.

"I believe they are keeping the priestesses down here." One of them said matter-of-factly.

I was ahead of them in an instant, running as fast as I could, shoving the torch I had grabbed from King Gavin's man ahead of me in desperation. The flame blinded me temporarily as I ran into iron bars and was knocked backwards, throwing the torch from my hands. My head ached, but I ignored it as I said Elise's name and spat blood from my mouth.

My heart sank when I saw the priestesses huddled against the stone wall behind them. They cowered and covered their faces and naked, bruised bodies. I called out again for Elise and when they heard the desperation in my voice, their startled faces looked up as one.

"They've just taken her!" One of them said, sniffing back tears. "Is that you Thomas?" She asked as she tried to make her eyes adjust to the brightening darkness.

"Yes! Yes! It's me!" I made short work of the chain and lock and opened the iron grating into the room. The stench hit me first. The women were embracing themselves, covered in their own filth but their sobbing turned from sorrow to relief. I unhitched my cloak and covered their nakedness as the other men behind me began to do the same. There were not as many as I remembered when we had left for Praxis Moors. "Where did they take her?" I asked and noticed that the closest woman had bite marks in her upper arm that were bright red and raw.

"They've taken her." She began to sob again. "Why are they doing this to us? How long have we been here?"

King Gavin issued orders for three of his men to gather the women and bring them behind us.

"Protect them with your lives."

My mind swooned in desperation and Fen Gisar had to restrain me from running up into the castle. "Let's do this the right way Wielder of the Sword. We'll lead you into battle but you must not let your heart rule your mind. Desperate men are dead men." His ice blue eyes calmed my rattled nerves. I nodded my head reluctantly.

Fen surveyed the group and then issued three of his men ahead down the opposite way toward a stairwell that would lead us up into the castle.

We quickly made our way up to the next level, encountering nobody as we moved silently from the stone covered floors of the castle foundations to the wooden floors of the upper level. King Gavin indicated a direction to the left that would lead us to the main assembly hall where the ceremony must have been taking place. I noticed a dark stain on the floor. The King followed my eyes. There were stains up and down the hallway that we stood in. He looked back at me and then tightened his grip on his sword. "Let's finish this."

Fen Gisar's men moved ahead of us silently, motioning to us as they reached a cross corridor. We passed stains more frequently as we reached the working rooms within the castle, stains that had candlesticks and tools lying nearby. The chanting was getting louder. Quinn Korid cautioned us and increased the umbra of his protection slightly with some softly spoken Lore. The strain of his concentration was beginning to show on his face. There were more white hairs in his beard than red from when I had first met him.

The Ren-Tigarians cautioned us from the end of the corridor as the pulsing light of a fire brightened the hall walls. They jumped around the corner and pulled back some struggling bodies that fell to the ground quickly in their deadly hands adding more stains to the floors. They motioned us forward and we fell in line behind them. The chanting grew louder and I knew that the ceremonial sights were just around the corner.

Elise.

My hands began to shake and I felt like I needed to vomit.

Augur began to hum to the same cadence of the chanting and the metal began to glow white as its heat grew in intensity.

"The Gods protect us." King Gavin spoke quietly, breaking the spell I felt I was falling under from the chanting. He rounded the corner and went ahead of us into his Hall. Lore Master Laird began to mouth words of Lore, creating a twisting whirlwind of air within the enclosed space of the hallway. As he stepped after the King, he pushed the whirlwind ahead of himself into the Hall.

I followed in behind both of them and stopped in my tracks as the scene unfolded before me. The men with me began to slice and cut the mesmerized hordes of men that swayed and chanted before the God of Death. Sitting on her ghoulish throne of bones, Queen Hadiya Mordeth smiled benignly down on her followers. In the middle of the room a large fire burned and turning slowly on a spit rod was a bound man, blackened and disfigured, but a man nonetheless. Beside the Queen, on a table covered with red velvet cloth laid a nude woman who struggled at the bonds holding her ankles and wrists.

Her slightly pregnant belly was noticeable.

Elise.

Priests, naked and scrawny clambered around her, mouthing and licking her body, pricking her with tiny sharp knives that drew blood and stained her white skin and blonde hair. One of the priests climbed on top of her, his hard-sex betraying his intention. A line of others stood behind him urging him on, administrating to their own sex in anticipation.

My eyes flared.

My mind sped up and the movements around me slowed to a crawl.

I moved as a liquid between the bodies being felled by our men.

Augur cut through any impeding body, leaving a trail of death behind me.

My throat hurt as I shouted Elise's name in a desperate plea to stop her from being raped.

I couldn't move fast enough.

Even as I shouted her name, the priest thrust his sex inside of her, smiled at me and used his knife to draw a thin red line across her perfect white neck.

Her head rolled towards me as she heard her name being called and I watched through blurry eyes as she recognized me and mouthed my name. A trail of blood dripped from the corner of her mouth as she smiled.

I found myself at the base of the dais. I leaped up and severed the priest's head in two through his grinning mouth, sending the top half flying backwards into the line of the surprised and excited priests who waited in line for their turn to rape. They scrambled after the skull and began to eat the offered snack. I stood over Elise protectively and swung my sword around in an arc at the other gathered priests, severing heads and arms that had been raised in a useless gesture of protection.

I looked down at Elise who watched me lovingly. After cutting her bonds, I put my sword down beside her and cradled her head in both of my hands, calling her name and reassuring that I had come back to protect her. I brushed her hair back trying to wipe the filth from her face, but I only managed to smear her white skin with more blood. She tried to talk, but blood welled up from the weal on her neck. I shushed her and told her not to talk. Tears poured from her eyes as I kissed her gently on the lips, telling her that I was here and that she would be okay. I told her that the Goddess Bashal was here and that she could heal her, but she had to lie still to stop the bleeding.

"At last," I heard a voice behind me, "the gift is finally mine." Queen Mordeth held my sword in her hand. Her voice sounded deep and sultry.

I put Elise's head down gently and turned to face the Queen. Fury burned within my soul as the beautiful and vengeful woman stood before me in all of her naked confidence. Her eyes burned with desire and were red to match the smoldering eyes glittering in the golden skull that adorned her brown hair. She levelled the sword until the tip touched my heart.

The God smiled and I wanted to kill her and kiss her at the same time.

Once more, I had failed those who I loved.

"Mortal, your life is forfeit." Her face *shifted* as the golden skull with its burning eyes fell lower on her brow. It became the focus of her features as her flesh melted away in lumps like a too-fat candle slumping in the hot afternoon sun. "I am at last reborn." The voice gurgled with delight.

The triumphant look on her face changed to shock as I pulled Laban's Mindstone from my satchel, grabbed the tip of the sword with my other hand and touched the Mindstone to the blade.

"Then let us die together!" I managed to say before my world exploded in pain.

TWENTY FIVE

Cataclysm

Suspicion of the treacherous,
Denunciation of the deceitful,
Condemnation of the contaminated,
The catharsis begins.
~Book of Eth

I floated outside of time and place within a void that was devoid of any light or life. I was surrounded by an all-pervading blackness that filled my being like river water bloating a corpse. Eth's presence was palatable, like movement in the corner of your eye, or the gossamer caress of a ghost that sends goose pimples up your spine. Hatred, pure and malevolent hid just beyond the ebon night I floated within. It pulsed and burned within my skin. I could feel it consuming the darkness as it searched for my soul, just as a hungry wolf will search a mountain path for an elusive scent. My body ached and burned with a searing, piercing pain.

My dead eyes opened to see Auger, pure and white-hot, penetrating the pale flesh of my chest and lying beside the flat of the blade, the amber light of Laban's Mindstone pulsed in-time to my slowly beating heart. Why was there no blood oozing from my chest? I looked closer and discovered that my life's blood was being drained into my sword. The gluttonous metal was consuming my life, just as it had drained the blood from the Terrok, and the blood from Jared's neck. I had hoped to use the Mindstone to kill Queen Hadiya, but it had betrayed me.

I smiled. The Queen was still gripping the hilt and her lifeless body lay across mine. I had stopped her. My body went cold as the last drop of blood was supped into the blade. I felt my soul travelling into the blade, leaving my bloodless carcass and the hunting God of Death behind. The all-encompassing blackness was replaced with the searing whiteness within my sword. I could sense all of the lives of the beings that had been taken by the blade throughout time, but where I felt solid in my mind, they felt like phantoms.

Except for one being.

She was here and I could hear her sobbing uncontrollably.

I approached her silently and stood above her.

"Hadiya?" I asked uncertainly.

"You!" She accused. "Why did you steal my son from me?" She continued to sob.

I reached out in comfort, and as my hand touched her shoulder, I experienced every moment of her life. I felt her pain and sadness as she was forced to leave the only home she had known, her mother's loving embrace and cede to her father's wish to marry a man she'd never met in a foreign land she'd never even heard of. Her only comfort was in being escorted by her only brother, but that all went horribly wrong. I saw their desperate escape from the bandits, their trek through the mountains during an early brutal winter and her eventual arrival at Lanera only to discover her brother's death when she awoke. That was nothing compared to her treatment by her husband Cadarn, but there was a light at the end of the tunnel of misery when she found out she was pregnant. Joy turned to sadness once again as Cadarn turned his malice against her son. When Dermot was made to leave, it threatened to rip the other half of her heart out, but instead of despair, she defied her husband and finally fled from his cruel grasp.

That was when it found her; a perfect and willing vessel to pour all of its hate into and someone who wanted to hear the promise of vengeance. It consumed her. It made her do things she could and would never do. It made her strut her scarred body around naked for all to see. It lied to her and only now did the realization of her actions sink in. She wept even harder.

But it had found its way here, into the relative sanctity of this sword-realm.

We both felt it searching, and knew what would happen when it found us.

"Don't leave me!" She pleaded desperately.

"I can't stay. I can't help you Hadiya." I argued. "You've made your own choices in this life."

"Choice was taken away from me the day I was born! Do you think I had any choice in coming to this god-forsaken land? Did I choose to be beaten? Did I choose for my husband to abandon me and my son? Eth forced itself into me!" She was shaking with fury. "It *made* me do those things. You must believe me that I had no choice!" She was digging her nails into my arms.

"No!" I didn't want to believe her. Kay's spirit told me not to trust her. "Let me go!"

"What about your choices? You *chose* to kill my son!" She screamed and dug her nails in deeper. "I saw you kill your friend!"

"NO!" I yelled back and pushed her to the ground. "I had to stop him! You turned him against me." I began to cry remembering Jared's dead-eyed stare. "You turned him into a monster!" I turned my back on her.

"You left Maura." Her words froze me. "That was your choice." How did she know about Maura? It must have had something to do with this place. She began to laugh, and as she did it turned into a gurgle. "Did you ever tell poor little Elise about Maura?"

I turned around slowly. She was on all fours. A puddle of blood was forming as her gurgling produced gouts of redness against the white floor. She looked up at me with red rancorous eyes.

"It is too late, I have won." Eth croaked. Hadiya's skin buckled under the possession of the creature, spilling blood from the many opening cracks. I backed away slowly as it continued to gurgle with delight. Her skin peeled away and was replaced with golden scales. It looked like a dragon.

I backed against something and turned quickly to discover what new evil the creature had thrown at me.

389

"Thomas." Jared was there, smiling benignly. "You need to return." My mind reeled with the implications of him being here.

"I'm sorry." Was all I could manage to say to the friend I had killed.

"I was already dead. You didn't kill me Thomas, you freed me." He grabbed my hand. "Now let me return the favour." He touched my forearm and I watched in amazement as his fingers slipped into my arm and began to pump blood back into my body. "The Gods contacted me within this sword-realm and told me how to return you to the land of the living. It turns out that in the great scheme of things, you were supposed to take my life so that I could be here now to help you."

I heard the creature's rasping laughter, malicious and venomous. "You can't escape me that easy, mortal!" It stood and shambled towards us, but as it did a green miasma began to filter down through the white ether. As it touched me, it calmed and soothed my fear, but it had the opposite effect on the creature. It raged back, clawing at the miasma Quinn Korid's Lore produced, buffering me from the creature's attack.

"You have guaranteed my eternal wrath upon your soul. I know what you are Thomas Cartwright. I know who you have loved and she will not be safe from me. Your progeny will end with the death of her child." Eth's vitriolic voice poisoned my ears as it vanished into nothingness. "But first I must repay this Lore Master's arrogance."

I could feel Quinn Korid's lamentation as the evil God took its retribution. His cries filled my mind as the green aura subsided, dissipating into the consuming whiteness.

"Thomas." I heard a soothing voice, but this time it was different, it was a woman's voice. Bashal was calling out to me. "Thomas, you must return now."

My eyes fluttered open slowly. I was staring up at white clouds drifting in a blue sky that was painted on the ceiling. The painting had black sooty marks smeared around it, like a battle was taking place in the heavens, but the painted figures sitting on the clouds seemed blissfully unaware. The sounds of fighting continued to grow and as I slowly regained my wits, I looked down at my chest and saw where my tunic was bloody and ripped open, and then I saw the red scar where my sword had in fact stabbed into my chest and drained me of blood. That further confused me as I knew I had died, just as I knew that I was alive due to the pain that coursed through my body. Sarha de Cent sat cradling my head on her lap and stared down into my face with those eerie green-glowing eyes.

"There you are." She said smiling down at me. "I thought we had lost you forever Thomas." She helped me to sit up slowly and as I did, I realized that I was on the floor, a fair distance away from the dais where I had tried to protect Elise and where the Queen had stabbed me.

Before the morbid throne of bones, Queen Mordeth stood holding Mai-Hon's staff in one meaty claw-like hand

and Laban's Mindstone outstretched in her other, daring anyone brave enough to touch it and die. Blood oozed between folds and flaps along her melting distorted flesh. The evidence of multiple stab wounds defied her ability to remain standing. The golden skull on her head had become animated, red eyes scanned the crowd while the jaws opened and shut spewing out dark words of mind-controlling power. Eth had begun its rebirth by trying to metamorphose the Queen's body, but Quinn Korid's interference had stopped it mid-way, and the evidence was disturbing to look at.

Meda, Donato, Laird and the Ren-Tigarians had the half-human creature surrounded on the dais. Meda held Quinn Korid's staff, protecting us from the creature with words of Lore. Fen Gisar stood behind him holding the unconscious body of Quinn Korid and then jumped from the dais to land on the floor beside us. Quinn Korid's eyes were rolled up into his head, showing white and his mouth frothed as he spouted madness, but he was still alive if barely.

"Heal him." Fen asked the Goddess then leapt back onto the dais taking up formation directly behind Meda.

The battle of the Gods began as power rebutted power, blue against red, hope against despair. Several of the Ren-Tigarians, sensing a point of weakness in Eth's guard, tried to breach its defences and attacked but were turned to lifeless dolls as Laban's Death-Mindstone did its work.

Behind the throne, towering above the dais between the columns appeared the same giant from the battlefield, answering an unseen call from its Master, knocked men back like insects. From my close proximity, I could see that the giant wore a polished metal cap on its head and it appeared to be clamped into its skull, pulling back the surrounding skin with imbedded metal hooks, which drew its mouth into a morbid smile, making it appear to enjoy the carnage it inflicted. The chain around its neck was still anchored, but the smaller man that I had seen leading it onto the battlefield was now just a dangling piece of meat. It reached out to either side, grabbing a column, and pushed, cracking the stone pillars. The floor jolted under the changing pressures, causing the standing men to sway in their attempt to remain upright. The giant looked above its head and snapped a huge wooden beam from the ceiling supports, then wielded it like a club, batting at the men that began stabbing at its feet and lower legs. Friend and foe fled the chamber in terror of the mindless beast's crushing blows.

Sarha de Cent stood and knocked a red-fletched arrow into her bow and loosed one arrow, then another, burying each to the feathers inside the giant's eye sockets. It flailed harder and combed at its bleeding face as it tried to pull the savaging arrows from its brain, even as it fell forward in its final death throes. Its massive body crushed the dais and sent gruesome bones flying in all directions from Queen Mordeth's destroyed throne.

The Lore Masters were thrown back by the body of the falling giant, but even as it crumpled onto the dais, the Ren-Tigarians, who had judged the giant's fall faster than any, pulled them to safety. I cried out and rushed forward, and saw that somehow, miraculously, Elise's body had been thrown clear of the debris. I tenderly covered her naked body with the velvet cloth that she had been lying on and carried her quickly out of the disintegrating room, cradling her closely as I reached the safety of the courtyard outside.

The night air cooled my sweaty face and body as more and more soldiers emptied out into the courtyard. We could hear the roof caving in behind us as the giant's destruction continued to take its toll on the castle. The Lore Masters and the Ren-Tigarians poured out of the castle and surrounded me, the questions were clearly written upon their faces. Fen Gisar must have picked up Quinn Korid as we had escaped as he placed him gently on the ground beside where I held Elise's body. The Lore Master continued to froth at the mouth. King Trevor walked up and surveyed the group. He raised his eyebrows when he saw me cradling Elise's body. One of the Ren-Tigarians, it looked like the last to leave the smoldering building, strode up to the King and whispered something into his ear.

"The creature has fled." He looked defeated. "Did any of you see where she may have disappeared during all the confusion?"

"Eth used Mai-Hon's Travelling Mindstone just before the giant collapsed." Meda spoke, but continued to look at me as he'd done since emerging from the castle. "It's probably just outside the castle walls as I don't believe it can travel very far in its present condition." Lord Trevor barked for horses and ordered his soldiers to begin a detailed search of the surrounding area. Meda leaned in closer to me. "Thomas, you battled a God and I believe you may have injured it." He looked nervous. "Mortals don't injure Gods without repercussions. It will want revenge for what has been done to it. Do you know where it may be headed?"

I couldn't stand looking into his measuring blue eyes anymore. How did I ever get involved in the world of Gods? Why did my actions and my life deserve the attentions and now the retribution of a Devine being? I held in my arms the lifeless body of the only woman who had ever loved me, and who had died because of me and within her was the baby I would never see. I didn't want anything more to do with the Gods. "Isn't this retribution enough?" I felt drained. I had lost everything. I didn't care about anything anymore. I felt empty and alone.

"No Thomas, it's heading somewhere. We both feel it." He said as Sarha de Cent stood beside me and placed a reassuring hand on my shoulder. "It is determined. Forgive my intrusion." Meda placed a hand on my head and gazed into my tear-stained eyes. I could feel him probing through my thoughts. He looked at Sarha de Cent, and then took his hand away. "I need to speak with the King."

"Can you help me?" I asked the Goddess.

"If I can." She smiled benignly down on me.

"I need you to bring her back to me." I kissed Elise's head.

"Thomas, what you ask is beyond my power. She is with the Creator now."

"NO!" I yelled it out louder than I had meant to. "No. I will not accept that. I have given you everything that you have asked of me. You are the Goddess Bashal!" I stood up and placed Elise's head gently on the ground to confront her. "You brought me back from death so you can bring her back too."

"Thomas, that was different." She said quietly as Meda returned with the King in tow. "There was life still lingering within you. It was important to save you because our work here is not yet finished."

"No! It's no different! I can't live without her! You owe me!" I pointed a threatening finger at her.

"There is a price you must pay for such a gift," her mood changed, "and for such insolence. Mortals do not make demands of the Gods without a cost." Her temperament became dark and brusque.

"Name it." I would do anything to have her back. To say I'm sorry.

"Thomas..." Meda began, but demurred under the intense green-glowing stare Bashal directed at the Lore Master.

"On your knees, mortal." I did as commanded. "Take hold of my bow." She extended it toward me, while still holding the other side.

"Do you give yourself freely to me?" The bow began to hum in my hands.

"I do." I was prepared for the worst.

"Then Thomas Gavriel Cartwright, I claim your life in exchange for Elise's. When our work here has ended, you will return to the Isle of the Crescent Moon and dedicate the remainder of your life in servitude and obedience to the High Priestess and to me, Bashal." Energy coursed through the bow and entered my body, which caused a spasmatic reaction in my hands where I could not let go of the bow. She bent down and touched a hand to Elise's forehead. Her dead body shook as the energy coursed through her. The priestesses had gathered around us and knelt before Elise's shaking body, shielding it from harm and from the eyes of the growing group of onlookers.

Elise suddenly sat up and drew her first breath.

I cried out with surprise and released my grip from the bow as the energy subsided. I gathered her limp body into my arms as she began to cough up gouts of clotted blood. I called her name over and over again and gently patted her cheek, like rousing a drunk when the barkeep is trying to close up. A low moan escaped from somewhere within her chest and she turned her head upwards to the sky. Her eyes were clouded with a milky-white residue.

"My love! I am here! Elise, please wake up, my love." I combed her hair and kissed her forehead which had finally began to warm up.

She moaned again, but this time she started to thrash about, as if in pain. I tried to hold her, but the priestesses pushed me out of the way.

"What's wrong? Why won't she wake up?" I asked.

"I warned you! I warned you, Thomas." Sarha said. "There is a difference between life and living. She lives, but she'll never be the same woman that you knew." Elise screamed and fought the priestesses holding her down. Blood began to pour from the various wounds that etched her body, but the priestesses had already begun to clean and wrap her. Her moans continued and one of the priestesses looked up at Sarha. Blood began to pool on the ground between her legs.

"NO!" I didn't know what to do. I couldn't lose her again. "What's happening? Why won't you answer me? Why is she bleeding?" King Trevor and Master Dirk held my arms and stopped me from lunging at the High Priestess.

"I have done what you asked of me!" She said, pointing an accusatory finger at me. "I brought her back, but I could not save your child." A look of sadness played across her face. "She is miscarrying, the child has died."

The men pulled me away from the gore as Elise continued to scream. I didn't resist them. It seemed to last forever, but eventually her screams ended, and they brought me back to where she lay bundled on the ground. The priestesses had finally dressed her and removed any evidence of our dead child.

"Elise?" I stroked her hair. She was lying still, staring at nothing with those milky-white eyes. I called out to her again but there was no reaction.

"Thomas?" Meda called to me gently and I left Elise to the priestesses. "We know where Eth is headed."

"I don't care." The Gods had ripped my world away from me, and I cared for nothing save Elise.

"You may." His answer lifted my eyes from the mud-filled courtyard.

"Where?"

"The Isle of the Red Oak." He paused. "Eth has gone to take revenge upon your family."

"Why?" I whispered to the old man.

"Thomas, we still have time to try and save them." He said, trying to reassure me. "But we need to leave immediately." He looked at Elise. "The Priestesses will take care of her until you can return to her." He grabbed my arm. "Thomas, we can intercept Eth, but we'll need help and a little luck. I won't let Eth take your family. I make this solemn promise."

"That promise costs you nothing and me everything." I shook off his grasp.

Appearing from beyond the gate walls, Wasil and Ginzo guided Captain Gill and his female guards into the courtyard, bidden by some unspoken command by the God.

"My God Thayer, ask anything of me. What is your need?" The Captain surveyed the bodies littering the courtyard with an ashen face. He began to sign a protective warding, and then stopped when he realized his God stood before him.

"We need your ship." The Lore Master pronounced. "Lore Masters Donato and Laird will give us all the wind we require." They nodded their assent and help. "Then we'll leave within the hour. Make the preparations."

The mounds of the slain priestesses would crown the hill behind us and the ashes of the Ren-Tigarians would be scattered on the winds when the warrior-priests whirled their strange stones above their heads and sent the souls of their fallen to the afterlife. Fen Gisar would be tattooing his face and the priestesses would head back to the Isle of the Crescent Moon with my beloved, still trapped within her mind and Quinn Korid still trapped within his own. King Trevor and the army had gathered the bodies of his dead brother and squire and were mobilizing for the longer journey home. He had wished me well and had spoken quietly with Meda but his eyes had betrayed the topic of their conversation. The sun was setting behind us as we galloped towards Wellspring and Captain Gill's ship.

My list of life-debts was getting longer, but for those that were still alive, it fell down to two people. My love's debt would be repaid when I returned to the Isle of the Crescent Moon, where I would also try to repay Quinn Korid who had sacrificed his mind to save my life. The priestesses would try and heal his fractured mind back in their Temple but his glittering Mindstone lay muted and dull to match his slack and lost appearance. Before we had left Castle Cragthorne's ruins, Sarha de Cent announced that she would not be returning to the Isle of the Crescent Moon and raised a Priestess named Gavriella as the new High Priestess. The other priestesses didn't bat an eye at this sudden revelation of losing their Goddess and one by one bowed before Bashal to receive a blessing for their faithfulness and sacrifice during their imprisonment at Cragthorne. Lastly Gavriella approached and bowed before the Goddess. Sarha de Cent's eyes glowed brightly as she placed hands on the younger woman's head. She spoke quietly, so that only the new High Priestess could hear her words, but judging by the tears that ran down the woman's cheeks, Bashal was imparting some of her godly powers within her. We left shortly after to nods and muted words of encouragement.

I wanted to know what the former High Priestess wasn't telling us, but I rode along in silence, feeling dead inside. My child was dead and my future bride might as well be. It seemed to me that every time I tried to make a difference or exact some kind of revenge, the people I cared for got hurt. I don't know what I could do to stop Eth and I cringed inwardly at who would die next. My mother? My father? My entire family? I should just keep riding when I hit the ocean and drown myself. Perhaps that would secure their lives.

I had briefly joined the search party for the escaped Queen but we had found little evidence of her passing. All that remained of her was a mound of bloody flesh that buzzed with angry flies and wasps. No Mindstone, no staff, no Skull of Power.

We reached the coast two long days in the saddle later and boarded Captain Gill's ship. I only noticed the name painted across the stern as I clambered up the gangplank, *Huntress*. I hoped her name suited the task. As the ship pulled out of the harbour and turned north, Lore Masters Donato and Laird decided to alternate their abilities four hours on, four hours off and began to fill the sails with their Lore-invoked wind. The Huntress lurched heavily as we began the journey home. The air was crisp with the first hints of autumn blowing in off the ocean and as the shoreline disappeared in a haze, I glimpsed the myriad colours of changing leaves exposed in the forest canopy.

When Donato wasn't filling the sails with Lore-induced wind, Meda had him sequestered below decks and he began to teach the young Lore Master the keys to unlocking the histories hidden within the Stone of Knowledge and how to access them. Just as Sarha de Cent had passed her mantle onto a younger Priestess, Meda was doing the same in preparation for the battle to come. He wanted to ensure that the Temple of the Sky would be rebuilt and that the books that had been lost in the fire could be re-written.

The Library would survive because the Tome of Lore was finally being read.

I sat in Captain Gill's cabin with the Gods and Lore Master Donato, eating my meal in silence. The sheep's stew and biscuit filled my stomach, and kept my mouth busy. I had not spoken with anyone since Cragthorne and I could tell by their glances that they desperately wanted to question me about the events, but had taken my silence as a rebuke for their failure to protect Elise. In part they were right, but I also thought that the less people knew, the better chances they had of surviving the upcoming confrontation with Eth. Eth had read my soul like a book and was targeting the people I cared for the most.

"Thomas," Meda began, "we need to discuss what happened to better know what we face."

"I thought you were omnipotent?" I let the question hang as I slurped the soup.

"These corporeal forms limit our powers, but we can still help you."

"I don't need your kind of help. People have died because of your so-called help. I don't want my family to die because of your help." I pushed the stew away, losing my appetite.

"That is unfair." Donato defended the other two. "Gods can't influence men in that way, only in the decisions they make."

"What's the difference?" I asked as I picked up the wine and poured myself a cup.

"If a man picks up a knife with murder in his heart, only remorse can help him put that knife down. A God may touch a man's heart or mind, not the weapon they hold in their hand." The Lore Master responded, the light reflecting off his glasses made him appear not to have eyes.

"Eth has been the cause of many deaths. It may not wield the knife, but it kills nonetheless."

"You are both right," Meda responded, "and wrong. Now that we inhabit these bodies, we may in-fact wield the knife that kills." He sighed. "Though only one of us is capable of murder. Thomas, we need to know what Eth knows. Please Thomas."

I left nothing out and retold the story as I drained the bottle of wine. Sarha comforted me and made assertions that there was nothing that I could have done. Bringing Elise back from the dead was only made possible because a small spark of life still existed within her. My unborn son. She explained that my son knew he couldn't survive the trauma they had both been through and was only clinging to that thread of life, so that he could give it up freely to save his mother. I began to weep. My son, the hero. My son.

The Gods tried to explain in words what they had attempted to do at Cragthorne. They tried reasoning with The Creature to cease in its attempt at destroying mankind, but they said It was unreasonable, and claimed that its bloodlust had not yet been sated. They then tried to control it as Quinn Korid sought to protect me, but the attempt had failed as the power within the sword had given The Creature greater strength. That strength had ultimately failed when it turned its attention to the Lore Master, and released its hold on me. That slip in judgement had given me enough time to regain control of the sword and use it against the Creature.

404

In the end, like a cornered animal, it had fought back fiercely but when the opportunity for flight appeared, it ran.

It needed the sword to complete its transformation and had learned the only way of getting it was to go after the ones I loved. It was speculating on human weakness and that in the depths of my despair, I would forfeit the sword to The Creature to spare the ones I loved.

I sat silently while I tried to judge these Gods and their motivations. I ran through the confrontation with Eth again in my mind and realized that I would indeed need their help. I couldn't face Eth again on my own and reluctantly agreed to help them in whatever way I could. Sarha placed a hand in Meda's and then each placed a hand in mine. The Stone of Knowledge and the Runes on *Silya* flared to life. I found myself back inside the white place within my sword but watching the events from a different angle. It was strange seeing myself from above. The whiteness blinked out of existence and we were once again back on the ship. I felt nauseous and looked around for something to drink.

"Why didn't you tell us about Maura?" The Goddess asked in an irritated tone.

"It was just a bit of fun before I left." I tried to sound glib. "It's none of your business."

"Thomas, we just witnessed The Creature's words; 'Your progeny will end with the death of *her* child'. It was not talking about Elise, as the Creature believed mother and child were already dead."

I was stunned. "What are you saying?"

"That you have another son, Thomas Cartwright."

Sarha sat silently and ran her fingers over the gilt runes marking *Silya* as her eyes glowed green. I heard the name of my village, Maura's name and the word 'seek'. Her mouth moved silently as her eyes moved back and forth seeing beyond the veil of our reality. The glow faded from her eyes and she smiled, confirming what she had suspected. Maura was indeed pregnant and would be giving birth any day.

"Are you absolutely sure?" I asked and was answered with a nod.

I stared down at my clasped hands on the table, as the knuckles turned white. Knowing about Maura and her pregnancy made me feel worse. My stomach turned with guilt. Not only had I left her alone and pregnant, but I had met Elise, got her pregnant and had chosen to settle down to a life with her. Everything had just changed. What was I supposed to do? I had already vowed my life in exchange for Elise's.

I had a son, and The God of Death was seeking him out.

I hoped Maura would forgive me for leaving.

I hoped I could forgive myself if Eth got to them first.

There was a knock at the door as Captain Gill poked his head in. He produced a tray of wine, cheeses and fruits.

"Those Lore Masters are simply amazing!" His smile spread across his face. "Do you know that we've just passed Praxis Head! That's unthinkable, even with the best winds it would take days, no, a week to travel that far!" He looked around the room at our sombre faces, and then gently backed out, apologizing for the intrusion, and closed the door quietly behind him.

I helped myself to the food and drink, pouring glasses for all. My hand was shaking and spilled some of the wine. It was amber in colour and quenched my sudden thirst. The colour reminded me of Laban's Mindstone, and how I had futilely tried to use it to kill the Queen. I asked the Gods about that and why the Mindstone hadn't worked when I touched it to the sword.

"In essence it did work." Meda began. "The Queen's body was being disfigured beyond description, animated only by the Skull of Power, the power of Eth, but you must understand that Eth is the *God* of Death. The Creature *is* Death incarnate. You can't kill that which is already dead."

"Then how am I supposed to stop it?" I stammered. "How are *you* going to stop it?" I slammed my fist onto the table spilling more wine. "You can't fail me again! You promised!" I felt embarrassed as the words left my mouth, as the truth came forth unbidden. Lore Master Donato looked uncomfortable and excused himself from the cabin, leaving me with the two Gods.

"Thomas," Sarha held a finger under my slumped chin, "we won't fail you." She prodded my head up. "We won't leave you to confront the Creature alone this time. We must do this together. We must embrace the consequences, whatever the outcome." She said this last to Meda who nodded in agreement.

For some reason her words didn't comfort me as they explained their final solution.

TWENTY SIX

Culmination

My heart is torn,
My soul has fled,
Land of the living,
Becomes tomb of the dead.
~Book of Bashal

We arrived in Ambrose harbour where I had set sail over nine months ago on a voyage that had only taken us two weeks of continued Lore-induced wind from Wellspring. The air smelled fresh and the harbour sounds of crewmen loading and unloading cargo was reassuring and gave the illusion of normalcy. I saw the *Merry Widow* tied up at the docks and still sitting on Mr. Mange's shoulders, like a swollen piece of meat, was his hairless cat Beatrice, still alive, still observant of all. It slowly turned its head and gazed at us with ancient grey eyes as I bellowed over greetings. Some things I supposed would never change and that gave me hope for the future.

Meda asked the harbour master if anyone or anything had arrived in the harbour recently that was untoward or bizarre. After looking around confused and pointing at various casks and crates of odd looking sea creatures, Meda explained slowly that he was referring about a woman, more than likely scantily robed and wearing a golden crown with ruby eyes. The wizened harbour master screwed up his face, studying the man before him for any hint of humour, then laughed and shook his head no, but promised if she did arrive, he'd send word onto the King that a beautiful harlot had set foot on his Island. He laughed once more and shared his joke with the men loading the ship beside us.

This was where our group decided to separate. Lore Masters Laird and Donato looked haggard and sapped of life due to the strain the sea voyage had exerted on them. They decided to head directly to Tyre with the news of King Arian's death and the imminent arrival of the new King and army. Meda exchanged a private word with Donato before the younger Lore Master managed a weak smile as I helped him into a waiting carriage. Somewhere during our ocean voyage, the younger Lore Master's hair had gone stark white.

I managed to secure horses for myself, Meda, and Sarha de Cent and as we prepared to leave, I was surprised as Wasil, Ginzo, Captain Gill and his women pulled up behind us on their own horses.

"We must see this thing through to the end." The smiling Captain said. "I want to see with mine own eyes, the end of this foul creature."

"Very well, but don't get in my way." Irritated, I kicked my horse on ahead, determined to make the two day journey before nightfall, which I knew was impossible and would probably kill the horse beneath me, but I didn't care as Maura and my unseen baby filled my thoughts. I could not fail them as I did Elise and my unborn son. I slowed my horse when I spotted something unusual lying in the tall grass at the side of the road. I recognized a pair of worn boots exposed on the side of the dirt trail. The image brought me back to our flight from K'Larn to Jahad's Rest and the bodies that had littered that trail. Flies and bees swarmed in the air over the corpse and the putrid smell of rotting flesh assaulted my nostrils. The others finally caught up as I dismounted and handed my reins to Wasil. Cautiously I walked over to the body, picking up a stick as I did. I gently tilted up and flicked off the hat that covered the body's face which released another torrent of buzzing flies.

The man was middle aged, balding and unfamiliar. I couldn't see any visible wounds on his body. I looked closer at his face or what was left of it. There was a bloody mark across his forehead and the flesh looked like it had been melted like candle wax.

I froze in my boots and dropped the stick.

Meda and Sarha sat their horses behind me and saw the evidence as clearly as I had.

Eth was on the Island.

"It is Quickening." Sarha spoke and when she saw my confused look she continued. "Eth discarded Queen Mordeth's body shortly after leaving Cragthorne. Judging by the state of decay, Eth discarded this body yesterday or early this morning. We can only speculate on how many people have died to bring It here so quickly."

"It increased the travelling ability of the Mindstone by consuming the host bodies faster." Meda's look was ashen. "We must hurry."

"Wait." Something on the man's vest caught my attention. "This man is wearing Scat's insignia." I held my nose and bent closer. "I do know this man. His name was Ulrich, he worked Scat's estate." I stood and approached Meda and Sarha. "His estate isn't far away, we should check there first." They nodded in agreement. I leaped back into the saddle and kicked my horse to a gallop. The others followed and soon we were thundering down the dirt road. The flies and bees went back to their feast undisturbed.

I led them down a left fork in the road onto a manor house estate which was situated northwest of Lillydale. Scat inherited it from its previous owners when raised to Lordship status. It was beautiful and sat picturesquely beside a river where its former owner, Scat's older brother, had been found floating face down in that river, halfway to Lillydale. The official cause of death was reported to be drowning, exacerbated by a slit throat, although that last part was never confirmed as the body had been found days later and was lodged under a log. The slit throat was blamed on the log. Needless to say our village began getting their water upstream for months after until the memory of the body's exact location had been forgotten and the winter swell had washed the log downstream towards the ocean.

Along the trail leading to the estate we saw the telltale lilies that gave our village its namesake. They were turning yellow with the season and as we crested the hill overlooking the estate which was nestled in the valley below, we saw smoke rising from chimneys which proved at least someone was occupying the manor. I reined in sharply when I realized something was wrong. The fields were littered with dropped tools and tacked horses ran amok, still tied to half-filled carts. It was a warning that all was not right on the Scat Estate.

I dismounted and slowly entered the outer fields, trying not to give away our approach. Meda warned me to take caution as we didn't want to walk into farmhands wielding scythes that had been turned by the Creature. I hesitated and asked if Captain Gill and his women could ride to the village to protect Maura and my family just in case things went wrong here. I described the Inn and Wasil and Ginzo agreed to go as well. They would wait until sundown and if they hadn't heard from us, they would escort Maura and my family to Tyre for protection. They left quickly as the God and Goddess joined me.

I could hear my heart beating loudly in my ears and closed my eyes to steady my nerves. When I did, I lurched unsteadily. I felt the Creature's presence. "It's here." I knew exactly where it was waiting and also that it could feel my presence as well. There was no need for stealth.

I realized belatedly that the rest of our group had been sent away uselessly because if the Creature was here and It wanted me to witness Maura's death, that meant that she was here as well. I tried not to panic and swallowed the bile that rose in my throat. I continued walking toward the house holding the hilt of my sword as it hummed in my firm grip.

"Thomas, while we distract the Creature, you can try to safely remove Maura and the baby."

That caught me off guard. I had forgotten about the baby.

"Your son is crying." Sarha said matter-of-factly. "He's hungry and scared." She tried reassuring me with a quick smile but it didn't work. I could only hear the rattle of tack and bridle as the horses walked around aimlessly.

There weren't just tools discarded in the fields. The workers who had been using them had been tossed aside like forgotten dolls. Their broken and bloody corpses lie in the fields where they had spent their lives toiling, becoming a part of their final harvest. Crows leapt into the air, startled from their feeding. I didn't want to see what they were dining on, my concentration was focused on the house ahead, and the God of Death that awaited within.

As I approached the pleasant-looking home, I tried to flush out my emotions, especially the feelings of anger which I knew Eth preyed upon. I steadied my nerves by bringing up the image of Elise to give me strength and courage. I missed her smile. No, I couldn't become filled with sadness as Eth would prey upon that emotion as well.

"Avenge me." I heard Elise whisper in my ear. "Kill the Creature! Avenge your dead son!" My blood began to pump hot as the feelings of fury began to well up in my stomach. The Creature was trying to control me. I calmed down and drained the feeling into my sword.

I heard the baby scream which broke my anger, and filled me with dread. The front door had been left open and as I placed my left foot on the first stair I heard It laugh.

"Welcome to my home, Deceiver." It was Scat's voice, augmented with a rumbling growl. "Come in and meet my family. My wife and *your* son I believe."

I looked to the Goddess for guidance but she placed a finger on her lips to keep me silent.

My hand shook as I pushed the door open further and followed the voice into a large drawing room. Sitting on a bright blue divan, Maura held a crying baby in her arms, gently trying to comfort it with cooing sounds. She was crying as well, the tears staining her beautiful face. She looked at me with a look of joy and fear and shook her head, denying my presence, a ghost from her past come to life.

Standing behind her and the divan, Scat had both hands on her exposed white shoulders, caressing her flawless skin with fingers stained red with blood. His fingernails were long and menacing. He shushed them, but kept his yellowish eyes on me. On his brow sat the Skull of Power, the eyes flaring red to the beating of his heart. The skin under the rim of the Skull was red and inflamed and had the look of melting wax. I didn't have much time before the Creature would need a new host, and Maura was closer than me.

"You remember Maura don't you? Beautiful Maura, supple Maura, juicy Maura? You may not know this, but she's been Scat's loving wife ever since you disappeared." It smiled. "Sharing his bed, his sex," he bent and licked her ear, "his whip." He taunted me to attack with those last words. Maura stifled a cry as he pinched her skin, dripping bright red drops of blood down her white neck. "Or have you forgotten her and replaced her in your heart with that Whore-Priestess, Deceiver." His mocking voice flushed the anger back into my veins. "Wasn't that whore carrying *your* son as well? My but you have been a busy dick haven't you? Scat actually believed that this was going to be his child, *his* progeny, but we know better, don't we?"

"Thomas." Maura stifled her voice. "I thought you were dead. We *all* thought that you were dead." She began to cry. "Scat told us that you had drowned crossing the sea, said he had word from Tyre." She heaved in distress. "I was pregnant and all alone. I had no one else to turn to." She held the baby up slowly, "This is your son Thomas."

He pinched her neck again forcing her to cringe as he tut-tutted, making the baby cry again at the sudden jerky movement.

"Eat it." Eth's voice crooned through Scat's clenched yellow teeth.

Maura blinked. Shock registered on her face.

"What?" She asked. "You can't possibly," Scat's eyes didn't leave mine.

416

He was watching my distress growing and was enjoying it. He was trying to get me to react, to draw my sword. He wanted me to hand it to him. The Creature knew that Augur's power could not be wrested from its rightful heir. It could only be given freely. My hand rested on the hilt. I could feel the heat from the blade in my hand, begging me to draw it.

It sensed the power within the God, calling to it, coaxing it from my grasp.

"I said *eat* your baby!" His smile disappeared. A drip of blood traced down his face from the oozing red weal under the Skull of Power.

The Sword of Prophecy was reacting with the Skull of Power, tempting it.

"Stop this, please." I pleaded.

"Eat it!" Eth ordered. "Now!"

"I'll give you the sword!"

"Oh I know you will, but I want you to watch her eat your son. Your bloodline *must* end here today." It purred words of power. I couldn't look away. "Once it is dead, then I will kill you, but you will suffer first."

Where were the Gods? Why weren't they helping me? Why had they betrayed me once again?

As he said 'suffer', Maura's eyes flitted back into her head as she fell under the Creature's control. She opened her mouth, exposing perfect teeth and raised the tiny squirming body, suddenly held taught between her hands.

417

Why had the Gods abandoned me? They promised! She lifted the baby to her mouth.

"NO!" I screamed, plunging the sword into her chest, impaling her to the divan.

Scat plucked the child from her loosened grip as she groped feebly at the weapon piercing her body. Blood poured from her mouth and down her neck onto the blade where it hissed and disappeared within it.

I fell to my knees and held her face. I called her name over and over again. Her eyes slowly flitted open as she was released from the Creature's power.

"Thomas?" She asked gently. "I thought it was you." She sounded tired. "I had the strangest dream." She smiled as blood continued to trail from the corners of her mouth. "You mustn't leave Thomas. You need to stay here and marry me." Her voice trailed off as she rested her head on my shoulder and died.

The baby cried.

I kissed her forehead and pushed her head back onto the divan, then stood and faced the Creature.

Scat held my son out at arm's length where it wriggled fitfully above the divan, his too-heavy head lolling back and forth just out of reach.

"Give me the sword." It said wolfishly.

"Give me the baby."

He smiled and began to squeeze. The baby flailed fitfully.

"Give me the sword." It said again, more forcibly.

"Thomas, give it the sword." Meda said from beside me. The Gods finally decided to show themselves. They had betrayed me. They watched me kill Maura and did nothing.

"WHY?!" I roared. "Why didn't you stop It?! You promised that you wouldn't fail me again." Shaking with anger, I drew the sword from Maura. Her body fell limply onto the divan. I leveled Augur at their necks. They backed away slowly to stand behind the divan on either side of Scat, hands raised in apparent acquiescence.

"We have unfinished business, brother and sister." Scat smiled. "Now give me the sword, mortal." Its derision spiked my anger.

I held the sword level, gripping the hilt so tight that my knuckles hurt. The baby cried out again uselessly. I could cut all three of their heads off in one scythe. Scat's face began to bleed and the skin began to melt faster in anticipation of finally getting the sword.

"Good." He said, his voice gurgling. "Now give it to me." He squeezed the baby harder as his ecstasy grew.

The baby had stopped crying. Its squirming had stopped.

Blood welled from the points where his fingers had penetrated the soft flesh. Red pools fell onto Maura's still body. Meda and Sarha moved to stand directly behind the Creature, holding up its melting body.

"NO!" I screamed and plunged the white hot blade through the heart of the beast.

He let go of my son. His limp body fell onto his dead mother's.

"Now Thomas!" The Gods commanded, so I pushed the blade deeper, until the hilt touched Scat, impaling the three of them together.

Scat's body shook as he spewed red froth from his mouth.

Augur drained the blood from their bodies.

Scat's shrivelling corpse slumped back into the High Priestess, his face a screaming silent mess.

"*As it was, so shall it be.*" Meda spoke the words of Lore.

The three bodies shrunk together, their life force sucked into the glowing white sword. The light was becoming too intense so I raised my hands to shade my temporarily blinded eyes. A concussive blast knocked me backward to slide across the marble floor, stopping only when I hit the wall behind me.

A miasma of light swirled where the Gods had once stood. The white light of the sword mixed with the red light of Eth, the blue light of Thayer and the green light of Bashal. It swirled and began to shake the foundations of the house. The roof and floor began to rip themselves apart. Sudden hands grabbed me from behind and dragged me out of the room and out of the house. I saw two bodies rush back into the house.

Ginzo dropped me on the grass outside as two of Captain Gill's women placed Maura's body and the baby's beside me. We watched in disbelief as the house crumbled in on itself around a vortex of light. A ball of multi-hued lights rose up into the air from the middle of the ruins and then crossed through the sky, tracing a path toward the sun that was setting in the east behind us.

I cradled my baby and Maura's body and then slipped into unconsciousness.

TWENTY SEVEN

Beginnings and Endings

I've killed friends.
I've killed lovers.
I've killed Gods.
When did I become executioner?
~Book of Thomas Cartwright

I sat on the porch of my parent's house watching birds find the last berries on the bushes as the new season began. My father had died shortly after I had left the Island, receiving the same grim news that Maura had, which left my eldest sister and my brother-in-law to run the family business. They had allowed my mother and other siblings to stay in the house, but my mother had aged visibly after the news of my death and then my father's and she had not been able to care for my younger siblings due to her broken state of mind. She passed away the night of my return as the shock of seeing me suddenly alive and covered in dried blood had driven her fragile mind over the edge. The next day we buried my mother next to my father.

Under an oak tree by the river I dug a single grave where Maura cradles our baby for eternity. A carved headstone reads 'Maura & Baby Thomas'. I cut a lock of hair from each of them before they were buried.

Later that day my sister told me that she was pregnant. I told her that I was happy for her. She told me that if it was a boy, she was going to name him Thomas in honour of me, her lost brother returned from the dead and if it was a girl, Lily, for our mother. But I didn't feel like the same person anymore. I felt this constant nagging in the back of my head to return to the Isle of the Crescent Moon to care for Elise, but I found myself puttering around the shop, helping where I could, but more often than not, I would wander down to the Salt Cellar and drink myself to oblivion. One day, after sharing one of my stories with Mr. Partridge he stopped shy of placing the frothy mug of beer to his lips and looked at me queerly.

"What the hell are you still doing here Thomas?"

"Waiting."

"For what?"

"I used to have purpose. First it was fighting the Queen, then it was having a baby and a wife, but that's all changed now."

"How? She's still alive isn't she?"

"Well yes, but she won't be the same..."

"Do you love her?"

"Well, yes, but..." Just then Mr. Salt walked over and placed the food I'd ordered down.

"Son, we need to talk." He seated himself beside Mr. Partridge. "Now I know you were fond of my Maura, and, well, things happened between the two of you, but when we found out that you were dead, she moved on and married

Mr. Scat and everything was fine." He helped himself to some of the sausage. "You need to move on too. I know you loved her, but she's gone son." He sniffed at some unseen tears. "It'd be best if you went to your other lady friend and leave us in peace with our memories." He stood and wiped the table with his apron. "We've mourned you once son, we don't want to have to watch you drink yourself into another early grave." He walked back to the bar.

I left the next week to my family's protestations. I tried to explain, but couldn't quite express the extent and depth of my loss or grief, and that staying in Lillydale would be too painful. I promised them that I would keep in touch as often as I could, then mounted my horse and rode out of town for good. I told them I was going to the Isle of the Crescent Moon to be with Elise. My sister gave me a loaf of crumbled goat's cheese bread as a farewell gift.

I still send her a letter at least once a year.

I made my way back to Tyre and was given a private audience with King Trevor. He looked like he had taken on the responsibilities of royalty with dignity as he led me into a private chamber.

"Thomas, we missed you at the wedding." He offered me a cup of warm spiced wine. "Heather wanted me to knight you at the ceremony for all that you've sacrificed for King and country."

"I apologize your majesty, but," I began.

"Call me Trevor. I'm still not used to this." He pointed at his crown as he sat opposite me.

"After the events of the last year," I paused, "well, I've tried to keep to myself."

"We can all appreciate what you've been through Thomas, but you shouldn't be trying to cope by yourself." He sipped his wine. "Time heals all wounds, but not as fast as laughter. My grandmother taught me that."

"I'd like to return to the Isle of the Crescent Moon to be with Elise."

"That's a noble cause, worthy of a knight."

"I'll never wield a sword again."

Just then a man entered the room and whispered something in the King's ear. "Excuse me, but I have urgent business to attend." We stood and shook hands. He gripped my maimed hand gently. "You'll always be welcome in any capacity you think fit." He embraced me, slapped me on the back and then left in a flurry. A servant entered behind the King and began to clear the glasses as Lord Fiongall walked past the open door.

"Thomas?" He ducked into the room. "What a pleasant surprise. I was just looking for my brother-in-law."

"You just missed him."

"As we missed you at the wedding." He had returned to the Island to attend his sister's wedding and to gather his family to return to Upper Doros. "I'll be leaving shortly to return to my duties as Clan Chief."

"How is the rebuilding effort coming along?"

"Slowly, but I've convinced the council that we need to build our own library." He smiled. "You can imagine the battle I've had as ours is an oral history." He touched his half-arm. "My daughter has become an excellent lute player to make up for her dad's shortcomings. Perhaps you'll attend dinner tonight? She's planned a small recital."

"Thank you, but I'm not planning on staying."

He regarded me with sympathy and then nodded his head in mutual understanding. His ordeal had been much the same as my own.

"Don't give up hope Thomas. Happiness will return in the least expected places." He turned to leave. "That reminds me, Master Donato wants to speak to you before you leave. Fare thee well." He whistled a melancholy tune as he disappeared down the corridor after the King.

I wasn't aware that the Lore Masters were still in Tyre or that they had been patiently awaiting my return. One of the servants directed me to their chambers and I knocked gently on the wooden door.

"Come in, come in." Both Lore Masters stood over a table with a large map laid across it. "Ah, Thomas, please have a look at this." They pointed to the map. "We were just trying to figure out the best place to discard something that no one should ever discover again. Laird thinks we should fling it into the fires of Mount Kali, but I think we should drop it into the depths of the ocean." The both looked at me with owlish eyes. "What think you?"

I was taken aback. Lore Masters asking for my opinion? "I don't know, it depends on what it is."

"He doesn't know what we're talking about." Master Laird said, poking the younger man in the ribs.

"Maybe you had better take a seat Thomas." Master Donato offered up a soft leather armchair. "A lot of things have happened since we departed company." I sat in silence as they recounted their story, beginning with the fact that Donato was now Master of the Temple.

When King Trevor and the Ren-Tigarians had eventually returned to Tyre, Donato ordered the priests to scour the ruins of Lord Scat's house for anything that may have survived the destruction and to return immediately with anything they found. Buried under the mountain of wreckage they had discovered Mai-Hon's Travelling Mindstone, the Stone of Knowledge, the Bow of Desire, the Skull of Power and most surprising of all, the Sword of Prophecy, all still perfectly intact.

They asked me to recount the events of that day, but only if I was up to it. He told me that Captain Gill had offered a brief description of the events, but there were many holes in his story. After proffering a much needed bottle of wine, I sat back in the chair and retold my version of that day. It sounded a lot shorter when retold, but in the moment, it had seemed to last for hours.

Donato let out a sigh and offered his condolences. "I still had so many questions for Meda," he leaned back, "not to mention secrets I wanted to pry from Thayer." Laird leaned in and whispered something to the new Master of the Temple. "Ah, yes." The younger man said. "The Ren-Tigarians would like to keep the Sword of Prophecy in their safe keeping, but require your blessing and offering of the gift. They vow to guard it vigilantly until the Gods deem it necessary to be unveiled once more."

"They're welcome to it. It's caused me nothing but sorrow."

"Interesting." Donato steepled his fingers together. "There is another name for the Sword mentioned in the Tome of Lore. *Soulblighter*, but I suppose that doesn't sound as romantic as *Sword of Prophecy*."

The silence was broken when the Lore Masters told me of their plan to take the Stone of Knowledge back to the Temple of the Sky where Donato would use it to rewrite the books lost in the fire. The Mindstones would be returned as well and would await new Lore Masters to claim them. The Gateway and the Death Mindstones were being searched for by King Gavin during the restoration of Castle Cragthorne and he had promised to return them to the Temple once they were found.

The item that had begun our conversation, the Skull of Power, would either be dropped into the ocean when they crossed over to the mainland, or brought back to Mount Kali and thrown into its molten core. No one was allowed to touch it and it had been padlocked within a wooden chest in King Trevor's treasury behind armed guards.

"It should be dropped into the ocean." I offered. "Eth was born under that mountain, it stands to reason that Its source of power should be buried as far away from that place as possible." The Lore Masters agreed.

"Which brings us to the Priestess' bow," Donato said, "it must be returned to the Isle of the Crescent Moon. Since you are planning to journey there, could we impose on you to return it to them?" The Master of the Temple asked.

"I'd be honoured." I needed purpose in my life, and they both knew it.

"That's settled then, now, why don't we partake in the festivities the King has planned for tonight? He's gone to great trouble and we may not be together as a group again." The two Lore Masters led me down the corridors and the noises and smells brought a smile to my face.

As I stepped into the hall, the King banged his dagger loudly on the head table and silence filled the room slowly.

"Let us all raise a glass and toast Thomas Cartwright, the man who faced the God of Death and survived, the man who sacrificed everything to bring peace to our land." The room erupted in loud hoorays. I felt my cheeks flush in embarrassment. Two men pushed their way through the crowd and approached me. I barely recognized Graham and Geoffrey through their full beards.

"By the Gods you're a sight for sore eyes." Geoffrey looked older and wiser. Graham looked the same, only bearded. "The King wants you at the head table and we're not allowed to take no for an answer." They grabbed my arms and led me towards the King's table. "We didn't think we'd see you again when you went after that foul bitch, but that sword of yours must have done the trick." We arrived at the table. "We'll talk later." They punched me in the shoulder and made their way back into the crowd. I smiled when I saw them sit down near the table beside two beautiful young women. From what they were discussing it was obvious the women didn't believe they actually knew me.

"Thomas, please have a seat." Heather dan Kalon said in her lilting voice. I sat down beside her. "You look like you've seen better days my boy. Maybe tonight we can help you to forget." She smiled knowingly. "Only the bad things and help you celebrate the good."

"The light in my life has been extinguished." She tried to comfort me with a comforting hand on my arm as the music started up.

A girl, younger than Elise sat on a stool in the midst of the tables and began to strum a lute that reflected the candlelight from its golden-blonde and highly polished wood surface. The haunting notes caught in my chest. A voice picked up the notes as Lord Fiongall walked up behind his daughter and placed a hand on her shoulder, harmonizing the tune with her. It was a sweeping saga that regaled our struggle with the Gods and the ultimate toll they demanded of mankind when confronted by the divine. I stared at my maimed hand when the song lamented the ultimate price of having to sacrifice those that you love in order to save them

430

from a greater evil. The tune faded and there was no applause. There wasn't a dry eye in the place. The King stood and thanked his brother-in-law and niece then called for more wine as a group of musicians entered and began a tune that made people want to get up and dance, which they did.

I excused myself and stepped out of the hall. I found a door that led to a balcony and sat down in the cool night air. I pulled out my pipe and smoked in silence.

"May I join you?" It was the King.

"It's your Castle my liege." I offered him some of my Lillydale weed which he accepted and stuffed his own pipe.

"So you're off to the Isle of the Crescent Moon?"

"Yes Sire. Sorry, force of habit."

"Well, I can't blame you. It's a spot nicer than this place, not to mention filled with beautiful women."

"I'm only interested in one woman."

"Of course you are. Please don't take offence." The glow of his pipe reflected from his kind face. "I suppose I can't talk you into staying?"

"I've made up my mind. I've also given my word to the Goddess." He harrumphed. "I know, I know. They never kept their promises, but I feel drawn back there."

"I know something about forced responsibilities." He laughed quietly. "Can I at least give you a gift? I want you to have this." He unbuckled a sword from his waist. "Please, accept this."

"But, this is the sword you received from the Temple of Ren-Tigar."

"It was passed down to me from my mentor, Barik N'Adir. It is the sword of a warrior-priest. You've proven to me that you are a warrior, and now you leave us to become a priest."

'This is too great a gift. You sacrificed so much for this."

"And you haven't?" His heated voice echoed off the walls. "The honour of a gift is in the receiving, not the giving." He sat back down on the rock ledge. "I have nothing else of more value to express my gratitude, besides, they are planning on taking your sword, it only seemed fitting that you should take one of theirs." He laughed again. "A last spit into their all-seeing eye."

"Then I accept it graciously." I strapped it around my waist. "Thank you." I shook his offered hand. "May I ask you a question that's plagued me for some time?"

"Ask away."

"Why were you sent to our village and not someone else? Surely spreading the call to arms should have fallen on someone else's shoulders, not the brother to the King."

"Scat. Rumours of his brother's death had reached Tyre and I wanted to meet him in person and decide for myself if he deserved the honour of a Lordship." He sighed. "If I knew then what influence he would have had on recent events, I would have drowned him in the river too." He placed his hand on my shoulder. "I owe you an apology for ruining your life."

"My life is not over quite yet. Elise waits for me on the Isle of the Crescent Moon." I smiled at him. "Who knows, perhaps she'll be able to bear more children."

"Well said. Now, let us visit the crypt together to say your farewells to Arian and Kay and then we'll return to the hall. I have barrels and barrels of Pandrosian ale that need to be drunk before this night's over."

Two days later I was aboard *The Huntress* once again. Captain Gill had agreed to drop the Ren-Tigarians, the Lore Masters and Lord Fiongall and his family off in Seacliffe then turn south and take me as far as Wellspring as he didn't want to travel around the southern tip with the winter season approaching. The crossing this time was a little less violent and I shared the final days with my friends in relative good humour. With a captive audience, Lord Fiongall sang more of his new music along with his daughter Lucinda as Captain Gill provided everyone with enough wine to drown our sorrows. The mood brightened when his women appeared in their brightly coloured gauze, swaying their hips and breasts to the assembled men and the fast music. Temple Master Donato even got up and joined the women in their wild dance to our applause and whistles.

We arrived in Seacliffe and said our goodbyes. The Ren-Tigarians bowed as one to me, fist to heart. Fen Gisar stepped forward as the rest of the Ren-Tigarians pulled out those strange noise making rocks and began to twirl them above their heads. He grasped me forearm to forearm.

"Thomas Cartwright, your name will be etched into the Wall of Legends along Ghazanfar and Al-Shidath." I had no idea what he was talking about. "It will be honoured for time eternal. We will protect, Augur." I smiled inwardly. "We will keep vigil." He returned to his men who put away their whistling-stones, then yelled Gisar at the top of his lungs to call his men to attention. They bowed once more, then turned and ran westward in their strange triangular formation, which was smaller now than when we had first met. The missing warrior names forever etched into the face of their grim leader.

The Lore Masters stepped forward next and we exchanged wishes for a safe and pleasant journey.

"Are you sure you wouldn't rather join our order in the mountains?" Donato asked with a grin.

"I'm sorry, but I couldn't be trusted around so many books again." I shook his hand in farewell and was surprised to find something in my palm. It was a smooth blue stone.

"It's Meda's Heartstone, found within the ruins of Scat's house." It looked unremarkable. "He would have wanted you to have it." I thanked him once more and bade them both farewell. They made their way down the gangplank, the younger Master of the Temple helping the older Laird and waited on the dock for Lord Fiongall and his family to disembark.

He approached and held my left shoulder, saying nothing, then embraced me warmly, patted me on the back and looked into my face again.

"A new name will be added to the Song of Warriors sung in the Mead Hall of Bleneth. Thomas the Terror of the Terroks." We both laughed. "Though it won't be easy coming up with a word that rhymes with Terrok." I wished him a safe journey as his family joined the waiting Lore Masters. Donato raised the Travelling Mindstone above his head and as a group they disappeared within the slash of light.

We sailed into Wellspring as the year's first snowfall blanketed the ground and melted into the ocean. I embraced Gillian and thanked him for everything that he had done and sacrificed for me. He didn't want to hear of it and told me that he now had a story to retell in every tavern in Perg. He even had a royal seal, given to him by King Trevor, which allowed him tax-free trading for life with Manath Samal. That was something no other merchant on the Isle of Holbrook possessed. Each of his women stuffed a coloured and scented silk scarf into my tunic, telling me where they had been worn, and that they would help keep me warm in even the coldest winter night. Wasil and Ginzo were beside themselves and wrested their hands asking for forgiveness as they had nothing to offer me as a farewell gift. I shook my head and thanked them for their unlooked-for generosity when I had needed it most. I gave Wasil my amulet of

Thayer, in remembrance of his unwavering duty to the God while he had been amongst us. He promised me that he would wear it for life, and tell people that Thayer's protector himself had worn it. I gave Ginzo my Terrok claw. The big man was so full of emotion that he couldn't speak, he just hugged me warmly. I stood on the dock and waved goodbye until I couldn't recognize anyone on the deck.

I ended up wintering in Cragthorne, helping King Gavin and his builders with the restorations. It felt good working with wood again and my talents were appreciated by all. We eventually found both Mindstones buried underneath the tons of rock and timber. The King planned to return them to the Lore Masters come spring, and under my suggestion, had them placed under lock and key. I visited the graves of the murdered priestesses every day and brushed the snow away. As the weather warmed and travel became possible, I decided it was time to go to the Isle of the Crescent Moon. King Gavin arranged a farewell and the townsfolk threw flower petals along the path as I headed out of Cragthorne Castle for the last time.

I avoided going south through Gilmouth, remembering how I had been treated before, and instead headed west through Keegan's Inn and south through Harding, using King Gavin's seal and letter to get the best rooms and permission to pass through Pandros uncontested.

I arrived at the Temple of Bashal just in time for the Spring Awakening Ceremony as new young women from off-island were being introduced to the New High

Priestesses. Gavriella welcomed me and was caught off-guard when I produced *Silya* from my belongings. I told her the complete story of my journey and as a reward for my service to the Goddess was allowed to live in the cabin by the sea that I had stayed in before.

"Elise is waiting for you within."

"How is she?"

"You'll have to judge that for yourself."

"Quinn Korid?"

She sighed. "He passed away this winter in his sleep. We could not heal his mind. It was far too damaged." She handed me something. "Perhaps you'll know what to do with this." It was his lifeless Mindstone. I bowed and left her to greet her new followers.

On my way to the cabin I tossed his Mindstone into the sea, returning it to where it had once come. I stood outside the door, afraid to open it. Afraid of what awaited me. I gathered my courage and knocked on the door. When there was no answer I pushed open the door and was surprised to find no one inside. I put my belongings on the bed and looked at the few objects sitting on the table, a comb, a shell and a candle.

"May I help you?" She stood in the doorway with the sun behind her so that her face was in shadow. "This is my room, if you are looking for something you need to check with the High Priestess first." As she entered, her face came out of the shadow and I realized why there were so few objects in the room.

She was blind and her blonde hair had turned as white as her eyes.

"Elise?" I started, but my voice caught in my throat.

"Thomas?" She stumbled and I rose to catch her. "It can't be." Her hands moved from my arms to my face where they deftly probed my features. She sagged into my arms and began to cry deeply. I moved her over to the bed and held her until we were both out of tears.

"I dreamt of you," she said quietly, "and the Gods. You were being eaten alive by Eth while Thayer and Bashal watched. You plead for their help, but they refused." She began to cry again. "When they wouldn't help, you cried out for me. I tried and tried, but I couldn't find you. I woke up just as you were consumed in light, screaming my name."

"They can never hurt us again."

Thirteen years have passed since that day, and I find myself sitting alone at the small wooden desk in our cabin by the sea, looking out at the tumbling waves and remembering those foolish words. We shared two happy years together in our cabin, before she fell asleep one night and didn't wake up. The priestesses told me that being reincarnated by the Goddess had shortened her life expectancy, but it was more than I expected after uttering that promise.

At the behest of the Master of the Temple, I have written down the story of my life as best as I can remember, and it should please Donato that I've left out most of the tawdry bits. It seems that I am the first Priest of Bashal (according to what he's delved from the Stone of Knowledge) and this fact, along with our shared adventure, deserves a place in written history. It still confuses those cloistered scholars why it took so long for me to take the vows after being offered the privilege more than a decade ago, but after spending thirteen years on the Island I finally feel old enough to accept the required vow of chastity that I forgot to mention in our correspondence. I've thumbed through the voluminous copy of the Tome of Lore delivered to me today, signed by Donato himself with the inscription, "In appreciation for your sacrifice." He's asked that I give a copy of my story to the acolyte who delivered the book so that it can be included in the Tome under the chapter '*Sacrifice*'. I wrap the pages carefully, closing the book of my life.

Perhaps Brother Equinos will live a quieter life than Thomas Cartwright.

Epilogue

Lore Master Donato,
Temple of the Sky,
Upper Doros
From Brother Equinos (formerly Thomas Cartwright),
Temple of Bashal,
Island of the Crescent Moon

Master Donato, my apologies for this late entry, but recent events require inclusion into my life's story that I have already sent on ahead of this letter as you can read before.

"Brother Equinos!" A voice startled me from my afternoon reverie, as I was seated on a chair outside my cabin. I tucked the golden locket back within my robe, which would forever contain three locks of hair, one blonde, two brown.

"Yes?" I asked, sounding disgruntled as I stood up and straightened my back. A priestess ran up the sand path and bowed reverently.

"You have a visitor." She appeared winded from running ahead of them to warn me of their approach. "Actually, you have visitor*s*." She pointed as a group of armoured men walked up the path. Sunlight glittered off the polished pieces of armour peeking under their weathered cloaks. I checked beside my open door for Trevor's sword and moved cautiously toward it.

Although many years had passed, I was heartened to recognize Graham and Geoffrey's smiling faces beneath their grey-streaked beards. They still wore the colours of King Trevor and from their finery, they must have risen quite high in rank.

"By the Gods, is that you Thomas?" I shook Graham's extended hand. "It looks like Island life has made you soft." He poked at my stomach.

"It's Brother Equinos now," I shook Geoffrey's hand, "and being around so many beautiful women has made me as soft as they are." I teased playfully.

"You lucky bastard." Geoffrey laughed. "Life on the road has made our only bedmates a rock-in-the-back and some painful saddle sores."

Following them up the path were Captain Gill and his women who smiled and waved greetings at me. They stepped aside as a young man shoved his way passed them and walked up to me.

"Are you supposed to be my father?" He asked incredulously. "A fat old Priest?" He looked at the two older soldiers. "I thought you said he was a great warrior?"

I looked at my two friends with incredulity. Graham apologized for the boy's behaviour.

"Thomas, King Trevor has been recently approached by Lord Scat's old housekeeper." He coughed into his hands. "She claims that this *boy* is your son." He stressed the word to chastise the young man, but continued when there was no reaction. "The King asked us to bring the boy and to convey the story told to him so that you could determine its validity. He said that he would have written first, but thought that meeting this *boy* in person might convince you better." He paused. "She told him that Lord Scat had been away from the Manor House for weeks before he reappeared, during which time Maura had given birth to their child. On the day of his return, Maura spotted him approaching the house and watched in horror as he began to kill his own people who were bringing in the harvest. She knew that something was terribly wrong and perhaps it was divine providence smiling upon her as a serving girl had died just that morning giving birth to a baby boy. The baby's father was rumored to be Lord Scat. With the housekeeper's help, Maura switched the babies and ordered her to leave immediately, never to return, and to keep the identity of her boy a secret from everyone, especially Lord Scat who would kill the baby if he discovered that it was Thomas Cartwright's son and not his own." Graham looked at the boy. "She fled to Tyre with her husband and raised the boy as their own, vowing to take Maura's secret to the grave. During the past fifteen years he's become a bit of a nuisance and the husband had threatened to tell the King of his real identity if she didn't. As Lord Scat was dead and Thomas Cartwright had left the island, she didn't think it would matter to reveal the true identity of the boy's father. When she told Lord Trevor, he chastised her for not telling anyone sooner and sent us here immediately to find you."

I was in shock and for once I didn't know what to say.

I stared at the boy, looking for something familiar, and then he smirked, and in his face I saw a younger version of myself staring back at me. I pulled Maura's hair from my locket and placed it against his head. It matched perfectly. I began to weep and pulled the boy into my embrace.

"What'd I do?" The boy asked shrewdly.

"You rose from the dead." Geoffrey said quietly.

Perhaps the Gods hadn't failed me after all.

The End

Acknowledgements

I took my first step down the path to fantasy novels when in Grade 3, my teacher read to us The Hobbit. I followed Bilbo back and forth to the lonely mountain and that journey changed my life. After The Hobbit, I read Lord of the Rings, and then the Thomas Covenant series by Stephen R. Donaldson. This was followed by Terry Brooks, Tad Williams, Robert Jordan, Melanie Rawn and the brilliant Guy Gavriel Kay. I didn't discover historical fiction until my adult life, and this genre breathed life into my fantasy writing, thanks to authors like Bernard Cornwell, Jack Whyte and Giles Kristian.

I would like to thank;
My wife Heather for being patient and supportive,
My sons Jude and Tristan for gracing my life with theirs,
My father who taught me what it meant to sacrifice,
And finally my mother, who never got the chance to find out that her son was an author.

Dan Melchior

About the Author

Dan grew up and still lives on Vancouver Island, the closest facsimile to Middle Earth outside of New Zealand. He got the chance to portray Bilbo Baggins in a stage production of The Hobbit in the 90's, thus closing the circle on the book that started it all. He's been a paperboy, an inventory clerk, a dishwasher, a waiter, an officer cadet, a home renovator, a tutor, an actor, and still plies his trade as an electrical engineering technologist in the construction industry. He's carried his younger brother who has MD up a mountain on his back, camped in the snow, fallen asleep in the rain with an 80lb pack strapped to his back, sailed an 8ft boat in gale force winds, ran out of air while diving, greeted a bear outside of his house and converted his garage into a haunted house for the past 6 years.

He's also been busy writing, directing and editing movies with his neighbours and family.

The ideas for a second novel have been written down in the notebook and soon will be making their way to the printed page.

The Tome of Lore continues to be written...